The Four *Aces*

◆ ◆ ◆ ◆

A New Children's Home Mystery

by **Marilyn R. Stark**

Workplay Publishing

Contents

This book is dedicated to Randall, Brian, Valerie, Christal, Sean, and their Dad, who used to be my first editor.

All of them supported my love of writing and believed in me before I did.

Author's Note

The Lord Jesus Christ and my Muse are my best friends with guidance from my patient, understanding Editor, Cheryl Mueller, from whom I took author's license, rather than lose my writing voice.

Chapter 1

Shannon Warren Donnelly woke at four a.m., thanks to a specific nightmare she had not had in years. She slipped out of bed without waking her husband, David, and grabbed her robe, slippers and sketchbook.

She had left the drapes at the patio door open the night before. It was a clear night. The full moon lit-up her kitchen, as well as the outdoors like daylight, and reflected off the brass closure of what had brought to life her nightmare. She questioned whether the dream had been an omen as she started the coffee pot as usual.

There were three photo albums on the table: her Children's Home Album, the Warren Family Album, and the brown leather hand-stitched storybook her nanny, Nanna Ruth, had made for her and her twin Sheldon when they were five years old.

Shannon and her twin Sheldon had lived at the Warren Family Carriage House with Nanna Ruth while their Dad was away in the military. Their mother had died when the twins were three years old. Their grandparents lived nearby on the Warren Estate and golf course.

Now, the kitchen filling with the aroma of fresh coffee, she drew out her sketchbook from the kitchen drawer. She recalled that morning Grandmother Warren had hustled Shannon out of her bed, and insisted she was to wear her new dress. "Hurry up. You are coming with me," she demanded, practically shoving her out the door.

When Shannon noticed her play suitcase, she was puzzled. She had promised Nanna Ruth she wouldn't go anywhere without her new leather storybook and the cloth doll Nanna had made for her. As she ran back into her room to grab them, she automatically glanced at the wall clock she had learned to tell time with. It had read four a.m....

"Shannon?" David asked, as he put his arm around her and set a mug of coffee in front of her. Just one glance at her sketches and he knew part of what was going on. "What is haunting you about four a.m. that you have circled?" he asked as he pulled up a chair next to her.

"I'm not certain." She pointed to and circled rough sketches of the layout of the rooms in the Main Building of the Flat Rock Children's Home—the office of the administration. "The church was a city block away. I remember she left me there, in his office. There was a clock behind Father Fielding that had stopped with both hands on four."

"Has your foreboding lessened any since you filled two pages of possibilities or is it Lori's standby four a.m. flight that has you concerned?" he asked.

Shannon rubbed her eyes. "Remember, the morning Lily and Lori were born? Before we could even tell them apart?

David smiled. "We felt a mixture of awe, instant love, and a premonition that these two would be our greatest challenge in life and joy. Is that about right?"

"They have been charming and demanding. They learned to walk holding onto each other. They learned to talk by finishing each other's sentences, and we questioned if the way they depended on each other would be a hindrance to their independence as adults."

"I think they've done just fine," David said. "Eight years of college, Lily's earned her Doctorate of Chiropractic Health, and Lori her Doctorate of Veterinarian Medicine." He grew more serious. "So, do you think your uneasiness has somethingto do with our daughters?"

Shannon shrugged her shoulders. "I'll fix breakfast."

Soon Shannon and David were having their usual at-home breakfast at their Winthrop Estate, just as a colorful sunrise appeared on the horizon. Early morning dew sparkled on blades of grass and petals of Shannon's roses and in view of the Shannon-Warren-Winthrop Golf green number fourteen. Patches of steam hovered over their coffee mugs. The scent of bacon and fresh-from-the-oven cinnamon rolls filled the air.

Hunter, their brown-eyed son, and for the most part, forever optimist, joined them. A gentle breeze from the window lifted his wind-blown hairstyle. Casual. "Hey, you two," he remarked as he filled his plate from the sideboard warmer. "Why so glum? I am excited about Lily and Lori's return home to stay and not just visit. I bet I'll be taller than either of them," he bragged, smiling.

He had inherited his sisters' ability to read people, so he knew something was wrong this morning. But he kept it to himself by using the gift of gab he acquired from his Dad. He retrieved the coffee carafe and asked, "Need a refill? Mom? Dad? Love you guys, you know," he added as he bowed his head for a silent thank-you-prayer, with the usual request for his family's safety. A special prayer for his Mom because he knew she was unusually concerned about something or someone—probably his sisters this morning.

"Grandma's rolls today, huh?" He smiled his usual cheeky smile and wiped a bit of icing off his chin with his thumb.

"All right, Hunter, your Mom is worried about Lily and Lori getting out of Chicago."

"Have you called them?"

"No," she replied softly, as she shoved her chair back and paced to the other side of the carpeted deck, her head down, her arms crossed tightly against her waist.

"Honey, we've talked about this," David cajoled. "Do you want me to call Jonothan? He's probably still in his office at the Turtle Crossing Airport, or he may already be in Chicago."

Hunter continued eating, having watched his Mom and Dad work out concerns in the past and waited. Sure enough, his Dad joined his Mom, put his arms around her, and said nothing more.

She looked at her watch, turned in her husband's

arms, glanced at Hunter, and announced, "You're right! This would be a good time to call Jonothan. It is imperative he pick up the girls as soon as possible for their trip home." Jonothan did not answer, so she left him a message and then, after a moment, dialed Lily.

Lily picked up right away, but she was already talking to someone else. "Just take the elevator to the second floor. You know my apartment number."

"Lily? Hello?" asked Shannon.

"Hello, Mom. Sorry about the mix-up. As you probably heard, Lori just arrived. She's coming up to my apartment and we will call you as soon as we have our itinerary, okay? See you soon."

***

Lily unlatched her door and held it open while her twin sister stepped through, carrying a single bag. They hugged, each overwhelmed with physically knowing the other was okay.

"Mom just called," Lily reported. "She wants us to contact Jonothan. He flew some business tycoon into Chicago and called me last evening around six. All we have to do is call him and he will be ready. The sooner, the better, so he can file a flight plan."

"Well, I shipped everything out except what is in my overnight bag. I cancelled my previous flight because mom had a problem with my four a.m. flight. It didn't feel right to her. So I booked a red-eye two days ahead of schedule, and here I am. Mom is probably right about us leaving yet this morning. The sooner we get home, the better."

"Here," Lily suggested. "I made an egg and grilled cheese sandwich, and you can eat the other half. I will phone Jonothan and my taxi driver."

But before she could pick up the wall phone to dial, it started ringing. "What do you bet Jonothan beat us to it?" Lori said. She answered because she was close-by. Brushing her shoulder-length, golden-blonde braided-ponytail over her shoulder, she announced, "Joe's Bar & Grill." She remembered playing secretary for Uncle Jonothan when she and Lily were probably four years old.

Jonothan replied, "I'll take a dozen chocolate cupcakes with raspberry icing to go in forty-five minutes."

Lori said, "Your excited, very blonde sweethearts are ready for travel," and hung up. "We are to meet our favorite pilot at Gate XYZ as soon as possible."

Lily phoned her taxi driver for pickup. "He will be here in fifteen minutes. I picked up two Chicago Cubs ball caps. Turn around so I can turn your pony-tail into a bun and tuck it inside the cap."

"If anyone heard you outside the building, or saw you, we're dressed alike, our bags are the same shade of blue, and …" Lily looked out her bedroom blind. "Our taxi is just two stoplights away. Five minutes earlier than I expected."

"You're leaving clothes in the closet and your high-school graduation suitcase?"

"My friends will take care of it."

"You have a lot of trust in this taxi driver."

"I'll explain later. Hey, Sis. Can you grab that brown paper sack on the counter? It's breakfast for our taxi driver. Thanks. Ready?" She gave her apartment a sweeping glance, unlocked the door, and relocked it on their way out.

The hallway was clear as they entered the elevator, and they saw no one when they got off. However, they were prepared to use their negative/positive shadow moves as they quickly slipped out the front door of the building, presently shadowed by street lights and a partially late sunrise.

They moved straight for the taxi. Lily recognized the green-and-white smiley face on the roof and the scratch on the passenger door. However, Lily still waited until he signaled, tipped his hat and winked at her. Lily nodded in return, opened the door, and motioned for Lori to slide in ahead of her, bag and all.

As soon as they were seated, Lori hit the lock button and Lily handed the driver his usual, plus their destination written on the front of an envelope.

He checked with her in the rear-view mirror before pulling into traffic. When she smiled and nodded, he noticed her hands were shaking when she handed him his coffee. He tipped the bill of his hat in return, twitched his mustache as though he was used to picking up two gracious, beautiful ladies at this address every day. But, by the thickness of the envelope and destination, he also knew this was her way of saying thank you for safe traveling and discretion. He would miss their conversations, but this would be the last time he would be stopping at this address.

***

Jonothan Carpenter was not surprised when his nieces Lily and Lori approached him at the airport as though they were on some covert assignment. They were wearing dark sunglasses, their blonde hair braided and coiled inside Chicago Cubs baseball caps, wearing matching powder blue tops, designer jeans, and jackets.

As soon as they were in the air, he asked, "You ladies made great time this morning. You apparently have better taxi connections than I ever have. It usually takes me twice the time it took you."

"That's because Lily befriended a very trustworthy taxi driver," Lori said.

"We felt uneasy the moment Lori entered my apartment building."

"Okay. You both know I do not take your instincts lightly. Apparently, your Mom has been on edge as well because she called me right after I placed my cupcake order."

"Really?" Lily asked. She squeezed Lori's hand and they visibly relaxed. When they cleared the runway, they removed their ball caps, loosened their hair, and boosted their sunglasses on top of their head.

Looking up, Lori smiled and said, "There is barely a cloud in the sky."

"We should have a smooth ride," Jonothan nodded.

"It's been a while since I've had the time to fly any more than the minimum required," Lily sighed.

"Lily, why were you so flustered when Jonothan called regarding the gate number where we were to meet him?"

Lily shrugged her shoulders and replied, "My only

explanation was when I had this itchy feeling in the back of my neck, I felt that I had become the mouse in some feral cat's trap."

"I had the same feeling, but it disappeared at liftoff," Lori added. "I haven't slept but a few hours all week. I probably should take a nap, but I don't want to miss a moment."

"Uncle Jonothan," Lily said, "your new plane is a smoother ride, but it's still hard to hear."

"Put on the headphones, ladies."

"Yes, sir," they replied in unison, looked at each other and smiled, as they complied and kept their eyes on the altitude, the altimeter, and the printout of his flight plans.

A few hours later, Lily exclaimed, "Oh. Wow! We are farther north than I thought if what I am seeing are the turrets at The Great-Stone Castle in Sidney, Ohio."

"Sometimes I have instincts as well and thought since we are arriving earlier than expected, you might like a tiny detour," Jonothan added.

"What a nice surprise," Lori commented. "It's beautiful. We have talked about taking the time to visit there again. Remember the birthday party we attended when we were in Junior High?"

"I do." Looking out the side windows, they were unusually quiet and appeared to be enjoying the small towns, farms, an abundance of recently planted fields, and were searching for the area where Lily's office had recently been built.

"Jonothan," Lori asked softly looking out her window, "How much farther to Eight-Mile-Centre's growing business metropolis which includes Lily's new office?"

"Eight-Mile-Centre is below on your left," Jonothan smiled, "and on your right is where Doc O'Reilly's Ranch begins, which includes his home, state-of-the-art O'Reilly expansion and Veterinarian Animal Hospital, where Lori will soon have her own office."

"On your left is the recent expansion of Granny Oates Estate—future headquarters for a shelter for women and their children."

"The community of Turtle Crossing has been growing as well due to the opening of The Welby Mansion Bed and Breakfast, The Welby Chapel, The Turtle Crossing Tunnels of Safe Passage and the adjoining Welby-Warren-Davies Golf Course. Each has helped promote this growth," he concluded.

"You sound like a tour guide," Lori exclaimed, excitement sparkling in her eyes and voice.

"From this bird's-eye-view, I feel humbled to be a part of this growth," Lily added.

"So much has happened while we were gone," Lori reminisced, as she reached around in her seat to hug Lily. "Well, you know we have visited off and on, but in short spurts, which didn't allow time for more than visiting with family."

Once Jonothan had landed at the Turtle Crossing Airport, he reminded them that their Dad had left the keys for a 1986 Lincoln Continental for their use.

Lori took the keys, threw Jonothan a kiss, a smile, and a wave as they stowed their bags and slipped into the vehicle. Lori turned the ignition. As the interior quickly cooled, the only sound was the purring of the motor and the click of their seat belts. "We made it. We're here!"

"Do you remember how to drive, or which direction is north?" Lily grinned as tears ran freely down her face.

"Jonothan said everything we need is in the cooler."

"Ah-ha," Lily exclaimed. "A local map with directions and our choice of Root Beer or Orange Soda."

"Okay, co-pilot. Where do I turn once we leave the parking lot? And once we're on our way, you can clear-up what happened with that guy you were dating off and on for the last three years, or more."

"That will take more time than we have right now."

"More than once, you hinted that the break-up wasn't an easy one," Lori replied.

Lily sighed. "Not at first. No. The first time he broke up with me I was wondering what I had done or said that he was so nasty with me. Then, looking back, I questioned if it was because I hesitated to give him all my test answers. There were times when I needed to study, when he wanted to party. He even said I was a party-pooper and he was going to find someone else who was more fun to be with."

"Here I was looking forward to meeting him," Lori replied.

"Then he suddenly needed help to study because he had to pass. Well, thanks to my friends, it appeared he had bragged about why it didn't matter if I passed because my family had money to burn.

"You know how careful we have always been about discussing our family's holdings. The only thing I could recall was quite possibly he slipped into my room when I was on the phone with Mom or intercepted one of my calls."

"He was dating one of the girls in the admitting office, when I broke it off with him altogether. Later, I heard he got caught cheating on one of his finals and dropped out."

"I was so angry with myself for not catching on sooner," Lily finished.

"He was the entire package though, right?" Lori asked. "Good-looking, sweet, and knew just the right thing to say?"

"Right. I even gave him leeway there. But he wasn't that good an actor. Even when he kissed me, I always felt there was something missing, or he was just putting on an act."

"The truth, no doubt," Lori remarked. "I can't wait to hear your story."

"I had forgotten how peaceful this drive is. Fields planted in winter wheat and corn. Smell that freshly cut green alfalfa. Are you speeding?"

"No. I thought I heard a siren, but was looking for it on that side road. Whoa! That was a Deputy Sheriff that just buzzed past us in one big hurry. No time to pull me over."

"I think that was Deputy Brandi Carpenter. It looked like her German Shepherd in the passenger seat."

"Oh, no. That looks like smoke and a fire truck. It's Granny's place!"

"Take it easy, Sis," Lily said.

"That looks like Doc O'Reilly directing traffic," Lori

added, with a sigh of relief. She knew if it was really bad he wouldn't be out directing traffic, he would be helping put out the fire.

As they pulled up, they heard him call, "Move along, things are under control here." Then, recognizing the sisters, he tapped on the window. Lori rolled it down. "Go on down to my place," he said, slipping something from his pocket into her palm. "Granny has been on pins and needles waiting for you."

They drove quickly on.

"What did Doc slip into your hand when he tapped on the window? A garage door opener?" Lily asked.

Lori passed the object over to her sister. It had a code number on one side, with a huge number three on the other. "The door opener for my parking spot at the hospital. The last time I was home he was extending the garage between the house and the bunkhouse. The hospital is getting so big."

"I am so excited for you," Lily said. "I know if I am having trouble sitting in this vehicle when I would like nothing better than to pull up beside the O'Reilley Veterinarian Animal Hospital and see you sitting in your new office. You have got to be feeling it's an early Christmas Eve."

A few minutes later they had pulled up to a series of garage doors running along a newly rennovated building. Lily punched the code #wow3 into the opener Lori had passed her. Garage door three opened and Lori pulled inside.

Lily stepped out of the car and said, "This is so new, it

still smells of fresh concrete and paint. It's so big I bet you could pull a semi-truck in."

"Yes. Spooky when our voices echo back at us."

An intercom telephone rang with a buzz and gold flashing light. Lori picked up the phone and smiled. She angled the phone so Lily could hear the voice on the other end. "This is Granny. Now, you girls, just hop into Doc's All-Terrain-Buggy, luggage and all."

But before they could take a step, the intercom buzzed again. Lori picked it up and listened, "Hey girls, this is Doc. Come out the door where the light is blinking."

They pulled their luggage across the expansive garage to the door Doc had indicated. It rolled up silently to reveal Doc's special-built black Ford pickup. Lori got behind the wheel of Doc's special-built black Ford pickup truck. Lori turned the key Doc had left in the ignition and the engine purred like a sleepy tiger. The sisters grinned at each other like the little girls they had once been.

The last leg of the drive passed in what felt like seconds, and then they were at the kitchen door, which burst open to reveal their their mom Shannon, Granny, and Doc O'Reilly, all beaming with excitement and relief at their arrival. Once inside, the greetings, hugs, tears of joy, and a feeling of safety was overwhelming. It wasn't until after soup, sandwiches and two huge mugs of coffee were devoured, that thoughts of what wasn't being discussed could finally surface.

The twins looked at each other, sat down, and quietly took a bite of their favorite carrot cake with cream-cheese icing, and took another sip of their coffee before Lily could make a comment.

"I know Granny promised us we could rent her farm-house until we find other accommodations, but I'm sure that has changed now that it's become a women's shelter."

Doc O'Reilly asked to speak. "I know you are young ladies now, but, humor me, okay? I can't give you a report on Granny's place because Brandi said she will leave a crew there overnight, and she and Jonothan will be stop-ping with a report. This includes updated reports on each of you, as well.

"On us? Why would Aunt Brandi have a report on either of us?" Lily questioned, looking around the table, waiting for someone to say something.

"I can tell you this much," Shannon said. "There was a fire in the apartment next to the one you left this morn-ing. Mainly smoke, because the ladies in the apartment on the other side of your apartment helped put the fire out. The insurance company tried to contact you about damage, through the Sheriff's office."

Before Shannon finished her statement, Lori noticed approaching lights of a vehicle in the drive about the same time Granny answered her phone. "It's Brandi and Jonothan."

Doc released the house security system and opened the door.

"How are my favorite nieces?" Brandi asked as she swept across the kitchen, her arms opened wide, thinking they weren't little girls anymore but their love was strong as ever.

"Aunt Brandi!" they chorused.

"What do I have to do to get one of those?" Jonothan asked smiling.

Lori raised one eyebrow directed towards him and added, "We hugged you before you rushed us through the airport. When you were granted clearance, we both felt a great weight just disappear."

"Then you both had a premonition that something wasn't quite right?"

"Yes!" Lori burst out. "We're certain we were being followed. Did you find anyone? Or were they your people?"

"The firemen found two pieces of luggage that matches yours—full of street-drugs," Brandi stated, sounding like the stern deputy they all knew she could be sometimes.

"Luggage?" Lily said, as she squeezed Lori's hand. "We brought our luggage. It's in Doc's pickup outside."

Brandi nodded. "I believe you, but that's not enough in police work. Luckily, the real culprits were in such a hurry, they—meaning more than one—left their fingerprints on the luggage tag and a copy of your photo I.D. inside the luggage on the sticky tape."

"What do we do?" Lori asked, pleading in her eyes.

The twins had already eaten their fill, but Granny and Doc laid out a platter of roast beef, more shredded chicken sandwiches, pickles, radishes, celery, cheese and another one of cookies. Plus fresh pots of hot coffee and chilled lemonade. Shannon and Jonothan helped themselves while they listened to the conversation.

"I'm still playing catch-up here," Brandi said as she

pulled out her notepad and pen. "Who knew what time you were flying out?"

"My closest friends at the apartment complex and the desk clerk," Lily replied.

"This was apparently well-planned, but if you had already left, why would you leave luggage in your apartment?"

"I just left some clothes and furniture that my friends wanted and planned to clear out," Lily explained.

"But," Lori added, "after Jonothan called the night before, no one knew we were leaving early. We were too busy packing last-minute things, and it was too late to contact anyone."

"Also," Lily suggested, "it was a weekend. Most everyone was still in bed at five in the morning."

"Besides," Lori added, "We left wet towels in the bath tub. The closet doors were left open. And the bed clothes were piled in the middle of the bed."

"Remember, Sis," Lori continued, "You mentioned your neighbors from downstairs brought their luggage up last week and set aside a few things they wanted."

"Did you make plans for later in the morning?" Brandi asked, glancing at Jonothan when he started to answer the question for them.

"We planned to have brunch around ten."

"And your scheduled flight?" Brandi asked. "The one you would have taken if Jonothan had not flown you out?"

"Four. Lily's friends planned to stop by around noon."

"Who ordered the box of donuts? There was a half-eaten box of donuts on the counter. A place called Ernie's."

"It must have been a gift." Lori covered Lily's hand as Lily responded. "My favorite donut shop, Ernie's. He knew we were leaving and must have sent a going-away present."

"Someone delivered the order," Brandi said. "Dum-Dums One and Two must have had a little snack while they were tampering with your belongings. That's enough for now." Brandi had known these two favorite nieces since they were still eating in high chairs. She closed her notepad and gave them a warm smile. "You girls have had a very long day."

"And the fire at Granny's. Was that because of us?" Lily asked.

Granny walked around her kitchen table, with an arm around each of the twins, and squeezed their shoulders. "No. I had to have a couple of old trees cut down and as they were cleaning up the area, one of the workers who was taking his lunch break flipped his cigarette into a pile of twigs. Some smoldering embers were still hot from earlier in the day, which erupted into a fire."

Granny kissed each of them on the cheek and felt their shoulders relax a bit.

Jonothan, Brandi, and Doc watched the bravado the twins had bottled up before they arrived accelerate into near tears until Granny explained about the fire. Jonothan and their parents were the only family that had kept in close touch the entire eight years they had been gone. "You both look exhausted," he said. "No one even knows you are here. So, why not spend the night here at Granny and Doc's tonight?"

"Your family will all be here tomorrow because

Granny's place has a mess to clean up after that fire in the driveway."

"He's right," Brandi said as she and Jonothan picked up their dishes and carried them to the sink.

"Where's your canine partner?" Lori asked, as she and Lily gathered up serving platters from the table.

"He has been checking around outside and visiting his family," Brandi replied.

"His family?" Lily asked, when she noted they were all smiling.

Brandi opened the back door of the kitchen to let in Lieutenant Pepper, a tall, alert German Shepherd police dog.

"Pepper," Lily and Lori cooed as they approached him.

"Aunt Brandi, he has filled out a bit," Lori remarked.

Lily scratched his ears. "Pepper, does this mean you and your lady have had another litter of puppies?"

"They are staying here for the rest of the week," Brandi replied. "He is on leave from the force, in a way. However, he is helping me train one of his own."

While Lori and the rest were discussing Pepper, Jonothan noticed that Lily's thoughts were elsewhere and motioned Lily to join him. He motioned to Granny that they were going out on the screened-in back porch. "Lemonade? More coffee?"

"Lemonade," she replied, massaging her neck with her fingertips.

"Do you want to talk about what else is bothering you, Lily?" he suggested softly, still holding the lemonade he had poured for her.

She settled into one of Granny's rocking chairs. While gripping the cool glass with both hands, she finally looked at him, felt the tears pool in her eyes, and took one careful sip, set the glass on the side table and asked, "Do you remember when I first started school, you came to our house with Aunt Brandi and I hugged you and then got upset with you when you put your arm around Brandi? I told you I loved you first?"

Jonothan smiled and said, "Oh, yes! You also broke your Aunt Brandi's heart," he chuckled, "When you told her I was your boyfriend, so she couldn't be your aunt anymore. You stomped your foot and ran to your room in tears."

That was a part of the memory she wasn't proud of, but felt she owed him an explanation. "I was a lonely kid. I missed you when you were away at school. Lori was really frustrated with me, and Mom and Dad were dealing with much more important things than me. You were our listening board in those days." She paused. "Have you heard anything about our friends' apartments? I hate to think they're in danger because of us."

"It's being taken care of," Jonothan said.

"Okay. So what does that mean? Does anyone know what or who was responsible?" Lily questioned, feeling left out of what his comment suggested.

Jonothan hesitated a moment too long but added, "I will call you as soon as I know. But regarding another subject, I heard you were still undecided about the location of your practice."

"I really want to open my practice at the Eight Mile

Centre; however, Isaac Pease hasn't decided what he plans to do with his practice. I heard he expects his son to join him in the fall."

"I heard there is another chiropractor interested," Jonothan added.

"The rumor is factual then? Does this person have a name? Should I call and offer my assistance?"

Jonothan had heard a rumor that one of the offers involved one of Lily's former professors, but had learned from experience not to put a whole lot of credibility on rumors. "Only rumors. But I understand they have a great deal of local backing. Why would you be concerned?"

"Well, you know the entire community is solidly behind Lori working with Doc, while I, on the other hand, have zilch when it comes to patients' trust. No amount of advertising, or even a brand new building can take its place."

He had seldom seen this side of Lily. "Hey. What has happened to my favorite niece? We both know that it isn't financial, and the business community of Turtle Crossing is really excited about the further potential growth your family continues to add."

Lily had kept her broken heart under wraps. That distraction didn't belong in her business decisions.

"Mind if I interrupt?" Lori inquired as she approached Lily and nodded to Jonothan. "How long have the lightning bugs been in abundance? Aren't they beautiful, Lily?"

Lily smiled. "It's still daylight, silly. I do still know the difference between a lovely lady bug and a flash code."

"Well, you know as anxious as I am to get started

working with Doc, I need to get some shut-eye. Join me, Sis? I've got some ideas that I want to share with you that are going to keep me awake until I do."

"Have a nice nap, ladies," Jonothan replied as he kissed each of them on the cheek. They disappeared into the house. Jonothon waited a moment before pulling out his phone and dialing Will's headquarters. "Will," Jonothan greeted. "How is the investigation going? Lily is really upset because she has no idea what happened at her apartment and is even more concerned about her friends."

"I know," Will's voice responded in his ear. "I have a couple of my semi-retired agents in Chicago now. There is no way I am going to leave this to chance. I did that once. Lesson learned."

"You're talking about your sister's daughter, Shannon? You know she does not hold you responsible. That was all her not-so-well-liked, jealous, misguided grandmother."

"I know. But all those years the twins' mother, Shannon, would have been raised by her daddy, instead of the children's home. It still haunts me at times. But, I add thanks to Nanna Ruth in my daily prayers for the handmade doll and nursery rhyme book she made certain Shannon treasured and took with her everywhere. Without those, she would have been lost to us forever," Will added.

"Will, I can't speak for my wife on a professional basis, but Brandi isn't about to let this be written-off without closure. As children's home sisters, their bond is unshakable."

Chapter 2

"I hope the two of you don't mind sleeping in twin beds in the same room," Granny teased.

"Not at all," Lori responded as she gave Granny a hug goodnight. Granny closed the door with a soft click. Lori turned to Lily, but Lily was momentarily caught staring at their images in the 'see-all-of-me' oval mirror. "Sis, you need to sit down before you fall down."

"It's coming back. Shoot! It's been hovering for years. Admit it."

They still hadn't spent any time alone—just the two of them with nothing or no one to be accountable to. Tears filled Lily's eyes, as she followed Lori to one of the twin beds and sat down. Facing each other. Silence sat heavy on their shoulders.

Gaining strength and control, Lily dried her eyes. As they continued to stare into each other's eyes, Lily asked, "Remember the first time we figured out how we knew what others were thinking or feeling—especially when we finished each other's sentences?"

Lori smiled. Lily smiled. "Our reflection!"

They grasped each other's hands. "Our Connection!"

"It has been eight long years of schooling," Lori added. "Mom suggested in no uncertain terms that we get some very much-needed rest, that she and Dad will see us tomorrow."

"Mom is always right," Lily replied, a smile lighting up her eyes.

"Shall we?" Lori added, smiling in agreement.

They turned down their bedding and shoved the beds together, pulled their covers up and reached out to hold hands as they had as children and before birth.

***

The following morning, they were giddy, as though they had stepped back in time. One showered while the other unpacked her luggage. Fun clothes and party clothes. Neither was surprised when their clothes matched.

Sharing the mirror, they suddenly hugged and each felt a wave so strong that when they backed away tears of laughter and joy filled the room.

Granny and Doc were sitting in their garden room when the twins entered with their hair in pony tails, dressed in jeans, blue-and-white striped western shirts, and western boots. Granny noticed Lori's left boot and Lily's right featured a beautiful delicate pink rose.

"Something smells like home," Lori announced.

"Breakfast in the warmer?" Lily asked, chipper and sweet.

Granny and Doc were stunned. "They're back," Doc said, as he winked at Granny.

"And stronger than ever," Granny added. "The greatest part is they appear to be unaware of how profound they truly are."

"Miss Lori, Miss Lily," Doc began, "Do you ladies wish to ride alone this morning, or would you like some company?"

"Doc," Lori suggested, "Last evening you encouraged us to ride the South Pasture Trail. I know we are a bit rusty, but if you feel we need a guide…"

"Not at all," Doc replied, a bit hesitantly. "But, you see, it's just that there are two young men who called very early this morning. They're quite anxious and excited and…"

Lily grabbed Lori's hand, their attention drawn to two young men whom they hadn't seen since Christmas day were jogging towards Granny and Doc's kitchen porch.

"As I started to say, Hunter and Storm just arrived," Doc added.

Hunter and Storm burst through the door calling their names. Lily and Lori stood, as their baby brother, Hunter, and cousin, Storm, stopped in their tracks.

"You're, ah, really back," Hunter announced.

"Welcome home," Storm added softly.

As Hunter moved in for a hug, emotion clogged his usually boisterous voice and the aura of his sisters was two-fold when the three of them hugged. Hunter felt the jolt as well.

Storm waited his turn and glanced over at Hunter when Lily and Lori hugged him, as well.

There were moments when Doc thought these two

young men also had the sight but kept their lights more closely guarded than the twins ever had. "Will you young men join us?" he asked.

They quickly complied and filled their plates with bacon, ham, scrambled eggs, pancakes, and of course, cinnamon rolls to go with juice and coffee. As soon as they were seated, Hunter graciously asked, "Will everyone join us in grace? Thank you, Lord Jesus, for this wonderful day. For this food so graciously prepared by our host and hostess, and for this connection and love of family gathered here. Amen."

They opened their eyes, all humbled by Hunter's words, and squeezed hands before letting go of this, their powerful connection. Silence filled the room momentarily as they ate and Granny topped off their coffee.

"We have orders from Mom and Dad," Hunter announced, looking directly at Granny and Doc. "You two are not cooking any more today. Marcie's Catering is taking care of it all."

"The meat is already in the roasters," Storm added. "We'll put them on the table of your screened-in porch before we saddle up."

As the girls helped Granny clear the table, Lily asked, "Do we need jackets for the ride?"

"Yes," Granny replied, and handed Hunter a thermos of hot coffee, laced with chocolate. "So. You have had plenty of room to park the RV's and campers?" Doc asked.

"Yes," Hunter replied. "I think this family celebration will be the first of many all-sides-of-the-family reunions."

"Before you ask," Storm added. "The barn is cleaned. The lanterns are in place and once the ladies do their decorating, the barn dance will just need people and the band. Tonight, the dance is for family and invited guests only. Granny's barn could not accommodate the number of people who wanted to attend."

The morning was cool under the clear, bright sky as they mounted their horses, already saddled and prepped by Hunter and Storm.

"What a wonderful way to start the day," Lily remarked.

"I missed the quiet of the country," Lori added.

"In addition, the awesome feeling of accomplishing what we set out to do," Lily confirmed, "plus the anticipation of using our knowledge and training to be able to help others."

"In my case," Lori added, "helping animals and their owners."

Nearly an hour later, as they approached a spring-fed pond and grove of trees, Hunter suggested, "Why don't we rest our horses and walk around the pond?"

"Thanks," Lori replied as they dismounted and loosened the reins. Then asked, "Hey, Storm, what are your future plans?"

"Dad approves of me finishing my degree to become an attorney, But Granny and Doc agree that I also have a unique talent training horses. So perhaps I will just have two careers."

"Okay, Storm then the more you learn about the legal field, the more passionate you are about it?" Lily asked.

Storm hesitated, looked at Hunter, and asked, "Are you a mind reader now, too?"

"Was this something the two of you worked on together?" Lori asked.

"Pretty much," Storm nodded. "However, my Dad suggested that our area is in need of some competition in the field of law and pharmacy."

Noting Storm was not only undecided, but was feeling torn about revealing something that he and Hunter had been working on, Lily turned to Hunter and asked, "Hunter? What about you?" She smiled. "It's so odd to be talking to you like an adult. It's been so long."

He smiled back. "Too long. I plan to be a minister like Great Uncle C.W. Warren. I feel drawn to teaching others about the life of Jesus and the lessons to be learned in the Bible."

"He puts together Biblical themes and combines art, visuals and music," Storm said. "I've been attending church since his first production because I want to, and every time I felt uplifted. I know I can be a drag sometimes, you know like worried about missing a basketball shot, or walking a batter in a baseball game. Sounds like a waste of time to some, but I hate to lose."

"Well," Lori added, "we know! You get that honest enough from your Dad."

They all fell silent, taking sips of coffee that steamed in the cool air. Each was quiet as they unknowingly took measure of each other, as adults.

"I have lived in other states," Lily said. "Sat in classrooms and talked with hundreds of students—but this is, by far, the first time I have felt such a strong connection of peaceful trust in my life since I was a little girl."

Her statement was followed by a whispered Amen from each of them. Their horses rested and watered, they decided it was time for them to return to Doc and Granny's. Their ride back was even more relaxing and fun, as Storm played the harmonica, and Hunter led the singing 'oldie' songs like, "Don't Fence Me In," for one.

Usually Lily hated the process of brushing Maggie, a three-year-old chestnut quarter horse she had ridden. However, Lori had taught her that this was really good for the horse's health. In a way, it was a thank you to the horse for an enjoyable ride. However, listening to Storm as he brushed Jasper, a buck-skin stallion quarter horse and harmonized with Hunter as he brushed Murphy, a red sorrel stallion quarter horse to a Willie Nelson song, changed her thoughts to enjoyable.

This is what I've been missing, Lori thought. *Family.* She watched Storm as he talked to his horse and filched an apple out of a nearby basket and held it out in his open hand. She followed Storm's directions as she made eye contact with the horse that had been so gentle with her, as though she knew the person in the saddle was a bit nervous and rode like a beginner. Instead they had become friends.

"She will always remember you," Storm said.

"Really?" Lily remarked. "Now you sound like Lori. Although it's not the first time I've heard it, it's that usually your mind is swimming in a dozen different directions, but today you were relaxed and focused."

"Then why the frown?" Hunter asked.

"I am so sorry I wasn't here to watch you grow up," Lily said.

"That's double from me, too," Lori added as she drew Hunter in for a sideways hug. "It appears the two of you both grew at least two inches since Christmas. What are you now?"

"Hunter is six foot two and I'm six foot three," Storm bragged teasingly at Hunter.

"Hey, ladies," Hunter hesitated, waiting for their attention. "You do know today's party is to celebrate the huge milestone the two of you have made in your lives? Thus there will be a lot of family attending, including our Oklahoma grandparents, and some from Mom's Children's Home family that she grew up with."

"Expect us 'ladies,'" Lori smiled and put her arm around Lily, "to break out our western clothes and fancy cowgirl boots!"

Storm and Hunter were both moved by not only their appearance, but their combined power, and wondered just how long they would be able to keep their own ability to read people from the twins.

Doc came out of the house to greet them when they returned. "Granny and I plan to splurge a bit. Join us in a strawberry milkshake, or chocolate?"

"I like the way you think," Lily agreed. "If memory serves me right, one summer evening, I was crying because a boy I liked broke up with me, and you helped me forget all about it with a milkshake."

"It has been years since you fixed us your hand-cranked

ice cream and strawberries," Lori said. "This time it didn't have anything to do with a guy or tears."

Doc returned to the house to make the treats. Granny came and joined the twins.

"You know, Granny," Lily winked at her as she pulled up a nearby lawn chair next to Lori, kicked off her boots and stretched out, as well. The horse ride through the country had made her feel nostalgic. "Were you aware of the trouble our Mom had with the school when the teacher insisted that Lori and I should be in separate classrooms and wear un-matching clothes, so we would develop our own personalities?"

"Not only that," Lori recalled, "Mom went to the school board so we could attend school in the same class-room, but on opposite sides of the room."

Yes." Lily added. "Then, when we turned in all our papers and tests in record time, she didn't have a choice but to allow us to sit in the back of the classroom. I always felt like a freak because we were the tallest in our class, as it was."

"We got even though."

Doc, emerging from the house with the shakes, snick-ered. He passed a frosted glass of pink milkshake to each one. "Here I thought you girls were such sweethearts."

Granny grinned. "Just how many times did you switch places?"

Lily glanced at Lori and replied, "Until it got boring. Then we got the feeling that she felt a little guilty because she picked-up on just how isolated we already felt with the other girls."

"It just made our bond stronger," Lori said. "We had learned that just because we continued to know stuff about people, there were times when we screened what we knew. You know, whether or not to say something, which might put us in a scary position. Especially when someone got hurt in an accident. What if? Would they have believed us?"

Granny and Doc both had tears in their eyes. "Have you ever shared this with your parents?"

They shook their heads back and forth. "We talked to Mom's Dr. Kate," Lily said.

"We did a lot of praying," Lori added. "Did it always work? No."

"We're not perfect, but for the most part it worked. If you leave out our quick temper, especially when it involves people who can't help themselves."

"I guess we didn't see what others did until the big day of the fight. That was my fault."

"Lori, please," Lily begged. "I was okay."

"I know that now," Lori continued. "Lesson learned. No matter how sick I am, everything else takes a back seat to being alert and being prepared for anything."

"I can't recall ever seeing you that angry, Sis. Granted, he was always a real jerk, and probably deserved what happened to him."

"We had seen Dexter Franklin's younger brother, Calvin, trip others, which he always thought was funny. But that day in study hall, when he rammed his size twelve shoe right behind your knees was totally inconceivable! Your knees buckled and your head hit something. I think someone's elbow could have broken your nose, but when I saw blood…"

"I wasn't knocked unconscious. He didn't break my nose. But the way you went after him was like nothing I have ever seen. One kick and he flew out of his seat and onto the floor. He was three times your size and weight. You screamed and went after him like a banshee. I've never before or since seen you move like that."

"You recognized it though, right?" Lori asked.

"Yeah. It's one of those moves Aunt Brandi taught us after Aunt Wendy hid us in the woods when those two goons tried to kidnap us."

Doc had heard comments about this but never from the girls. "How old were you?"

"We were three."

"But it wasn't until the eighth grade," Lori recalled, "that I retaliated because Calvin had hurt my sister. I can still see him tangled up in his desk on the floor. The room was quiet after he hit the floor."

"When you put that hold on his free arm and demanded he apologize; everyone—guys included—were afraid he would hurt you," Lily added.

"Then, he got his second wind swore at you and yelled, 'You broke my finger and my nose!'"

"You yelled right back, 'Blame the floor and your desk. That's what you hit. Not me!' When he said, 'My dad will see you in court. You women are all crazy.' Then you stomped on his shoulder and twisted his arm until he flinched and said, 'Okay. Okay. I'm Sorry!' We all were so amazed when he apologized."

"I remember," Lori admitted. "I let go of him and walked away and got sick. I know. I felt foolish for not stopping, and I prayed for patience and forgiveness to never get that angry again."

"What were the odds," Lily said, "That his dad would just happen to be across the hall and saw everything that happened, plus the aftermath."

Lori spooned her milkshake thoughtfully. "Could he be the one who has been having us followed, just because we're back home?"

"All I know is that we need to get back in shape. Studying and riding a stationary bike isn't the same as running and riding outdoors," Lily added.

"You are so right," Lori said. "I am looking forward to today. The family is also celebrating Hunter and Storm's accomplishments. Hey, who was that one doctor who taught one of your classes? Wasn't he interested in you?"

"It's so good to see you together again," Doc said. "I'm sure all the others are looking forward to meeting you again at the party tonight.

"Speaking of people coming in," Lily asked, "Granny, I thought I heard vehicles during the night. Are those Will's new buses? Security here and your estate?"

Granny nodded. "Just so you know, his Oklahoma family is bunking in one of his old on-site-buses. Others are sleeping in the hay-loft adjacent to Will's additional headquarters."

"Do you suppose that was what was bothering Hunter and Storm?" Lori mused. "Doc, are you expecting second and third generations here this weekend?"

"Yes. Several campers were brought in for the week-end overflow," Doc said.

"That sounds great," Lori added. "That's a relief because we missed being here with family. Hopefully, they will all be wearing name tags."

Chapter 3

Doc O'Reilly slowly cruised into Granny's Estate driveway, nodding to one of Will Fox's security team members, professionally dressed in their Blues Security Apparel. Granny rode in the front passenger seat while Lily and Lori shared the back seat of Doc's black special-ordered sleeper Ford pickup truck.

"Granny," Lily asked. "Who made the reunion banner?"

"It's amazing! " Lori added as she read the names plastered in twelve-inch letters: *CARPENTER – DAVIES – DONNELLY – FOX – OATES – WARREN.* The Banners were strung from tree to tree in alphabetical order along the driveway entrance of Granny's Oates Estate.

"Once each vehicle and its family members are properly identified," Granny explained, "and are listed in the reunion journals, they will be issued name badges. The boys helped Doc with the vehicle parking, so no one can crash our reunion, like last year."

"This will be the first reunion we've been able to attend for more than a single day," Lily commented, as Doc drove at turtle speed behind the barn toward his personal parking space.

"This is the first time we have been chauffeured," Lori said, "Instead of driving our get-away-vehicle. Thanks to the two of you, no worries today."

"No worries today, Ladies," Doc repeated.

"Worries?" they replied in unison, joined hands, looked at each other and smiled. The last time they had said that was high school graduation. The feeling caused goosebumps that melted into warmth like the frost of overnight melted when the morning sunlight boldly sparkled on each blade of grass. Unshed tears of welcoming pooled in their hazel-blue-green eyes. The color depended on what they were wearing and feeling. This was a homecoming that wasn't just about family but each other.

With a deep sigh, Lori said, "It's okay to relax a bit and sharing a visit at Doc and Granny's house has become a wonderful, unexpected, stress-free vacation. Especially knowing we will have a place to rent closer to work."

Ahead they noticed someone standing in the lane, speaking to the driver of each car in turn through their open windows. "Granny, why do *we* need to wear badges?" Lily asked.

"To set an example," she replied, and smiled when she read their badges: Lori R. Donnelly DVM and Lily A. Donnelly, D.C. Granny knew why Lily had asked as Doc inched forward toward the one person they were hoping to ignore at the reunion.

"Good afternoon, Dr. Dexter," Granny said, making an issue of reading his official badge.

"Good afternoon, Granny O'Reilly and the ladies of the hour, Lily Anne and Lori Rose."

"See, Granny. Doc," Lori pointed out. "He ignores our titles."

Dr. Dexter moved on to the car behind them with a sour look, and Lily saw a friendlier face. "Uncle Kristopher! You look like your brother, Charlie."

"But you are taller than he is," Lori added, with a teasing smile, as he handed them a copy of the Oates/O'Reilly ALL-FAMILY Reunion Program Schedule.

"I look forward to spending more time with the two of you later," Kristopher Donnelly announced. "Doc. You will park in your assigned slot?"

Doc's reply was a casual salute and a smile because Kristopher knew Doc had been in charge of the parking.

"Granny," Lori asked studying the grounds more carefully through the window, "When did you have the fence along the drive installed?"

"About six months ago," she replied. "It's a project that has been in the works for several years."

"Does this include your entire estate or just part of it?" Lily asked.

"Just part for now. I am sorry that you haven't had a chance to look over your boxes, trunks, and luggage that Jonothan delivered here a few weeks ago. They are locked-up in the blue bedroom until after the reunion. One of the families flew into Turtle Crossing and found the Turtle Crossing Hotel was booked, as was the Welby

Mansion Bed and Breakfast due to a wedding."

"Oh," Lori commiserated, "We are still undecided which one of us is the worst cook, so we are enjoying being spoiled by you and Doc this week."

"But we are also excited that you are allowing us to rent your estate home until we get our businesses up and running and can afford to either buy or build other accommodations," Lily concluded, as they climbed down out of Doc's truck.

Their feet barely touched the ground when squeals filled the air. Lori and Lily were suddenly made aware of the increased security. "Aunt Marcie," Lori quickly grabbed her hand just as Lily handed Lori her new dressy western hat when one of Will's men stepped out of the shadows.

"Sorry," Marcie whispered. "I don't think I will ever get used to Will's security, but you girls have to admit I got their attention," she chuckled as she hugged them.

"Really, Aunt Marcie," You may hear from Uncle Will about this," Lily remarked. "Good thing you are wearing your name tag."

"Where's Mom and Dad?" Lori asked. "And how are you and your family?" she added as they followed Marcie to the farmhouse. The twins both turned around and waved to Doc and Granny, then blew them a kiss and thank-you wave.

Doc hugged Granny as soon as they disembarked from his beloved truck. "With those two, plus Storm and Hunter, this weekend will be a well-remembered, first-time combining all-sides-of-the-family reunion.

The twins' trek towards the farmhouse smoothed out when they decided to walk on the drive rather than the lawn, which was filled with family clusters of folding tables, play pens, and lawn chairs of every description, under every shade tree.

Lily called out, "Have you seen our Mom and Dad?"

Several pointed and replied, "On Granny's porch!"

"Thanks," Lori added and waved.

"Well. That just melted a huge iceberg," Marcie said.

"My, oh, my. Look what little brother has done to Granny's plain white garage."

"Mom's pictures do not do it justice," Lily added. There's Granny's favorite sunflowers. They look exactly like the real ones, bending forward like they are sheltering a bench, a rocking chair and antique baby cradle with Mom's roses in the foreground!"

"I take it," Hunter greeted, "My famous big sisters approve?"

"What's not to approve?" Lori remarked as she gave him a hug, followed by a hug from Lily.

"We would like to talk to you about your future plans, and visits with our infamous Shadow Angels & Aunties later," Lori said. "But you felt my presence long before I said a word, didn't you?"

"Yes," Hunter replied. "So did Storm," he added softly, the moment Will walked away.

"Anyone observing us would think we hadn't seen each other just less than an hour ago," Lori smiled, as Storm reached out to shake her hand.

"That isn't even cool," Hunter chuckled as he

buddy-punched Storm on the shoulder.

"Beautiful job on the garage," Lily commented, "and as we walk towards the garage, I might add awesome screened-in porch and sunroom. No further discussion until later."

"But we do have a proposition," Lori suggested. "We would like the two of you to join us secretly at first anyhow."

Together they turned around and faced Hunter and Storm. "We could become the Four Aces later," they added and walked towards the house.

"They're back," Hunter smiled.

"This is so exciting," Storm added. "Oops, we're being paged."

"Yeah," Hunter agreed, as they jogged back to help the family crew with setting up a few more chairs and tables inside Granny's three-car garage.

"Hi! Mom, Dad," Lily said. Lori echoed her greeting, as they took turns hugging their parents.

"Everything is okay," Shannon nodded.

"Yes," David hedged, not saying a whole lot either, as he warmly hugged each of his daughters. "But, Lily, please remember, both of you have been greatly missed. Remember, if you ever get in a tight spot, we're just a phone call away."

"It is pretty awesome to be home." Lily choked back tears and righted her hat.

"Knowing we don't have to leave early to get back to school is a dream come true," Lori said. "We can finally move forward with our lives. I know I already have a job, and Lily is dealing with a few challenges; but we'll work them out."

Lily glanced at their dad and he tipped his hat. Message sent. Message received. "We are looking forward to spending more time with Hunter and Storm, too," Lily added.

"Why didn't you ever answer my letter?" Hunter asked a bit brusquely.

"When did you send me a letter?" Lily asked, puzzled by his tone of voice.

"A month ago!" he replied.

"What was the exact date?" Lori asked.

"The exact date? Why are you asking? Surely you believe me?"

Lily and Lori hesitated. They had not planned to get into this today.

Shannon looked at David and David suggested, "Son? Why don't you and I get the ladies some lemonade?"

"Sure, Dad," Hunter replied, and they strode off toward the refreshment table.

"You see," David began, "It's been about three months ago that someone started stealing mail from Lily's—and several of Lily's friends'—apartment mail boxes. She found out when companies started demanding payments that were overdue."

"She would have told us if she had received a personal letter from anyone back home. Not necessarily the contents, of course, but your sisters have always been excited when anyone from home, especially family, remembered them anymore."

"I had no idea," said Hunter. "Maybe we better take these pitchers and glasses back to the ladies."

When they returned to the table, Hunter was contrite and said, "I apologize. I should have known better, but…" and shrugged his shoulders.

"Now can I have another hug?" Lily asked.

Hunter's eyes lit up and when he smiled, his dimples were more noticeable.

"Are you sitting on a deadline, Storm?" Lily asked.

"Nothing pressing that I can't reschedule," he replied. Storm had tried to stay in the background during the misunderstanding, especially because it involved the twins. He wasn't used to interacting with anyone who had the sight except Hunter.

"Are you two serious about us teaming up together?"

"Absolutely," they replied. "Will you be at the dance this evening?" Lori asked.

When they nodded, Storm said, "Can the first waltz be mine?" he asked, smiling. "Don't want my girl getting the big head, you know. Later."

"Wow," Lori remarked, "Will and Wendy have their hands full with that one."

"So true," Lily agreed. "He's feisty, polite, stands his ground, and is movie star handsome; but he also has that deep dark brown hair and eyes with a studious mysterious look about him."

When Lily was describing Storm, Lori noticed the painful distance Lily was hiding from everyone—the former professor who had broken her heart. "Have you heard from him since graduation?" Lori asked.

"Not a word," Lily replied softly. "But I have to keep moving forward, you know. He has someone else now." She swallowed hard, blinked away wasteful tears, and turned into Lori's arms.

Hunter had been watching them, waiting, hesitant to approach, but felt his Mom's approval and her nod. He loudly cleared his throat and asked, "When you are free, I would like to introduce you to my girlfriend, Harmony."

"Of course," Lily replied. "Hmm, baby brother," she teased, "this sounds serious,"

Lori smiled and winked at him.

"I think she is pretty special," Hunter said, "I may be biased. Some women don't like her and commented that she doesn't fit in."

"Is she here yet?" Lily asked.

He nodded. "She just arrived."

"Okay." Lori said. "How does she feel about your introspective side?"

"Well," he hesitated and answered, "I'm doing much better. Mom insists I set aside time for daily meditation and accepting who and what I am. And having you two as my big sisters is a miracle I am thankful for every day."

"Well, should we go meet her?" he finished.

"Sure," they replied as they turned to follow him toward the barn.

"Wait," Marcie called out, cameras in hand. They hesitated and turned towards her, when she caught up with them. Marcie remarked, "Storm is waiting for your approval on the Barn Dance Hall—Country Style this evening."

"We're on our way," Hunter announced.

When they arrived at the barn, Storm called out, "I'm double-checking the lighting."

"Tables and chairs in the old hay mow are a smart touch," Lily commented. As she climbed the stairs, the sound of her boots echoed back in the emptiness.

Storm quickly left the ladder he had been on and raced up the opposite set of stairs to greet them. The twins quickly became distracted by a large dog sitting at attention outside the door while two small children happily stamped in the dirt around it.

"Whose kids are they?" Lily wondered aloud.

"Not sure," answered Hunter.

"And what about the dog?" Lori asked. "Scruffy, but could pass for one of Rosie's grand-pups." She immediately changed course to visit the animal.

"Wait, where you going?" Storm demanded.

"It's okay," Hunter intervened. "Lori has a way with animals. The four-legged kind at least." If Lori heard him, she ignored the jibe.

Hunter announced his approval of the decorations and exited the barn too. Marcie met him at the door. "Sorry to have sidetracked you," she said. "I know Harmony just arrived and is looking for you."

"Lots going on," Hunter agreed.

But Marcie didn't hear him. She had just noticed a scarecrow in one of Granny's gardens, and thought her imagination was on over-drive. *What just happened? Is it a memory that feels a bit out of reach? Why here? Now?*

Meanwhile, Lori was approaching the scruffy dog

with a coat full of burrs, and with the intelligence in its eyes that was heart-warming. When the little boy, still young enough to be wobbly on his legs, fell over, the dog snatched hold of the straps on his trousers and tugged until the little boy was on his feet. He was barefoot. Dusty. Both kids were in need of a bath and haircut, and the baby's dirty diaper was drooping between his little legs.

Hunter joined his sisters, who were now crouched by the dog and the children.

"There you are," Harmony's voice said behind him.

The older child, who looked to be about two years old, heard her and cried out, "Harmony, Harmony, Harmony!"

If someone could be struck dead from shock, it was Harmony. Her face turned white as chalk.

Hunter turned. "You know these children?"

She merely nodded, then straightened her shoulders and with an almost challenging look, replied, "They live in a nearby mobile home park. Their parents were talking of leaving because they haven't been able to find work. I've made friends with the mom since I dropped off some left-over stew and clothes from the church rummage sales."

"What about the dog?" Lori asked, studying it with a veterinarian's practiced eye.

"Don't know. I've never seen it before."

Lily picked up the smallest of the children, who was reaching up to her for just this purpose, and asked the older one, "Where are your mommy and daddy?"

"They go bye-bye." A tear slipped out but was quickly

fisted away, leaving a streak of dust across her cheek. Then she reached up to Harmony, saying "Harmony, Harmony."

Harmony stooped down and swept her into her arms. As she brushed the child's wet, stringy hair away from her face, the little girl said, "Me, Little Missy, and he, Baby Blue." Then pointing to the dog, she added, "He, Troop."

Unnoticed by the others, Storm had followed them outside and had tracked the children's footprints, and the coming and departure of adult prints which were just beyond the wood's clearing. The dog's prints appeared nearby too.

The little girl watched Storm as he exited the barn and walked toward them. He paused several yards away and bent to lift something out of the dirt. The girl held out her hand and stated, "Mine!" when she saw a pink purse the size of her hand, with a make-shift chain, dangling from Storm's hand. Storm handed her the purse and she hugged it close to her chest.

Marcie and Shannon arrived with questioning looks. While Shannon took pictures of the children with Lily and Harmony, Storm motioned Marcie to join him. "There are some interesting footprints in the lane I would like you to photograph," Storm suggested. "Dad's always bragging about how you know what to photo in a case."

"What led you to the conclusion that this is a case?"

"See here, for instance, is where the children were picked up by Lily and Harmony. Before that, they were with this scruffy dog that joined these two children. Before the dog, the footprints appear to be a woman's with one child. Then, her footprints head in the opposite direction alone and disappear into the woods."

"I see what you mean. Your Dad will be proud," Marcie said, as they headed back. "But your Dad's team has checked out this entire area. How did they miss this?"

"In the beginning, my reason to follow the footprints was to find the parents, to let them know where their children were. I also contacted the nearby mobile home park," Storm added.

"I'm sure they will be in touch," Marcie said. "In the world we live in, the parents would be turning this place upside down to find these two beautiful children; but these footprints tell a different story, don't they? No matter what, we need to figure out where they came from and why before too many others notice and start to interfere, especially Dr. Dexter. He'll do anything to center this party on himself."

As Storm and Marcie joined the crew around the children, Marcie suggested, "While we distract a certain doctor, you ladies take these children to Granny's for a bath and fresh clothes. You know the huge walk-in closet where she collects donations for the homeless and church rummage sale."

They nodded. While Storm threw Dr. Dexter off their trail by telling him that one of his Dad's security team might need medical attention, Hunter corralled Granny and Doc.

Families were busy visiting. Children were playing and unaware of the scenario that was happening within a few feet of them, which was a true blessing. The children fit right in, and during all this, Troop meandered away from the crowds.

"Here we go," Lily said. "Bathtub, clothes, and food, in that order."

Agreeing, Lori added, "I'll see what's available for the dog Little Missy called Troop. There wasn't a collar, so we don't know if it has had its shots." As they approached the farmhouse, they were surprised to see Brandi still in uniform pull in and park between the updated garage and driveway entrance.

Missy whimpered when she saw one of Turtle Crossing's Deputy Sheriffs. Lori quickly filled her in on what they knew of the mysterious children's situation. "Lily, Harmony, and I are taking them to the downstairs bathroom to clean them up and get them into some clean clothes."

"Mind if I join you?" Brandi asked. "You all know, I am required to report to children's services whenever children have been abandoned."

They nodded, but Brandi wasn't taking any chances. In Granny's big closet, she grabbed clothes, diapers, shirts, a bag of shoes that looked to be the kids' sizes and rushed around the corner when she overheard Granny talking to Dr. Dexter. That meant that sparks were about to happen and soon. "Lock this door. I will wait outside."

Murmuring and giggles drifted outside the bathroom, and Brandi had some ideas floating in her mind, when Dr. Dexter spotted her.

"Deputy," he said, as he puffed out his chest, "I need to check those children over to make certain whether they need to be hospitalized or possibly are victims of child abuse."

"Well, Dr. Dexter, those children are healthy. The dust has been washed down the drain and they have also been checked for lice. There is no sign of broken bones or bruises."

"By whose authority?"

"As you know, I am a Deputy Detective with the Turtle Crossing's Sheriff's Department and Lily has checked them over as well."

As Harmony started the bath water and laid the twelve-month-old on the floor, grabbing soap, towels, and whatever else she would need, Lily shut the water off. Teasing Harmony, Lily suggested, "Do you have a change of clothes?"

"Why?"

"Because this young man is going to be splashing water all over us."

Marcie and Lori slipped into the bathroom with Little Missy. Harmony whispered to Blue, "Just wait till you see your big sister, all dressed up with her hair swept up in a pony-tail. Harmony set Blue in the bath tub and asked, "Lily, can you hold onto him while I shampoo his hair?"

Lily was already in position before Harmony had the baby shampoo ready. "How did you know what I planned to do?" Harmony asked, then shrugged her shoulders.

Little Missy was still standing just inside the door when Dr. Dexter started banging on the door and demanded, "I need to see those children!" Apparently Brandi had been called away from her post.

Missy tiptoed away from the door and grabbed Lori. By this time, Lily and Harmony had Blue dressed, their dusty clothes were bagged and stored in a bucket behind the door. The bathroom was spotless.

Marcie let herself in through the side door off of the kitchen as they were finishing up. "We need to figure out what's happening with these little ones before Dr. Dexter whisks them away in to protective services," she whispered to Lily, Lori, and Harmony, who all nodded. "Little Missy, will you hold my hand while I pick up Blue and carry him out the door? That man knows I have two children; however, he has never seen them. Can you pretend to be my children? Your friends Lily, Lori, and Harmony are going to go fix you both some food and meet us at the picnic table. Ready?" Marcie threw a diaper bag with a few diapers, a couple of bottles, and a change of clothes over her shoulder and unlocked the door.

Dexter was winding up for another round of pounding on the door when Marcie stepped out with the children. "What is all the ruckus out here?" she demanded, looking around to see if anyone else was about or paying Dexter any mind.

Dexter stepped inside momentarily, turned around, and left.

By the time Marcie arrived at the picnic table in the garage, she was steaming about Dexter and his pompous attitude. "These children were so well behaved, neither one of them let out a peep," Marcie smiled proudly. "Granny cornered me and offered to read to them on her porch swing with her and Doc as soon as they eat."

"Harmony, I barely recognized those children when you ladies left them with Granny and Doc. Are you free for a while?"

"Yes," she nodded. "Hunter, I assume you and Storm have been busy, too?" she added after they were settled in a shady spot away from the crowd.

"Storm and I have been making room for more parking, and reminding people to mark their lawn chairs so they don't get lost; you know, stuff like that. People have been really helpful. They're even emptying the big trash cans into the dumpster."

"May I assume you two are ready for this evening's dance?" Harmony asked. "You are so lucky to have such a wonderful connected family. I was drawn especially to the family trees. From what I know, Little Missy and Blue may never have that."

"In what way?"

"I met their dad once. When I asked their mom where they were from. She was hesitant and cautious when she replied, 'Oh. Here and there. We travel a lot. I had both my children right here in this mobile.'"

"There were no family pictures anywhere. Little Missy and Blue could be most anyone's children."

Hunter clasped Harmony's hand. "My family has connections and never give up when a search is put in motion. Especially when it involves children. So it's okay for you to enjoy the rest of the day and evening. There will be a Sunrise breakfast and a Sunday service tomorrow. I hope you will attend. The barn and the double-garage-sized attached tent that we put up will be filled."

"Hunter," Harmony added, "Dr. Dexter isn't going to give up either."

"Well, he's off the trail for now, and I need to focus on tomorrow. My great uncle, Rev. C.W. will be giving the main sermon."

"Does this mean that you will be doing the second one?" Harmony asked.

"Yes. Will you be there?"

"I can't wait," she murmured.

Hunter looked at his watch, and whispered, "I have to go now, sweetheart," followed by a hug and a kiss on her cheek.

Lori had stayed on the sideline, mingling with family. So far, each family member and their guests were accounted for. Marcie was still taking family group photographs and the adults' horseshoe games had quieted down to cards.

Closing her notebook, she glanced up and noted that Dr. Dexter was doing everything to drum up his business. Anything to make himself look important. "Dr. Dexter, what are you still doing here?" Lori asked.

He stood up, shoving his shoulders back to prove he was still one-inch taller than she, which didn't minimize his dislike of her. It was because of her that his father had pulled him out of school and enrolled him in military school. They moved away, which kept him from being expelled, however his dad also changed jobs, but this was never mentioned. "As a matter of fact, I was just leaving."

"Thank you for stopping by," Lori said in her most

respectful voice that she used for recalcitrant horses and dogs.

"Do you even know who I am?" he demanded, as he brushed miniscule dust specks from his sleeves.

"Of course I do," Lori replied. "Come on. We're all older. The past is in the past. We can't go back and change it. Right?"

He was stunned. She didn't act overbearing or act high-and-mighty. Was it really that easy?

"You are aware that your sister isn't a real doctor."

"Lily is a Chiropractic Doctor of Health! I have no doubt that Lily and I attended required classes that you didn't. So get over it! We both went to school, including summer classes, eight years. You did say you were just leaving?" Lori tossed him a two-fingered salute goodbye, turned around, grabbed a sandwich, an apple and a lemonade, and walked away.

"Hey, Sis," Lily asked when she caught up with Lori. "Are you okay?"

"Yes. Thanks. I felt your love and support. Your strength helped me to reach out to Dexter, to help resolve the past issues, instead of using the past as a crutch. I came real close to telling him to grow up, but then realized any more words from me would be a waste of time. Instead, I'm going to meditate and get ready for the dance this evening."

"Thank you! I am looking forward to it, too," Lily added. "Mind if I join you?"

They had just showered, dressed and were doing their hair when Lori asked, "Were you aware of Hunter and

Storm during the Dexter confrontation when he tried to collect those two darling children?"

"Yes. What an awesome feeling! It has been so long since I even felt this awareness connection with you, Sis. Until you walked into my apartment in Chicago, it became real again, and continues to grow. But, now it is pretty darn awesome with Hunter and Storm too!"

"I know. Dexter was surprised and frustrated that his plans to 'show-off' his newly acquired title, but I don't believe he is finished with us even though Brandi was not about to back down."

"While you were stuck dealing with Dexter, Jonothan stopped by with exciting news. The Shadow Angels have called an emergency meeting, which will include: Will, Jonothan, Hunter, Storm, the two of us, plus the first and second generation Shadow Angels."

"Interesting. You don't suppose our plans as a Foursome will be limited?" Lori asked.

"We'll work it out. Hunter and Storm have asked for the first dance this evening, but how about another horseback ride early Monday morning?" They high-fived, stopped side by side in front of the full-length mirror and smiled—with just a little bit of mischief in their eyes.

"Also, I overheard a few comments today about some plans that have been in the works for the last two years about Eight Mile Centre."

"Uncle Will hinted," Lori added, "that he has been working towards helping our dreams come true."

Lily answered the timid sounding knock on their door with, "Come in."

"May I have a word with you?" Harmony asked. "Have you seen Hunter? I wanted him to know that I never mentioned this huge party scheduled this weekend here to anyone!"

"Thank you," Lori replied, "For sharing that, but I'm certain he is around some place."

"Yes," Lily asked. "Are you planning to attend the dance this evening?"

"Hunter asked me, and—" Harmony gave a deep sigh, "—I'm so glad you are wearing jeans. I only have a few dresses."

"We're eating light if you would like to join us," Lily encouraged as they grabbed the jean jackets Granny had helped them decorate when they were in high school.

"The embroidery on your jackets is exquisite," Harmony remarked.

"Thanks," Lori said. "We did all this one summer when we stayed with Granny while Mom and Dad went to Alaska with friends."

"Yeah," Lily added, "We had to practice on a pillow case first. If you're wondering, we left our jackets here with Granny while we were away at college."

When their feet hit the bottom of Granny's stairs Hunter and Storm were waiting with broad grins on their faces. "Do you two always leave your dance partners waiting?" Storm teased.

"Come on," Lori teased right back. "Have you been eating all day, or do you have time to join us for a snack before we hit the dance floor?"

"We have a table reserved at the barn if you would like

to join us," Hunter added, "plus your choice of pizza or hot dogs, or both? We're here to escort you to the Barn Dance. Harmony, I've been looking all over for you."

"Really? I thought you two were practicing with the band?"

"Can't fool you for one minute, can I?" Hunter replied. "Are you going to join us now or were you planning to check on Little Missy and Blue first?"

"I promised Granny I would help her get them ready for bed, but I will join you at the dance a little later," Harmony replied.

"I noticed your bicycle by Granny's back porch," Hunter commented.

Hunter caught up with the rest of the Foursome walking towards the barn. "Lori, you and Lily were awesome with Dr. Dexter this morning regarding those two children."

"It was the four of us," Lily clarified.

"We like the idea of the four of us," Storm added, catching up with them, glancing at Hunter not wanting to speak out of turn, or speak for him, because they had not had a chance to talk about his feelings.

"Are you two free in the morning?" Lily asked. "Lori and I enjoyed our ride yesterday and would like you two to join us again if possible."

Hunter couldn't believe their luck. "We have security service tomorrow, so that would be a great way to start our day."

This Foursome plan was working out in more ways than one, and he prayed his sisters never found out that

Uncle Will had assigned him and Storm to 'look out' for them.

"Here's our table," Storm said, as he pulled out chairs for the ladies. Once they were seated, Hunter brought a tray of food and drinks.

In the meantime, Lily and Lori were on overload. Lily leaned over to Lori and suggested, "We know part of this reunion is about us about to launch our careers, but the mix feels a bit weird."

"I agree." Lori slathered mustard on a sandwich and hid her reply behind a mug bubbling with frosted, aromatic root beer. "Who does that gorgeous red-haired young lady belong to?"

"She's Brandi's niece. Brandi's brother Mason and Autumn Davies's, daughter, Allison," Storm replied.

"And," Hunter added, "Allison sings in the church choir and once in a while sings with our Donnelly-Davies Band."

"She is lovely," Lori smiled, "You say 'our' like you are a part of this band."

"We wanted to surprise you," Hunter said. "Yes, I play guitar and sing part-time."

"We've had to cut back," Storm added, "the past four years, with college and I help Hunter at the church."

"Mom wrote us about your interest in the church," Lori replied.

"Yes." Hunter hesitated, and then apologized, "I have been helping C.W., Reverend Cecil Warren, with Sunday services every other week at his Evangelical Community Country Church in Winthrop."

"Oh, I always loved that church," Lily commented. "Then will you be doing our service tomorrow morning?"

"We are doing a thirty-minute Sunrise Breakfast service tomorrow morning at six, before the campers pull out. Marcie and some of the other women will be taking care of the breakfast."

"Is the Sunrise Service on our programs?" Lori asked.

"No," Storm responded. "C.W. and Hunter decided to do this after talking to some of the families. They can eat breakfast during the Sunrise Service and save time on the road." He glanced around the tables and announced, "The band will be playing the Tennessee Waltz to encourage the adults to dance. Come on. We discussed this. This reunion was a celebration party for the fabulously famous Donnelly Twins."

Hunter held his hand out and drew Lily to her feet. Storm did the same to Lori. The lead singers introduced them and began harmonizing with Allison Davies. Hunter teased Lily, "Have you been practicing?"

"Have you been practicing?" Storm asked Lori. "See. Just like riding a horse. You never forget."

"It always helps when the partner doesn't hesitate to take the lead," Lori replied, a smile on her face as Storm added a smooth turn around the dance floor.

"Lily," Hunter suggested, "Just relax and enjoy, or make believe I'm someone else," he chuckled. "Sorry, Sis. If he walked away, he didn't deserve you."

When the band switched to a fox trot, the nerves disappeared. Anyone watching would have thought they had to have been practicing for months when they kicked it into overdrive and decided to have some fun. The ladies followed. Never missing a step.

As soon as the music stopped, Allison stepped up to the mike. "How about a ladies-only line dance, which will be followed by a men-only line dance."

While the ladies were lining up, Hunter and Storm stepped away from the crowd. "We're going to have to change the evening's venue," Hunter suggested.

"I got the same feeling," Storm nodded. "As long as we are on stage with the band, Lily and Lori will stay, but otherwise we are not going to be able to 'fudge' a reason to stay with them."

Chapter 4

After the band took a break, Lori looked at her watch, and said, "Storm, We are really enjoying the music, dancing and watching the family having fun, but it's been a long day and we have to get up early for the Sunrise Service in the morning."

Hunter overheard her request as he approached from the stage and suggested, "We must be on the same wave length because it appears that most of the family agrees with you."

"Can we catch a ride with you guys over to the ranch?" Lily asked. "We'll stop by and let Granny know that we're leaving with you."

Hunter stopped by the stage and talked to a member of the band. "My sisters are tired, so Storm and I are going to take them back to the ranch. Uncle Will, if the band needs anything, can they call you?"

"I'll still be here," Will replied. "They still don't know you two are assigned to them, right?"

"No. But I won't lie to them if they ask," Hunter replied.

"Understood," Will nodded.

A few minutes later, they pulled up by Doc's front door.

"Lori," Lily asked. "What's taking so long? Do you need help remembering the code?"

"Of course not." Lori smiled, and when she punched harder on the code pad, the door moved.

That was when she immediately shoved Lily at Hunter off the west side of the three-step porch and took Storm with her in the opposite direction, his body in protective mode. No one said a word, but Hunter & Storm sent an alarm on their walkie-talkies to Will's headquarters parked behind Doc's barn. Within minutes, all of Will's team would be descending on their location.

The quiet was, or could have been, unbearable except this Foursome was at risk of the unknown, yet there was a bond of growing trust. The porch lights spilled out between them. At first, Lori thought the darkness was their friend, but maybe not. She knew Lily would be recalling lessons since childhood: Remember. Remember. Listen. She placed her hand on the brick. Cool, as expected for this time of day. The deck was dark except for a splash of light from the patio door. Perhaps it was partially open, but that was around the back corner of the house. The security light halo was too far away and towards the driveway.

Lily threw a clod of dirt onto the porch, then Lori threw another, and they waited. Patience. They had already scanned the immediate area when they had arrived from habit. No vehicles. Not even a bicycle.

However, all of the lights were on inside the house. Lily hadn't practiced the tree shimmy for years; but when she heard a twig snap—and smelled dog on the light breeze—she pulled Hunter down into a squat position. Then, when Storm started to move forward, Lori grabbed his shirt and whispered "NO." When they saw a moving flash of light, Lily and Lori knew it was Brandi accompanied by her German-Shepherd, Lt. Pepper, and motioned stop on the guys' open palms. They nodded. Always assume the worst until proven wrong.

"What is your assessment?" Brandi asked Lori.

Lori replied, "We didn't see or sense people or animals inside the house."

"Is that why you are barefoot?" Brandi whispered.

"Well, the guys weigh more than we do, so we climbed on their shoulders; otherwise we couldn't see in the windows.

"I prayed for a dog, and look who showed up? Troop and Pepper," Lily said.

"Troop," Lori encouraged, "What do you have there?" She held out her hand and he dropped something at her feet.

In the distance, they heard a siren and, and soon thereafter a police car with lights flashing pulled in Doc's driveway so fast, he barely missed hitting a light pole beside the main entrance. Storm and Hunter blinked a look at each of the twins and traded places. Of course, the dogs felt the change as well.

"Herman," Brandi acknowledged in a belligerent tone of voice. "What in the world are you doing here?"

"I heard the break-in call on my radio, and I don't need you questioning my right to be here." He turned to Lori and with his hand extended, demanded, "Now, Little Missy, you will hand over whatever that excuse for a dog dropped at your feet."

"You crossed the county line," Brandi said, taking a deep breath and added, "twenty-five miles back."

"Well!" he blustered. "How about I take this Little Missy here?" But he made the mistake of grabbing Lori by the wrist. Suddenly his gun flew out of his hand. He was on the ground unable to move, and for an instant he thought he was seeing double Missies. Then that female, Deputy Brandi Davies, had her size ten boot on his jugular, and there were two K-9 dogs slobbering all over his pant legs.

Meanwhile, two of Will's men in blue and a couple of deputies from Turtle Crossing had moved the twins, Hunter and Storm, into the shadows.

"Herman," Brandi repeated, "This entire visit of yours is still being recorded. Your guns will be returned to your office by courier within twenty-four hours, and the State Patrol will escort you back across the county line. Unless you would like to spend the night in the Turtle Crossing Jail."

Once the paperwork was completed, one of the State Patrolmen leaned forward for Brandi's hearing only, and remarked, "No doubt his fifteen-year-old son was involved here."

Brandi just shrugged her shoulders. The Foursome were very much aware of why she had moved them out of the spotlight and of the approach of Dr. Dexter.

"Are Lori and Lily okay?" Dr. Dexter asked.

"They're fine," Hunter replied.

"I wasn't asking you," Dexter said.

"I need to talk to the four of you," Brandi clarified.

They nodded. As they turned to follow her, Dexter commented, "Since I'm the doctor on call this evening, perhaps you need me to sit in on this?"

"No, Doctor," Brandi replied.

As he walked away, he mumbled, stomping his feet and saying, "It still all comes down to money and privilege every time that bunch is involved."

"Dex!" Will demanded. "Follow me! That's my family you were mumbling about. So, what's the big deal? You served in the military, and I applaud you for that. You now have a family medical practice and, from what I hear, you are a very good doctor. You need to let go of your 'poor-me-childhood'. I understand your parents were well-liked and well-respected in this community."

"It sounds like you have a file on me. Why?" Dexter asked.

"I have a file on every person who works for and with me," Will stated. "I also have a file on your brother, Calvin. When you were kids, how many times did you take the heat for what he did?"

"He was my responsibility!" Dexter stated, as he threw his shoulders back and looked Will in the eye .

"No, Dex," Will said. "Man to man here, okay? That's

where your parents made the mistake. They paid your brother out of one episode after another. Then they sent you to military school? But, Calvin followed you into the military and served overseas, didn't he?"

"What does all this have to do with me not being allowed to talk to your family?"

"It's their story to tell. Deputy Brandi has a job to do. And that includes this entire evening!"

"That means they were..."

"You have a good evening, Dex. You're already off the clock. We appreciate your volunteer time," Will said as he headed towards his traveling office.

After they had answered questions for Brandi, Lily and Lori walked over to Will's second home and office. "Thank you, Uncle Will," Lily whispered and then broke down crying. Lori sat beside her, tears falling like rain.

"It was like when we were little again. We've both gotten hurt a few times when we intervened to help each other, but we and the boys had been patient all evening; and then I prayed, and Lori said she had prayed for Pepper or one like him; and there was Troop. The Lord answers prayers, and we weren't foolish, or careless."

"But why were you both barefoot earlier?" Will asked. "Were you playing cheerleader?"

Quiet settled while the girls dried their eyes. "We were eliminating the possibilities, Lily said. Someone had dismantled the security system and could have been armed."

"So what made you go to the back door?"

"Troop!" they all four replied.

"That's where he found the billfold."

"All of you trusted the cunning of a dog you've known for less than twenty-four hours?" Will questioned.

"We also trusted each other," Storm replied, surprising his dad by his no-nonsense, authoritative tone of voice.

Although Will was surprised by Storm's answer, he had to admit his son's self-confidence had grown by leaps and bounds since his nieces had returned home. They had good hearts and helping others was in their DNA. And Storm and Hunter had been assigned to be Lily and Lori's bodyguards. So why wouldn't they trust each other?

His nieces were pre-kindergarten when they had insight that was astonishing, and just announced what they knew. For a while they just assumed everyone was like them.

Not my son, Will thought. *Surely he wouldn't keep something like that from me?* Okay, so Doc had mentioned how remarkable those four were getting along.

But then, it was the way Granny described them. "They appeared to have this inner circle, especially when they danced the Fox Trot. They were so in-sync with each other that when they were whirling around the dance floor, they changed partners twice and never missed a step. The smile and challenge on their faces had everyone clapping with the music and the enjoyment of watching them dance." To his knowledge, they had not practiced this dance.

"I'm sorry, Lily," Will apologized. "My mind was elsewhere. What were you saying?"

"Uncle Will," Lily began. "If you had seen the way Troop picked up that fifteen-month-old little Blue by the straps of his britches and then let the baby hold onto him this morning so he could keep walking, you would trust him, too."

They heard a bark, scratching, and a knock at Will's door. They all looked up and waited.

One of Will's men said, "I take it he has found you. I told one of my men to tie him up."

He looked out the door and added, "This dog is like a ghost. Not only did it chew the rope through, but he led us on a merry chase."

Troop had already made his way between the twins and lay at their feet. He was wet and muddy, content and tired, but still alert.

A report came through to Will from Brandi. "You might like to know. The prints that were lifted from Doc and Granny's home belong to three men from Herman's county. It was Herman's fifteen-year-old son's billfold that Troop found."

"We also heard the phone ring inside before Troop arrived. It rang again and continued ringing. Any idea who it might have been?" Lily said.

"They are still checking numbers," Brandi continued. "But no doubt that is how Herman knew where they were because no calls went out, unless someone called to warn them."

Will turned up the volume on his radio/phone and heard, "This is Sheriff Herman reporting. Please disregard that call at O'Reilly's Veterinarian Animal Hospital Ranch. It was a false alarm."

"Deputy Davies, we have three truckloads of volunteers

here wanting to know if Doc and Granny O'Reilly are safe."

"Hey, Will," Doc asked, "One of your boys directed me back here. What's going on?"

"Someone broke into your house and had a little party," Will replied. "Everything appears to be all right, but Brandi is insisting that you look through the house in the morning and report to her if anything is missing. In the meantime, you are going to have to go out front so your friends and neighbors can see that you are alive and well."

"The girls left hours ago with Storm and Hunter. Are they okay?" Granny asked.

"They are all in here, and they are fine," Will replied.

"Good." Doc replied.

"Doc," Brandi suggested, "If I just jump on your running board, can you drive me back to my car? Then the three of us can thank all your friends."

"Do you mind if the four of us hop in your truck as well?" Hunter asked.

"The more, the merrier," Granny agreed.

The moment Doc and Granny appeared, the welcome was astounding, as their friends applauded. "Boy, Doc," one of his patient's owners announced. "You gave us a start. And, Granny, it's good to see both of you are okay."

"Deputy Davies," Doc asked. "Can you fill everyone in, because we just arrived home."

Brandi, who had never needed a microphone, announced, "Good Evening, ladies and gentlemen. The good news is Doc and Granny's home wasn't damaged.

My team has been through the house. We won't know if anything is missing until they check it out personally."

"I can't thank you all enough for showing up here so promptly," Granny added. "We'll certainly know who to call, if we ever do need help."

"Wait a moment, please," Doc stepped forward. "Will, is it all right to introduce Lori?"

Will tapped on the back window of Doc's truck and asked, "Lori, Doc would like to introduce you. Why don't all four of you come out and join Doc?"

"Lori," Lily suggested. "This will give Doc's friends and clients a chance to meet you."

When they stepped out in front of Doc's truck, Doc proudly presented Lori, "Ladies. Gentlemen. I would like you to meet my new veterinarian, Dr. Lori Rose Donnelly."

A patter of good-natured applause erupted from the crowd, along with shouts of support and congratulations.

"Doc," Lori was still shaking inside, "I am overwhelmed. All your friends were so welcoming. All this before I had the chance to move into my office or help any of your patients yet."

"May I add something?" Lily suggested. "Apparently these people are unaware of the Eight-Mile-Centre's existence."

"That will be changing soon," Granny added. "Buildings have been under construction, but the owners have held off putting up any signs."

"The first building to be completed will be the clinic, though. The public is excited about the Turtle Crossing

Clinic being built; and the hospital has been advertising it, so people will know they won't have to travel as far for medical care, especially for after-hours emergencies.

"Goodnight, all," Lily smiled as she and Lori turned on the bottom step and waved, they dashed up the stairs to close themselves in their room.

Once in their matching pajamas, Lily approached the subject that she knew had been weighing on Lori's mind most of the evening. "I have to assume that your stomach has finally settled down after the issue with that Herman deputy character who assumed you would go meekly into the next county with him."

"Yes. I've continued to work out while I was in college, but after the take down as a result of him insulting me in the beginning, then grabbing my wrist and assuming I didn't have the sense I was born with, I know the reason why I reacted immediately. It's self-preservation. Fear of the unknown. And, in my mind, I know the Lord says, 'Don't worry about tomorrow. Today is already taken care of,' but...But I still can't describe how I disarmed him—for instance, to show Hunter or Storm that move—because I can't recall it in detail."

"Mom could tell and show you better than I could," Lily added. I have practiced it in front of a mirror. But I miss some of it too, you know."

"Aunt Brandi shoved us away and let Herman believe that she took him down."

"I know," Lily added. "At first I couldn't believe she did that, but she had already told Mom, Aunt Marcie, and Granny that she didn't want this type of attention on us."

"You asked how I am feeling," Lori began, "I'm still a bit jittery and excited and looking forward to start working as a veterinarian, along with Dr. Matthew Denver O'Reilly."

A timid knock on the door could be only one person. "Come in, Hunter," Lily suggested.

"Would either of you be interested in a bedtime snack? Say, a strawberry milkshake?"

"How did we survive," Lori teased, "without you to take care of us all these years?"

"Oh, I tried not to worry too much," Hunter replied. "But, I not only missed you both, I asked the Lord and his angels to look out for you guys, as well," as he handed them their shakes.

"Thanks," Lily responded. "There were times when I got into a few tight spots, and suddenly an opening appeared. So, no doubt your prayers, combined with Lori's, mine, and Mom's kept a few angels busy."

"I take it you aren't ready to share any of this right now?" Hunter asked.

"When the time is right, possibly," Lily replied.

"Lori," Hunter asked. "Can you teach me the move you used on that stupid Herman tonight? It was all I could do to restrain Storm from getting in the middle of that."

"But you knew I could protect myself, just not which move I would use?"

"I will put it this way," Hunter explained. "With the four of us, there was no way he was leaving with you."

"Would you like to explain just one thing you did to prevent it?" Lily asked.

"We locked up his steering and disconnected the temporary flashing light he pops on top of his vehicle. We had blocked both driveways. You forget, Storm and I were in high school track and that jerk and his partner were both out of shape."

"Very efficient. But, what about his gun?"

"The safety was still on."

"Ah. You noticed that, too," Lori commented. "I'm proud of you."

"Thanks to Uncle Will and Great Grandpa Warren." Hunter added. "Also, to those volunteers who left Doc's private drive open, though. On a personal level, Lily, what interest do you have in Dexter? He acted like he was very seriously worried about you today."

"I've been too busy to give him the time of day," Lily replied. "I am anxious to introduce myself to the Turtle Crossing business owners, and at the same time check on where my equipment and furnishings are so I can start seeing patients. I hope to have an appointment with a local chiropractor who may need some short-term assistance."

"I still didn't like the way Dexter treated you, though."

"Don't worry about it," Lori replied. "It's in regard to something that happened in high school. He can't seem to let loose of the fact that he still blames me for practically getting him expelled from school. But, his dad intervened and they moved away."

"This milkshake was exactly what I needed." Lori smiled and winked at Hunter. "I should have awesome dreams."

"Yes," Lily added. "We have to get some sleep if we're going to make it to the Sunday Sunrise Service."

"Goodnight, ladies. See you in the morning," He collected their empty glasses and left.

Chapter 5

"It doesn't seem possible how quickly I have acclimated from the classroom and hands-on testing to determining the treatment to keep an animal healthy. It won't be long till you are doing the same, on people of course.

"I know, Sis, and as usual, we both woke before dawn. Not for finals, but what Hunter calls a Sunrise Service. I'm anxious to hear Hunter preach a service with Great Uncle C.W."

"Apparently there have been a lot of changes," Lily added. "Granny said that Storm's girlfriend, Madison Grace, will be singing a duet with him and leading the congregation. Hunter and Storm have chosen well, don't you agree?"

A few minutes later, down in the kitchen, Hunter, Storm, Doc and Granny turned when they heard the echo of two sets of cowboy boots clumping a staccato beat down the stairs. When Lily and Lori entered, the four observers exclaimed, "Wow!"

Lori smiled and said, "I'll tell you a little secret, Granny. I bought my bluebells blue dress in Denver." She twirled around, winked at Granny, and bowed.

Lily followed suit. "I bought my matching dress in Chicago," as she joined Lori and cut a piece of Granny's gooey breakfast sandwich to go, a cinnamon roll, juice and coffee.

Lori winked at Granny and whispered, "Thank you for the wake-up this morning. Granted, you were a bit sneaky. However, that door still squeaks its own greeting."

"Undoubtedly, you were already awake. Hey, you young people go ahead. We'll be there shortly."

"That's okay," Storm replied. "We'll follow you over."

"Wouldn't have it any other way," Lori agreed, as she took her cinnamon roll with her.

"Hunter," Lily asked. "I hope you reserved our seats up front. We don't want to miss a moment."

"Of course," Hunter nodded. Three minutes later, they arrived at Granny's lane. "You both are our guests of honor! Love your cowgirl hats, as well." And parked in the mowed field behind their stage area. Looking at his watch, he remarked, "We're right on time with twenty minutes to spare." He and Storm escorted them to a table marked 'Reserved'.

"We'll talk after the service," Storm said, as they headed back stage.

The tent extended beyond the barn, and every seat was filled with parents and children singing songs directed by Madison Grace. "May we have a round of applause for the lovely children's choir?"

"Thank you, Madison," Hunter remarked. "Please stand for prayer and join us in song."

Madison played keyboard as the families sang with gusto. After two songs, Storm announced, "We have a request for Lily and Lori. Harmony and David on the flute to Amazing Grace." When they finished, there wasn't a dry eye among the adults.

C.W.—Reverend Cecil Warren—kept his sermon to fifteen minutes, followed by Hunter's fifteen minutes. The service concluded with "Till We Meet Again."

Then Lily and Lori brought out their Great Grandma's fiddle and Grampa Charlie's harmonica. Storm had taught Harmony how to play the flute, and Will's daughter, Summer, played the haunting Dolby guitar—using a bar with sounds similar to an electric steel guitar.

Marcie and Sheldon's son, Kristopher Charlie Donnelly, known by all as Kris CD, brought his Dad's banjo and joined the unexpected jam session. Uncle Kristopher and Nancy's twins, Jacob and Jordan Donnelly shyly found a seat in the back and joined in with mandolin and bass. Hunter and Storm brought out their guitars and joined the jam session, moving from one song to another.

Those who had planned to leave early got another cup of coffee and settled in for an enjoyable session. A few in the crowd started singing along with parts of songs they knew, and it was a toss-up as to who was enjoying this music more, the performers who kept looking at one another and smiling, or the audience.

But when Grandpa Charlie sat down at the keyboard, they all knew they were in for a warm, inspiring surprise.

They had all heard the story of how he had been on the missing-in-action World War II veterans list while on his way home, and had been hospitalized after an auto accident. At first, he had been too injured to play piano.

Now, no one wanted to leave, but after about twenty minutes, Charlie encouraged Little Missy to sit beside him and play a few chords after he played them. Harmony was astounded.

Later, as the instruments were being stored away, Marcie grabbed her brother, David, and asked her mom, SaraBeth, and Granny, "I had the silliest dream last night after wondering all day yesterday, what is it about the scarecrow in your garden there, Granny, and costumed lambs?"

Granny and SaraBeth chose a pair of white wrought-iron padded chairs and bench and sat down. Granny nodded to SaraBeth, "Well, you've heard how overpowering my dad, better known as Uncle Henry Carpenter, was. He was known for his shady deals all over Turtle Crossing, and many feared him, including me."

"You both were there at the old Turtle Crossing Library the day I showed you how I got away from him down that staircase in the wall and how Miss Bea snuck me out of Turtle Crossing to Lima. Marcie, you were a baby, and you and I shared the lemon-colored room at Aunt Tressie and Uncle Fletcher Brown's house in Lima. That's where you were born, Marcie.

"Then my dad found out where we were living and threatened to file for custody of my children because I was working in a factory to support us. That is when Aunt

Tressie drove us here to Granny's farm. But somehow he found us again. I had no choice but to get you out of the area to a safe place where he couldn't find you."

"Granny and I dressed the two of you," SaraBeth murmured, as tears fell into her lap.

"And," Marcie spoke up, "you dressed us up like wooly white lambs."

"And," David recalled, "You hid us in the garden beside the scarecrow and big, tall, sun-flowers. That must be why I've never liked sunflowers. Don't cry, Mom," David continued, "Please."

"At first," Marcie continued, "When I saw Little Missy and Baby Blue walking up the lane, I felt as though that was David and me. But that doesn't make any sense, does it?"

"Yes, it does, Marcie," SaraBeth added. "I carried David, and you ran along beside me, helping me carry your suitcase in the lane towards the woods, where some-one picked us up in their car. I could hear the police sirens coming closer to Granny's with your Grandpa Henry in the lead.

"I moved back in with Aunt Tressie. I missed you and Charlie, of course. He was still listed MIA—Missing In Action. I worked all the overtime I could get and only ate because Aunt Tressie insisted. They finally sat me down and forced me to look in the mirror.

"I saw him one day, when I got off the city bus. He was parked across the street and smiled, pleased I was alone. He nodded, and with an eerie satisfied smile, drove away. It would be two weeks before I could see you and David."

Marcie turned into Sheldon's arms. "Sheldon, you heard?" He held her as she wept. David and Shannon were stunned. "Mom. Granny. Why haven't you ever told us this story?"

"I think we prayed you would never remember it," Granny said. "And If there is any satisfaction, he was in such a hurry to grab SaraBeth's children, he shoved open the only barn door that wasn't locked and literally fell face first into buckets of cow manure I had piled there. That's where I left him."

Doc, Will, and Jonothan stood off to the side, drying their eyes. Brandi and Charlie joined them. They had never heard it either.

"Marcie," Granny asked. "Has your Mom answered all your questions?"

Marcie lowered her head, and whispered, "Yes, but on second thought, I've always wondered why Mom's mom, Jewel, never did anything for her daughter?" Her question was met with silence.

Breaking the uncomfortable silence, Will said softly, "Marcie, your family's strength is your love for one another."

"Later," SaraBeth said, "when he saw that I was alone and my children were no longer with me, he dropped the suit. He didn't really want you; he just didn't want me to be happy. He succeeded. If there would have been another way, to this day, I don't know what it would have been. And, I can't change it. But, I couldn't take the chance that he really could get custody of my beautiful children."

"We love you, Mom," David said, as he reached out

and hugged her. "Marcie and I had each other at the children's home, and you came to see us as often as you could. Many of the children didn't ever have family visit them. So, see, because of you, we turned out okay, don't you think?"

"I couldn't be prouder," SaraBeth replied.

"Are you going to be all right, Marcie?" SaraBeth inquired.

"Yeah, mom" Marcie replied. "I was so afraid the nightmare was a precursor to something that was going to happen to my kids, even though they are grown."

Hunter approached them, and said, "Granny. We'll finish up the barn and tent later this evening. Storm and I promised to take Lily and Lori horseback riding as soon as we grab something to eat. If you don't mind, we look forward to tomorrow's Shadow Angels meeting and tour of Turtle Crossing."

"Sounds like a great plan," Granny added.

Doc O'Reilly joined the ladies. "Are you ready to call it a day, Granny?"

Granny squeezed his hand, then hugged David, Marcie, and SaraBeth, before telling each of them, "We love you like you were one of our own," before rejoining Doc.

***

By the time Granny and Doc arrived home, the Foursome had saddled-up and headed out. Granny leaned against a tree and felt at peace. She watched lightning-bugs golden/green fluorescent lights appear and disappear, flashing gracefully on-and-off around her. The background quiet was interspersed with the gentle creaking of leather saddles and the memorable sound of horses' hooves in sync with their riders.

"Storm," Lily asked, "Have you and Hunter given any more thought to us becoming a Foursome?"

"What's to think about?" Hunter asked. "Especially after the way we have been picking up vibes with you and Lori."

"Is Mom aware of any of this between you and Storm?" Lori asked. When he didn't reply, she continued, "I think, once we get serious, we can become a powerful unit. But it will require most of your personal time. That won't matter to Lily and me, but both of you have ladies who are going to be upset if you have to cut back on your dating time, without knowing why."

"We'll keep that in mind," Hunter replied. The change of subject brought out his charming smile, which helped him get away with a thoughtful response, and no answer at all.

"And I hope you have already cleared your calendar for tomorrow because we have a surprise for the two of you."

"I have a question," Storm began, his voice so soft it was apparent he had been struggling to even talk about himself. "Did any of you talk to my dad after the fiasco at Doc's?"

"No," Hunter asked. "Why? What's going on?"

"I'm not sure," Storm continued. "Dad stopped in the barn and sat with Granny and Doc for a while. And I started to speak to him right after we did that fun fox-trot and he walked away as though he didn't even see me."

"You know how intense he can get at times," Lily added. "It's hard to tell what they were talking about. He may not have even seen you standing there."

"Hey, Storm," Lori began. "You guys really do need a break. After all the work you did for the family reunion. Especially the impromptu jam session. As they were pulling out today, everyone said they hope we keep it as an annual thing because they all had so much fun."

"Trust us. Tomorrow will be a fantastic gift!" Lily added, as she smiled at him. "Hey, Hunter, Great Uncle Kristopher was looking for you yesterday. Did you get a chance to talk to him?"

"Oh, shoot. Every time we got in two words, that nosy Dexter just popped into our conversation. Uncle Kristopher finally turned around, stuck his business card in my pocket and marched off."

"What did it say?" Storm intervened.

"Call me."

"Oh, wow!" Lily exclaimed. "I heard he is looking for extra help in his legal pool."

"It's been a while since I talked to Uncle Kristopher. His office is in Turtle Crossing, isn't it?" Lori asked.

"Yes."

"Lily and I checked with Miss Bea about an apartment to rent in Turtle Crossing but she didn't have anything available."

"Mom and Dad have plenty of room in their new place they built just off the golf course," Hunter said, a mischievous look on his face. He knew the reason why their mother didn't want her daughters to live under the same roof. She was afraid they would never marry because, in her mind, what man would want to compete with the two of them as a team?

Lily and Lori were unusually quiet. "Are you living at home?" Lily finally asked a bit cautiously.

"No," Hunter and Storm replied softly.

"You know, guys, Lori and I were really hoping to live together for a few months. If nothing more than to get back that twin sister feeling. No one seems to understand. It's not forever. We have discussed this. In the future, we hope to marry and have children, a family of our very own, someday. Finding an apartment was our backup plan in case something happened to Granny's offer. Of course, Granny's place is closer for Lori."

"Close for you too," Hunter reminded, "When your office is up and running at Eight-Mile-Centre."

"True," Lily agreed, "Once all my walls are painted and my equipment and office furniture have arrived, I hope to be very busy. I am beginning to think someone has absconded with two semi-trucks which have just disappeared. How is that possible?"

When they returned from their ride, Lily volunteered to run into Granny's cooler and pick up some drinks. She stopped in her tracks on the deck off the kitchen when she heard Granny and Miss Bea discussing expanding her Estate Farmhouse into a women's shelter.

"You mean," Miss Bea continued, "How can you ask the Donnelly twins to give up the plans you promised them? That they could live there between college and when their new businesses take off."

When their voices diminished as they left the kitchen and went back outside to sit in the squeaky swing, Lily dashed inside to get their drinks. Granny had left her notes on the kitchen table with the headline, *The Cradle of Roses,* with a list of names. "Is that the reason for the picture of a cradle on the outside of Granny's garage?"

As soon as Lily slipped inside the barn and handed off the drinks, they found a bench and a couple of stools to sit on. "All right," Hunter began, his voice deepening, the way it did whenever his sisters were hurting. "What's happening?"

"It appears we do not have a place to live after all," Lily replied.

"Since when?" Storm demanded. "Granny wouldn't go back on her word."

"Hunter," Lori suggested. "*The Cradle of Roses* you painted on Granny's Garage. That's it?"

"Yeah. Hey, Granny hasn't received any calls since she was coerced into it when she did some extensive remodeling for Doc O'Reilly's Veterinarian Hospital where guests can stay when their pet's surgery requires several days' recovery." Hunter looked up and saw Granny and Doc standing in the doorway.

How much had they heard? Lily wondered. Troop wandered over past Granny and Doc and meandered up to Lori and dropped a piece of paper at her feet, then lay down in front of them.

As if a heavy fog had dropped the temperature, the Foursome was speechless.

"Hey, Troop," Lori asked. "What have you got here?"

Lily read the note aloud. "Mrs. Pease, wife of Isaac of Chiropractic Medicine in Turtle Crossing, asked me to call her immediately."

"I don't understand," Lily remarked.

Doc O'Reilly said, "Isaac has been scrambling to find someone to take over his practice temporarily because he broke his arm. It appears one of the volunteers who was at Doc's last night told him to call you. He said he can be there to coach you on his patients' needs and would welcome working with you."

"Can I use your phone?"

"Of course, Lily."

"Can we set all this aside until our trip to Turtle Crossing tomorrow?"

They all nodded.

"The names you read in bold print are contact people, not women presently needing help," Granny added softly.

"That's okay. Some of my lists don't always work out as I plan them either," Lily added.

Chapter 6

Granny slid a stack of her Sunrise Pancakes and sausages in the warmer at a little past six and smiled when she heard the noisy anticipation of her young guests that matched her own to attend the emergency Shadow Angels meeting. "All those planning to ride with me, be ready to leave by seven sharp!" she called. "Anyone within miles around is used to seeing me drive everything from a tractor, my Lincoln, and Doc's four-door pickup truck."

Lily, Lori, Hunter and Storm smiled. They were almost too excited to eat. The official Four Aces Foursome replied, "Yes, ma'am." They knew this meant that if they planned to attend, this would be a requirement. Although Granny would never admit it, she was looking forward to the rare Shadow Angels invitation.

As they joined Granny in the screened-in-back-porch, she asked, "Did you young ladies draw straws this morning?"

They just smiled but nodded as Lori climbed in the front with Granny and Lily joined the guys in the back. "We feel honored to be invited to this special meeting of the famous Shadow Angels," Hunter began, all the while memorizing each turn Granny made.

Storm teasingly asked, "Are we being followed, Granny?"

"You catch on quick. I never take the same route arriving or leaving," she added as she slowed down and turned into a nondescript-looking drive which appeared to be a break in the woods creeping towards the road.

Lori motioned to Granny—left, right—left, right—left, right, left. Granny's eyes sparkled as she slowed around a sycamore tree when she heard comments from the rear. "Wow!" Storm exclaimed.

"Ditto from Hunter here. I can't wait to—"

"Explore?" Lily added and smiled.

Granny grinned and suggested, "Another time. We won't have time today."

The ladies, so used to faring on their own, allowed Hunter and Storm to assist them from Granny's Lincoln.

"Just follow Miss Lori and Miss Lily," Granny advised as they stepped down the concrete entrance steps that took them around to the back of the house where the spacious patio disappeared into a shaded expanse and towards a cleverly disguised boat ramp and dock. The curious little-boy excitement was apparent on the faces of Hunter and Storm. However, they were tugged towards the casual seating near the door that Granny had disappeared into.

Lily and Lori turned towards the guys and Lori began, "Storm, I know you have heard the stories about the history of the Shadow Angels, which in the beginning were known throughout Turtle Crossing and beyond. The four of them were tired of doing just what was expected of them and decided to expand on housekeeping, laundry, and personal chef when a couple of young ladies approached them about a problem they were having and asked for their help.

"In secret, they became the Carpenter Aunts' Card Club who supposedly played euchre in their spare time. However, they seldom played cards. The original four were your and our great-aunts, Jewell Carpenter, Opal Carpenter, Willi Carpenter Roberts, and Tressie Carpenter Brown."

"They became the Shadow Angels when they asked our Mom, Shannon, your mom, Wendy Fox, Aunt Marcie Warren, and Aunt Brandi Carpenter to join them."

"Now," Hunter began, "regarding the two of you. You have a well-known mystic connection, which I always thought was because you were twins. But Storm and I are cousins, and have accepted the fact that at first we thought stuff happened only when it was just the two of us; however we have sensed things were going to happen before they did when Harmony was with us.

"We hadn't talked to anyone about what happened at Doc's place," Storm continued. "We're not little kids anymore. Last night was so strong, it was rather scary, but exhilarating, too. Was it because the two of you were there, too?"

"Lily and I felt it as well. It is something we need to set aside some time to explore and work on, but Granny just opened the door, so, later. Essentially, the four of us are guests, so if someone does ask, Lily?"

"How about, it's a work-in-progress. I hope you understand that Lori and I have only been home about forty-eight hours." She watched and felt the stress drain from his stance, and they both smiled. "Agreed?" They nodded. "We're all here to learn."

The Shadow Angels' business meeting had taken a brief break and as soon as they were seated, Aunt Willi announced: "To save time, will each of you please put on your name tags? I know. We're all family, but humor us today, okay?

"Sorry, guys," Lily added. "This is our fault because some people have always had trouble telling us apart. But, if I start wearing cowboy boots, that might give us away. Not today, though, because we both wore our matching boots."

Hunter could always tell them apart, so being their baby brother might have its advantages.

Willi continued, "Help yourself to the snacks and lemonade or iced tea. We will eat in approximately thirty minutes as scheduled."

Hunter elbowed Storm and pointed to a well-worn plaque on the wall behind Chairperson, Aunt Willi. *To Protect our Clients and Each Other—What is Discussed Here—Stays Here!*

Storm had memories of conversations between his mom and dad after similar Shadow Angels' meetings over the years, which made today very special. If asked, his response would be: Respect. Dignified. Elegant. And, they continue to be physically and mentally sharp.

Straightening his shoulders, he sat up even straighter and listened. A couple of projects had requested security for an upcoming festival, a wedding, and a retirement party, Marcie reported. "One was at the GreatStone Castle and another at the Welby Mansion B&B."

"Any other requests at this time? If not, we'll move on to more recent happenings."

Hunter and Storm had trouble hiding their surprise when Will Fox and Jonothan Carpenter walked in the door.

"Gentlemen." Aunt Willi announced. "You have the floor."

They each pulled out a notebook and nodded to Lori and Lily. "The Chicago Case has been turned over to the local D.A. & Drug Unit," Will stated. "The flowers, donuts and coffee were a delivery from Dr. Dexter on the day before your friends knew you were scheduled to fly out. Jonothan?"

"Lori, your early arrival and your Mom's request to pick up you ladies a day early happened because my other assignment cancelled and I was already in Chicago at the time."

"Lily, your college friends apprehended the perps who had just broken into your apartment—trashed it and some of what you had left for them. The perps claimed they were scheduled to frame someone else and were on the wrong floor. They didn't know your name, nor could they describe you," Jonothan added softly. "The apartment building has been sold and the younger classmen have found other accommodations. I have a bundle of cards and letters for you because you didn't leave a forwarding address."

"Also, Granny," Will began, "The issue of a break-in at your and Doc's home has been settled. The young man who drove a couple of friends to your place is the son of the sheriff in a nearby county. The sheriff is handling his son, against mama's tears, etc. The boy has to eat his meals at the jail and sleep there every night for six weeks. No visitors allowed. During the day he is mucking-out barn stalls for a friend."

"Does anyone have anything to add to these reports?" Aunt Willi requested as she looked directly at Lori and Lily, Hunter and Storm. If not, thank you, Will Fox and Jonothan Carpenter. You are all welcome to join us for an after-meeting-lunch."

"Thanks," they replied. "We're expected elsewhere."

After Granny introduced the Foursome guests to members of the Shadow Angels, she delcared that they also had other plans. Once outside, Doc pulled in and parked beside Granny's Lincoln. Unbeknownst to the young people, Doc and Granny had made special plans for their guests.

Granny asked, "How would the two of you like a trip down memory lane at Turtle Crossing? Just us ladies?"

Lily and Lori replied, "We would love it!"

"We love hanging out with you guys, but..." Lori quickly clarified to Hunter and Storm.

"Yeah," Lily added. "But we also look forward to a full day tomorrow."

Hunter looked at Doc and Storm, then the girls, and stammered, "Well, Harmony did ask me to stop by."

"Stormy," Lori said with a cheeky smile, "you did promise Madison Grace you would stop by her place on your way home."

"Well, boys," Doc suggested, "it looks like the ladies don't need us to look after them with Granny at the helm." Storm and Hunter joined Doc in his pickup and the women watched them drive away.

"Granny," Lily began. "It's been awhile since we have had the time to just cruise down Main Street."

Granny obliged, and soon they were all driving down Main Street of Turtle Crossing, the twins pressing their faces to the windows.

"Oh!" Lori exclaimed. "Sadie's Diner. Suddenly, I am so hungry." Granny maneuvered the car around back and parked.

"Dare we go in the back door like we used to?" Lily impishly suggested.

"You just want to peek in her kitchen," Granny admonished, her eyes twinkling.

"Sadie!" they called out the minute they stepped inside the back door.

"As I live and breathe," Sadie remarked, as she carefully hugged them, so as not to get flour from her apron on them.

Memories of childhood moments with Sadie, caught them unaware, as tears sparkled in their eyes. Granny led them to their favorite table marked 'Reserved!' It had long ago been their favorite because they could see the front and back door and were close enough to the kitchen that Sadie might join them for a coffee break when she could.

Miss Bea was already waiting. Once seated, their waitress served Sadie's sweet tea, bacon-lettuce-tomato on light-as-air sourdough biscuits with cups of creamy potato soup sprinkled with chives and cheese. Once the waitress left, Granny made a toast: "To Sadie and Miss Bea for heading up the committee and plans for Eight Mile Centre."

"Congratulations, Doctors Lily and Lori Donnelly, for setting your goals and accomplishing your dreams," Miss Bea announced. "Please accept these honorary membership certificates to the Turtle Crossing Business Women's Association." The framed certificates had been signed by Sadie, Miss Bea, Granny and Dr. Kate.

"You young ladies look well rested," said Miss Bea.

"Thank you," Lori replied with an appreciative smile. "Miss Bea, so nice to see how some memories remain the same. You still wear the same perfume." Lori smiled at Lily when she made the comment.

"You remembered!" Miss Bea exclaimed.

"How could we forget?" Lily added. "Of course we remembered. The compacts you gave us, of 'Evening in Paris' solid perfume, is still one of our treasured high-school graduation gifts. "

"Would you believe," Lori continued, "It has held its fragrance all these years." Then Lori's voice softened when she asked, "Why is it that you nor Sadie never remarried?"

When a strange silence followed Lori's question, Lily added, "You see, our Mom worries that between the time we spend together, and the hours we invest in our professions, we'll never marry and have a family of our own."

Sadie handed Granny and Bea coffee of their choice and placed tall glasses of iced cherry lemonade with a maraschino cherry on a stick in front of Lily and Lori. Finally, Sadie began, with a bit of mischievous teasing smile on her face revealed. "First of all, we never found a man who cared enough about us to offer romance. We are still looking for a love like Granny and Doc found, but we've not given up."

Granny blushed. "I know you girls are looking forward to walking down Main Street with Sadie and Miss Bea, so I'll meet you at the Veterans' Museum in about an hour?"

Lily nudged Lori's knee under the table, reminiscent of a childhood prank to play hide and sneak from whoever happened to be their superior at that time. Then shrugged their shoulders, smiled at Granny, checked their watches, and Lori agreed. "We look forward to it."

"Hey, Sis," Lori asked, "What do you think Doc meant about…"

"Us being safe with Granny?" Lily added. "I guess Miss Bea and Sadie feel we can take care of ourselves."

"We have a surprise for you," Miss Bea shyly admitted. "We've been dating the Bixby Brothers for about six months. They opened an all-men's clothing store. You can purchase everything from sportswear to tailored suits and tuxedos."

"Their sons took over the business in their East Coast City store," Sadie continued, "and they now consider themselves semi-retired. They like Turtle Crossing's slower-paced lifestyle."

"Their store is just two blocks away," Sadie added. "Let's go check it out. You'll love it."

Less than ten minutes later, the four of them stepped inside Bixbys. The shushing of the doors and the silence inside drew them into the elegant ambiance that was not the norm for the average businesses in Turtle Crossing.

"Even the air," whispered Lily, "Is reminiscent of finely woven imported wool, silk, and butter-soft leather."

"I know," Lori replied. "I'm glad Granny talked us into wearing our new boots instead of our more comfortable ones."

"So," Lily teased, "Was that a moment out of habit when you looked around for a place to clean off your boots before entering?"

Then the Bixby Brothers appeared like they were programmed from a movie script. "Alfred Bixby," he greeted them with a genuine smile and offered a handshake. "You must be Shannon and David Donnelly's famous daughters, Lily and Lori Donnelly? My friends call me Al."

"Hello, I am Joseph Bixby, Al's brother. I go by Joe. We are honored to meet you."

Lori swallowed hard to keep from teasing Joe and Al, certain they were prepared to bow, as though greeting the Donnelly Twins as royalty.

Lily nodded, but felt there were other customers in the store. She glanced towards a shadowed area beyond their conversation. Lori cautiously elbowed Lily as Sadie and Bea picked up on Lily's lack of attention.

When the background music changed to a romantic ballad that Donovan had sung to her when they had danced together eighteen months earlier, Lily was aggravated that her thoughts were of him. She had to forget him. He had someone else. But she still felt someone was observing them. What if someone from her apartment complex had followed her?

Lily glanced towards a dimly lit area beyond the display of shirts and ties, and was impressed with the indirect lighting, when the man straightened and looked directly at her. She was spellbound. It couldn't be Donovan. He was taller and she had never seen him in a hat. She quickly turned away.

Lori cautiously elbowed Lily and remarked, "Lily and I recently commented on Uncle Jonothan's trendy clothes when he picked us up in Chicago. We can see why he would be a Bixby regular." Alfred and Joseph Bixby smiled when they heard Jonothan's name, but did not comment.

"Are you ladies looking for something specific today?"

"Thanks for the offer, Mr. Bixby," Lori replied, "However, we really don't have the time today."

Before he could reply, Sadie said, "We wanted them to meet the most dapper gentlemen in all of Turtle Crossing."

"Well," Lily commented, "Mom and Dad have an anniversary in a few months. So now we'll know where to shop. But today, we are looking forward to seeing the display about our Grandpa Charlie at the Veterans' Museum."

Then Sadie puzzled them when she all but pushed them out the door. "We are immensely proud of these two young women," Miss Bea added. "We have already accepted them as the newest members of the Turtle Crossing's Women's Business Association."

"Their parents are certainly proud," Joe replied. "David and Shannon have supported us since the day of our grand opening, and their golf course is bringing in an impressive number of out-of-state golf weekenders."

"Miss Lily and Miss Lori are beautiful young women," Al added, "There is a special depth to those two that also sets them apart, which speaks well of their heritage."

As they headed towards the Veterans' Museum, Lori asked, "Hey, Sis, What happened in there? You acted like you had seen a ghost."

"I thought I saw Donovan."

"Inside the store?" Lori demanded.

"What would he be doing in Turtle Crossing?"

"Hey. You want to go back inside?" Lori asked.

Lily was tempted, puzzled, ticked off, heart-broken, and not quite ready to see him yet, and replied, "NO."

***

Donovan Michael James had just arrived in Turtle Crossing and had stopped in at Bixby's on his way to the Welby Mansion B&B, before his interview with Chiropractor Isaac Pease.

He was stunned, puzzled, and confused when he heard Lily's laughter. She had been adamant that she was going home to open her own office in Winthrop, where her mother also had several art installations.

Joe placed a hand on Donovan's shoulder and said, "Young man, if you're looking for a special lady, a man would be making the mistake of a lifetime walking away from either of those young women."

Donovan wished his mother could have heard this conversation about Lily and her twin. He had quit listening to his mother's reasoning about why he should marry the girl next door because her family could trace their heritage back to the Mayflower.

Quite different from children of parents who had both grown up in a children's home and probably "welfare" couldn't possibly be anyone she would want added to her genealogy chart. She refused to say where she had acquired her information, but he also knew she would always find fault with anyone or anything that didn't fit into her plans.

Which was why his mother had no idea where he was or why. He had arrived in Turtle crossing a few days early, to learn about the people and local businesses before his interview with Isaac Pease, of Isaac Pease Chiropractic.

***

As Lily and Lori left Bixbys and started walking down Main Street, business owners offered a "Good afternoon," and welcoming smiles.

"It sure is great to see the downtown thriving," Lori said.

"I know, it's been so long since we've gone places together. I forget."

"I did, too," Lily added, as she tugged Lori to stop. They stared at their reflection in the pharmacy display window. Then smiled. "No wonder people slowly turn around and look a second time."

"We're going to have to ask Aunt Marcie to update a photo of us together," Lori suggested. "I haven't had time to appreciate that we're going to be living close enough to schedule a coffee break together." Tears filled her eyes as they hugged.

***

Donovan looked forward to helping out a friend for a few months while Isaac recuperated from a broken arm. He was excited to get the chance to find out first-hand if his childhood memories of his Great Uncle's chiropractic business were all he remembered them to be.

Isaac's receptionists greeted him and asked him to be seated. About that same time, Isaac led an elderly gentleman out the door.

"Good to see you again, Donovan," Isaac said, awkwardly shaking hands with his left hand. "How long do you plan to be in town? I only need one assistant, and I have another interview early in the morning."

"I see." Donovan replied, hiding his disappointment. "No rush, I reserved a week at the Welby Mansion B&B."

"Good choice," Isaac said. "I'll contact you before the week ends. Sorry to be brief, but I'm taking my wife out to celebrate her birthday this evening."

***

Changing the subject, Lily asked, "Did I ever tell you how Donovan and I met?"

Lori shook her head no, as they found a beautiful

white lawn bench under a huge sycamore tree, in view of the Veterans' Museum and waited for the Pennsylvania passenger train to blow her whistle and zip through Turtle Crossing station. "Okay, Sis," Lori said, "You have my undivided attention."

"I—we, had just graduated high school and Winthrop was having its annual Arts Festival. A troupe of college students had written a play and we had tickets. Then you had a date that night, so I went by myself and turned your ticket in. I arrived early and spotted an artist friend of Mom's across the center of the theatre. I hadn't seen her for a couple of years. When I felt as though someone was staring at me, I glanced across the theatre.

"I looked around, though. I thought perhaps I wasn't the person he or she was looking at. I was tempted to ask Mom's friend if she knew who he was because she was always so connected with the artist groups, then he turned and greeted a young woman in the aisle, and I turned back to Mom's friend.

"I noticed the theatre was filling up, so we hugged and I returned to my seat. The people on my left were excitedly glad someone (meaning you) had turned in their ticket, which meant their entire family could sit together.

"I was surprised that whoever had the aisle seat beside me was either late or maybe was working the lobby— so I relaxed, ready to enjoy the evening when the lights dimmed and the curtain opened. Imagine my surprise when the usher flashed his light on the floor, and then the row and seat number before a gentleman sat down in the aisle seat next to me.

"He didn't look at me or nod any recognition so I just shrugged my thoughts away, when the usher was standing at my aisle again. Someone needed to get through, so I stood and folded my seat back, so this couple could quickly be seated. Over the please-excuse-us gracious comments the couple made as they squeezed through, I glanced past them.

"He, in the meantime had stepped out into the aisle to let them in, and I glanced up into the most compelling misty green eyes. He smiled, nodded and commented in a husky, deep voice, 'Hello again,' and sat down. My very next thought was that maybe he knew you, and was just being polite, because I knew I would have remembered meeting him before. I wasn't very polite. I didn't smile or reply."

Lori teasingly added with a gentle smile, "I'm trying to imagine you speechless."

"Then as intermission began, a woman one row behind us got a bit anxious, and it became apparent she was definitely heading towards the exit. She continued on as she swung her ample bag into people. Others stood up to protect themselves after one woman's hat was sent airborne several rows towards the stage. When that happened, the man beside me moved me into the aisle beside him.

"You know how I am about a stranger touching me, but, although it was unexpected, my waist was warm and tingling where his hands had gently guided me back out of this woman's way as she turned towards the stairs. Then, when her purse swung out from her elbow as she arrived at the stairs towards the exit, I realized how glad I was he had moved me. Otherwise, at the speed she was moving, she no doubt would have dumped both of us onto the floor. As she left, the smell of alcohol hovered and dissipated up the aisle, as well.

"When I attempted to turn away from him, I realized I had not paid close enough attention; but he was one step lower than I was, and we were suddenly nearly eye to eye." Lily hesitated a moment, then continued. "It was the most surprising feeling. It was like we could see into each other's souls. It felt like I was under an earth-shattering spell, when he softly asked, 'Are you okay?'

"Then some woman several rows up called out his name. 'Donovan, Donovan James! Up here!'

"He acted reluctant to let go of me, politely nodded, and I headed up the steps to the lobby." Lily suddenly stood up and suggested, "We better go into the Veterans' Museum and see what's been added since we were here last."

"Fine." Lori replied, "But there is more, Sis. Right?"

"Yes," she replied. "I returned for the last act. He did not."

Chapter 7

Lori knew when to leave well enough alone and signed the register. Silence had been their way of skirting around painful moments since childhood unless one or the other's safety was at risk. However, silence this time had more to do with breathless appreciation.

"Wow! I see they have improved the entrance of the Veterans' Museum," Lori began. "Including, these wall-paintings of tanks, jeeps and interesting uniforms of past wars."

"I wonder how long Mom and Wendy have been working on some of these murals," Lily whispered.

They wound around a section of antique home furnishings, transportation memorabilia, and musical instruments that fit the appropriate time period of the different military conflicts and wars.

They stopped in their tracks when they approached the entrance of the Naval segment display that featured a life-sized photo of their Grandpa Charlie, in full uniform and Grandma SaraBeth Donnelly. "Oh, wow," Lily remarked, her voice filled with reverence. "They look so young in their wedding picture. Or this one where Dad was just a baby."

"Do you feel like you just walked into a real battle?" Lily added. "Are we on a treadmill or is it moving? Oh, wait. There is Grandpa Charlie. Impressive. I remember he only wore his uniform for special occasions."

"Look who sponsored this display. Ms. Bea Longacre."

"That's no surprise," Lily added. "Ms. Bea and Sadie fought our grumpy, crooked, great grandpa Henry Carpenter tooth and nail for women's rights to be successful women in business."

"You had better add Granny to that list," Deputy Sheriff Brandi Carpenter added from behind them.

"Hi! Auntie Brandi," the twins mimicked in their little girl voices.

"Are you on free time or volunteer undercover?" Lily whispered.

When Brandi didn't reply, Lori added, "I get the feeling that no matter where you are, your choice of career becomes a part of who you are."

"You know, that's what I respect about the Shadow Angels," Brandi explained. "It's been exciting to watch my fabulous nieces with Hunter and Storm," she added. "The Shadow Angels, your Uncle Will and I will do everything we can to support you, but…"

They all looked around to make certain no one was within earshot and Brandi continued in an even more serious voice, "In addition to your careers, keep in mind that the Shadow Angels were very cautious, secretive to a fault, knew the law, and how to skirt it, and when to call for help, when they took it upon themselves to help others. The four of you have a strength, very similar to the Shadow Angels: trust."

They fell silent as they read headlines listing people and historical happenings in Turtle Crossing and nearby towns. They were drawn to the recent changes in the mile-long Turtle Crossing's Tunnel of Safe Passage. It included entrances to the underground tunnel from many of Turtle Crossing's businesses and upgraded those that had been in existence for years.

"Does this put us in the remember-when category?" Lori asked. "Because we remember when Aunt Alex was the first to 'use' the tunnel in secret between The Welby Mansion Bed and Breakfast to visit her parents in Turtle Crossing. Now it's open to the public for the Welby B&B and our Mom and Dad's golf-course and housing development."

"I wonder how long Mom and Uncle Will's Wendy have been working on the Veterans' Museum background murals?" Lori questioned.

"Remember when we were in grade school and watched Mom stand so still in front of a blank canvas. Then with a sweep of what she called background colors, with several brush strokes, a person, an animal, flowers appeared to come alive—like magic?" Lily murmured.

"Yeah," Lori replied, a contemplative look on her face. "Mom and her art never gets old, does it?"

They had just finished reading detailed information

about a huge impressive-looking tank, built in Lima, Ohio. Then just a few steps away they stopped and stared—in awe—at a life-sized portrait of their Grandpa Charlie in full uniform. "Wow!" Lily exclaimed. "Mom caught his charm, his wit, his strength plus the strained sadness in his eyes."

"Yes," Lori whispered, as she grabbed Lily's hand. "I think that shadow in his eyes is because he was in prison overseas, and when he thought he had lost Grandma."

"Let's go this way," Lori suggested. "I am trying to find where Mom is supposed to be on this map, but I don't see Granny either."

"I looked at my watch when we arrived," Lily added, "but since she wasn't at the entrance, we probably should let her know we're here."

"No doubt we're close, Sis," Lily suggested, when they heard piano music that could only be their Grandpa Charlie playing in the next room.

"Maybe we can tiptoe inside," Lori whispered. "Remember how we used to dance for Grandpa Charlie when he played the piano? Was it Aunt Marcie who told us playing piano helped Grandpa Charlie when he returned from the military hospital?"

The music quieted as Grandpa Charlie saw them enter. He stood, smiling.

"Hi, Grandpa Charlie," the twins greeted him in unison.

Charlie reached an arm around each of them, kissed them on the cheek, and in his deep rustic voice chuckled and said, "Your Mom made me look pretty handsome in that portait, didn't she? Now, may I escort my lovely, famous granddaughters to the show room?"

Charlie swept his granddaughters, Lily and Lori, up the aisle past rows and rows of people seated and apparently waiting for the meeting where they were scheduled to meet Granny. They had arrived with just a few minutes to spare, thanks to their Grandpa Charlie who had seated them in the front row next to him.

With a quick glance at their program, they both smiled when Miss Bea opened the festivities. "We would like to thank Shannon Donnelly and Wendy Fox with this bronze plaque, which will be placed in the museum entry, as the artists responsible for all of the detailed displays in this Veterans' Annex."

"As of today, this annex will be titled the Charles Donnelly Veterans' Museum of Turtle Crossing. Would you join us, Charlie?" He squeezed the girls' hands as he stood and joined Shannon and Wendy on stage.

"Keeping it in the family," Miss Bea announced. "We would like to introduce Doctorate of Veterinarian Medicine, Lori Rose Donnelly, and Doctorate of Chiropractic Health, Lily Anne' Donnelly, as the newest members of The Business Women of Turtle Crossing Association."

After the presentations were concluded, people gathered in discussion clusters, not quite ready to leave, when Isaac Pease's wife, Leona approached Lily and Lori. "Ladies, Isaac and I heard about the conflict you've been having with finding a place to live."

"Well, we are in a quandary about what to do with my mom's home here in Turtle Crossing. Would you girls be interested in house sitting it for us for at least a year? Here are the keys. Look it over, and if you are interested, we will draw up the papers. Your only cost will be minimum utility costs over what we presently pay with it empty. Do you know where it is?"

"Are you talking about the two-story brick showplace on the corner of Red Brick Lane and Mountain View Road?" Lori asked.

"Yes," Leona replied.

"So. House-sitting means practically rent free." Lori said.

"How soon could we move in?" Lily asked.

Lori had been clutching the keys in her hand so tightly, she nearly dropped them when she opened her hand to give a set of keys to Lily.

"Anytime," Leona replied. "And, if your brother Hunter and Will's son Storm would like to move in as well, we would agree to that. Perhaps you ladies would feel a bit safer on the estate with them there. It has five bedrooms."

At that moment, Lily and Lori glanced up—immediately aware of the look on Uncle Will's face. It was apparent he had been aware of the Pease Family's gracious offer.

Granny approached Lily and Lori and asked, "Where would you like to eat? Doc and the boys mentioned getting a pizza."

"You choose Granny," Lori suggested.

"I think this would be a good time to reserve a table at Alexa Welby's B&B."

"The boys and I agree," Doc added.

Chapter 8

Monday evening, the day after the weekend All-Family Reunion and celebration for Lily and Lori's return from college, was quiet and relaxing, but still exciting. Lily, Lori, Hunter, and Storm gathered on Doc and Granny's back porch for coffee and Alexa's special cheesecake.

"It's decision time," Lily said. "We have the rest of the week open."

"Well, if it helps," Lori began, "Granny slipped me a note that one of my college classmates had left a message on their answering machine. She plans to visit GreatStone Castle in Sidney, Ohio, with a neighbor friend of her mom's tomorrow morning at ten. Something about a bridal party venue. I should call her when we arrive at Granny's."

"Well," Lily added, "My interview with Isaac Pease isn't until Friday, and our house-sitting contract should be ready then, as well."

"So. Tomorrow morning," Lori continued. "Leave at eight-thirty? Destination – GreatStone Castle, Sidney?"

The following morning, as they rushed through breakfast in silence, Granny and Doc were amazed. "Thanks for the note about your projected plans for the rest of the week," Doc said, chuckling.

"Have a safe trip," Granny added, to which they nodded, threw her a kiss, and rushed out the door with the thermos of coffee and cups. The four of them piled into the waiting car, with Hunter taking the wheel.

"Going to the castle today works out best," Hunter began. "That will leave Wednesday and Thursday free to visit Dr. Kate, and stay a couple nights in the house we grew up in. And walk around the golf course in the evening after the golfers have left for the day. I have missed that peaceful feeling. And look forward to visiting Mom and Wendy's Art Gallery in Winthrop."

"Storm? How do you feel about these plans?" Lori asked.

"I can't wait to work out at your Mom's studio," Storm replied. "And maybe play a round of golf? You know, there are times when I feel like a vagabond. Dad's business takes him on the road a lot and mom's art and the Winthrop News keep her pretty busy, too. I know. I have been away at college, so I didn't notice the distance until I returned home from college."

"We've noticed a change in our parents, too. It's like they're uncertain how to treat us as adults," Lily added, "But now, we'll finally have a place of our own to come back to for at least a year."

"You're right." Lori said, as the excitement bubbled over in the tone of her voice. "No explanations! The Four

Aces finally have a place to roost! Privacy, top notch!"

"The main thing I will miss is our morning ride," Lily added.

"Well," Storm suggested, "Our parents are out of town for two weeks. I'm so used to staying at Doc. and Granny's and coming and going, but I never thought to share my plans. Thanks."

"See?" Hunter said, "Now you sound just like your Dad. And that's a compliment, by the way."

"That's awfully nice of you," Lori added. "But Lily and I noticed the Business Women of Turtle Crossing had their heads together shortly before your dad led us in the direction of Isaac and Leona."

"This is the first time," Hunter said, "I have ever heard of that organization."

"That is because," Lily added, with a sparkle in her eye teased, "Because you are a guy."

"No kidding," Storm agreed as they pulled in the drive behind the castle.

"It is separate from the Shadow Angels," Lily began, "They organized when Uncle Henry was loose and nasty. 'Fight fire with fire!' was their motto. Women only."

"Drive around to the front entrance of The Great-Stone Castle," Lori announced. "I'm not being a backseat driver, by the way. I'm reading the directions my friend sent me.

"Wow!" Lily exclaimed, "This castle sits pretty high up."

"Even when Jonothan flew us over it," Lori recalled, "It looked like it was perched on a mountain top."

"When we were in grade school, it seemed like it was part of a mountain," Lily added as Hunter followed the drive around and parked at the front entrance. They exited the car, staring up at the castle.

"This is quite impressive," Storm remarked as he ran his hand along the limestone porch rail, and climbed the steps to the porch.

"Granny mentioned the five-foot-wide screen door and sculpted glass front door were no doubt built to allow room for ladies wearing their ball gowns with hoops and layers of petticoats to enter gracefully."

"Well! I for one am glad we're not expected to wear those long dresses with dozens of petticoats," Lily continued.

"Not to worry," Hunter chuckled. "It appears this porch wraps around at least two-thirds of the castle. Wouldn't it be nice to relax in one of these swings in the afternoon or evening?"

"And you wouldn't be alone?" Lori teased. Hunter smiled and raised an eyebrow in response.

"These trees are as old as the Warren Estate," Lily commented as she walked around a curve of the porch, leaning against the two-foot-high and one-foot-thick limestone railing.

"Granny reminded us as we left earlier to look at the garden area," Lori added. "The horseshoe shaped space is a natural elevated bowl for seating guests for an outdoor wedding. It is centered at the bottom of the elevation near an ivy covered garden arch. Beautiful setting for a bride and groom."

"Is your friend just shopping around for a wedding venue?" Lily asked.

"Could be," Lori replied, as they headed back to the castle. "Now that we're here, I'm anxious to tour the inside."

They meandered inside and felt a moment of stepping back in time. A guided tour was already in process, and the four of them quietly joined the group. "The wainscot is red African mahogany on the walls in the Reception Hall," the guide repeated as about thirty ladies gathered in preparation to head to the second floor. Hunter and Storm waved to Lily and Lori as they followed the tour in progress.

In her haste to move out of the way of the tour group, Lily backed up one step too far, and suddenly felt herself tipping backward, completely off balance. Just as suddenly, someone behind her placed their hands at her waist. Leaning close to, but not touching, her neck, he said softly, "Hey. Good morning, beautiful lady. Watch your step here. We can't have you falling."

Disbelief shook her to silence. Otherwise she would have screamed. Her heart pounded as she finally braced herself against the wall. She couldn't turn around. *It can't be him*, she thought. He hadn't spoken to her since college.

Then the hands were gone. Her waist felt warm where he had touched her. She spun around. A nearby office door was closed, but the Side Hall exit door was ajar.

Lily hurriedly slipped out the Side Hall door. She looked left and right, and at first saw no one, then spotted Lori talking to someone in the direction of the garden.

She wrapped her arms around her middle in an effort to calm her insides that were shaking like she had just stepped from an outdoor, steaming ninety plus degree temperature into a walk-in freezer. She collapsed into a nearby chair.

She looked up when a staff member approached and asked, "Are you ill, Miss Lily? Your sister, was looking for you, and I noted that this door had been opened, but not secured. Odd that she asked me to check this area."

"Lily!" Lori breathed as she rushed to Lily's side. "Are you okay?"

They thanked the staff member, who returned to the office. Lori bent down, took one look at Lily's face, and suggested, "Shall we walk to the garden or take a drive?"

Lily didn't move, but her hands were cold as ice. Then Lori used the voice she used for recalcitrant animals, slipped her arm around Lily, and barked, "Now. You will stand up and march!"

Lily stood up, gave a weak laugh and leaned on Lori, tears coursing down her cheeks, as they walked past the windows of the office.

***

Donovan had been hired by the owner to take photos of the castle and outdoor wedding garden area. He had been stunned when a willowy blonde turned and walked right past him. She didn't recognize him. But by the time he recalled Lily mentioning to him that she was a twin, the young woman had walked on. He decided to stop by the office to clear his thoughts when he spotted a duplicate willowy blonde near the steps of the Side Hall.

He responded without thinking. To keep her from falling backwards down the few steps into the Side Hall, Donovan reached forward and the moment his hands touched her waist, he knew she was his Lily. He hadn't been close enough to touch her for over a year, and the way his heart pounded was a response he was not prepared for. His voice caught in his throat. He didn't want to startle her and leaning close to her but not touching her, he said softly, "Hey, beautiful lady. Watch your step. We can't have you falling."

Memories flooded his mind as he reluctantly dashed into the owner's open office and closed the door. "If I could just go back," he thought, "But there are no do-overs."

"Donovan?" his boss inquired. "Are you ready to explain what just happened? The Donnellys are very special around here. That family is tightly knit. Sharp, courageous, business owners. And from the expression on both of your faces, it seems like you have some history with that young woman. Grabbing her and then running away is no way to behave, even if you did keep her from getting hurt. Frankly, from where I was standing, you're lucky she didn't turn around and deck you."

*****

Hunter called out when he caught up with his sisters as they were walking around the exterior of the Castle, "Hey, you two. This place is awesome. Especially the defunct ballroom/attic that is filled with whatever holiday decorations, extra chairs, just whatever needs repaired or replaced."

"Wait until you see," Storm continued. He could tell

Lily was upset about something by her odd silence, and added, "The solid pocket doors, the workmanship, the restoration and care that has gone into the rooms."

"Did your friend arrive yet?" Hunter inquired. "The guide said we could still walk with you on our scheduled tour." He finally asked. "Okay, Sis. What's wrong?"

Then a woman called out Lori's name, waving her arms to get their attention. Lori and Storm joined her friend who led them in the direction of the garden. Hunter motioned to Storm that he and Lily would wait for them near the front porch entrance where their tour would start.

"Lily?" Hunter asked.

"I'll be fine," Lily replied. "I'll bet you're beginning to wonder about your big sis, falling apart like this, right?"

"It's a guy, right?" Hunter asked as he took hold of her shoulders, his voice gentle, yet not demanding to know more.

She nodded her head as she wiped away a lingering tear. He wrapped his arms around her and added, "You want me to punch his lights out?"

She giggled and backed away. "Thanks. Let's just sit on that porch swing and wait for Lori and her friends."

***

Peering at them from the office windows, Donovan remarked to his friend, who was also working the photo shoot, "You're on my case about Lily, but it looks like she already has someone else anyhow."

"You don't see the likeness? That's her brother."

A woman's familiar, high-pitched laughter carried

inside the Castle. Donovan shivered. He was not ready to see this woman just now. He asked, "Do you know where I can hide out?"

"Really, Donovan. When are you going to learn? Stop running from shadows before you lose Lily forever. No matter who your mom thinks you should marry, you can't please everyone, and I think you have jumped through enough hoops for your parents."

***

As the Donnelly tour prepared to leave, they stopped when strains of Bach's "Air on the G String" softly began playing; and they were drawn into the happy occasion. As they started to turn away, the mother of the bride motioned them back inside.

The music stopped and then began again in earnest, as the bride's attendants lined up in the Gallery at the approach to the second floor of the Staircase. As they carefully began their one last practice descent of the stairs in their whisper-mint green spike heels, and wearing ankle-length full skirts.

The tips of their spike heels disappeared into the lush thickness of the deep rose-red carpet as they proceeded seven steps down to the landing. As expected, the moment the music had started, on que, their demeanor changed. Each was the picture of a princess, as they gracefully turned to face and admire their destination. At the bottom of the steps, they proceeded through the Reception Hall to the lovely Parlor where family and friends, the groom and his attendants would be waiting.

The bride waited on the last step where her dad would

assist her for their grand entrance, all the while framed in the artistically carved Red African Mahogany open staircase.

"Lori," her friend, Julie, asked as they prepared to leave, "Are you certain you need to leave now?"

"Yes," Lori replied. "Thanks for the exciting invite, but we have a pretty tight schedule."

The staff member from earlier was standing nearby, once again with his clipboard, and approached them when he heard they were leaving. Shaking hands, they each shared how much they had enjoyed their tour and visit. Then Lily added, "It looks far different as an adult."

"Most things do, I guess," he said. "Please give my regards to your Mom and Dad, and Will," he added when he shook hands with Storm.

Once they were on the road, Hunter asked, "Lori, thanks for running interference with that blonde on the tour with us. She was hitting on me to the point of distracting everyone else. Was she a friend of Julie's?"

Lily shook her head. "The daughter of her mom's friend. I don't know how well Julie even knew her before today."

Hunter said, "I begged Julie to please not share our names with her."

"Julie knows better," Lily added, "I would love to be a little bird when she nails her mom for insisting Julie invite her along. Julie was so embarrassed she may not even stay for the wedding this afternoon."

Silence fell inside the car, filled with the hum of the road passing beneath them. Lily's stomach was still churning. She knew they all wanted to know more about what had happened to her earlier, but respected her right to tell them when she was ready.

"Lori, you are wanting some answers, right?" she began. "I can't remember what I told you early on about my professor."

"Just start at the beginning, Sis," Hunter said.

"Okay." After taking a deep breath, Lily continued, "Well, I had a week off from school. Instead of going home, one of my classmates had a family emergency and asked me to go to this exclusive vacation spot in her place.

"When I realized it was a honeymoon destination, I double-checked the address certain I was at the wrong place. I looked like a fish-out-of-water signing the register by myself."

Lily sighed, and continued, "That's when Donovan appeared at my elbow, acting like he was with me. It was their newest bungalow, built with families in mind with a connecting door. I, of course, was unaware of this until we each parked our rental cars in front of the bungalow."

"This is the same guy you spent practically every moment with for an entire week and then he left without even a goodbye or explanation?" Lori asked. "I have never heard you talk about anyone in that tone of voice, ever."

"I thought I was over Professor Michael Donovan James, until today," Lily spat with a tightness in her voice that belied how he could make her feel.

"Wait a minute!" Lori demanded, as she grabbed Lily's hand. "Was he wearing a powder blue dress shirt and blended vest, and dressed more like he was part of the wedding party than a professional photographer? He looked at me at first like he knew me, and then disappeared, and when we went inside the castle, we got separated when some of the early tour group ahead of us all tried to get closer to the tour guide."

Lily nodded. "That was him. It was my own fault. I was looking through my guide map, when someone bumped into me. I was close to the side hall exit stairs, and he kept me from falling backwards down those four steps. But I was upset because I thought I had put him out of my heart, you know. All he had to do was touch me and I felt like I was on that frustrating merry-go-round again.

"It was like watching a silent film strip in black and white, in slow motion. The word *NO* raced through my mind, but before I could turn around, his soft, low voice came back on rewind. Then he was gone."

Hearing the pain in her voice brought Hunter around, and he reminded her, "Don't forget, Sis, I did offer to punch his lights out."

His comment brought giggles from the back seat. "I remember," Lily replied. "Lori, I know I called you that last morning of checkout, and when I saw that his rental car was gone, I thought it was strange that he would leave without telling me because we had spent the majority of our time together, except at night, of course.

"The night before checkout, he kissed me on the cheek during a dance. I thought he was going to kiss me goodnight, but was interrupted by a noisy group walking past our bungalow. However, when I returned to class, you'll never guess who my replacement professor was for my last quarter?"

"Donovan?"

"I always got the feeling that there was a rule, whether in writing or not, no fraternizing with students," Lily continued, "He totally ignored me. Never made eye contact with me. Of course, all the girls were drooling over him, but I kept quiet. Rumors abounded, from he was engaged to be married, married, or widowed. You know, he really does have a beautiful smile; but when he took over my class, I never once saw him smile."

Lily took a deep breath. "But I think that's enough about Donovan for now. I would rather focus on the four of us. Where else but home should we be free to be who we are and discuss where we are headed?"

Outside, the sign announcing the corporation limit of Winthrop slid past their windows.

"The first place we're headed," declared Lori, "is grocery shopping. We'll need supplies for our new place." The others agreed, and Hunter parked in one of the open spaces along the main road.

The Four Aces had bonded so quickly that they were unaware of the impression they made. However, their charismatic appearance was infectious, especially with Winthrop business owners who were excited to see them and didn't hesitate to stop them on the street.

The Four Aces were seldom anxious to draw attention to themselves; but when the owner of the grocery stopped them outside his office, they felt like four-year-olds when he offered them penny-candy as a special treat. Their laughter and smiles were so genuine, the other shoppers and clerks applauded.

"We've put it off long enough," Lori said as they filled the trunk with bread, milk, fresh fruits and vegies.

"Most of the fields are planted by now," Hunter added, as Lily slowed down her approach to Shannon's Haven Golf and Country Club and lowered the windows of the Lincoln. A groundskeeper was headed towards the maintenance shed with the mower. The scent of fresh-cut grass hung pleasantly in the air.

"What a surprise," Lori said, "I see George is the gate-keeper today and has already opened the gate."

"Someone called you," Lily admonished when she saw the excited expression on his face, when he stepped out-side of his security entrance building.

"We wanted to surprise you," Hunter admitted.

"Well, Granny not only suggested when you might arrive, but..."

"She gave you the description of the car and license plate number," Hunter chuckled.

Lily and Lori clambered out of the car and gave him a hug. Of course, Hunter and Storm offered a hand shake; but he then hugged each of them. They had known him since they were children. He pointed them in the right direction and they climbed back into the car to make their way to their final destination.

"I understand your Mom and Dad knew nothing about your plans?"

"No," Hunter replied.

"Well, welcome home!"

"Lily? Lori?" Hunter asked. "How does everything look?"

The purr of the Lincoln was barely audible as she turned left at the Private Drive sign, past the Carriage House towards the house they grew up in. Home.

"Pull in the far right garage door," Hunter said as he opened the garage door next to it.

"I see we won't have to go to the Clubhouse Garage for a golf cart," Lori added, as they unloaded their groceries and luggage. She started opening cupboard doors. "I found the fridge," Lori beamed as she helped Lily empty the grocery bags.

"So, little brother," Lily asked, as she hunted for the built-in refrigerator. "When did Mom and Dad renovate the kitchen?"

"About six months ago," Hunter replied. "Mom was so excited about getting it finished before you two finished college."

"These are oak, right?" Storm asked. Hunter nodded and motioned Storm to help bring in the luggage when he saw his sisters about to get a bit emotional.

Lily and Lori were near tears as they wandered into the living room and were pleased that their mom and dad hadn't changed it from the pale oak colored leather couch and matching kick-back type chairs.

"It appears the only change in here is the carpet," Lori said.

"And our bedroom appears to have withstood the test of time and our non-use," Lori added.

"Let's take a look at Mom's studio," Lily suggested.

Their expectations high, they opened the door and were surprised their Mom didn't have one canvas started or completed.

Hunter turned on the lights. "It appears," Lori began, "We may have to run the dust mop. I didn't realize Mom had quit working here."

"She left her workout music, though," Hunter said as they set the dust mops aside and started the music.

Between the music and all the time they'd spent in the car, a little bit of movement seemed in order. It took Lily and Lori twenty or more minutes to go through their warm-ups, when they noticed that Hunter and Storm were standing still.

"What's wrong?" Lily asked.

"Are you two okay?" Lori asked.

"You lost us in the last fifteen minutes," Hunter explained.

"Sorry," Lily replied.

"Storm," Lori said, "you'll notice some of these stretches are similar to what I did in volleyball, except nearly in slow motion."

"Stormy," Lily asked softly, smiling her quirky grin because she knew he only allowed family to forget he wasn't a two-year-old anymore. "Have you been lifting weights again?"

"Ah! You noticed," Storm replied, smiling.

"We need strength," Lori agreed, but the main components are durability, tenacity and extension. Ready?" Which was one of the action words they had practiced. With hand signals, the moment the door knob moved and even before that, the Foursome were already in the "on-guard" position.

Hunter and Storm couldn't believe it. They were supposed to be protecting Lily and Lori, but instead they were working as a unit.

Lori moved forward swiftly and yanked the door wide open. There was a moment of stunned silence. "Mom? Dad?"

A flurry of happy shouts and hugging followed. Storm stepped away and shut off the music.

"You all didn't waste any time with training, did you?" David remarked.

"We needed to work out some of the kinks as a team."

From what we just observed," Shannon said, "I think your response was impeccable!"

"Really, Mom?" Hunter asked, proudly.

They gathered in the living room and Shannon began, "As you know, Lily, the body has its strengths and weaknesses."

"What your Mom is referring to is that we used to work out together," David added.

"This is a story we never thought to mention before. Yes. Before I joined the Army, I had found a job cleaning at a dance studio similar to your Mom's and was told had I trained in ballet in grade school, I might have made it a career. The only ballet would have been basketball, track and gratefully working with the girls' volleyball team in our children's home gym. But a semi-retired ballet coach worked with me after hours. I loved it."

"Dad," Lily began, "Would you consider … umm …

do you have the time to work with Hunter and Storm?"

When he didn't answer, Lori interceded "Hey, Dad. Mom and Lily and I need to finish organizing the kitchen. We'll let the men catch up here." Lori, Lily, and Shannon filed out, closing the door behind them.

"Dad?" Hunter asked. "Storm and I need this. We don't have to be better than my older sisters, but..."

"But how do you keep them safe when...they are capable on their own?"

"Yes."

"Let me tell you something," David suggested, "Except for close family and friends, your sisters are first and foremost like their Mom. The run-of-the-mill jerks see them as lovely women who surely are weak because they are not muscle-bound like a ball player, for instance.

"You're saying surprise and speed, in their case, is in their favor?" Storm asked.

"Yes, however, after watching the four of you dance together at the reunion, no one there would have believed it was the first time. You challenged each other and loved every minute of it. Your strength and fitness were astounding. Don't ever lose that in-the-moment, aware-of-your-surroundings proficiency."

"Dad," Hunter commented, "now you sound like Lily and Lori."

"And my Dad," Storm added.

"I'll grant you one thing," David continued, "what the four of you did just a moment ago impressed your Mom. And you know she doesn't hand out compliments like that on a whim."

"I wish my Dad was as understanding," Storm added.

"Your dad was astonished and proud when he watched the connection the four of you have acquired since Lily and Lori returned home."

"Is there time to work with us on a few moves, Dad?" Hunter asked.

***

After the Donnellys and Storm enjoyed a dinner of chili prepared by the twins, Hunter drew his dad aside and suggested he and Shannon take them all on a tour of the winery with maps describing their expansion.

"What brought about your interest in wine-making?"

"Sadie and the Tunnels' expansion."

"They forced her out?" Lori asked.

"Pretty much. When she refused to sell, someone found an old rule on the books. But she fooled them all. She called me and a crew of us moved her out of Turtle Crossing to our place in the suburbs of Winthrop."

"I know our family has always had close ties with Sadie, Dad," Lily began. "But why did she call you?"

"Because of your Mom's connection with the Turtle Crossing Business Women's Association."

"So, where is your market?" Lily asked.

"It's a work in progress," David replied. "Your great uncle C.W. is excited about what we have started. And our expansion includes the acreage where his trial vines have been planted. If production continues as we expect, we're going to have to expand our operation here or move it entirely to C.W.'s. He's even used some of our wine for communion before."

"Mom?" Lori asked.

"We have good people running both of the golf courses. You girls are just getting your careers under way. Hunter, it won't be long before your career takes off."

"Your painting, as well?" Lily asked.

"Wendy and I are both exhausted because the board at the military museum kept coming up with ideas and changes. Six months became twelve. That's never happening again!"

"We would love to see your operation," Lori requested.

"Honey?" Shannon asked of David. "We have time to show them our vines right now, don't we?"

"You're interested?" David asked, puzzled and excited at the same time. A smile spread across his face, and he popped up out of his chair—in his rush to share this dream of his with his daughters.

"Of course we are," Hunter quickly responded, nodding to their Dad, the look reminding his Mom and Dad of the numerous times he had begged them to tell the girls.

"What about Warren Enterprises?" Lily asked.

"Well, Brandi's little brother Mason Davies has shown interest and has been working with your Grandpa Richard Warren. You would think Mason was Richard's son. You remember Richard's connection with the navy and Mason's with the Coast Guard and a conversation between the two is why Mason arrived and stayed in the Carriage House for several months."

"I take it none of this is for publication? " Lori asked.

"No."

"I remember some acreage beyond the golf course," Lily recalled. "But, I never paid much attention to it because I thought it belonged to the Parkers."

"Your Grandpa, Mom and I bought it after your abduction," David replied softly. "Because you both admitted you still have nightmares of those two incidents."

"Dad, Mom," Hunter suggested, "As you know, the four of us plan to continue working as a unit with the Shadow Angels."

Storm had enjoyed listening and watching the interaction of the Donnellys and planned to schedule more time with his mom, dad, and sister. "I cannot thank you all enough for including me in your plans and am excited about moving into the Pease Victorian tomorrow."

"I understand the ladies are going in to Winthrop to visit Dr. Kate?" David asked, smiling at Shannon.

"Yes, and you and the boys are headed over to C.W.'s?"

"Yes, we'll drop the car off at the dealership on our way."

"Sounds like a plan," Shannon said. "We'll pick it up after our visit with Dr. Kate. I must admit, I haven't stopped by for a visit since she retired; but when I called, she was excited we were stopping by."

***

Dr. Kate greeted them warmly, but a bit slower than usual. "Thank you girls for coming to visit. Lunch is chilling in the refrigerator. I have a pitcher of ice-cold lemonade with a pinch of mint to start our visit."

"Lori," she asked. "How are you feeling about your choice as a veterinarian?"

"I love it. Did you hear Doc O'Reilly is ready to open the O'Reilly Veterinarian Animal Hospital?"

"Yes," Kate replied. "I read the newspaper article about the grand opening. How wonderful to be a part of such an exciting venue."

"I know," Lori replied. "But it's a bit overwhelming, too."

"Ah! Come on, young lady. Once you save the life of a child's pet, or assist in the birth of a possible grand champion colt, lamb, or steer, your passion will return, tears and all."

Just listening to Dr. Kate describe how she would feel brought tears to her eyes, as she scooted her stool closer to her ninety-three-year-old-mentor she had loved since she was a little girl.

"Lily?" Kate suggested, "come a little closer, dear. Something has changed between you. What is your number one fear right now?'

Lily pressed her fingernails into the palms of her hands and shook her head. "I can't believe you're asking me a question like this. My office has to open in a month. I'm sorry, Sis, but I've envied how your career has progressed so quickly. I don't know if I can do this on my own."

Lori started to say something, but Dr. Kate squeezed Lori's hand and shook her head. "Lily, when was the last time you attended church?"

"It's been awhile. Not until I returned home a little over a week ago," Lily replied. "But I've enjoyed listening to Hunter and Rev. C.W. at the All-Family Reunion."

"What was the message?" Kate asked.

"I don't recall," Lily replied.

"But you still believe in the Lord?" Kate asked.

Lily and Lori replied, "Absolutely. Yes!"

Kate motioned Shannon to come closer. "Do you remember how we used to join hands and pray together when negative thoughts brought us pain and things didn't go as we thought they should?"

Shannon, Lily, and Lori pulled their chairs closer to Kate to make a circle and sat in silence for a few minutes. They each felt a warmth that had been missing for the twins for several years. "Dear Jesus, please come into the hearts of these very special young women, Lily, Lori, and Shannon," Dr. Kate prayed.

"Help them to see that only you can show them they are never alone. That all they need to do is believe in you and your compassion and trust that the Lord has their back. To understand they can't control everything or everybody by themselves. All they need to do is ask You for help and most things are possible. We ask this all in your blessed name. Amen. Amen. And Amen."

They felt the strength and power of the Lord. Their hands tingled. "My heart feels lighter," Lily commented, smiling.

"So does mine," Lori added.

"Dr. Kate," Shannon said, "I, too, agree with my daughters. I didn't realize the stress I have been dealing with until just now. Thank you."

"Having retired," Kate admitted, "I miss interacting with my patients. I, too, must get my act together. This prayer was for myself, as well," she admitted. "Do you have other plans while you are in the area?"

Lily looked at Lori and her Mom and replied, "Lori, Hunter, Storm and I have an appointment this afternoon in Turtle Crossing to pick up keys for the…"

"Ah. I heard," Kate added. "Wendy and I had tea yesterday and she told me about your house-sitting the Pease Victorian home. What a wonderful blessing. Before you leave, I have a gift for you ladies. Remember, the special oils you played with one day that you thought was my perfume? You will find a college graduation gift bag for each of you on my dresser. Would you mind getting them?"

While they were gone, Kate took Shannon's hands in hers and softly asked, "My dear Shannon, how are you doing?"

"I am doing really well. Much better after stopping here today to see you, Kate. Please feel free to call me any time. Even if it is just to talk about the weather." Shannon leaned in and kissed Dr. Kate on the cheek. Then asked, "Would you consider allowing me to do your portrait for my art gallery here in Winthrop?"

Lily and Lori were just about to join their Mom and Dr. Kate but waited patiently for her reply.

She bowed her head and whispered, "I am honored that you would even consider asking me to sit for you. Thank you. Oh, my, but what does one wear for a sitting?"

"Your choice."

Chapter 9

The Foursome awoke Friday morning at the Warren Estate, five miles west of Winthrop, to flute music Shannon's and Will's grandmother had recorded just for the family.

"Amazing, isn't it?" Lori began, "That these two days here with the boys have been…"

"As special to them…"

"As it has to us," Lori remarked.

They recognized Hunter's *tap-tap-tap, tap-tap* knock on their bedroom door and smiled. He hadn't changed that knock since he was four years old.

Lori opened the door to find Hunter and Storm in the hall.

"This has been an awesome visit home, hasn't it?" Hunter said.

"Yes. We were just talking about that," Lily nodded.

"Maybe it's contagious," Storm suggested, as he crowded Hunter out of the way. "Remember the reunion dances? I stopped in at Dad's after the fiasco with that other county sheriff and Dad was playing this same recording. It's his favorite, too."

"We already hit the showers, so both bathrooms are free, ladies." Hunter smiled his quirky, cute smile. "Hey, you're the ones who wanted to hit the road early this morning. We just might save you some breakfast," he warned as he quickly shut their door, just before Lori's pillow hit the door.

"Now we know for certain we are home," Lily said, as they gathered what they planned to wear and headed towards the showers.

After breakfast and hugs were shared all around, they loaded up their luggage and Hunter took the wheel. They rolled down the windows and soaked up the nostalgia of the sound of the engine, the tires, the whack of a golfer teeing off, the low murmur of a golf cart, and the distinct fragrance of peony and rose from their Mom's flower garden that extended to Nanna Ruth's Carriage House.

As they headed towards the gate, Hunter slowed at the Gatekeeper, Milton Merryweather's hut, which had a welcome stop sign on the entrance side of his building. It was apparent he knew to expect them. "You all have a safe and blessed journey, and come back soon," he said, as he tipped his hat goodbye and opened the front gates.

As they rolled their windows up, it was apparent this visit was a stamp of approval from their parents for following their dreams. Yet they were scrappy enough to fight for beliefs instilled by them and had become stand-your-ground adults.

"Be careful through here, though," Storm reminded Hunter. "Your Dad said he had to move off the edge of the berm of Summerville Road for a farmer's two-third's-of-the-road piece of farm equipment and into a pot-hole filled with muddy water."

"Didn't Mom tell you why they came back here?" Hunter asked.

"Just that they had a flat tire and the spare was too bald for driving back to Turtle Crossing safely," Lily replied.

"Right along here," Storm said. "They pulled ahead into the next side road and found a piece of a golf club stuck in their tire. A guest golfer was so angry when his ball went out of bounds, he must have thrown his club into the concrete corner-post. The club head and part of the shaft were hidden in a puddle along the edge of the road."

"Then, according to the relative who brought him along to play, told him there was a possibility he could be banned from playing here again because he not only threw his driver across the road, he apparently had a confrontation with one of our groundskeepers about out-of-bounds posted rules."

"Sounds familiar, doesn't it?" Lily murmured as she opened her briefcase.

The silence, reminiscent of his Dad, troubled Storm. "If I said something wrong, I apologize."

"You didn't say anything wrong. Brandi's first husband, Justin, confronted groundskeepers and kidnapped Lily and me," Lori recalled. "It's one of those momentary memories we leave in the past," she added. "On a lighter note, Storm, have you ever studied a contract for someone who, like the four of us, considered house-sitting, as opposed to renting?"

"No." Storm replied. "But I have heard of it and I called Uncle Kristopher. He said, "The simpler, the better. Apparently my Dad and Miss Bea discussed this matter."

"Miss Bea has been in real estate since she was a toddler and followed her dad around long before he passed," Lori added.

"Isn't our appointment with Mr. Pease at eleven o'clock?" Lily asked.

"I'm not an attorney," Hunter appealed to Storm," but shouldn't all four of us sign this document?"

"Absolutely!" Lily and Lori replied, as all four smiled in understanding.

Hunter, using the rear-view mirror, winked at his sisters. Storm, catching onto his charming cousins, loved being a part of this Foursome. Which, also, reminded him that he needed to have a talk with his Dad, especially since his mom and dad always had their own business interests, Storm had been searching for a place to fit in. Being one of the Four Aces with plans to help others made him feel like a piece of his heart had been missing.

***

"We're a half-hour early, but surely we can pass the time in his waiting room," Lori suggested as they entered the Pease Chiropractic Office Building.

The assistant, Chloe, greeted them as the Donnelly Family when they entered. "He expected you would be on time," she added. "He's with a patient. Just take a seat in his office." She held the door for them to follow. "His office is the first door on your left."

Meanwhile, Lily was mentally checking the layout. But Lori looked further down the hall and was certain she saw Lily's Donovan talking with Isaac Pease and wondered if he was also Lily's competition.

However, Mr. Pease quickly joined them. "Good morning. Correct me if I'm wrong, but with the four of you going in different directions for work and college, I hope you don't mind if Oliver French, the groundskeeper, stays on at the cottage."

"If you require her, his wife, Peaches, has cleaned our home once a week for years. She, also, works at the Turtle Crossing Main Street Bank."

"Unless we get in a bind, we're all used to taking care of the housekeeping," Lori noted, to which the others nodded in agreement. In the back of her mind, she made a note to find out more about the Frenches, a silent message that was shared.

"The attached page lists who to call if you need service. However, don't hesitate to call Oliver. He knows more about repair than I do," Isaac admitted.

"I can't thank you enough for helping us out," Leona added. "It was just what I needed to exchange the bedroom linens. We had been waiting on the replacement drapes and bed-covers to arrive and they just came in this week."

"Here are your two extra sets of keys, and gate security remotes. Any questions? No? Well, you have our personal number, as well as the office number."

"Lily?" Isaac asked. "Do you have a moment?"

Before Lily had time to reply, Lori said, "We'll wait for you outside, Sis."

Hunter immediately questioned Lori's quick reply, but waited until they were outside.

"Lori," Hunter asked, "what was the rush?"

Lori wanted to discuss seeing Donovan in the hall with Lily first.

"It's something I need to talk to her about first."

"You're worried."

"Concerned," Lori remarked just as Lily opened the door behind them. "He hired someone else."

"Yes," Lily said. "However he was very forthcoming with his reasoning. First, he's afraid of losing his clients to me. Second, the person he hired is a nephew of an old friend of his."

"Does this person have a name?" Hunter inquired.

"D. Michael James," Lily replied as they all piled into the Lincoln.

"I called Granny. She suggested we use Doc's truck to move our stuff out of her Farmhouse," Lori added. "And Storm, apparently your vehicle is parked behind your Dad's vehicles."

"Does half of Turtle Crossing know we've moved in?" Storm wondered.

"I don't think so," Lily replied. "But it's a small town. Rumors abound."

Granny and Doc had lunch waiting for them. Excitement sparkled in their eyes as they dished up lasagna, salad and drinks.

"Do you mind if we help you move in?" Granny requested.

"We would love it," Lori replied. "You're wanting to see the place?"

"Busted!" Granny said. "It's been years since we had a reason to be there."

"Lori," Doc began, "you always have a place here regardless. Until you decide on a vehicle, our business just purchased a nice five-year-old Ford pickup with our names as Veterinarians and the O'Reilly Hospital for you to drive. Would you like to take a look at it?"

Lori was speechless when Doc handed her the keys and led her outside. "How did you know? This is my dream truck, blue as the sky on a warm sunny day. With my name on the side! With a trailer hitch and a place to store new and used boots. And a gun rack."

"The guys from the bunkhouse helped us move your luggage and boxes this morning," Granny added.

When it was time to drive out, Storm led the caravan, followed by Lily, Hunter and Lori. Doc and Granny brought up the rear. Their caravan followed Storm, who opened the side road gate. "I had forgotten how beautiful this house and grounds were," Granny exclaimed.

"It certainly is steeped in the history of Turtle Crossing," Doc said.

"They left us a list on their bulletin board," Hunter read. "*Feel free to make use of our personal library. Reorganize the Antique Furniture in the Parlor however you like. Please make this house your home. Thank you for putting life back into this house again. It's a blessing not to have to check it daily. P.S. Please feel free to call if you have any concerns or questions. Signed, Leona & Isaac Pease."*

The Foursome quickly moved boxes and luggage into dressers, chests and spacious closets while snacking on an assortment of Granny's apple dumplings and peanut butter cookies. When they had finished, the Foursome gathered in the family room with their notebooks and calendars. Their silence was filled with satisfaction and disbelief.

"This seems so surreal," Lily finally commented.

"I know," Lori added. "We are lucky to have family and friends."

"Most of all," Lily continued, together we are so much stronger.

"So, tomorrow," Hunter suggested, "We'll look at our schedules?"

"And," Storm added, "We'll each practice the Security System. Agreed?"

"Lily," Hunter asked. "We were all on pins and needles at the chiropractor's office. What did Mr. Pease say to you today?"

Lily pondered how to answer Hunter's question. "I've gotten so used to dealing with everything by myself, except for the help of our twin-connection-calls. But to answer your question, Mr. Pease thanked me for offering to assist him until his arm heals; however, he hired the nephew, of a friend who needs this experience to decide whether to continue teaching or pursue his lifetime dream of working with patients."

"And," Lori added slowly, "each of us tried our best to

ignore the fact that Donovan was there with a patient."

Lily nodded, sighing. "That's all the proof I needed to know that Donovan is here and will be in Turtle Crossing for a while. My question is why here? And why be secretive about it? Why not call?"

"We can run a background check on him," suggested Lori.

"That's okay," Lily replied. "Maybe I just need to focus on an all-out search for my office equipment, and stop waiting for something to just happen. That's what I paid insurance for, and it is long past time when delivery was promised."

***

Saturday morning, each of the Foursome was awake by five-thirty in their new residence, the Pease Victorian. With a freshly brewed mug of coffee in one hand and one of Granny's cinnamon rolls in the other, they wandered out onto the front porch. Each chose a rocking chair as the early morning sun warmed their toes.

Silence. Except for the creak of the antique padded rocking chairs. Storm stood up and turned to face the Donnellys. "I've been in every nook and cranny of this house and grounds while working with my Dad, but being here with all of you, like this, is amazing."

"We feel the same way," Hunter encouraged. "What a way to start the day. We've been on this roller-coaster of venues and visits, but this—today—together is such a reward, maybe even more so for my sisters."

Lori nodded. "There are no words. I am still reeling that any time I drive that truck on a veterinary call, I will be humbly gratified that I get the chance to help a child's pet mouse or a grand-champion horse starting Monday morning. Then when my day is finished, I have a safe place to sleep at night with people I love and trust."

Hunter cleared his throat and smiled. "I agree with both of you. I now have the chance to study without having to jockey for space or time, or not having to hide or explain how or why I feel the way I do."

"Acceptance is a pretty special feeling," Lily added. "I have some ideas on how we can launch our first real assignment for the Four Aces. Set up a plan to find the trucks that appear to have disappeared. Two weeks before my graduation, they were scheduled to deliver all of the equipment I need to see patients. The sooner, the better! At this rate, Donovan can build and open his own office or take over the Pease clientele if he decides to retire or go into practice with their son."

"I have started with a list," Lily continued. "Who wants to see me fail? Where could the culprit store two semi-trucks? I know of only one person who owns a trucking firm, Brandi's half-brother, Jace Carpentier. He is a Deputy Sheriff in Sunrise and owns a trucking firm. My personal deadline is in fifteen days."

"Dexter wouldn't go this far, would he?" Lori asked.

"I don't know, but Great-Grandpa Henry's nephew would have no qualms about it. If we don't have any leads in one week, we bring in the Shadow Angels and your Dad, Storm, okay?"

***

Michael Donovan James, on the other hand, had

overheard the secretary's comment to Mr. Pease regarding the imminent arrival of the Donnelly twins, their brother, and cousin. Donovan watched them as they strode towards the lobby entrance.

In high heels the twins were nearly as tall as the young men with them. Their approach was impressive. The twins were tall, willowy, beautiful blondes. The young men were film-star handsome, tall, muscularly fit, with deep, dark eyes and hair. However, it was their personality, their direct approach and stride full of expectation that demanded a respect they appeared to be unaware of.

Any of them alone would turn heads. There was an aura about them as a unit that made his heart ache. If he could prove himself to Mr. Pease, perhaps he and Lily could become partners in life and business. Okay. Not all dreams come true. But where to start?

However, he wondered why when they left the Pease office, Lily marched ahead, with certainty. She appeared to be one angry lady.

***

Their second full day in their new home, Lily woke early once more. "Sunday morning sunshine!" she exclaimed. "What a way to celebrate this exciting new chapter of our lives!"

"As corny as that sounds," Lori added. "Being thankful for all our blessings in church this morning is a super way to start our new lives."

"Good morning, ladies," Hunter greeted as he finished his omelet. "Storm is driving separately this morning. He plans to visit with his mom and dad after church."

"I assumed you would take Madison Grace out to eat after church," Lily teased.

"We are just getting our wings, little brother," Lori added. "Our curfews are our own. I believe you have a meeting with Uncle Kristopher at eighty-thirty in the morning, don't you?" She winked at him in her saucy way, and thought, how good it was to be able to tease him.

"Hey, Sis," Hunter asked Lily, "Are you okay?"

"Yes, I just didn't get much sleep."

"Working on a backup plan?" Lori encouraged.

Lily smiled. "Absolutely!" One of her backup plans was to call Miss Bea and Dr. Kate on Monday. "All I need is an adjustable exam table until this company fills my reorder, Lily decided. She dropped her office keys in her purse with plans to stop by her office after church.

"Okay if we follow you?" Lily asked, then added. "New tie, Hunter? You do look pretty spiffy this morning too, by the way."

"Thanks," he replied as they locked up, keyed in the security system, and followed Hunter on their way to Eight-Mile-Centre.

"It takes a little getting used to, seeing our little brother, all grown up, doesn't it?" Lori began as they found a seat where they could see Rev C. W. inside his favorite chapel that had been moved here and added to the new church.

"Yes," Lily replied. "I'm also excited to see you in your new office. I can picture you in your new hunter green shirt with your name, Dr. Lori Rose Donnelly, Veterinarian, the *Doc O'Reilly Ranch and Animal Hospital* printed on the back."

"You are going to be wonderful. Well-known through-out your field of expertise!" Lily put her arm around Lori's shoulders. "So why do I feel a need to ask the Lord for his help in my evening and start of everyday prayers?"

***

Donovan found a seat in the last pew. The stained glass windows not only told a story but gave the new church a feeling of history and permanence, he thought as he listened to Hunter and Madison Grace in a duet to start the choir and morning service.

He knew exactly where Lily and Lori were seated, but from experience knew not to focus on Lily or she would sense he was there. Instead, he gave Rev. C. W. his complete attention because C.W.'s message always made him feel like it was meant just for him.

"If you are feeling like there just might not be any-thing you can do to change matters, look at them in a different way and don't get discouraged. Consider what you would do if a friend or the Lord needed advice from you, regarding a similar predicament. Be gentle with your advice now. Simplify. Can you change it? Suddenly, sit-ting on the sidelines of what others will think just lost its power, didn't it?"

Donovan smiled as he took notes and thought, *I need to put together a plan on how I could pay off my Great Granddad's I.O.U. in increments and share this plan with Lily and her family so we can start fresh. Wow! Where have I heard that nothing worthwhile has ever been easy?* How true.

***

They arrived a little early at the O'Reilly's and upon their arrival motioned to Granny at the kitchen window that they were headed towards the larger-than-life weeping willow tree between the master farmhouse and the creek.

"Those two beautiful young ladies," Granny began with Doc, "are much more relaxed than the day they returned to Ohio and home."

"I know," Doc replied. "That Foursome represents the children we were never blessed to have."

"I agree," Granny murmured. "The few days they shared as a family with their Mom and Dad was a healing they all needed."

"Let's not forget," Doc added with his arm around her waist, "what you and your Professional Women's group presented to Leona and Isaac regarding their empty Victorian was beyond fantastic for all involved."

"She thanks me every time I see her," Granny smiled. "And if I don't turn down my potatoes, they will boil all over my stove."

"I'll turn them down. You know, I still regret waiting so long to ask you to marry me. I just didn't think I could go through losing another loved one again."

"I know. And I never thought I would live it down that I married a younger man."

"Lily," Lori began, as they sat on the special bench Doc had made for Granny. "Remember all the plans we used to make when we were little about what we wanted our weddings to be like?"

"I know," Lily laughed. "Our weddings were going to be perfect. Not filled with so much drama and security, like so many others in our family."

"Well, you know how Uncle Will is."

"I do," Lily smiled remembering. Aunt Brandi is as well. But then not everyone understands all the horrible things our Great Grandma Warren and Great Grandpa Carpenter were responsible for."

"That's why he ended up in jail," Lori continued. "What do you say about a ride this afternoon with Granny and Doc?"

"We can at least ask," Lily replied as they headed back up the hill to Granny and Doc's kitchen.

"After we eat and look at Lori's office and the animal hospital," Lily suggested. "Would the two of you consider riding with us out beyond the pasture this afternoon?"

"I'll have to call the bunkhouse just to make certain we have someone on call," Doc said.

"This is a really good idea. In fact, Lori," Granny asked, "How long has it been since you were on a range?"

"Several months," Lori replied. "That is one thing I forgot I needed to be comfortable with, as well as accurate."

"Do you still have your license to carry a gun?" Granny asked.

"I will have to check with Mom. But Lily, you may as well do the same. It isn't like we'll have any county support at the Centre."

"If I recall," Doc commented. "The two of you used to compete against each other when you were in high school."

"That was Mom's idea," Lori said.

"But that also involves self-defense," Lily added, "Which was a life saver on campus once, and I've never forgotten that momentary feeling of helplessness." Lori reached over and laid her hand over Lily's.

"We can ride out to the practice range, and I'll notify my men where we'll be," Doc added as they quickly changed their clothes into western boots, jeans and hats and were soon riding out.

Each of them had taken several shots with a hand gun and rifle, and then checked their target sheets. As they gathered them, Doc started back to where Granny had stayed with the horses. "Now this is important. Do not look around—just at me, and your target sheets."

The look in Doc's eyes was all they needed to realize they could be in a real dangerous position. They had proved they could be really good at pretense and Lily shook her target sheet at Lori.

***

They all saddled up, and Lily and Lori argued back and forth as to who won today, while Doc and Granny were unusually quiet.

Doc stopped by the bunkhouse and informed his ranch hands about the incident. "Also," he added, "The boot prints were three inches longer and two inches wider than mine."

"Lori, are you free until tomorrow morning?" Lily asked.

"Sure," Lori replied, pleased Lily was ready to talk about what had her fired up. "What's on your mind?"

"I need to take a look at my section of my building at the Centre. I just have a feeling, you know…"

"Granny," Lori called out. "Lily and I are going to the Centre. To Lily's office. Catch you later."

They had just left when Granny phoned Will.

"How were they dressed?" Will asked.

"We just got back from the practice shooting range. So, jeans, western hats and boots. Why?"

"Did Lori drive her new truck?" Will requested.

Granny looked out the kitchen window and replied, "No."

"Good. Storm just pulled in. We'll follow them. I would like to see how it's coming along anyhow."

When Lori turned into the Centre, she drove in around the church and parked in the shaded parking area for business owners. Lily started to get out and Lori grabbed her hand. "Look! What are those strangers doing coming out of the open door of your office?"

Words were not necessary as they rolled down the windows in the Lincoln and shimmied out of the vehicle. "Okay." Lily began. Cowboy boots would not be conducive to a night time venture, let alone afternoon. But, shade from these trees is helpful," she added as she lifted her huge shopping bag out of the backseat.

Lori shouldered her purse and smiled as they whispered, pretense. They made their way through the grassy area alongside the fence that bordered Eight Mile Centre, changing their appearance as they went and strode through the alleyway two buildings beyond Lori's office.

Storm spotted them just as they left the alley, and Will

was so angry when Storm pointed them out, he gripped the steering wheel in frustration. "Dad, park in the church parking lot and let's go."

Will stared at Storm, surprised at his son's confident tone of voice, but nodded and followed.

Meanwhile, when Lily finally managed to walk on the concrete alley, she asked Lori, "What else in the world do you have in this shopping grab bag? Something keeps poking me in the ribs."

They heard the sound of an engine across the Centre and turned around pretending to be window shopping, when in reality they checked out who they appeared to be. Lori had grabbed a brown wig and topped it with an out of state rodeo hat and an 'Annie Get Your Gun' kid's water pistol and holster.

Lily had rolled-up her jeans, replaced her western boots with a pair of black tennis shoes. She looked like she was over two inches shorter than her partner, with a Shadow Angels reversible wrap-around black skirt, and a black wig topped with a black hat with a white spooky looking ghost on the front. "Sorry, but that is my fold-up cane that keeps poking you in the ribs. I probably should pretend to need it."

A man's blustery loud laughter was their cue. They both whispered, ready, and turned away from window-shopping while checking out the area around them. "I will never be able to thank the Shadow Angels for this one-of-a-kind bag gift," Lori added.

"Ok, Sis," Lily stated, "here goes." She pulled a map out of her purse. "Action!" and pointed across the Centre towards the pharmacy and grocery. All the buildings around them were closed on Sunday. Two burly looking men spotted them, argued a moment, and went back inside.

Lily pointed out and added, "Did you see Stormy is nearby?"

"Yeah," Lori confided as she re-arranged her pony tail.

Storm as he strolled out of the Centre's central median park area with binoculars, a cane looped over his arm, acting like he was an avid bird watcher. For anyone watching, they were not together. Will had followed his son's directions. He had parked the vehicle and sat on a bench in front of the pharmacy eating a crumbling stale cookie and popcorn.

There were no stop lights, but stop signs, parking areas and pedestrian cross walks. Then, Hunter and Madison Grace appeared in a pristine 1953 White Mustang with red leather upholstery, and pulled up close to the curb. Hunter and Madison Grace's conversations were silent as the couple used sign language. No one looked around, and everyone but Will was aware of what they were doing.

Madison Grace moved closer to Hunter and held up a Just Married sign and beeped his horn and waved at the men gawking out the windows and front entrance.

If anyone were asked to describe him, it would have been an elderly guy with a black mustache, a wig of curls, and jockey hat with one arm around a redhead with long curls and a wedding veil topped with a flowering crown.

While their attention was on the just-married couple, Lily and Lori moved swiftly to their destination. Lily kept her sun glasses on, and Lori had plopped on a pair of coke-bottle glasses with her western hat pulled down over her ears. She had re-buttoned her western shirt so that one half hung longer than the other.

"Hey. We visit here every Sunday afternoon. What kinda business is goin' to be here?" Lori asked bobbing her head.

The men at the entrance merely glanced at them. "It won't interest you, ladies. It will be a night club with pretty girl dancers, a bit of gambling and plenty of booze."

"What you goin' to name this place?" Lori raised her head acting like she was trying to see inside.

"The boss left early, but everyone will know on opening day. He's real excited about it!"

Lily sensed Brandi and Pepper nearby; consequently, Lily slipped past the entrance and knocked on the bathroom door. Brandi caught Lily's reflection in the opposite window as she approached the open room counter which was covered with sketches and other papers.

"Gentlemen we have been having a problem with break-ins in the area, so I need to see your papers that prove you have a legal right to be in this building," Brandi said. "I have driven past this building numerous times and the sign is still posted: *No Trespassing—Private Property.*"

"We just work here, officer. Our boss said to keep busy. He has papers right here that show he owns it."

"May I see them?" Brandi asked politely, stalling for time and wondering what in the world Lily was doing.

"Okay. I'm the owner," a man in a suit and tie blustered. "Here. I have the papers to prove it."

When he handed the contracts to Brandi, she breathed a little easier when she noticed two cruisers drive up, and Pepper stared down the man who claimed to own the property. Lori leaned forward and asked "What's the date on his paperwork?"

"Butt out, old lady," another man puffed his chest out and brazenly moved closer, then balked when Pepper growled.

Will kept his counsel when he recognized one of the men in the background.

"Sir?" Brandi asked Will. "Take a look at this."

Will held the contract up to the overhead light and remarked, "Dates have been erased and this contract was not filed or recorded in this state. Also, the address is wrong. The number for this property is engraved in stone on the front of the building."

"Hey, ownership is nine-tenths of the law. I paid good money for this building, and we're not leaving!"

"Is this your signature?" Brandi asked.

"Of course," he replied.

"For confirmation, may I see your driver's license?" When he acted offended, and started to reclaim the contracts, Brandi added, "If you refuse, we'll have to ask all of you to leave, unless you would rather spend the night in the Turtle Crossing Jail."

He looked around at his men and at Brandi, Will and Pepper, then challenged, "You and who else?"

While two other officers replaced Will, Storm, and Lori, two men started backing up when the door behind them closed and locked. One of the men held his hands out and announced, "Hey, boss. Maybe you ought to re-think this place. I think it's haunted. I heard someone whistling in the bathroom and that broom closet. Where is Bubba?"

Two more officers came around the corner with another man in hand-cuffs. "Is this guy part of your operation?" Officer O'Keefe asked. "He claims he just stepped outside to smoke a cigarette."

"Bubba," his buddy asked. "Did you ever find that ghost you told me about?"

"No," Bubba replied. "Boss, you don't want this place. I tell you something blew on my neck and stole my glasses. Then it turned out the light and shoved me out the back door."

***

As soon as they drove away, Lily unlocked the connecting door, looked at Will and asked, "Well," Lily announced, "I found out how they got the keys. That guy, Bubba, worked on the paint crew we hired, and bragged about it."

Will looked angry. "Storm and I will change the locks right now and the code as well. Lily, you've got to move something in here that will pass for an office."

"Okay, Uncle Will. I do have several ideas that I planned to implement tomorrow if Hunter is free," Lily replied.

"I can reschedule my meeting with Uncle Kristopher," Storm suggested.

"Two of my men are here and will stay on as Security Guards until further notice," Will said as he walked with

Lily throughout the rooms. "I'm glad Lori didn't drive her new truck here this afternoon. Justin here will follow you ladies home."

"Uncle Will," Lily appealed, "Dr. Kate mentioned that she is planning to sell her entire office. It's early yet. Can you help me move all this into my office before midnight?"

"I already contacted a friend of mine regarding my telephones here, and they are scheduled for their first appointment in the morning," Lily continued. "I need some change for the pay phone next door. Does anyone have any change?"

A few minutes later, Lily ran back into her building. "Doc said we can use his new rig to transport just about everything."

"All right! Let's get this show on the road tomorrow!" Will held up a sign that read, *Silence.* "There's nothing we can do here! I'll lock up and set the security." Once outside, Will said, "Just in case, except for security, follow me to Doc's."

Upon arrival at Doc's, all the vehicles were clean. Lily had found two 'bugs' in one of the drawers in the office space she had chosen and left them there.

"It was apparent they weren't expecting any opposition," Lori said.

"This has been," Lily said, "one of the most incredible days in my life."

"Oh! I agree," Lori added as they unloaded Doc's rig and set up each room according to Lori's floor plan posted on each door.

Granny chuckled, "Hey Lily, when did you have these blinds designed?" She and Lori finally finished hanging the last scenic blinds.

"Oh, Granny," Lori answered. "She ordered them around last Thanksgiving."

"You remembered," Lily teased.

"How could I not? Nice to finally see the gift I bought you for Christmas. Pretty good taste!" Their smiles and repartee were contagious.

"You have a guest, Sis," Hunter called out.

"Mom?" Lily greeted, "What do you think?" she asked spreading her arms wide.

"It's really taking shape," Shannon replied. "Dad and I brought something for your grand opening.

"Oh. Wow!" Lily exclaimed. "A sign! It's beautiful. You had my certificates framed."

"Wendy framed them," Will added.

Tears gathered and trickled down Lily's cheeks. "They're beautiful," she added as she ran her fingers along the oak frames. "It makes this moment so real," she sniffed, drying her eyes. "And the fact that she did all this work makes them so very, very special," as she hugged her Great Uncle Will.

"Thanks to all of you, I will proudly open my office tomorrow, even though the equipment I ordered is still missing."

However, due to the unusual happening at Lily's office building at Eight Mile Centre, Will insisted the announcement that Wendy and Marcie had finished putting together for possibly a front page announcement later, became a Turtle Crossing News Special Edition and actually covered the entire front page Monday morning.

Lori and Lily started their first day at work the following morning and were astonished to read the front page of the *Turtle Crossing News* Special Edition: "Grand Opening of Long Awaited Board Member of Eight Mile Centre, Lily Anne' Donnelly's Chiropractic Office," plus a photo of her wearing a white smock with her name printed on the front pocket.

On the other half of the front page: Lori Rose Donnelly, DVM, partnered with Dr. Matthew Denver O'Reilly, Veterinarian and CEO of the O'Reilly Ranch Animal Hospital. She was wearing her new hunter green shirt with her name on the front. She was standing beside her blue truck featuring a unique advertisement on the doors that matched the back of her shirt.

Chapter 10

Lily and Lori were excited about finally having the chance to work a full week at their careers, as each approached the workout bar on the second floor above Doc's new garage, with Hunter and Storm in tow.

"When was the last time you ate lunch with Dr. Dexter?" Lori asked.

"Oh, my. It's been over a month, but it wasn't a date," Lily began. "He just happened to sit next to me at a counter."

"He stopped by earlier this week trying to get Doc to come to his office for a checkup."

"But Doc won't see him," Lily replied.

"I know. Then he said you and him had been on a hot date the previous night and that you had told him quite a story about me."

Lily shook her head in amazement. "He's up to his old tricks again, is he? The jerk stopped me at the pharmacy when I was looking for a card and was whining about the way you and I always stick together like glue."

"Enough said!" They high-fived each other and hugged as tears gathered in Lori's eyes, her temper simmering.

"He's not worth wasting time over, Sis." Lily continued her usual stretches.

"There was a time," Hunter said, "when I would have been ready to deck him, but I've learned to ask the Lord for patience and consider the source. However, that doesn't mean I am happy when someone tells lies about my fabulous, intelligent, almost perfect, loving sisters."

"Thanks, Little brother." Lori winked and smiled. "But we can't allow that jerk to spoil one more second of our day."

"But he also bears watching," Storm added. "Dad said the smart thing to do is to stay quiet for the moment and check him out."

"Our first assignment as the Four Aces," Lily exclaimed, "We'll organize that after our workout. Meditation first."

They unrolled their floor workout mats, sat down in position, and closed their eyes. Silence ensued.

After their usual stretches and a series of what Storm equated with martial art and self-defense moves, he asked, "You all have discussed a handful of the Shadow Angels workouts before, but I'm not familiar with them. Would it be possible to experience some of the advanced moves like the squirrel, the twist, or the rope?"

"Funny you should ask," Hunter replied as the sound of soft footsteps on the steps outside drifted through the room, "I believe our special guests have arrived."

A moment later, members of the Shadow Angels were

filing into the room. Storm had met these women on many occasions during his twenty or so years and had overheard his mom, and dad, make comments about them. Of course, today would be far different than a business meeting. And they were all here. Which was the reason why his dad had his full crew on site parked behind the new Veterinarian Animal Hospital.

"Well good morning," said Shannon, greeting each of her children a brief hug. "Seems like the four of you have become just about inseparable."

"We're a rustic group, Mom," Lily announced, turning toward the assembled Shadow Angels. "Ladies, good morning. We're calling ourselves the Four Aces, or just the Foursome: Storm Fox, Hunter Donnelly, Lori Donnelly and myself, Lily Donnelly."

Shannon nodded, taking her turn to address the group. "And may I once again introduce the original four Carpenter Aunts' Card Club Members: Jewel Hendrix Carpenter, Opal Fields Carpenter, Willi Hendrix Roberts, and Tressie Carpenter Brown. They later became the Shadow Angels, and without them, none of us would be together today."

She turned toward another small cluster of women, younger than the first. "But soon the Shadow Angels were swamped with people needing help and requested the following younger ladies to join them. They became the Little Angels. Brandi Davies Carpenter, Marcie Donnelly Warren, Wendy Warren/Sands Fox, and myself, Shannon Warren Donnelly. Once we gained strength, knowledge, and proved ourselves, we became a part of the Shadow Angels."

She faced her children and Storm, her expression full of meaning. "We know your Foursome will do well because we have already seen you in action. Of course, you have a head start. You grew up observing family members doing what we do, and have done, since your childhood."

Many of the Shadow Angels nodded and murmured their own encouragement and approval.

"Today," Shannon continued, "will probably be the only time all of us get together again in one place. Unless any one of us feels the need. This includes the addition of the Four Aces. Of course, the need for discretion is just as important as trusting one another. In the beginning, even our husbands were unaware of what we were doing. Jewel's ex-husband, Henry, never did. And Storm, you undoubtedly noticed your Dad has a crew here. That's for our protection and yours. So, we will not be staying long."

Tressie stepped out to attract their attention and only because the Four Aces were facing the mirror did they see Opal, Jewel and Willi follow her slower routine.

"You will notice that because of their age, their movements are like a film in slow motion," Marcie began. Suddenly one of them made two simple moves and Storm couldn't believe just how limber, strong and talented these ladies still were.

"Oh!" Storm exclaimed. "Wow. Those moves were so amazing. I missed the transition and the final because I got caught up in the almost casual approach."

Brandi moved around Tressie and revealed a few of her self-defense moves she had taught Lily and Lori before they started grade school, then stopped in the center of the room and said, "I have to leave early. The rest will follow. When you work out together, you will be able to determine each other's strengths. One of you may be more limber than the others. The twins, for instance, are double-jointed." Brandi looked at Lily and Lori and suggested, "You will have to ask them about that sometime."

Hunter smiled as she left. "I remember stuff about Deputy Sheriff Brandi, before I was in grade school, and it had nothing to do with who could bench press more weights than another."

"You're right, Hunter," Opal remarked, "it has to do with timing. Choosing the moment. Being aware of where you are. And control."

"In other words," Marcie added, "use your mind. Your street smarts. Don't think you have to prove what you are capable of, just because you are. We have been successful in this county and some others, because we work as a team. And we do our best to stay within the law."

The Four Aces moved through several what-if scenarios with former Little Angels plus coaching from the sidelines by the elder Shadow Angels. When Shannon left the room to change, Lori and Lily prepared the guests for their Mom's presentation, taking it in turns to tell the story.

"The first time Mom used this move, her life and that of her friend were in jeopardy. Her moves, in addition to distractions by others helped distract the man holding a gun on her," Lori announced. "We will briefly set the scene. Two men were waiting behind the massive desk for the right time to grab the guy with the gun, who was also holding onto the woman who they planned to use for ransom."

Lily took up the story. "Then he was spooked when he saw two men who were not only dressed alike, they could have been twins. He let go of Shannon and swung his gun towards the second one and yelled, 'You. You have to be a ghost.' Meanwhile, a well-trained lady was hiding under the office desk and another was in the employees' commode-sink bathroom nearby."

"These two guys," Lori said, "really thought their boss would be anxious to pay them for capturing the lady they said was named Bea. They mistook Mom for Bea, and proudly announced her as Bea, when they brought her into the room. Mom was shuffling her feet because both of her ankles were roped together."

"Her movements were subtle. Calculated. Practiced," Lily continued. "As the lights in the room were dimmed and instead were focused on Shannon with the mirrored wall behind her, silence filled the room. One moment there was a rope around her neck—to around her waist— then tightly around her wrists behind her back and to her ankles, but loose enough so she could shuffle her feet."

"One of the Shadow Angels who had been hiding under the desk took advantage of their attention on Shannon and had slipped behind the floor-to-ceiling drapes. She yanked on the cord so hard the drapes opened wide. The sun shone in, blinding the guy with the gun who had once again imagined a ghost and spun around towards the window," Lori added.

"Mom shimmied out of the ropes, then appeared halfway across the room like a ballet dancer butterfly with wings and slipped behind the heavy wine-colored drapes in the corner," Lily softly added.

Meanwhile, this guy was pointing his gun in all directions, screaming that they were all ghosts. Then he wildly spun around, slipped on the coil of rope, fell back and hit his head on the corner of the desk, slithered onto the floor, passed out, and dropped the gun," Lori added.

Her audience, who had listened silently in awe, applauded. Storm glanced at Hunter and his dad and excitedly remarked, "Show us how you got out of the ropes!" To which Hunter and Will nodded their heads in agreement.

Then Shannon explained, "I met with a magician several times who taught me this maneuver. It's good to have this as a backup in your mind when lives, including your own, are at stake. Even better, when you have kept your mind alert and body in shape; otherwise, you will be needing a few chiropractic sessions with Lily. I speak from experience. After my first practice sessions, I had more than one appointment with Dr. Kate. By the way, Lily is very good as well."

***

David Donnelly was especially proud of his wife and their children this morning. He joined Will, who appeared to be gathering his thoughts as they slipped out the door before the ladies.

"Will," David began, "did I ever tell you that I have been in love with Shannon since the first day she arrived at the Flat Rock Children's Home? I can still see her when she bravely walked into the dining room for breakfast."

"I know. I was only seven and she was six, but I wanted to protect her, you know. Of course, you know Shannon and my sister Marcie became friends. You've probably heard this story from Marcie."

"No, not really," Will replied. "Marcie and I will always be lifetime friends. We still trust each other, but not many people understand that the passion was missing. We figured that out when we found it with someone else. But, as Shannon's uncle, I have gone back and questioned why didn't I recognize her? So much of her childhood was stolen from her."

"But not her birthright," Will remarked.

"In what way?" David asked.

"First of all," Will continued. "There are times when I see so much of her mom, my sister, in her. In her smile. In the way she enters a room."

"Her beauty is from the inside as well," David added. "And I've noticed since my daughters returned to the area after eight years away while they acquired the education and degrees they sought. There's still that cautious, lack of trust, if you will, with strangers."

"So," Will questioned, "are you worried about the times they were held for ransom?"

"Yes." David replied. "Shannon and I have been so very careful, but I overheard them talking about the kidnapping at Granddad's, when Brandi's ex-husband worked with Shannon's grandmother."

"What about Hunter and Storm working with them

now?" Will asked. "I have seen the four of them working, planning, training, and dancing together. According to Storm, it's amazing."

"Thanks, Will."

"David, I can never thank you for being there for Shannon, at the children's home and most of your life. However, that doesn't make it right that you and Marcie had to be there either."

"I know. Shannon and I plan to meet them for lunch after church on Sunday. They want to see their grand-daughters' new offices."

***

Lori finally had her office in order. File cabinets were one-quarter full of empty folders and her licenses and degrees were framed neatly in one space on the wall off to the side of her desk. Unobtrusively, yet with pride.

She was in the middle of filling out some paper-work for Doc when there was a knock on her door. Slid-ing the paperwork into a folder, she turned it over and announced, "Come in."

A man about her own age entered the room with a scowl and scrappy tilt in his posture. He finally spoke when Lori asked, "How can I help you?"

"So," he began, angrily motioning with a sweep of both arms at her framed licenses on the wall. "Just goes to show you what lots of money can accomplish!"

"You do not speak to me in that tone of voice," she demanded, standing up. When her anger simmered, her voice went up an octave, "Perhaps you should leave and return with a more respectful attitude."

Lori suddenly felt claustrophobic. Her office didn't feel quite so large, after all. The clod acted like she was in this office because her family, or Doc, had financed her position and title.

Doc recognized the change in her voice and tapped her door as he entered her office. "Is there a problem here?" he asked, as he removed his dusty western hat and gloves. Then he froze.

Lori had only seen Doc speechless once or twice before. He looked away for a moment to gather his thoughts. Finally, Doc said, "So, Denver O'Reilly in the flesh. The nephew who is planning on suing me for a million or more. I hear you believe my money is your birthright."

As the two men stared at each other, Lori quietly hit the button to buzz Granny at the stables. The silence was thick as molasses in January.

Denver threw a glare at Lori. "Does she have to be here?"

"Indeed she does. We're partners!" Doc announced and raised that one eyebrow. An expression he used when he meant business.

Denver turned his back on Lori in a huff and faced Doc. Granny slipped in through the office door. Denver's mouth turned down but he did not object to her presence.

"So," Doc began. "You have sent me several special delivery letters. May I also assume you have legal papers to back up your claims against me?"

"Yes. I do." Denver once again acted all pomp and bravado. Smiling like he had won something over on

Doc, "I have deeds that prove your brother, Lewis Avery O'Reilly, my Dad, owns fifty-per-cent of everything you have here!" he proclaimed as he slapped the papers on Lori's desk, almost hitting Doc in the process. When he stood and leaned against Lori's desk, Lori started to move forward to protect Doc.

But when Denver tightened his fists and raised his voice to a yell, Granny reached over and held Lori's hand. Then surprised herself and everyone in the room as she stood proud and walked around behind Lori's desk beside Doc with her hand on the holster of her 45. "You packin', kid?"

Denver's face turned white as the paper in his hand, which was visibly shaking.

Granny's voice even sounded like Annie Oakley. "Sit. Down!"

Denver sat back down and, more respectfully, replied, "For as long as I can remember, my Dad said you cheated him out of his half of this huge ranch. So after he died, I found these papers in a metal safety box along with his, my mom's, and my birth certificates, their marriage license, and this picture of you, my dad, and your parents."

Granny apparently had heard the rest of the story, as she, like Lori, was taking in Denver's appearance. His clothes were clean but thread-bare and hung on him like borrowed clothes. His jeans hung in gathers from his makeshift belt. The buttons on his shirt didn't come close to matching and were all stitched on with black thread. His shoe laces were knotted together in places and appeared to be holding the shoes together.

Her whole demeanor softened. "How did you get here, son?" Granny asked quietly.

"Hitched a ride from time to time. Walked part of the way."

"From?" Doc asked.

"Pennsylvania," Denver replied.

"Have you had anything to eat today?" Granny asked. "I've had beef stew simmering all morning. Lori? Would you mind?"

"Granny," Doc said. "I've been looking forward to a bowl of that beef stew all morning."

As Lori exited to get the food, Brandi pulled up in her Deputy Sheriff's car right outside Lori's office. Lori understood Granny must have called for her before coming up to the office. Jonothan was with her, and he quickly agreed to help Lori with the stew.

"Morning," Brandi greeted, as she looked Denver over a little closer than she would any other stranger, and waited—waited until he made eye contact with her and asked, "You here looking for a job?" When he didn't reply, she waited.

He finally replied, "Yeah."

"What's your name?"

Denver's Dad had always hated the police, but Denver had never found a reason to because after both his parents died, the police befriended him. "My name is Denver Avery O'Reilly."

"Well. Any relative of Doc's is a friend of mine too," Brandi announced as she reached towards Denver for a handshake. Denver didn't move.

Doc saw red for his nephew's rude lack of manners and started to say something, but Brandi waved him off.

"Stew's ready," Lori announced. "Guess what's for dessert? Granny's prize-winning peach cobbler. Lori set up a card table, added more chairs, and Granny asked Jonothan to say grace. When all the people in the room closed their eyes and bowed their head, Denver resisted. But one look at Pepper who was staring at him like he was a criminal, followed their lead. Besides, if he didn't eat something soon, he was certain he was going to pass out.

Denver hesitated as he leaned over the bowl and just let the scent wash over him. Doc then handed him a packet to wash his hands. "We'll continue our conversation after we eat," Doc suggested. He couldn't help but question why Lori suddenly exclaimed, "Uncle Jonothan, Aunt Brandi. What do you think of my new office?"

"This office is really nice, but I'm anxious to take a ride in your new truck," Jonothan smiled.

Granny handed Brandi, Jonothan, and Lori bowls of stew and suggested, "Why don't you eat in Doc's office where there's more room?"

They had barely sat down in Doc's office when Brandi asked Lori, "What's your take on this Denver O'Reilly?"

"Well, it is apparent Doc and Granny are already nuts about him."

"I'll do some research on him just the same. How is Lily doing?" Brandi whispered.

"She has had a few nights when she got up and checked the security system before she could go back to bed. Other than that, she is eating and has had a few new patients from out of town. Of course, at least half of the other Centre business owners have stopped by and have been surprised at her knowledge and admitted to friends how much she had helped them."

"That's wonderful, kiddo, and is Doc keeping you busy, as well?"

Lori nodded, smiling. Brandi set down her bowl and dabbed her lips with a napkin. "I'm sorry I have to cut out so quickly, but it seems like things have settled down here."

"That's okay. You'll keep an eye out for Lily's trucks too, right?"

"We've got some feelers out," Brandi replied, as she finished her stew, hugged Jonothan, and left. Lori and Jonothan gathered their things and returned to her office, where the others were finishing their meal too.

Lori's heart went out to Doc. Neither he nor Granny had ever had any children of their own and here was a nephew. She prayed his appearance wouldn't turn into a nightmare.

Doc didn't mention that Denver's hair was so like his, the way it waved behind his ears. Even his eyes were as blue as Doc's. Lori studied them sitting at her desk, side by side, and was certain by the loving way Granny was looking at Doc she saw the resemblance, too.

Lori, in her best professional voice, stated, "We need to see your driver's license."

Denver ignored Lori and looked at Doc. "Do you have a driver's license?" Doc asked.

"Sure do," Denver replied, as he pulled a much-worn billfold from his hip pocket, withdrew his driver's license, and handed it to Lori.

Lori quickly scanned his birthdate, and Pennsylvania address. The tattered photo revealed a man so many years younger than he appeared today. He was twenty-seven.

"Denver?" Doc asked, making certain he had Denver's attention. "Let's just put all our cards on the table. I have my copy that matches the one you have here as well. However, there were more papers that followed. Your dad was a gambler. Whenever he got in too deep, he came by, and each time he sold off acres and acres of land. The last time he stopped here, he begged to borrow half of what my house was worth.

This is a copy of the original cabin, and a receipt for money I loaned him, which he never paid back. I never heard from him again."

"These are just copies," Denver hesitantly challenged.

"Yes. The originals are in a safe. When did your Dad die?"

"Shortly after my mom, about two months ago." Denver replied. "I've been working out of state as a farrier. I just lost my job, because my boss's daughter married and wanted my job. I spent most of my savings on my parents' funerals. Then some guys thought I should pay Dad's debts as well." He cast about, looking lost. "I should probably be moving on. I don't want those creeps causing you trouble."

Lori demanded, "Are you certain no one followed you?"

"No. I haven't been in one place long enough to pay rent anywhere," Denver replied.

"Doc," Granny said, "Buck needs to know if you have a new hire, so he can ready a space for him in the bunkhouse. Is Denver your new hire?"

Doc appraised Denver for a moment. "What do you think, son? It'll be hard work."

Denver looked edgy, like he was expecting a trick. "I'm not afraid of hard work."

Doc looked at Lori for confirmation, noting that she was also aware Pepper hadn't growled at Denver. Plus Granny had taken a liking to him too. "Okay. I'll give you a week, Denver. We'll see how you work out."

"Thanks," Denver replied.

"There's paperwork," said Lori. She retrieved the required three sheets from her file cabinet and placed them in front of him.

As soon as Denver had finished the paperwork, Buck arrived at Lori's office to take Denver to the bunkhouse where he would be staying.

"Denver," Buck greeted as he shook Denver's hand. "Just thought you would like to know you will be spending time with me for a few days, at least until you learn the ropes here. Granny sent over a change of clothes, a jacket, hat, shirt, and shoes for a start. I don't know what else she put in there, but I guarantee, you'll be treated right as long as you put in the effort."

"Thanks.

"We can talk more tomorrow, Denver. As you can tell, the bunkhouse isn't that far from the main house and the new O'Reilly Ranch and Veterinarians' Animal Hospital and Stables. I've got your bunk ready."

When Denver hesitated to enter the bunkhouse, Buck noted the fear in his eyes and put his hand on Denver's shoulder. "Young man, you are safe here. The wranglers have made O'Reilly's their home for years."

Denver entered and followed Buck to his living space. The few muscles Denver had left were tight as a Saturday night fiddle.

The man in the bunk next to the one with his name on the chest at the foot of his bunk greeted Denver. "My name is Midnight. Yours is Denver?"

"Yes."

"What was your last job?"

"I am an educated, well-experienced Farrier," Denver replied.

"Well. I don't believe I have ever met a bona fide Farrier before. Doc will be pleased. I've heard him say a talented one is few and far between, even though he can do it himself. For my notion, it appears to be a pretty dangerous job, trimming a horse's hooves. Hey, time to eat. We turn in early."

Denver nodded, as he laid down on the first real bed he had slept in for over three months.

***

The next morning, Buck had to wake him. The kid looked worn out, but he couldn't coddle him. He had asked Doc and Lori to meet him in the stables in an hour. "Denver, shower is free. Your breakfast is in the warmer. Then, we have a meeting with Doc, Lori, and Granny in the stables in an hour."

Denver jumped as though he had been fired out of

a cannon. For a moment, he didn't know where he was. He scratched his head, shoved his mop of whacked hair out of his face, and immediately contrite said, "Sorry, Mr. Buck. I can't recall when I have slept so soundly."

"When we get your hair dried, I can trim it if you like." Denver disappeared into the shower and Buck smiled when he came out with the beard shaved off. "They won't recognize you." Buck chuckled. "Do you want to throw these old clothes away?"

"No," Denver replied. "Souvenirs, you know, my mom hand-sewed all those patches on my shirt and jeans." He smiled as he stuck his harmonica and his Dad's white pearl pocket knife in his clean jeans and wiggled his toes inside a pair of almost-new work boots.

Denver and Buck arrived five minutes early. Doc, Lori and Granny kept looking beyond the entrance to the stables. "Mr. Buck," Denver asked, "are we waiting on someone else?"

Even when they heard his voice, everyone but Buck and Denver were having a problem recognizing the new Denver. "Our apologies," Lori said. "Sorry we didn't recognize you, but you do look a bit different minus the beard and a haircut."

"You listed that you are an experienced Farrier. May I assume your experience extends to shoeing as well? We would like your input on a horse we found hobbling about in the grazing field about a mile out from here."

Denver immediately asked, "Do you have him on any pain meds?"

"No. We just brought him in three days ago."

"Has he eaten?"

"Yes." Lori answered, as she opened his gate. Denver grabbed her arm and ordered, "What do you think you're doing?"

Doc looked at Denver and said, "Let go of her." His voice was deep and demanding.

Denver shook his head, and added, "Surely you know what could happen?"

Buck motioned Denver to back away.

Lori pulled on her heavy-duty leather gloves she had been using in place of a brush and started brushing the back of the horse's neck and humming to him. Not a specific melody, but more like a shushing sound. The horse relaxed and allowed her to carefully brush further down his back, skipping the scars, as she talked to him in a soft angelic tone. "Now, sweetheart, you better eat and drink some of this fresh water I brought you earlier."

Denver let out the breath he had been holding and gently said, "Okay. Lori, I apologize. This horse acts like he is hypnotized."

"Thanks."

"He has been abused," Denver commented in a gruff sounding voice. "Were you skipping around the scars?"

"Yes," Lori replied. "When he finally allows you to look into his eyes, you will note he is in pain but whoever did this didn't break his spirit."

Denver would never admit it in a million years, but he was certain he had fallen in love with this beautiful angel. He had never met anyone who had such an in-depth understanding of an animal.

"Lori has had a special way with animals since she was very young," Doc proudly added.

"When he is further along, would you allow me to play a soft lullaby? I am not that adept with a harmonica yet, but Buck gave me a lesson this morning."

"Why?" Lori asked, still doing her best to balance the scruffy, impolite Denver from yesterday with this handsome, apparently caring Denver.

"I play. But my only experience has been playing for a neighbor's dog so he would quit barking all night," Denver said. "I take it you haven't had a chance to even take a good look at his hooves?"

"Briefly," Doc replied. "Talk to him. We'll be here on standby."

Denver lowered his voice and asked Lori, "Do you have a pick and a flashlight?"

"Right here in my bag," she replied, as she handed him what he needed.

Gently patting the horse's thigh, Denver began, "I don't know what your name is, but it looks like you are okay with Lori calling you Sweetheart. Is it okay if I take a look at your hooves? There is a possibility you might have a pebble in a soft crack in this hoof. I know I do not like walking on stones barefoot myself."

All the time Denver brushed him lightly here and there, then Lori took over the light so he could gently raise the horse's foot and use the pick. Denver began talking softly once again. "Well, Sweetheart, with your permission, I will do my best to remove two stones. I am warning you ahead of time because this may be painful.

There you are," he said gently, as he put the horse's foot down. "If you don't mind, we might take a look at another one in the morning."

Chapter 11

Donovan had a checklist as to where he ate his meals. Today, it was Sadie's Diner on Main Street. The differences appealed to him, or perhaps it was his new lifestyle. Here in Turtle Crossing he might rub elbows with a police officer, a truck driver, a business owner, a teacher, a waitress, a nurse, traveling families on the road for vacation, or retirees about any time of day.

In between placing his order and before he even took a sip of his morning coffee, he opened the Special Edition of the *Turtle Crossing News,* half-listened to the undercurrent discussions, and quickly realized he truly was not in the minority here. But, just seeing Lily's picture on the front page of the newspaper caught him unaware.

He planned to stop at the general store for a picture frame. Especially when Miss Bea entered and went straight to the kitchen.

"Hi, Miss Bea," the owner of the Donnelly Hardware Store greeted. The shared recognition as Turtle Crossing business owners and a nod said it all, as he held the door for her on his way out.

Isaac joined Donovan for his usual order before he even sat down at Donovan's table. "Well Donovan, it appears someone set a fire under that girl!" he remarked as he opened his Special Edition copy and pointed out Lily. "Congratulations, Miss Bea," he added as she reemerged from the kitchen and walked past their table. "Your newest professional members are moving forward like a runaway train."

Without slowing, Miss Bea replied, "Yes," and joined the most dignified ladies in Turtle Crossing three tables away.

"Isaac," Donovan asked, "I have seen those ladies out and about in Turtle Crossing, but seldom all together in one place."

"They have the distinction of being known as members of the Carpenter Aunts' Card Club," Isaac said.

"I am a people watcher, but then these ladies are an excellent example of don't judge a book by its cover," Donovan said.

"Yes," Isaac agreed. "They are patients and friends of mine, who have been in my office since you arrived. They are alert, graceful, and well-trained, disciplined dancers."

Normally Isaac would not have described them in this way, except that if they came into his office and Donovan took care of any of them, he wanted Donovan to be aware of their special needs. "You know, Donovan, regarding Lily, I have always found the best way to find out something, is to ask."

Since Lily isn't even speaking to me, Donovan thought, *there has to be another way.*

The diner door opened and two surly looking men Donovan had never seen before entered and seated themselves at an empty table. Miss Bea and her companions eyed them suspiciously. The whole mood in the diner shifted.

Lowering his voice, "Isaac, I am not asking you to reveal any Turtle Crossing secrets, but the silence in Sadie's is as thick as smoke right now."

"I will expect you in the office in an hour," Isaac announced, clearly evading the question. He did not make eye contact, which was unusual for him.

As Isaac passed the two cocky men sitting in the last booth, one of them commented, "See you've still got that arm in a cast, huh, Doc?"

The man's tone of voice when he made that comment to Isaac rolled goose bumps up Donovan's spine. It was time to leave. But just as he shoved his chair back to follow Isaac and the ladies, a young couple in the first booth put money in the juke box and, acting a bit nervous, took a lot of time making their choices. They had barely sat down when the two men appeared to have a disagreement of sorts. The one facing the street motioned towards the front of Sadie's. Donovan couldn't see what caught their attention, until he spotted the reflection of a Deputy Sheriff's car in a discreetly posted mirror, which led him to the conclusion that the only others still nursing their coffee cups were a table of farmers or construction workers in the rear of the diner.

***

Although it appeared that Isaac left by the back door, in reality he took the tunnel exit, followed by the Shadow Angels who caught up with him. "We've got your back, Isaac," Opal whispered as they led him out through Johnson's Garage tunnel exit.

Once they hustled him into the backseat of Willi's station wagon, Isaac finally felt safe enough to take a deep breath.

"Your office is closed today, Isaac," Jewel declared.

"What about Donovan? He doesn't know what's happening."

"Don't worry, we're taking care of him now."

***

New signs appeared on the front door of Sadie's Diner that read: *Closed. Beware. Wet Paint.*

When Brandi entered the front door, with an attitude of intimidation personified, she approached Donovan, winked at him and read aloud, "On your feet, buster, you are under arrest for driving a stolen vehicle."

That was when Donovan realized the couple who had been dancing and the so-called noisy trio of men in the corner were an undercover security team from Sunrise.

The two men in the last booth were unaware of the officer who had entered Sadie's by the back entrance. While one man was being handcuffed and being read his rights, the second man clamored over the back of the booth. When he found the kitchen door locked, he shoved through the exit door and was arrested before the back door swung closed.

"Lieutenant Carpenter, may I go to work now?" Donovan asked.

"No," Brandi replied. "Isaac's office is closed for the day. We don't want it to appear that either of you was involved in this arrest. Also, I would like to introduce you to my half-brother, Jace Carpentier, of the Sunrise City Police Department."

"Owner of Carpentier Trucking?" Donovan inquired.

"Yes." Jace nodded and asked, "Are you Isaac's assistant chiropractor, Mr. James?"

Donovan nodded. "I've left several messages regarding Lily Donnelly's lost shipments."

"Yes, Professor James. Can we compare lists of possibility?"

"Of course," Jace complied as they moved into one of the booths and spread their papers on the table.

"Wait a moment, you're saying she opened for business with just one day to spare?"

"No," Donovan clarified. "This was her personal deadline, not her contract deadline."

"How do you know this?" Jace requested.

"Isaac. Her contract deadline is two weeks from today. It appears someone put a hold on these deliveries."

"Miss Bea," Donovan asked, as he shoved his notebook across the table.

"Here's part of the problem. Look at the entry dates. They are all on a Sunday. This outfit doesn't work on Sundays," Sadie said. "Did you show any of this to Lily?"

"Show me what?" Lily asked. She and Lori had strode through the front door in spite of the sign.

"Yeah, guys," Lori chimed in. "I don't smell any paint in here either."

"Sorry, Lily," Donovan spoke up. He slid the chart they had just started examining in front of Lily, as Lori slid into the other side of the booth.

Jace felt the electricity snapping between Donovan and Lily and wondered if they were even aware of it.

Donovan was at a loss for words. He hadn't been this close to her for almost a year.

Lily was curious. Why and what was he doing here? She had missed how his professor's voice turned soft when he said, "Sorry, Lily. A belated congratulations on getting your business up and running, ready for patients."

She nodded and half-smiled her thank you.

"We're on the hunt for your equipment," Jace stated. "Do you have any of your paperwork from the company or the trucking firm?"

Lily retrieved the paperwork Miss Bea had suggested she bring in case it was needed, unfolded the receipts, laid them on the table, and glanced around at papers with Jace's name on some, and Bea's as well.

Jace and Sadie exclaimed, "The handwriting is different."

"The dates don't match up," Jace added.

"Jace, look," Bea suggested. "This delivery cancellation order is your office number, and, here it appears someone forged your initials."

"My mom has been bragging about a new boyfriend. But I've never met him," Jace replied. "However, it looks like her hand writing."

"Wait," Lily asked. "Don't receipts usually state where the trucks are routed?"

Lori held the forms up to the light and read the lettering aloud. "Sounds familiar doesn't it?" Lori added.

"Absolutely," Lily confirmed. "Same as the illegal contracts those guys used at my building at Eight-Mile-Centre Sunday afternoon."

Donovan was stunned and asked the questions no one here wanted to discuss. "Sadie, were these the same men Turtle Crossing's finest arrested here today?"

Sadie started to nod yes but left the Diner's Dining room without answering.

Brandi cornered Lily and Lori away from the crowd. "I've watched you grow up; and even though you have lived out of state during your college years, I feel you haven't been open regarding other people you have been acquainted with and dealt with on your own. A boyfriend, for instance, who perhaps became a bit aggressive?"

"Okay," Lily sighed.

"Lily," Jace asked, "do you know of anyone who is upset with you or possibly has a grudge against you?"

"A guy from high school who would like to see me fail, and has made derogative remarks to me. But that was in high school, and you already have a file on Dexter Franklin. I haven't seen his younger brother, Calvin, since high school."

"Anyone else?" Lt. Brandi asked.

"Lily," Lori intervened, "you should tell Aunt Brandi about that guy from college."

"Lily," Brandi suggested, "Just tell me and let me at

least investigate this guy. If nothing else, it will ease your mind if this person proves not to be involved."

"All right," Lily began, "this guy was dating one of my best friends and study buddy. The first time I met him was at the library where we were doing some research. He even had the gall to ask me out when he and my best friend had been dating over a year. Of course, I turned him down and he went ballistic. He even made comments about my parents being wealthy business owners. My friend and I later checked with admissions, and they admitted that he had been trying to get my home address and went so far as to act like he was my boyfriend and needed to contact my parents about a medical issue that involved me."

"I wasn't the first person he offered money to for test questions. My friend called me later and informed me that he had been forced to leave college."

"This isn't the whole story, is it?" Brandi asked gently.

Lily looked at Lori and continued. "During my interview with Isaac Pease, I noticed a photo on Isaac's desk of his son Andrew and college friend. If this friend does not have a twin, it could be the same jerk. The picture is in a frame titled, *Best Friends.*"

"What is his name?"

"He went by more than one name: Paul, Curtis, or Arthur. No last name."

"Did you mention any of this to Isaac?"

"No. What if I'm wrong, Aunt Brandi?"

"If we're finished here, can we leave now, and take these papers with us?" Lori asked. "We just stopped to pick up a birthday cake and four dozen cupcakes for Grandpa Charlie and Grandma Sara Beth's party later this evening. Hunter and Storm have been itching to use the outdoor oven, grill and warmer." Sadie brought out their order and hugged Lily and Lori.

On his way into Sadie's, C.W. held the door for them as they had their arms full. "Just thought I would stop and have a cup of Sadie's coffee. See you ladies later."

"Hi, C.W.," Donovan greeted.

"Are you busy this evening?" C.W. asked.

"No," Donovan replied. "Isaac closed the office for the rest of the day."

"Well, I'm just on my way to the church. I left the hospital after visiting a couple of my members who had surgery today. Also, that book I ordered for you came in if you would like to follow me."

"Sorry. I didn't drive today. My vehicle is parked at the Welby B. & B. The Safe Passage Tunnel is really handy. I don't have to find a parking place, and the walk into Turtle Crossing is minimal."

"That's okay. You're welcome to ride along just the same, Donovan. You see, I don't like to wear the same clothes to a party after I have spent that much time around the hospital setting."

"I understand, but I don't have an invitation to this party, let alone a gift," Donovan added.

"Come along. If you are working in Turtle Crossing all summer, it wouldn't hurt for you to meet some of Isaac's patients in a relaxed atmosphere, and that way I won't have to arrive alone."

Once they arrived at C.W.'s Chapel, Donovan suggested, "I'll just wait here in your chapel, while you shower and change." Donovan chose a pew at random, closed his eyes, bowed his head, and said a blessing for Lily and her family.

When he opened his eyes, the sun filtered through the stained glass window. The reality took his breath away and drew him closer to the details. He picked up a brochure describing how a group of college students had just returned from Europe after studying restoration of damaged buildings. Through the assistance of friends and family, three of the four walls had been saved, as well as the stained glass windows.

However, what caught Donovan's attention was the bronze plaque beneath the life-size portrait. "Reverend," Donovan asked, "I've never heard of the artist of the painting behind the altar, and the stained glass window is astonishing."

"Yes," C.W. clarified, "the artist of the painting was Shannon's mom, Will's sister, Spring Flower Fox. The central part of the stained glass window was restored by Jonothan's mom, Opal Carpenter."

"An unusual craft," Donovan remarked. "The colors are so photogenic and realistic. I sat here and expected the children at His feet to speak."

"Would you like me to drive to the Pease Victorian," Donovan asked.

"Sounds like a great plan," C.W. replied.

"Thanks for sharing the history of your Chapel, C.W." Donovan said, once they were on the road. "It reminds me of a time when I was in grade school and attended a revival meeting one summer while I stayed with my grandparents. One of those feelings that lasts a lifetime."

"You are certain it will be okay for me to 'crash' this birthday party?"

"Donovan, I already checked with the family. It was an overwhelming yes. I believe you have met most of this family anyhow."

***

"Uncle Will," Lori exclaimed, "thank you for taking charge of the Pease Victorian main gate, and Hunter and Storm for not only parking our guests' vehicles, but taking care of the grill as well," Lily added. "Everything smells fantastic. We picked up the baked goods from Sadie's."

"Everything in the kitchen is under control," Hunter remarked as he hugged Lily.

"The two of you can get your showers and kick back for a while. Before you go back outside, you've got to taste Grandma Sara Beth's sun tea and lemonade twist."

Lori looked at Lily momentarily when they headed towards their rooms, "I know," Lily commented smiling, when they noted the bouquet of roses in the family room and, a single rose on their desks.

"Work just got left outside the gates. Thank you, Lord, for family, especially Hunter and Storm."

"Amen," Lori added.

Donovan was pleasantly surprised when he arrived at the home that belonged to his boss, Isaac and Leona's Pease Victorian Estate, and pleased that Lily would be living here. However, after introductions, he did his level best to stay on the fringes of her lovely family.

"C.W.," Donovan asked, "was this Victorian built in about the same era as the GreatHouse Castle in Sidney?"

"Perhaps about that time, but GreatHouse had some restructuring after their big fire. The windows here aren't quite as deep, either."

"What about the fireplace?" Donovan asked.

"The mantel in the parlor has similar carvings with a depth that is interesting," C.W. said.

"You sound like my Mom," Hunter commented.

"Mrs. Donnelly," Donovan began, his voice softer than usual, with respect in his voice. "Do you know anything about this fireplace? You knew R.J. Pease, did you not?"

"Not personally, of course. Just casual discussions."

"C.W.," Donovan asked, "Did you know him?"

"Yes," C.W. replied. "He was quite the financier in his day."

"I am fascinated and appreciate the details of carpenters of this time period," Donovan said as he ran his fingers along the top of the mantel.

Lily and Lori joined their Mom, their curiosity piqued, with flash lights because the afternoon sun was dipping in the west. Shannon was intrigued with the mantel, just as she was with her Great-Grandpa Warren's.

Shannon was certain her daughters recalled her stories of treasures found in another fireplace mantel in the home where they grew up.

"Wait, Lily," Lori announced. "Look at this. It's a series of knobs. What if the top could be lifted up like the cover of a piano keyboard?"

Hunter saw what Donovan had suggested. "Wait a minute, Sis. Donovan, if you have that end and I have this end, Storm, can you push it up with the knobs?"

Shannon handed her flashlight to Hunter. "What do you see?"

"I see several books, but we should probably call Leona and Isaac," Hunter announced.

In very short order, Lori returned from the kitchen. "Isaac said to do whatever we wished with the books. They apparently found books stored all over the house."

"I am just a guest, but I love old books," Donovan said. "Do you mind if I look at them?"

Hunter looked at his Mom and sisters before answering. The combined nods were all he needed. "Sure. Then later, we'll decide what to do with them."

Excitement sparkled in Donovan's eyes, and Shannon handed her flashlight to the boys while the books were removed and the mantel replaced. *So,* Shannon thought, *This is the young man who broke my daughter's heart.*

"Uncle C.W., haven't Leona and Isaac lived in Turtle Crossing their entire lives?" Shannon inquired.

"Yes, but it appears after working at the Veterans' Museum for the past year, you've also been doing your research," he chuckled.

"You know me so well," she added, as she kissed him on the cheek and led him towards the front porch. "Join me?" she asked.

"Sure," he said. "They have a half dozen rocking chairs out here."

"They do," Shannon replied. "However, rocking chairs

appear to have caught on ever since these four spent over an hour one evening relaxing out here."

"And, you also want to know what I know about Donovan. Shannon, all I can tell you is that I trust him. He reminds me a lot of your Uncle Will, who has never forgiven himself for not following his gut feelings years ago regarding the possibility you were at the very same children's home the day he stopped there, when he was searching for you. But, under an assumed name. Right?"

"He still carries a photo in his billfold of his sister holding you and Sheldon in her arms. It was taken shortly before she passed."

"Dad has an eight-by-ten of the four of us hanging in his office. I think Sheldon and I were about four years old," Shannon said.

"You know, Shanni, we all have regrets. I know you loved your Great-Grandpa Warren almost as much as he dearly loved you, and your grandmother was jealous. I overheard one of their last arguments regarding you and I left. I often wonder if I had stayed, maybe..."

Shannon reached over and gripped his hand in hers. "C.W., you knew her better than most. I've heard when she set her mind to something there was no stopping her."

"If you don't mind my asking, did they treat you well? You know, at that children's home?"

"They treated me well. I felt truly blessed to have had Marcie and David as friends. And, remember, I had my doll and book that Nanna Ruth had made for me," Shannon added.

"Ah, yes. I remember. Without them, you would have

been lost from us forever." His eyes sparkled with threatening tears. "Also, if you catch Will studying you from time to time, it's because you look so much like your mom."

"Really?" Shannon exclaimed, which was followed by a warm gentle smile as she stood, leaned over, and hugged him.

"You know it's nearly past my bedtime," he chuckled.

"Hey, C.W.," Donovan intervened, "you said I should remind you of the time. It appears you have your choice of destinations: the Welby Mansion B & B or Eight Mile Centre," Donovan smiled as he assisted C.W. to his car.

Donovan was stunned into silence for having waited and listened to C.W. and Shannon, not wanting to break up such an emotional conversation, and understanding why Will hovered around his family.

Donovan had boxed-up the twenty-five books and carried them out to C.W.'s car.

"Donovan, would you mind driving to the Welby this evening?"

"Not at all, C.W.," Donovan replied. "I'm staying in a suite, so you will have all the privacy you need," he encouraged.

"I appreciate it, Donovan," C.W. added. "Today has been a whirlwind. I just need some one-on-one, Thank You Jesus time."

Donovan parked at the registration entrance and suggested, "C.W., if you don't mind waiting on this bench, and I'll leave this box of books and your luggage here as well, while I park your car?"

Walking back from the parking area, Donovan noted dew gathered on fresh cut grass and the scent of climbing wild roses that reminded him of Lily.

When they reached Donovan's suite, C.W. remarked, "I believe I'm almost as curious as you are about those books you young people retrieved from that fireplace mantel. A few of them appeared to be journals."

"R.G. was a very private man, and, like you, worried over things he could not control, but worked to change."

"There are a few one-room school books in this collection. Was he a teacher?"

"Yes. But, storytelling was his passion. And, I would guess that is one journal that will pique your interest. I was invited to the old Welby downstairs piano-room once. What a treasure."

A knock on the door distracted them. Donovan answered the door. "Hot cocoa with marshmallows as ordered and a bowl of fresh popcorn. Have a good evening," Alexa, the owner said.

"Look at these one-room school books: *Ray's New Practical Arithmetic*—printed in New York or Cincinnati, copyright 1877. *McGuffey's Sixth Eclectic Reader*—copyright 1879. *McGuffey's Eclectic Spelling Book*—copyright 1879, just to name a few."

Donovan read the introduction aloud from one of his Story-Teller's Journals and almost dropped the Story-Telling brochure. "'A special thank you to a friend of mine for allowing me to borrow this sword for my presentation on the Civil War this evening.'"

"C.W.," Donovan remarked, as he handed him the

brochure with a picture of the Sword Bayonet. "This is my favorite picture of my Great-Great-Uncle Michael Micheal James, standing in front of the fireplace of his home on Christmas Eve. This same sword that was displayed above the mantel of his home is presently on display in a glass case above the Pease Victorian Mantel with a brass plaque with the same description. This Sword Bayonet was manufactured in Europe in 1909."

"Amazing," C.W. added. "How the Lord leads us in directions and down paths we normally could never have imagined, isn't it? And one more thing, Donovan. Did you read the plaque in its entirety? To be returned to the Owner or Estate of Michael Micheal James."

"It appears that this Great-Great-Uncle didn't initially have the money to pay off his debt, so this Sword Bayonet was used as collateral until the debt was paid. Interesting."

Chapter 12

Lily felt the silence in the Pease Victorian before she opened her eyes. While her coffee was dripping into the pot, she called Lori. "Lori? The Dr. Lori Rose Donnelly, the new O'Reilly Veterinarian?"

"Yes," Lori clarified, smiling.

"And were you up half the night again with that injured mare and her colt?"

"Yes, and it looks like I had better stay an extra night here at Granny and Doc's, even though my patients are doing well."

"That is awesome, Sis, to hear the excitement in your voice. Congratulations."

"Thanks. Doc has been on the phone bragging about how well they are doing."

"I'm not surprised. Did you hear that Hunter and Storm are checking on those summer jobs they mentioned?"

"Oh, no," Lori teased. "You are rattling around in that

huge Victorian all by yourself? Enjoy it, you silly goose."

"I'll do my best, Sis."

"See you soon."

"I just might bake something with those blueberries."

"Thanks for calling, Lily. Love ya."

"Love ya back," Lily murmured.

Taking her coffee with her, Lily climbed the stairs to the attic to follow up on a feeling that had been bugging her since the birthday party when the family was seated in the screened-in Florida-type room. The colored screening blended well with the brick, giving it a distinctive appearance.

Uncle Will had complimented Lily more than once that she was always good at seeing things from a different perspective. She questioned why the square footage in the Carriage House at the back of the estate was not what it appeared to be on the blueprint.

Lily's Dad had given her binoculars to help her deal with the memories of when she and Lori were hunted in the wooded area near their home by two men planning to abduct them. The stand of trees was between two fairways.

However, she was above the trees in the Victorian attic, and noted from the southwest side of the Pease Victorian home, the Carriage House appeared to have an additional fifteen by thirty feet than was shown on the original blueprint.

***

It was past time for breakfast when she returned to the kitchen to heat up the griddle for pancakes when the

208

phone rang. She stretched the cord as far as it would go and answered.

"Lily, Isaac here. Would you mind if Donovan James stops over to borrow a bicycle out of the Carriage House?"

Lily didn't have time to talk as her pancakes were ready to turn, replied, "Not at all. Does he have a passkey for the rear gate?"

"Yes. I loaned him mine."

"Okay, I'll unlock the Carriage House when he arrives."

With Isaac's keys for the Pease Victorian Rear Gate, Donovan thought of seeing her alone, one-on-one, his nerves as jumbled as a cook tossing garlic and onion into cookie dough instead of pizza topping.

Donovan drove up to the house and parked under the portico near the back door. Before he had a chance to knock on the door, Lily opened the screen door and asked, "Have you had breakfast? I just finished making a small batch of blueberry pancakes."

"You remembered?" He followed Lily to the kitchen.

Lily had been in such a befuddled state, she stacked the pancakes on the pedestal glass cake plate and covered them with the cut glass cover, then placed it in the center of the table. Donovan poured their coffee. Plates, silverware and napkins appeared on the table, with glasses of juice and water.

Neither spoke, even when he assisted her with her chair and they were both seated. Lily offered prayer as though programmed. Neither made eye contact until they both took a sip of their coffee. As Lily cleared the grill of the last of the pancakes, she added, "Your visit is timely."

"How so?" he asked.

"I'm expecting a delivery from the Donnelly Appliance & General Store this morning. The stove and refrigerator in the Carriage House kitchen needed replaced."

"When do you expect him?"

"He is due within the next hour or two. I was just planning to open it ahead of time. How soon do you need the bicycle?"

"No rush. I could just sit here all day and talk to you."

They cleared the table, rinsed their own dishes, and placed them in the dishwasher. Lily locked the Victorian, and they walked to the Carriage House. "Did Isaac say where the bicycles are?" Lily asked.

"Yes. He said they are stored under the open staircase."

"Guess we'll look for them together then," Lily replied, knowing she sounded like a retired, but strict, school teacher.

"Haven't you checked it out yet?" Donovan asked, a bit of laughter in his voice.

"No. We haven't had time." She smiled, and realized how good it felt to just hear his voice, with no one else around. Once inside, they were surprised when they felt for a light switch. She felt his presence, and her voice was soft, a tenderness that not only surprised her, but Donovan as well.

"Do you feel like an ancient explorer?"

"What an analogy." Their hands found the same switch. The fluorescent lights in the kitchen area blinked out of sync, which was so like their lives whenever they were alone together. *So why does his touch feel like a new beginning?*

"Perhaps. I'm not certain," he replied, as she turned around to face him. "I don't have a common-sense answer." He brushed her hair away from her face. Then he smiled and suggested, "It's apparent where the stove belongs, but shouldn't we know where to put the fridge before they arrive?"

"Definitely. But I'm not letting you off the hook, Mr. James!"

"Not this time. Knowing you, you asked Isaac if what he ordered would fit," Donovan remarked, when she pulled out a tape measure from the tool apron she was wearing, a sheet of graph paper, and blue prints of the Carriage House.

"Originally only the carriages and buggies were stored in the Carriage House. The barn burnt where the horses were kept stabled. After that R. G. Pease parked his antique vehicles here over the years. And instead of building a garage closer to the house, he built an addition onto this Carriage House."

"What are we looking for?" he asked.

"There is a small front entrance and window, one window in the back, but no windows on the far side. Why is there no access into the main Carriage House itself?"

Donovan merely shrugged his shoulders and asked, "I take it that is one thing you plan to find out?"

"Yes," she smiled. "However, I am curious about the metal circular staircase here at this end of the room when they already have a regular staircase at the other end."

While Lily felt the designs in the paneling from the knotty-pine kitchen cupboards to behind the metal staircase, Donovan climbed a few steps up and suggested, "Come on up. Lily, haven't you always wanted to climb a circular staircase?"

She chuckled. "Is this the little boy in you?" she teased.

Again, he shrugged his shoulders, uncertain how to respond to her and started up another step. Lily followed, momentarily looked down, and suggested, "Donovan, look at this." She sat on the step and reached over towards the top of the paneled section of the wall behind the circular stairs.

"Be careful, Lily," Donovan warned as he gripped her other arm. "You could slip right between these rails."

She leaned back into his arms, hesitantly. "Okay. I agree with you."

"Where should we look for a ladder?" he asked.

"The gardener/caretaker replaces light bulbs and such, but I think I noticed one in the screened-in porch closet before we walked back here."

"You're right. I didn't give it a thought at the time. One ladder coming up," he announced as they left the stairs.

What are we doing? she wondered, then turned and studied the lovely, unusual paneling in front of her.

When Donovan returned with the ladder, she remarked, "Does this have the look and feel of old barn siding?"

"Perhaps it is," he replied.

"But neither of the blueprints shows a door here," she added.

"It could be a pocket door. Did Isaac give you keys to the addition of the Carriage House?" Donovan asked, smiling.

Lily shook her head no, then went through the belted apron she had brought from the house and laid the contents on the kitchen counter. "Flashlight," she remarked as she joined him.

As he felt along the corner segment for an indentation, he suggested, "This corner could either be the start, or Lily, say aloud what you're feeling and or disregarding."

"Okay. From what I've heard since I was a little girl, the Shadow Angels have built-in hidden spaces, for whatever reason. There was a lot of secrecy in this town."

"Yes, I heard about Sadie and her daddy's use of the tunnels."

"Donovan, look at this. It is smoother here and when I shine the light, it picks up a patch of oil."

Donovan proceeded to tap on that area, but when he pushed with the heel of his hand it moved at least a half inch.

"Unusual," she remarked. "Two doors. The doors meet in the middle? One slides to the right and one slides to the left?"

Neither spoke as they laid the ladder on the floor as a brace to keep it from closing while they investigated. "Donovan. Those boxes are MY equipment!" Lily stated in a voice he prayed he never felt the need to use with him. "My receipts are in that blue envelope in my apron."

"Hold on," Donovan said. "I'll get it for you." All the numbers and company's descriptions matched.

"Donovan, what do you think of this? When Uncle D. Donnelly's appliance truck arrives to deliver the stove and refrigerator, instead of leaving with the old ones, I asked Uncle Will to transport my equipment to my Eight Mile Centre building. However, we are going to need help."

The wall phone rang and Lily rushed to answer it. Storm demanded, "Lily, where are you?"

"Donovan and I are in the Carriage House."

"Stay there. Hunter and I just pulled in the gate."

Donovan shoved the Carriage House pocket doors closed.

"We're following Uncle D. Donnelly's appliance truck and pulling in behind the Carriage House. Can one of you open one of the patio doors at the back?"

When Lily and Donovan opened the dining-room patio door, Hunter and Storm ran up to the door before the driver could get out of his truck. "We've been calling you on the house phone for hours," Hunter announced. "Then Storm remembered the phone number for the Carriage House."

"It's all my fault," her uncle remarked. "My helper called in sick this morning, and I ran into Will, and well, here we are to deliver a fridge and stove."

"Please come inside," Lily encouraged. At that moment, Lily felt Donovan behind her and was surprised she liked him there.

Hunter looked past Lily and nodded his head, and

asked, "Donovan, did you find that bicycle you were looking for?"

"Yes. The bicycle and much, much more."

"See, Uncle, you didn't need us for clean-up, after all. Once we get that new refrigerator and stove hooked up and balanced and the old ones moved out of the way, we're good to go."

Storm wasn't as patient as Hunter. "Okay. We know you both act like you're going to burst, but neither of you is that good as actors. So what is going on?"

"First of all," Lily began. "Storm, I know you and your Dad have been in and around the Carriage House when you installed an entirely new security system six months ago. Yet, somehow, someone still got in the Carriage House."

"No way, Lily," Storm argued. "Dad and I checked it and gave Isaac a price, but the Carriage House wasn't really done until after the Family Reunion Grad Party. To which, I might add, are you planning on doing some painting? We noticed the sheet hanging on the wall over there."

Lily shook her head. "While we were measuring for the appliances, something didn't add up, so I went up to the attic to get a bird's-eye view of the Carriage House and compared notes with the blueprints."

"Then," Donovan said, "we decided to check out the second floor here, but we didn't get that far."

"We questioned differences in the paneling," she added.

"We're dying of curiosity here," Hunter teased when

he recognized she was angry and yet excited about something.

"Just show us," Storm asked in a husky voice.

"And the rest of the story is…" Lily announced, while she and Donovan opened the pocket doors.

"Secret pocket doors?" Storm inquired. "Boy. Dad is not going to be happy about this."

"Nor is he going to be happy about this either."

"Well, I'll be," their Uncle D. Donnelly added. "I've attended parties and meetings here a few times, but never would have guessed."

"And the rest of the story?" Hunter asked.

"There's my equipment!" Lily announced as the family entered the hidden room, not even noticing when Donovan slid the ladder in the opening. "Here's my paperwork."

"That sounds like your dad's truck outside, Storm," Lily suggested.

"Yeah," Storm continued, "Dad planned to stop over to help."

Then Lily turned to Donovan. "Of course, he didn't know we already had a foursome."

When Hunter let Will in, he insisted on looking at Lily's shipments. "Will," Uncle Donnelly began, "I backed in and so did you. Just in case someone is keeping their eyes on what is going on here, we could make an issue about my appliance truck not starting and wrap the crates. Load some on my truck, then load the rest on yours. Leave the old fridge and stove in here for the time being."

They all knew Will, and for him to be so quiet was not good for whoever interfered with his family.

"Dad," Storm suggested, "why not have Hunter and me split up, so you and Uncle Donnelly are not alone."

Will's frustration sometimes manifested in his voice and he gruffly agreed with a nod, "Donovan, why not leave your car here. You and Lily take Hunter's car. It's good you parked where you did."

"Eight Mile Centre is our destination?" questioned Hunter.

"Definitely," Lily replied. "By the way, Uncle Will, we're returning the empty crates," she demanded.

"Agreed," Will nodded. He recognized the steel in her voice, and her hands on her hips. "You're more like your Mom and Grandma Fox every day." When Will left, he stuck a hidden camera in the creases of the barn-siding panels that framed the pocket doors.

Lily had acquired the habit of locking and setting the security alarm anytime she arrived and left. "You know, Donovan," Lily started talking once they were on the road, "if you hadn't already guessed, I forget you are new at this, but each vehicle will be taking a different route. Lori and I always trusted each other with our thoughts and actions, no matter what. That trust has to be earned, not granted."

"Even when it was merely a hunch or a gut-feeling?"

"Especially then!"

"And with Lori's late hours," Donovan asked, "there hasn't been time?"

"Exactly. You know, because of our past and you

keeping your distance since you arrived in Turtle Crossing, would you mind helping me sort out this hunch?"

"Listening," he replied softly. "I am anxious to earn your trust back, so what we discuss stays between us."

"Thank you. This means a lot to me; however, I'll try not to put you in an awkward position, okay?"

"Understood. But Lily, just so you know, if you remember anything about me at all, you are my number one priority and the reason I get up every morning."

Lily was stunned. But they were out of time for them right now, as Donovan pulled down the alley behind her Eight Mile Centre office. Both trucks were quickly unloaded and had installed Lily's equipment exactly as she had planned within record-breaking time.

"The appliance truck is needed for other deliveries, so we'll ride back with Uncle Will," Hunter commented, "Are you ready to leave?"

Lily looked at Donovan and he replied, "Yes. Thanks to this team, everything will be ready for your patients by eight tomorrow morning."

Once they were back on the road, Donovan asked, "I hope you were okay with my reply."

"Yes. Everything is happening so quickly and my head was spinning. I didn't even think of getting fingerprints, but Uncle Will said they must have worn gloves. But just in case he missed something, we all wore gloves."

"Could finding your missing adjustment tables, office furniture and necessary office supplies to support your business right there at the Carriage House cast a shadow on how you do everything?"

"I will definitely be more on the alert wherever I go, and plan to work out daily for a few weeks until I am as fit as I was in in college. Mom taught us better than a few hours three times a week."

"You're serious," Donovan said. "I've always been impressed with how fit you are."

"Thanks. But, the unknown reason why someone is trying very hard to put my business in jeopardy also makes it all the more frustrating to know how to fight them. I know how my Uncle Will thinks. He will move heaven and earth to make certain his family and friends are safe!"

"You are so right!" he added. "That goes double for me as well."

"Regarding that hunch," Lily asked, "I wonder. Have you noticed the photo on Isaac's desk of his son, Andrew, and another man in a frame that reads *Friends*? Has Isaac ever mentioned having met his son's friend?"

"The way he talked, this friend was a college room-mate," Donovan replied.

"Does he remind you of anyone?" she asked.

"You mean, a time when you meet a person, and you feel like you should know him or her, but not from where?"

"Exactly. Are you free the rest of the weekend?" she asked as they arrived back at the Victorian.

Donovan parked Hunter's vehicle next to his and turned to Lily while they waited for Hunter and Storm to arrive with their pizza and root beer. They rolled the windows down to catch the late afternoon breeze.

"It's really quiet and peaceful here," he continued. "There's Hunter. It looks like our pizza has arrived."

Hunter handed their pizza order to Donovan, then turned to Lily, and announced, "Storm and I are helping Uncle Will load up the old stove and refrigerator into his truck and plan to join our ladies with a night out. Catch you later, Sis," Hunter remarked.

"Thanks for all your help," she replied, then asked Donovan. "Let's eat at the Victorian. The Carriage House air conditioning isn't set up."

"We'll lock up, Sis," Hunter added. "Storm and I are planning to stay at Will's tonight. We'll probably throw a few burgers on his grill this evening."

"Thanks," Lily replied as she joined Donovan inside, her keys and tools jangling in the tool apron on her shoulder, reminding her that now they were finally going to be spending some time alone. Her nerves were a mess.

Donovan felt the heat through their pizza carrier and prayed he wouldn't say the wrong thing to her this time. The fear of losing her for the rest of his life ate at his heart. He stumbled on the first step and almost dropped the pizza.

Lily grabbed his arm. "Hey, are you okay?" Her feelings had continued to build all day. Even at the circular stairs, she had momentarily felt his warm breath on her neck. She knew she had leaned over the railing too far, when he drew her back against his chest. She was so flustered, she had rushed down the steps away from him.

He used her key to unlock the Victorian, and she held the door for him and immediately locked the door and set the security in place.

Later, in the kitchen, Donovan commented, "Lily, this pizza was the best, and your cottage cheese, with crushed pineapple, swirled in lime Jello is so refreshing. I can't recall a more special time than spending the entire day working and exploring with you today. I lost you once," he murmured, as he drew her towards him. They were facing each other, as he loosened her hair from the fancy hair clip she so often used. "Dance with me?" When Lily backed away with hesitation in her eyes, he stated gently, "You're afraid."

"Yes," she replied. "You left. Without a word. And broke my heart. I know, that was a long time ago, and I don't need to know the reason why."

"So, can we start over? Hello. My name is Donovan Michael James." He bowed, winked at her, smiled, and, taking her hand, raised it to eye-level and kissed it as softly as the touch of a butterfly.

Lily actually smiled for the first time all day. "Hello. My name is Dr. of Chiropractic Health, Lily Marie Donnelly." She curtsied, shook his hand, and smiled shyly.

"Very nice to meet you, lovely lady," Donovan added, as he found the music he was looking for. "Miss Lily, may I have this dance?" The eye contact between them was electric, as she placed her hand in his open hand. "Relax and feel the music," he directed, as they slow-danced around the room. The sensation of their blended touch, his arms strong and warm on her back.

"I've missed you," Lily whispered.

"I've missed you more," he added, as he kissed her cheek, and backed away to look into her eyes again. He kissed her other cheek, then spun her around, and drew her closer.

Lily wanted more as she reached up to frame his face and kissed him on the lips. Tentatively, she backed away to see if he was okay with her kissing him, and with her hand on his chest, she could feel his heart race.

The telephone rang three times before either of them moved. The sun was setting as Lily answered, "Hello."

"Lily," Lori said, "I'm too tired to drive home this evening. I'll see you in the morning."

"Thanks for calling, Lori."

"Is Donovan still there?"

"Yes. Why?"

"Encourage him to spend the night. This is a request from the Four Aces. We want you safe. Is the security still on?"

Lily looked around as Donovan closed the blinds and continued checking all the locks.

"By the way, part of Will's team is already in place. So get some rest. I understand you both had a pretty upsetting day. Good night, Sis."

"Goodnight, Lori. Thanks."

"Your family wants me to spend the night?" Donovan asked. "What about your reputation?"

"We're consenting adults," Lily replied. "Even if we were engaged, the people who count wouldn't care for two reasons. One, because they love me. And secondly, our safety is more important than gossip."

"Hey there, beautiful lady. May I repeat your comment? Even if we were engaged, I would be sleeping in the spare bedroom or the floor. Besides, I believe you were wanting to talk? Right?" he smiled and nodded.

"First things first. Popcorn, hot chocolate, and then we can talk."

"By the way, I have been working on the presumption of assuming I know what others are thinking."

"Be grateful. It's not a luxury I can claim."

Donovan's attention was a double-take.

"Sorry. Sometimes I forget that you are not from here and would be unaware of the special sight Lori and I were born with. Those who knew us then were used to the Donnelly Twins because we were open about it. We didn't know we were different. However, it saved our lives more than once."

"So, your ability to read people and situations is a talent you've learned to hide?"

"Yes," she replied. "But that isn't what I wanted to discuss with you this evening."

"Are you referring to the photo Isaac has on his desk of his son and a friend?"

"Yes. The friend got upset with me for not helping him cheat on his tests and later got caught anyway. He boasted about dating me and did some research on my family and their businesses. The dates he mentioned were times when he squeezed his chair between my roommate and me a few times and continued to brag that I was his girl. And my gut feeling is I wonder if he might be involved with the disappearance of my equipment."

"People do strange things. I agree with you there. However, I will pay more attention now that I know a little bit more about him. Thanks for warning me about Will's men being on the grounds tonight. Does this mean Will has plans to add to the security here?"

"He is always working on something. But just so you know, If you plan to spend more time with me," Lily challenged, daring him not to look away, you might want to brush up on your self-defense," she added, smiling and winked at him. "In case I need a personal bodyguard."

"Are you really challenging me?" he asked.

"Perhaps," she replied.

"I never thought you could be such a tease," Donovan added, "but it's not something one puts on a resume."

"Ouch," Lily murmured. "If that's too close to home, I apologize. You know, this has been one topsy-turvy day. Why don't we check out the refrigerator for that cold chicken and fix a bit of hot chocolate?"

"Lily Donnelly, you are one very classy lady. Much better than I deserve," he added as he piled some chicken and chips on paper plates and napkins on a tray. While Lily heated the milk, she turned to Donovan, and filled two mugs with hot chocolate and grabbed the marshmallows. When they were finished eating, they curled up on opposite ends of the sectional, lingering over their hot chocolate that had cooled.

"You asked why I backed away from you?" he replied, "Two reasons. One, I didn't want my mother to find out who you were. She tracked me down that week we spent together; but when she found out it was a honeymoon destination, she assumed I was having an affair with some woman. She faked a heart attack and had the police on the lookout for my car. We've barely spoken since. No. She doesn't know where I am this summer."

"Can you imagine my embarrassment when I found out who your Great Grandpa was when C.W. heard my name he asked me if I knew an Andrew James. I admitted that he was my Great Grandfather. Then I admitted that part of my reason for coming to this area was to learn if my ancestor ever paid off the loan your Great Grandpa was owed."

"C.W. was aware of the business loan because he did all of his brother, W.W.'s books. It's hard for me to put into words how relieved I was. The I.O.U. was marked paid in full."

"Donovan," Lily commiserated as she reached over and clasped her hands with his. "Surely you know I would never have walked away from you."

"I know, sweetheart. But, I left a note," he replied. "Why the tears?'

"I don't know. I haven't had a full night's sleep since I returned home," and yawned. But the two of us together feels so right. I'm exhausted, but I don't want to be alone just now."

"Well," he suggested, "this sectional sofa seats six so looks like it will have to do."

***

Lily woke with sunlight barely peeking between the blinds and was not surprised to glance at the other end of the couch and find it empty. Amazed, also, she had not only slept so late, but had fallen asleep after letting down her guard where he was concerned. She quickly gathered up her pillow and blanket and headed for the shower.

As soon as Lily was asleep, Donovan had moved to the kick-back chair where he could watch her, waking every two hours, wondering how he could help her when she already had so many people to protect and support her. As he watched the sun come up, he prayed it would chase away the shadowed edges of the Pease Victorian Estate and wondered if she would offer him a chance to train in her office now that Isaac's cast was off. Isaac wouldn't need him.

***

"Good morning, Ladies," Storm greeted. "We started early to work on some of the moves Dad taught us,"

Hunter added. "I know six-thirty is early, but we're all heading to work."

"Looking for someone?" Granny asked Denver when he practically ran her down as he sped around the corner of Doc's garage where the Four Aces had just finished a practice session. The Foursome played music during their workouts so anyone listening would believe they were practicing music, not training to work as a Foursome team.

Denver skidded to a stop, when he realized Granny could read the guilt he felt for getting caught sneaking around here, when he was scheduled to be mending fences. His entire body felt as though his morning shower had suddenly turned to melted ice. Shuddering and stammering, he asked, "Where's everybody going in such a rush?"

Granny put an arm around his shoulder. With a look

that had stopped bigger men than him, she answered his question with a question. "How long have you been here?" When he didn't answer, she continued. "May I assume you have finished the list of jobs Doc handed you this morning?"

Once again, Denver wasn't used to working with people who appeared to genuinely work as a team. His dad had taught him to never trust anyone, especially family. But, he missed not having any family, and was tired of being alone.

Granny patiently waited as his face turned from shock to fear, to anger, as his stubborn jaw tightened to an ungracious attitude, when Lily joined them.

"You know, Denver," Lily said. You remind me of that sad, stubborn saddle-bronc with its fierce block-headed attitude. And, Lori is still trying to tame it."

"You're comparing me to that lazy, hurting bronc out there?"

"That's right. Lessons in life aren't always visible. Like the scars on that bronc as you call him. I heard you whistling the other day. Why don't you try letting the bronc know someone cares about him? You were upset that he needed a pedicure."

Granny hid her smile when Denver's fists relaxed as he tried to swallow his pride, and headed for the paddock where bronc stood waiting.

I can't believe I stood there and felt intimidated by an old lady and put in my place by Lori's twin. Okay. A fascinating, no-hold- bars, queen of this outfit.

Yet he also felt loved for the first time since his mom

had passed. And that didn't make any sense at all.

As Granny and Lily continued towards the O'Reilly Ranch house, Denver spotted Lori leaning on the gate of the paddock. "Mind if I join you?" Denver asked softly so as not to startle her apparent focus on bronc.

"Denver," Lori said. "Bronc definitely needs those hooves trimmed, and we both know he isn't going to be cooperative if we confine him. Confinement still terrifies him. So, are you comfortable with me restraining him with a chain-lead-strap over his nose while you trim his hooves?"

Before Denver could answer Lori's offer, Buck joined them. "Here's Doc's leather farrier's apron and tool box," Buck said. "I'll be Lori's backup or yours," Buck added, winking at Lori.

Denver didn't miss the teasing admonition in Buck's voice and said, "I hope you don't expect me to sweet-talk this grayish/yellow buckskin bronc in the process?"

"Not at all," Lori remarked. "I'll take care of that because it is me he will be looking at."

"When do we start?" Denver requested, knowing the answer before he asked it, as he put on the apron and pocketed the tools he would need. "You know, bronc, the two of us are stuck with this team. They have gone out of their way to help us. So you and I have something to prove today. But just so you know, you're not my first feisty rodeo on tour. Why, you'll feel like dancing when we're finished."

Chapter 13

Reverend Cecil Warren, best known as C.W. to his family and parishioners, was calmer than his musical gospel team, who would be an integral part of his Renewal Celebration Church, which had been moved from its former location near the corporation limit sign of Winthrop to become a Chapel wing of the Eight Mile Centre church.

His Winthrop church, with its unique stained glass windows, went from the possibility of becoming a pile of rubbish to a Renewal Chapel, as an integral part of a growing community. Today was special because of a crew of students who had just returned from a tour of Europe where they had studied construction and preservation of buildings much older than his chapel. The entire front row had been reserved for these students.

He was unaware that the film and photos the students had taken during the restoration of his chapel, were as much about him because CW had given them a chance towards their degrees. The film was a historical documentary of his Renewal Church and Warren Chapel.

The Four Aces had promised C.W. they would take care of the music for the main service. The only difference in the opening would be Lori's and Lily's voices backing-up Hunter, Storm, Harmony, and Madison Grace.

After their morning warm-up, Lily squeezed Lori's hand, "Did you notice?" And motioned towards a guest. They recognized the fear in her eyes and the protective way she held the child on her lap.

"Yes," Lori nodded. "The only time she smiled was when C.W. approached her."

After greeting several other parishioners, C.W. joined the twins and, while he hugged Lori, he slipped a piece of paper into Lily's hand and whispered, "The young blonde woman with a little brunette on her lap needs help."

"We'll take care of it," Lori replied, smiling, and Lily kissed him on the cheek.

Aloud, CW added, "Congratulations!" Then turned around and asked, "Hunter, do you plan to help lead the music every Sunday?"

Hunter nodded, and shaking C.W.'s hand said, "We would love to, Uncle C.W."

After the service, Storm and Madison Grace approached the young woman. While Madison talked to her like they were old friends, Storm crouched down and talked to the little four-year-old for a moment, before they walked her to C.W.'s Garden of Peace in his chapel where they would have more privacy.

Granny caught up with Shannon in the church

parking lot. "Those students certainly surprised C.W. with an album of photos and film," Granny commented. "You no doubt miss his Winthrop church, having lived so close, when your children were growing up."

"Yes, but the last few years we have spent as much time in Turtle Crossing as we have in Winthrop."

"I can never thank you for the lovely mural you painted in the entrance and waiting room at Doc O'Reilly's Veterinarian Animal Hospital. It certainly is a big hit," Granny smiled.

"As you know," Shannon began, "Will's Wendy is especially talented when it comes to her whimsical touch with animals. Not many know this, but my Lori used to draw some pretty interesting sketches of animals when she was in school."

"I would love to see them sometime," Granny added. "Doc is so excited to have her in the business. He commented the other night that she mentors him as much as he mentors her."

Except for a few stragglers, the church had emptied when Lily and Lori caught sight of Hunter as he cornered a man who was clutching a woman's tattered hand-bag. Lori approached the woman who was screaming in the far aisle about the second row from the back of the church.

"Stop that man! He stole my handbag."

"Please, ma'am. We can't help you if you don't stop screeching."

Hunter heard and felt his sister's calming, but strong presence, and when the woman quieted, the silence in the church was deafening.

Lily nodded to Harmony, motioning her to back off. Harmony stepped outside and gently closed the heavy oak entrance doors and stepped back into the shadows.

"Just give the woman back her purse," Hunter calmly coaxed. "I'll let you go," Hunter quoted from his hundred or so statements he had written in his what-if journal.

"Get real, mister," the scrappy-looking purse-snatcher growled. "You really expect me to give up a few thousand dollars that old lady carries around in her purse? That ain't all. She has a gun in here, too. I can feel it." He reached inside her bag that had her husband's military emblem stitched on the outside.

The woman had stopped yelling and appeared to calm down until the purse-snatcher yelled at Hunter, "You don't believe that there is a gun in here, do you? I'll prove it!" The pistol he pulled out was rusty, but the barrel was shiny.

"Miss, miss," the woman tugged on Lori's arm, and said softly in Lori's ear, "The firing pin is missing."

Lori turned the woman around, leaned down and gently flattened her against the wall, eye-ball to eye-ball, and whispered, "Are you certain?"

The woman was suddenly more frightened of Lori than the guy who had grabbed her purse and she merely nodded a fearful, "Yes."

Lori murmured, "Thank you, Jesus. This is my baby brother, Lord." But she had always been taught to assume any gun is loaded until proven otherwise.

Lily spotted Troop crawling under the pews towards Hunter and saw a couple of women sitting in a nearby pew shadowed where the lights had been dimmed and for everyone's safety, motioned them to, lie down on the pew, close their eyes, and zip their mouths shut.

Then she felt something change. She noticed Storm as he slowly closed the door to C.W.'s Chapel which had been painted to appear as though it was a gate to the garden.

All the while, Hunter continued to question the purse-snatcher. "Is it really worth jail time? I mean, are you really certain she has real money, and not some of your old Uncle's worthless play money?"

"Shut up! You just march, mister," the well-dressed perpetrator demanded, shaking and waving the gun in Hunter's face.

All right. They knew the time had come. They had worked on this type of scenario when Storm's deep baritone voice blasted over the surround system: "This is God's servant speaking! This is HIS HOUSE!"

Okay, thought Lori, This is a new twist. A not-ever-trained-for scenario.

Meanwhile Lily had worked her way towards the man Hunter had cornered, who was fiercely eyeing him, and never saw the kick that sent the gun flying through the air, ripped the purse out of his hand and disappeared through the basement door. Troop had latched onto his leg, jerking him back and forth growling fiercely.

Madison Grace had disappeared into the church secretary's office and phoned Lt. Brandi Carpenter, who quickly handcuffed the purse snatcher. Lily, Troop and Hunter slipped out a side door of the church while an undercover officer Lori had attended school with, took over, explaining as they went out the side door. Harmony had carefully scooped up the handbag into a paper bag which she handed to Lt. Brandi's half-brother, Jace Carpentier, from Sunrise.

***

Brandi and Jace had just placed their lunch order to celebrate the Grand Opening at Eight Mile Center.

After Brandi had the full story, she asked, "So this woman attended church here, and she didn't actually see how this perp was disarmed?"

"No." Lori replied, "Although, I blocked her view, she could have heard Hunter's voice when he was talking to the perp."

"No," Harmony commented.

"From my standpoint," Madison Grace added, "I was close enough to hear Lori when she demanded the woman repeat her statement that the gun couldn't hurt anyone because the firing pin was missing. The look on Gertrude's face was pure fear."

"What else did you say to her, Lori?" Lt. Brandi asked.

"I said, 'Gertrude, you were hiding up here the entire time by yourself, right?'" Lori repeated.

"And she agreed?" Brandi asked.

"Yes. Why? What did she tell you?" Lori asked.

"She said, 'That's between me and God,'" Brandi repeated.

"And," Jace added. "The two women you motioned to lie down, close their eyes, and zip their mouth, apparently did just what they were told. They did not get up until I told them who I was, and they turned their heads and peeked at my badge."

One of the women replied, "These are Rev. Cecil's family. That makes them God's family. They saved our lives today. Is everyone safe now?"

"I told them yes," Jace replied.

"Can we leave now?"

"I told them yes," Jace repeated.

"Then one of the women said, 'Okay sir. We've spent this time praying. You see, God does answer prayers.'"

***

The following day, Hunter murmured softly, "The Four Aces," as he punched in the code for the second floor of Doc's garage practice room for their necessary practice together. Lily and Lori arrived simultaneously and Storm grabbed the door before it closed.

"Sorry, we have to work out here the rest of the week," Lily said. "Lori, prepare to be surprised when you stop by the Pease Victorian."

"We can attest to that," Hunter added.

"Indeed," Storm confirmed. "The entire landscaping, as well as inside the Victorian, the Carriage House, the grounds-keeper, tool shed, and garages." All the while they were discussing info, they were working on their warmup stretches.

"Guys," Lori began, "I like what Dad shared with you. Have you been practicing on your own?"

"I noticed it, too," Lily agreed. "Your movements are smoother, that's for certain."

"Yeah," Storm added, "But maybe it's the landscaping

staff Dad assigned to us," he laughed. "You know digging, shoveling, planting, clearing dead wood and hauling."

"Are you expecting sympathy?" Lori smiled. "But that may be helping because the pictures in your mind appear to be stronger, or perhaps it's your confidence."

"I need to tell you about a personal experience," Lily continued. "I was in my second year in college and because my room-mate was running late, I was alone. And, in a hurry. I carelessly let down my guard. My mind on my next class. When three guys came out of nowhere. I'll skip over their bragging and language."

"But, before they could grab my other arm, I reacted on instinct. I used Mom's 'rope' combination, now-you-see-me, now-you-don't-moves." Hunter and Lori gripped each other's hands. "I was sore for weeks and finally went to a local chiropractor."

Storm, in a gentle voice inquired, "So, what happened to the guys?"

"They were lucky. Two ran away after my backpack connected, dislocating their shoulders, and the one who had initially grabbed me showed up in class after he stopped at the ER with a broken nose, dislocated fingers, and limped for weeks where my boot bruised one of his thighs."

"I was so exhausted I could barely move, but the flight-or-fight wasn't an option. Each of those guys outweighed me by at least fifty to one-hundred pounds."

"So that's the reason you organized the self-defense classes at your dorm?" Lori inquired.

"Yes."

"What explanation did these guys come up with?" Hunter asked.

"They were certain they had encountered a host of ghosts. But just in case they might remember something, I threw my hat and green plaid winter jacket in a downtown garbage truck and bought a three-quarter-length plain navy wool coat with matching knit hat."

"And they didn't know if you were blonde or brunette," Hunter said.

"No. And I was wearing my old sunglasses," Lily added, "I threw them away because the frames were bent beyond repair. After that, I wore reflective ones, which I discarded before I left college."

"Could you identify any of them?" Storm inquired.

"I lost track of them." Lily murmured, looked at Lori, and replied, "Let's hope it never comes to that."

Hunter turned on some music to stretch to when they were interrupted by a knock on the door. Granny announced, "Jonothan just called. That storm cell has escalated with the possibility of tornados. Wildlife senses these things long before we do. Buck just rode in and said that the stock has already taken shelter on their own. You better slide the wooden panels over these mirrors."

As they slid the panels into place, Lily commented, "I think I will wait out the storm at my Eight Mile Centre office. I've locked the doors to the rooms where my new equipment is set up and am only using Dr. Kate's just in case a patient happens to discuss their experience at my office; except for my new desk, which is in my private office."

"Hey, Sis," Hunter said, "We will find the mastermind behind all this, you know. And, by the way, Donovan is a good guy."

Lily blushed and hugged Hunter, "You'll never know how much I've missed you, little brother."

"Hey guys," Lori yelled, "we need to do something now because this storm has moved in fast. I couldn't open the downstairs door."

They joined her on the first floor. "Did Doc put a basement in when they built this garage?" Lily inquired.

"Oh, wow," Lori recalled, "Yes. The snack shop, under Garage Door Number Three."

"We're just a few feet away. Where?" Hunter asked.

"Behind the chips and cookie display," Storm announced as he released three hinges, one easy tug and whoosh, Storm lifted the door on the floor, and down the stairs they went.

"Hunter," Storm yelled, "help me throw these lock-down bars."

"I'm not worried about Granny and Doc. They will be in their basement, and Will and his men will be in the storm cellar or in the bunkhouse," Storm added. "When Doc built the Veterinarian Hospital and this garage, Buck insisted reinforcement for his men; so he not only had extra supports around the building, he also had a storm cellar similar to this one installed in the center of the bunkhouse."

"I now know why this looks so familiar," Lily explained, "it's plastered at the entrance of this garage and I never took the time to read it."

Hunter turned on the weather radio. The reports were not good in Sunrise. The tornado had skipped Turtle Crossing and dipped down in a rural area west of town.

"Jonothan and Brandi's half-brother, Jace Carpentier, is in Sunrise," Lily commented. "Thanks to Alexa, owner of the Welby Mansion B&B, most of Turtle Crossing businesses have access to the Turtle Crossing Tunnel of Safe Passage, which would include Mom and Dad and golfers on the course."

"Madison Grace and Harmony were working at Granny's Cradle of Flower' today," Lori added.

"I never talked to Harmony about anything like this," Hunter said.

"Don't worry about it, Hunter," Lori added. "Anyone who stays or works for Granny is given the drill on where to go in her basement and, if caught outside, about her root cellar."

Sooner than they expected, they heard voices and pounding on the floor door above the stairs. Storm and Lily released the bar and the door flew open, almost taking Storm with it.

"They're all down here!" Will yelled, as he pulled Storm halfway up the stairs and hugged him. "Harmony, Madison Grace, Doc, Buck, plus the ranch hands are all accounted for," he added.

Denver shyly approached Lori and reached out to grasp her hands as she climbed the stairs. "Happy to see you are safe," he said and smiled. Lori was surprised to see such emotion from Denver, of all people.

Donovan rushed into the building, hesitated, then

hugged Lily so tightly, she whispered, "I can't breathe."

"Sorry. I thought for certain I had lost you."

"Oh my," Lily asked, "where is the garage door?"

"The tornado sucked it out and dumped it a half-mile down the road," Donovan replied.

Lily felt her stomach catch in her throat and embraced him, recalling when Lori tried to open the garage door and it wouldn't budge. "Lori, did you hear what happened to that garage door you couldn't open?" They stared at each other. Neither spoke. It wasn't necessary.

Hunter turned to Harmony and hugged her. "Today was too close. It will hit all of us later just how close. I picture tornado drills on the horizon," he added.

"Doc," Lori asked, "My truck? I parked it in the East Garage." She had yet to admit how the pressure changed, just for a moment, when it took all her strength to jerk away from the suction hold the tornado had had on her against the garage door.

"It's fine. The county is clearing the roads for medical personnel in Sunrise. Some will be needing shelter. We'll be needing to set up for a BBQ a couple of weeks early, boys. Not all of the markets have generator backup. And the Rochesters have huge roasters to loan out as soon as the roads are clear. His excavating equipment is already being put to use."

Lori kept hold of Denver and asked Donovan, "Can you let go of Lily, just for a moment?"

Lily and Lori hugged and a dam of tears followed. They reluctantly backed away, but Donovan finally saw in their eyes what this entire community had been aware of for years. Love. Their twin connection was pure honest trust.

Lily turned and kissed Donovan on the cheek and suggested, ""The men are going to need your help. Take Denver with you. Lori and I will be helping organize meals for an army."

Donovan tipped her face towards him, kissed her on the cheek, and murmured, "We're going to be okay." Then he and Denver joined Doc and Will on Doc and Granny's enclosed back porch which had become headquarters, where people could go in and out, posting the checklists of families that were okay, their location, those who were needing temporary shelter, and those who were still missing.

As Lily and Lori walked hand in hand towards Granny's kitchen, Lori stopped Lily momentarily and added, "I have to check with the police and volunteers to see if there are any animals in distress."

"I know," Lily replied, and we're both going to be smart and safe, right?"

"Agreed," Lori nodded.

They hugged and separated. "What about Mom and Dad?" Lori asked.

"Mom, Dad, and C.W. are all okay."

***

The following morning, a sight to behold, truly drew a crowd. The Pied Piper was the only traffic on the road. They recognized Troop walking beside a donkey with a straggly-looking rooster on his back, pulling a homemade rustic-looking wagon, which was bedded with straw, overflowing with a menagerie of animals. Two young freckle-faced boys, age ranging from eight to ten-year-olds, were following behind and pulling a smaller homemade wagon with side rails.

Followed by two horses, a Dam and her filly that appeared to be in shock, two white goats with red heads were tied to the second wagon, and three fawns brought up the rear. The only sound was the squeaking of the wagon wheels, the rustling of straw, and plodding of the donkey.

Each and every person on the O'Reilly Ranch would remember today as the Pied Piper Day, as a memorable aftermath of the 1986 Sunrise Tornado that resulted in how two young boys took charge of their animals and others on their journey.

Crisis mode with humility and compassion. Denver patiently led the horses into the stable; but when he started to lead them into separate stalls, they refused. They had apparently bonded. Even though they were splattered with mud, he just talked softly to them and left them with water and something to eat.

When Denver returned from the stables, he helped one of the ranch hands unhitch the donkey. The boys sat down at the picnic table for a few minutes and each drank a glass of water. But when Granny offered them a sandwich, they said, "We ate an apple a while ago, but we better wait until our animals are bedded down."

Doc and Lori made use of the Veterinarian Hospital recovery pens for the first time. The cowhands pitched in, making use of the walk-in animal showers. Following the directions of these two young adventurers as they insisted taking care of Tilly, the mother sow. They talked to Tilly about her babies as they walked her into the nursery cage, which had a heated area for her babies. She flopped inside and guzzled water from the spigot. Then, she nuzzled her squalling babies as they were retrieved from their temporary bed and feed sacks that had kept them warm. They were gently laid beside her and quickly started nursing.

"What else do you have in this wagon?" Lily asked.

"A robin with a broken wing that Troop spotted along the edge of the road. And the little girl our rooster found."

"*What?*" gasped Lily.

"Oh, my gosh. I forgot about her," Harvey stammered and rushed to uncover the child. "She's been awfully quiet. Hey, sleepy-head," he announced.

"We only spotted her on the ground behind the tree because this rooster here flew up and down the tree, flapping his wings and making such a racket. We investigated, and there she was on the ground behind a tree."

The younger of the two boys, Bart, continued, "There was a pile of twigs and dried-up corn stalks piled up on both sides of her. She was dry and so was her blanket. She held up her empty bottle and smiled. So while my big brother picked her up and found a safe place for her in the wagon, I rinsed out her bottle with water and then I milked my 4-H project, Josie, my Boer goat, and re-filled her bottle. It didn't take her long to finish it. You know, she never cried once. When she fell asleep, we were busy with our east/north-east directions for a while, but trusted Troop. He just seemed to know where he was going, and here we are."

Everyone stopped what they were doing to look at this little miracle. Lily reached inside the rails of the rustic, over-sized wagon and lifted the baby out. But the baby was not ready to let go of her bottle.

"I'll take her in to Granny's nursery and clean her up," Lily stated.

But before Lily could leave, the eldest boy Harvey asked, "Please," he requested, as he touched the baby gently on her cheek, and said, "Hey, Little Miss Sunshine, may I have your bottle so I can wash it in soap and water while my little brother, Bart, milks Josie and refills it for you. Will that be okay?" The baby raised the bottle up for Harvey to take. "You remember the story I told you about Bart's goat, Rosie? She won Grand Champion Rosette at the County Fair and a first place banner for her milk." The baby smiled at him.

"Is it okay if I take her inside for a bath and dry clothes?" Lily requested. "I will bring her right back out. My name is Lily."

"That's mighty nice of you, Miss Lily. Thanks."

Denver murmured, "I guess there really is a God."

Harvey approached Doc and pleaded, "We haven't seen a road sign all day, Sir. We couldn't find our mom and dad."

"Well, boys," Doc replied, "we will check into the next counties if necessary."

"Where are we now?" Harvey asked.

"We're north of Turtle Crossing," Doc said.

"They have a hospital, right?" Harvey inquired.

"Yes. Where were you when the tornado hit?"

"We were making certain our 4-H animals were safe under the barn hill, but the tornado was moving too fast for us to get to the storm cellar."

"Did your parents make it to the storm shelter?"

"We don't know. We couldn't find it," Bart replied.

"Parts of our barn and house were missing. It was a tangled mess with trees uprooted, and fields of wheat looked like someone had mowed a path right down the middle," Harvey added.

Bart handed Lily a fresh bottle of milk for the baby, and Lily joined their circle with the baby in her arms.

Donovan set a glass of iced tea on the stand beside her and murmured, "You look content holding that baby in your arms."

Lily was at a loss to respond to Donovan's surprising comment.

"So where were you planning to go?" Doc asked.

"Our Aunt was living in a mobile home park north of Turtle Crossing," Bart recalled, "But my compass was in my room and that part of the house was gone."

"And Troop?" Lori asked.

"You know," Bart replied, "Just before this storm hit, this dog—Troop?—showed up and pushed the animals and us farther under the barn hill where it was really, really dark."

"We were really scared. That tornado sounded as loud as an angry bull. Even the ground shook and parts of the barn siding were torn into pieces, and then it rained all night. The donkey belonged to our neighbor but we couldn't see any buildings, so we bedded all the animals we could."

"What about the cart?" Denver asked.

"Oh, we found it in an old shed and added sides to it for the county fair parade. It was right where we had put it—in an empty stall in the barn."

"Where were the horses?" Denver requested.

"The horses and fawns came out of a woods and followed us," Harvey concluded.

"Yeah," Bart added, "a fox followed us for a while until we stopped at a spring for fresh water; then it left us."

"You boys must be starving," Granny suggested.

"Yeah, a little bit," Harvey replied.

"We had packed our school backpacks for the storm shelter, but I'm ready for some real food," Bart added. "But we're too muddy to track into your kitchen."

"Why don't you join us in the shade at one of our picnic tables," Granny suggested.

Harvey and Bart looked like two worn-out, hardworking little heroes as they pulled off their caps and one hand-pumped water for the other, dipped their heads in the chilling well water, washed their faces and hands with the homemade soap nearby, and dried on paper towels nearby. A light breeze kicked up and dried the moisture off their necks.

"How about some chili with cornbread muffins and freshly baked chocolate chip cookies for dessert? " Granny suggested, "We'll join you. We eat out here quite often." Hunter carried the roaster filled with chili, and Harmony brought out baskets of cornbread muffins. "After we eat, the boys can take you to the bunkhouse to shower and put on some clean clothes that I collect for the church rummage sales."

The boys waited until everyone was served. Then Harvey announced, "Please bow your heads. Thank you, Jesus, for Troop and our safe arrival into the wonderful arms of people who have welcomed Bart and me and our collection of tornado survivors. Please help our friends and search teams find our mom and dad. Especially thank you for this food. Amen."

"Can we check on our animals before we clean up?" Harvey requested.

"They're our responsibility," Bart added proudly, straightening his shoulders back even though it was apparent they were worn out.

Denver went to check on the horses and found Lori quietly talking to them and one of the boys.

"You're an animal doctor, right?" Harvey asked.

"Yes." Lori said.

"I think it might be a Dam and her filly. They ate pasture grass after they joined us, and we didn't stop often, except to collect water and eat. The filly's ears perked up when she heard Harvey's voice and moved closer to the stable gate.

"Well," Denver said. "That's a good sign, don't you think, Doctor Lori?"

"Yes. Perhaps by morning, they will be ready to go outside in the paddock."

"See you both in the morning," Harvey added.

"Denver," Lori asked. "Have you ever dealt with a horse that has been traumatized like this?"

"Not personally," he replied.

Lori nodded, pleased with his relaxed honesty. "Can you explain something for me? I haven't been able to forget the look on your face when you saw that I was safe after the tornado went through."

"No one was more surprised than I was," he replied. "I've learned to keep my distance from women."

"Does this mean someone stole your heart? And it's not happening again?"

"Yes, have a good night, Miss Lori," he added, his voice soft and husky with emotion. He was chastising himself over and over with each step as he headed for the bunkhouse. "Walk away. Stay away," he mumbled.

"Talking to yourself again?" Will asked, a bit of a chuckle in his voice.

"Evening, Mr. Fox," Denver nodded respectfully.

"My dad was Mr. Fox. Friends, family and co-workers call me Will."

"Thank you, sir...um, Will."

"Problem in the stables?"

"No. It's pretty quiet this evening," Denver added. "Just wondering and wishing."

"You know, Denver, that's a bit like dreaming," Will added. "Without action, you're still stuck where you were yesterday, a month ago, and a year ago."

Will waited while Denver moved his hand over the harmonica in his pocket. "You would never make a good poker player. Buck says you do a lot of reading in the evening."

Denver looked calmly at Will. "You investigated me?"

"Indeed, I did. Your last employer was upset that you left. It appears his daughter and her new boyfriend were all talk. When it came time to actually shoe a horse, they failed miserably."

Denver nodded, and continued, "But from what I've seen, you and Doc act like brothers and you would move mountains to protect your family, especially your nieces. I can see why. Not many know this, but I met Lily before Lori, before I arrived at Doc O'Reilly's."

Will was intrigued and surprised this had not come up. He thought the twins told him everything.

"I was sitting on a bench in front of that new soup-and-sandwich outfit at Eight Mile Center when she came out and sat at the same bench where I was sitting, and asked me how long I had been sitting there. She offered me half of her sandwich and soda. During our conversation, her attention was focused clear across the parking lot, on what I now know is her office. I was mesmerized by her. She asked if she could help me. I told her I was looking for my Uncle Doc O'Reilly. And she gave me directions. Then I walked into Lori's office, and the moment I saw her, I was stunned. Especially when she moved to protect Doc from me."

"Why are you telling me all this?" Will asked.

"I really can't believe I did. Maybe because I can't ever tell her how she made me feel that day," Denver murmured as he turned to walk away.

"Well, I wouldn't wait around too long," Will remarked. "You're not the only one interested in her, you know."

"Goodnight, sir." Denver added.

Later, Denver joined the adults sitting around a fire. "I've never been around little kids, but those two act like miniature adults. They wanted to sleep in the bunkhouse and Buck had already marched Troop through the animal walk-in-shower, so Troop could sleep in the bunkhouse beside the boys."

***

The following morning, the air was clear, and the sun was waiting behind the trees and the nearly full moon was merely an outline in the West, as Lori checked on her patients, and was not surprised to hear Harvey sweet-talking the Filly and Denver playing a sweet lullaby on his harmonica. The stable smelled of fresh straw, sweet alfalfa, and Denver's after shave. She was puzzled why she noticed Denver's aftershave. "Breakfast is ready on the back porch," she suggested.

"We'll see you there," Denver replied.

"I have to go to the office. Doc's been on the phone since five this morning. I have to relieve him."

Lori grabbed two large cups of coffee laced with Granny's hot cocoa and set a basket of warm blueberry muffins on her desk and shoved them in front of Doc.

He rolled his eyes and held up his clipboard and hung up the phone.

"Wow, Doc!" Lori exclaimed. "This list looks like volunteers and first responders worked all night!"

"Hey, Sis," Lily said. "I'm here to answer the phone."

"The boys' parents are safe and on their way," Doc reported.

"That's great news," Lori said, the lack of sleep apparent in her voice.

***

The following day, Lily sat at her desk, in her office in Eight Mile Centre, contemplating why she was feeling antsy, and as she went through her day's schedule, the number of times she had promised herself, *Lori and I will spend quality time together, no excuses.* She dialed Lori and asked, "Lori, can you get free tomorrow?"

"Yes, but hold on," as she turned to Doc and stated, "Lily and I need a day, just the two of us."

"Go," Doc motioned.

"Yes," Lori confirmed.

"I was just closing the office," Lily replied. "Shall I pick you up?" Lily asked, excitement in her movements as she locked up her files and called out, "Harmony," and turned the open sign over to closed. "Take the weekend off. Lori and I are taking a much needed visit."

"You haven't been yourself for a couple of days," Harmony added, as they each checked the back door and the security.

"This is the second week that those same vehicles have parked illegally in the handicap spaces," Lily remarked.

"Dutifully noted," Harmony replied with a smirk.

"Thank you, Miss Harmony," Lily said smiling. "You and my little brother make a great team. Dear friend and office manager, see you on Monday," Lily added as they locked up.

Lori was waiting with two cups of her special coffee and her medical bag. Lily didn't even shut off the engine as Lori fastened her seat belt and they waved to Granny and Doc. "What's going on?" Lori asked.

"I don't have a clue," Lily replied. "Maybe a lot has happened recently, and I made myself a promise, okay we made a promise. This is good coffee really good, by the way."

"Feeling unsettled?" Lori requested.

"Yes. You, too?" Lily questioned, her voice lowering just a bit.

"I have been hungry for fresh green beans, potatoes, and ham," Lori mentioned, thinking to change the subject.

Lily didn't comment, just smiled. "It didn't take me long to notice the basket Granny slipped in the back when you put your medical bag in, Sis. How could one miss her fresh peach cobbler, but do I also smell chocolate, too?"

Lori laughed as they approached the Pease Victorian. Lily hit the remote to open the gates, and barely cleared the gates when she hit the remote again.

Once inside, Lori stopped Lily and hugged her. "I have really missed this place, and you. I overheard Granny talking to Doc just yesterday about my extended hours and feeling it was easier to just stay overnight. This feels more like home now."

"I agree," Lily said, "but I think it's the privacy, too. And since we're on 'holiday', how do you feel about taking the Safe Passage Tunnel tomorrow? Sadie commented that a recent tourist had to be careful in the sun and on her visit here she didn't have to carry an umbrella, but could pop in one store and out another using the tunnel, like the subway she was used to using in some cities."

"Hey, I love this sectional," Lori remarked.

Lily was hesitant to comment because she kept remembering Donovan on one end for a few hours, but later moved to a kick-back sleeper-chair. "This is where I slept that night when Donovan stayed overnight. He had held me in his arms earlier because I had been over-whelmed with everything that had happened that day. I hate the unknown and have been working harder on keeping myself ready, alert, and on-guard all the time."

"That's understandable, but there's more to how you're feeling, right?" Lori questioned.

"Guilty. We're so used to dealing with emotional stuff alone, but Donovan and I spent the entire day together. A reminder why other guys I met over the years didn't measure-up or something was missing in me."

"Haven't you always been just a little-bit in love with Donovan?" Lori said.

"I can't be. He could just leave again, like he has other times," Lily stammered, as tears threatened. "How about a hot cocoa?"

"Maybe later," Lori said. "I'm going to have some of that cobbler with vanilla ice cream. Oops. Do we have any ice cream?"

"Sure do," Lily smiled. "But it's a different brand. Donovan got Sadie's Rootbeer Float recipe."

"Oh, Lily. Really? But I thought she would never share," Lori said.

"I know."

They were back on the sectional listening to Willie Nelson's "Blue Eyes Cryin' in the Rain," when Lori asked, "What's your thoughts on Denver?"

"I don't know him well enough to say, Sis. He has always treated me with respect. Always listens, but seldom states his view on anything. Except the day of the tornado, the expression on his face in those gorgeous blue eyes, when he saw you were okay, was monumental. It was apparent he was smitten with you."

"Are you serious?" Lori asked.

"Oh, yeah," Lily replied.

"I'll take care of our dishes. I need a moment," Lori added.

"Okay." When Lori left the family room, Lily relaxed a bit, but that feeling was still edging into her thoughts. *Lord, if I just knew what is or could happen, perhaps we could derail it in some way. I believe and trust you, but somewhere I have heard, God takes care of those who take care of themselves. But, what about those who can't?*

Lori returned from the kitchen with two frosted glasses of rootbeer topped with two dips of vanilla ice cream floating, tantalizing.

Lori continued. "You said you spent one full day and night here with Donovan. Multiply that with working side by side, together lately, every day! Denver's better than Doc with most of the animals. He senses what they can't say."

"And when he plays that harmonica, I want to dance with him. We have a couple of times. I know, Sis, I haven't known him that long, but he treats Doc and Granny like family. I know Doc really is his uncle, but it's more than that. He loves them. But I think he is still dealing with trust issues."

"Has he ever kissed you?" Lily asked.

"Almost. But it is like there's a wall, a step he can't or won't take. So, then I question if he really feels the same way I do, you know," Lori replied.

"Well," Lily added, "it appears we're both at an impasse with the men in our lives, but on another note, do you remember how before the tornado we both had this feeling? The air was heavy, our personal barometers were close to rock bottom, but we both ignored it."

"I know. I am still trying to figure out what is in the offing," Lori added. "You know how clouds can be a prediction of a storm? Well, this feeling is oppressive, personal."

"Have you noticed anything out of the ordinary?" Lily asked.

"You know, I've been so busy," Lori replied, "Until we left Doc's Ranch, I felt that depressing pressure fall away. But Denver has suggested more than once that we can't ignore the fact that the horses are skittish. You know the fight or flight instinct they are born with. The hens aren't even laying."

"Oh, did I tell you that Bart left his prize goats at Granny's so there would be milk for the baby?"

"I did not know that. So the search is still on for the parents of Little Missy and Baby Blue? That is so sad. What about the possibility that they are related to Harvey and Bart? At least Harmony had met the children's mother. The way Harvey talked, their destination was their Aunt's at the nearby mobile home park. Their aunt was their mom's sister."

"Granny talked to the boys' parents, and they want to adopt the children as soon as their home is rebuilt," Lori said.

"That would be good. Mom was in tears when she heard about the situation. I can't imagine what she went through as a child," Lily commented.

"Granny mentioned that Aunt Marcie talked about it at the reunion. She was talking to Granny about how Sheldon, Mom's twin, was always looking for her. Marcie said he still has memories of looking for her, especially since he has children of his own," Lori commented.

"So," Lily said, "that must have been what he meant when he remarked to Will at the all-family reunion if he could, he would erase his grandmother Warren off the family tree."

"Two things come to mind for tomorrow," Lori began. "We're due a Four Aces emergency meeting."

"Undoubtedly!" Lily replied.

"And, hey! Touring the tunnel is not going to take all day," Lori suggested.

Chapter 14

Lori had just dried their peach cobbler bowls when the telephone rang. She picked up the phone, and on second thought didn't say anything because her usual answer at the office would have been, "O'Reilly Veterinarian's, Dr. Lori speaking." But the phone went dead. Puzzled, she hung up the phone and then picked it up. There was a dial tone, so they still had service.

"Lily, have you been having any trouble with your phone?"

"No, but—" the ringing of the phone interrupted. "Don't answer it," Lily demanded.

"But, it might be important," Lori replied and had turned away from the phone when it rang again, and Lily picked it up.

"Lily?" Hunter asked, puzzled that she hadn't even said "Hello," as usual.

"Hunter?" Lily questioned.

"Storm and I are at the carriage gates. But we left our

remote in the other car. Can you hear me?"

Lily smiled, as she looked at Lori and winked. "Yes. I can hear you now. One moment, please."

Lori spoke into the gate-speaker, "Please pull ahead. Blink your lights when you are clear, and I will close the gates."

Hunter blinked his lights, and Storm yelled, "We're clear."

"That was Stormy!" Lori said.

"On the gate speaker?" Lily wondered.

"Yes!"

The security light came on before Lori could turn off the security system inside. "Are the two of you looking for a handout as well as visiting with good news?" Lily questioned.

"Hey, did you call here a few minutes ago, not say anything and hang up?" Lori asked.

"Yes. Sorry. I accidently hit the wrong button on this cell phone," Storm replied.

"Well," Storm said, "we were so excited after leaving Dad's, but wanted to get both of you started right away, that we forgot to stop and get something to eat!"

"You two are in luck," Lori said, because Lily fixed more than enough of your favorite, Hunter." A millisecond later, while Lily heated the leftovers, Hunter, Storm and Lori set the table.

As they gathered around the kitchen table, Hunter's prayer ended with, "Thank you, Lord, for these cherished moments together in our new home, and for this food, Amen."

"Will had a meeting this afternoon with Doc, Granny, Buck, and Denver on how much time it would save on the ranch. As we were leaving," Hunter remarked, "the strangest thing, in a way, you know, was that Denver was the first one to mention your safety, Lori.'" Hunter winked at Lily when Lori turned her head. Nothing more was said when Lori's blush said it all.

"Finally, Lily responded. "Apparently our talk with Will must have made a difference. Especially for you, Sis. We all have been concerned about you being out at night, by yourself, and answering calls that take you all over the county."

"Are you both free tomorrow?" Lily said. "Lori and I have claimed tomorrow a 'holiday' and are planning to take the Turtle Crossing tunnel express to just get a feel for the business owners and maybe shop a little. Stop by and see Mom and Dad. No deadlines, you know."

"And practice on our new phones, just in case you get bored with our girlie stops," Lori added.

Storm and Hunter looked at each other and nodded in agreement. "Oh, we don't mind the girlie stuff," Hunter admitted. "Harmony has a birthday coming up soon anyhow."

The next morning, Lily was surprised when she woke up to the smell of coffee. *How nice,* she thought, as she showered and dressed for the day. She heard Lori's shower, but not the guys' and wondered how early they were used to getting up.

"Thanks for the coffee," Lily and Lori remarked.

"I'm not used to service like this," Lily commented.

"I am," Lori countered, "however this is so much different. It's like coming home, you know."

"Where do you want to eat breakfast?" Storm requested.

"If I park my car in Sadie's garage, we should at least stop by," Lily said.

"If you don't mind allowing me to drive your Lincoln," Hunter suggested.

Before Lily replied, Lily and Lori looked at each other and smiled.

"What?" Hunter questioned.

"Oh. Nothing," Lori admitted, "because even though you are the baby, you still like to take the reins as our protector."

Hunter and Storm just smiled.

"Did everyone put their phones on the charger all night?" Storm asked.

They were at Sadie's in five minutes, and were glad for the garage parking.

"Wow. What a crowd," Lily mentioned, as they entered Sadie's by the back door.

"Not to worry," Lori added. "Our table is on reserve for seven."

"Good Morning," Sadie greeted as they walked in the back door, with two minutes to spare.

"Good morning," the Foursome replied.

"The family special?" their waitress asked, as a pot of coffee, juice, and water arrived.

"Yes." Hunter nodded, having read the note that Lily had posted on their billboard. The only post since she had been living here by herself he noted. It had been their plan of sharing household responsibility when they had moved in.

"We can use Sadie's private entrance to the Tunnel. She doesn't have basement seating for her business, because it isn't open to the public," Lily added.

"Hunter, you know your way around better than we do," Lori said.

After they entered the Tunnel, Storm requested, "Hunter, is the Town Council still trying to buy her out because she doesn't have public access?"

"Turtle Crossing's public doesn't mind one bit." Hunter said. "It's one blowhard who wants to buy her out."

"This is our first visit to the Tunnel since we returned," Lily admitted. "I heard that it is easy to get turned around."

"That's another thing. Test our phones. Do you have any bars on your phone here in the tunnel?"

"No," was the combined reply.

"So, let's try Bixby's," Lily suggested. "Have you checked it out yet?"

"I am excited to see the owners again," Lori admitted. "If they're open."

"I hadn't thought about that," Lori said. "We could always run over to see Mom and Dad. You know the Seniors League will already be out."

"Do you want to ride through the Tunnel or walk?" Hunter asked.

"Ride! Maybe we could try nine holes this morning," Lily suggested.

Storm paid their tickets, and Hunter drove the electric golf cart advertising the Warren—Donnelly—Welby Country Golf Club.

"Hunter," Lori reminded, "there is a speed limit in here."

"Thanks, Sis," Hunter smiled.

"It's remarkable that the walls still have those golden lines of 'fool's gold' that sparkle here and there," Lily remarked, a feeling of disbelief and magic in her voice.

"We take so much for granted, don't we?" Lori added. "I'm looking forward to seeing the wedding chapel."

"Something we need to know?" Hunter asked, teasingly. "That must be the falls I am smelling."

"I believe you would be right," Storm chuckled. "The scent of fresh air. The outdoors and the wedding chapel, which is closed. No doubt they need security to be open. I've never arrived at the golf course by way of the Tunnel," Storm admitted. "How far is it to the golf course?"

"It's not far," Hunter replied. "But, we're not concerned about our time today."

As soon as they cleared the Tunnel, all four of them checked their cell phones, and Hunter immediately called their Dad. When he answered, they felt like kids with a new toy. "Put it on speaker phone, so we all can hear," Storm suggested.

"The girls and Storm are with me, Dad. We took the tunnel. Do you have time to visit, or do nine holes?"

David Donnelly knew there wouldn't be any problem getting them on the course for even eighteen. He knew his regulars would help him make it happen; and for the first time in his life, he asked, and players responded. But one of the guys suggested, "On one condition. We get to meet them as they go out."

"Well, here they are. May I introduce my nephew, Storm Fox; my son, Hunter Donnelly; and my daughters, Lily and Lori Donnelly."

The scheduled Foursome insisted on shaking their hands and the member golfers made a huge fuss about meeting some of the owner's family.

***

Shannon stepped out from the behind the counter and suggested, "If you don't mind sharing clubs, we have a couple of sets that have been donated for guests, so hope these come in handy. Girls, these are men's clubs, but still best for your height. Have fun."

But she didn't let them leave before giving them all a hug and said, "You have about thirty minutes before you can tee-off, so you can try out these clubs before you hit the course."

They lined up and started hitting a bucket of balls each. "All right," Lori asked, besides the stance, bend my knees, do a mini-squat, address the ball, and try to keep it in the fairway."

"I'm with Lori, but I forget the grip. We stood behind you, Hunter, and saw the way you brought the club back and swung forward and hit the ball square with the driver?"

Donovan was just leaving and was surprised that they grew up living on a golf course, but never played. But he couldn't take his eyes off Lily. And, wondered why they hadn't had private lessons, yet still weren't embarrassed to line-up in front of anyone on the practice range.

"Okay." Lori began, "maybe you guys should play. I'll just hit some balls on the practice range."

Then the first ball she hit only went about three feet. And Lily's didn't even go that far.

"No, Sis," Hunter replied. "We're playing together. You're on 'holiday', right?"

"Right. But maybe I can do better on the putting green," Lily suggested.

They pulled out their drivers and, with deepening concentration, hit their balls the distance of the practice range. "Now that was pretty good wasn't it?" Lily asked.

"You were both spectacular," Hunter admitted. "What were you aiming at?"

Both of them replied, "The trunk of that tallest tree."

Storm smiled. "Well. That's what you hit."

Lori and Lily both squealed. "Do we have time to hit a few with these irons?" Lori asked.

David and Shannon stood back and smiled. "I understand," David shared with Shannon, "that the four of them have discussed their plans with Will. That by taking the initiative, to be open and be seen by the public, perhaps someone will slip up and say something that could help with their search to find who highjacked Lily's office and business equipment. I almost laughed when they pretended to miss-hit like that with those new drivers."

"I know," Shannon reminisced, "It was frustrating at first when they weren't interested in playing on the high school team, but preferred volleyball instead. Maybe we'll be seeing more of them, after all," Shannon added.

One of the golfers standing by watching Lily and Lori yelled out, "Hey, Hunter. You gonna just stand by and let your ladies there beat you?"

Hunter didn't bother to turn around, but bit the inside of his mouth to keep from retaliating. Instead, he got into position and hit his driver better than he had in years. His ball hit that same tree. No one could have been more surprised than he was. He didn't need to be better than his sisters. But the one thing he did know: he wanted to see them find something they enjoyed doing besides work that they could do together as a family.

They never did go out on the course. They practiced chipping, hitting out of a sand trap, drove it out of the tee box, and excelled on the putting green. "We have used up our time," Lori said.

Lily was quick to respond. "I agree. We still have some shopping to take care of as well. Do you mind that you guys didn't get the chance to go out on the course today?"

"Another time," Storm added. "I've enjoyed watching the two of you acting like you didn't even know how to grip a golf club and proud that we're cousins."

"What do you think, Dad?" Lori asked.

"About what?" David frowned.

"About Lily and me at the golf course?"

"We love to see our children anytime, anywhere," Shannon replied.

"We may take more 'holidays' like today!" Lily added. They hugged and headed back to the tunnel entrance.

***

Shortly after the Foursome left, Dr. Dexter and his brother, Calvin, stopped by the club-house for something to drink after finishing the front nine. Calvin asked David, "We heard your professional daughters were out hitting a bucket of balls. How embarrassing for you, as one of the owners here." It was apparent Calvin's attitude echoed Dexters.

David asked, "Dr. Dexter, do you plan to finish the back nine?" David's demeanor was professional, but Dexter knew the Donnellys had a business to run. "Not today, sir. Here's the key for the cart."

"Aww, come on, Dex. I thought we were doing eighteen!"

"Not today." Dexter just hated to be bested by a woman. Especially the Donnelly women.

***

Once the Foursome returned to Turtle Crossing and window-shopped in several stores to help Hunter find something for Harmony's birthday, they decided to visit Alexa at the Welby Mansion B&B another time.

"How about steak and baked potatoes on the grill?" Hunter questioned.

"We'll need stuff for salad," Lily admitted. "I needed to go to the grocery anyhow."

As they started gathering what they needed at the grocery, Hunter remarked, "My apartment lease is up at the end of the month. I miss what we agreed to at the Victorian. Each of us would share expenses. Driving a few more miles to church and work and proving I can make it living on my own isn't all that important anymore."

"Grab hot dog buns. We can have hot dogs and potato salad for lunch, and the steak for our evening meal," Lily suggested. "I've been packing my lunch to save time at the office. And, I found this local farmer's garden stand carries veggies and fresh fruits. It's on our way home."

"Remember?" Storm said. "Live in the moment. Perhaps another time, we could invite Madison Grace, Harmony, Donovan and Denver."

***

For the past three days the twins had been on edge. The air around O'Reilly's Ranch felt like a storm was in the offing, but there wasn't even one tiny white cloud in the sky. The horses were even off their feed. The birds were in hiding. Denver stopped by Lori's office after he had paced up and down the hall so many times he had lost count. As had Lori. Troop had stuck to her like glue. Anytime she went to double-check something in her file cabinet, she had to step over him.

Denver finally knocked on her door. "Come in, Denver. Can I help you?"

"Were you planning to stop by the stables before you go home?"

"Lily and I were hoping to ride out to our favorite pasture and shaded pond."

"I'll see you there?"

"Sure. Give me time to change my boots. Lily should be pulling in the drive any minute."

Denver had no more than stepped inside the stables when Lily walked in. "Hey, Sis." Lily asked. "What's going on here? I parked inside the garage and waited until

Denver left your office. He looked a bit befuddled. You know, I haven't seen that perpetual frown he had when he first arrived for quite a while. It appeared he was looking or listening for something."

"You would be right on with that appraisal," Lori agreed as she locked up her office and joined Lily on their short walk to the stables. Before they arrived, they stopped and listened to Denver playing "Home, Home on the Range" on his harmonica.

"Thanks for playing songs that sound like some of the Old West black and white movies our grandpa Charlie likes to watch," Lily commented.

"Thank you, Ma'am. But, come on. I'm not that old," he added as they joined him, taking their time walking down the aisle past horses that normally would be at the stall entrance expecting and sometimes getting a favorite piece of carrot or apple, but instead were acting a bit stir-crazy.

"That's for certain," Lori agreed. "The only good part of this right now is that Buck has made certain that all his wranglers are expected to have their cell phones on them at all times."

"Earlier in the week, I heard on the news that a mountain lion had been spotted, but the person who reported it has never seen one except in a zoo," Lily added. "When I asked Doc about having his annual BBQ, he said he trusts his men and Will's, and if need be, there are sharpshooters who are trustworthy he can call."

"Denver?" Lori asked. "Have you seen any strangers or animals that appear to be out of their element?"

"No," he replied. "You're asking me if I or someone else is assuming someone or something is not what they appear to be because we're looking past the ordinary. Are you referring to me?"

"Absolutely not. Why would you think that?"

"Well, I don't have a college degree for number one."

"Denver, you were born with a talent that you have honed. You also have worked in this field for several years. I worked with a well-known farrier for weeks and I still didn't master shoeing."

"I'll see you in a bit," Lori informed Denver.

"Lori," Lily asked when she joined her. "Hunter and Storm were motioning frantically. They went up to the training room and found Madison Grace and Harmony waiting inside, looking a bit frazzled."

"What a nice surprise to see the two of you here." Lily greeted as she looked them over with a bit of frustration in her voice. "Where have you been? You have mud spattered all over your jeans and boots."

"We took Misty and Sandy out for a short ride. You said we should learn the terrain and not go far. I had the binoculars, and Harmony had her compass."

"But when Madison spotted someone on Invisible Ridge," Harmony added. "We dismounted and walked our horses back to the stable."

"Unless Will or Doc recently signed on Henry Carpenter's nephew who goes by Sarge is the same one who was target and fast-draw practicing a week ago. He has been bragging that he is going to be a famous western movie star."

"Did he see you?" Lori asked.

"I don't think so," Madison replied, "we were late because we dismounted and followed the river back."

"No wonder Storm and Hunter were upset," Lily said. "Where are they anyhow?"

"Sorry, ladies," Storm began.

"My apologies as well," Hunter sheepishly agreed.

"First of all," Lori stated. "We are glad you are both safe. However, they were already organizing a search party when you came trudging up the hill behind the horse stables."

"Now, are you certain that's who you saw?"

Harmony and Madison Grace sat down on a bale of straw drinking water as the facts started sinking in, but they kept their emotions under control.

"What time was that," Denver asked gently.

"Three-ten," Madison said.

"But that's within a half hour, give or take a few," Storm began.

"One of these days…" Hunter turned around, and the possibilities set his teeth on edge.

"I know," Lori remarked. "When we were looking for the girls, someone was robbing the bunkhouse."

"Sorry, ladies," Hunter clarified, "a few moments later, we found Buck fuming because whenever Doc hosts a big shindig, he expects it to be neat and tidy. Buck had just finished mopping the floor when he heard unusual foot-steps, but when he called out a fake name, they skedad-dled. That snoop was wearing brand new western boots with unusual tread, stamped with a number or letter in the dusty footprint."

Lily and Lori clasped hands momentarily and suggested, "Hunter, you and Storm share our uneasy feelings, so please allow the ladies to shower and change out of their muddy clothes and please, keep in touch."

"Hey, Sis," Lily said, "Donovan is wanting my attention. Are you going to be with Denver?"

Lori nodded and put her hand on Denver's arm, "Do you need some help cleaning up those two muddy critters?" They led Misty and Sandy inside, collecting special cloths and sponges to clean up the horses, as they went.

"This doesn't make any sense," Denver said. "What are we missing here?"

Lori ran through her mind all the things that could result in such strange behavior and commented, "Misty and Sandy are as calm as they were before their ride!"

Then Lori went into action, and demanded, "We need to bag up all their feed immediately and replace it with today's fresh delivery. Just to be on the safe side, change their water into clean buckets, as well."

"And keep this quiet?" Denver ask. "This includes bronc?"

"Yes! We'll have their feed tested. I'll check with Doc," Lori added, as they frantically removed their feed, bagged and tagged it for testing.

***

"What has you so upset, Donovan?" Lily asked.

"I can't believe it," Donovan stormed. "You know how Buck has always encouraged me to change at the bunkhouse? Well, guess what? After helping unload tables and chairs for Doc's big party, I went to change and someone had stolen my brand new western boots, western shirt and jacket I just bought at Bixby's today."

"I just heard that someone not only tore into most of the wranglers' trunks, but lifted the mattresses as well," Lily said. "What a loss. Where had you put your clothes?"

"In Buck's office," Donovan replied. "Oh, hey. Have you heard from Harmony and Madison Grace?"

"They just returned. They were delayed, but they're okay."

"Lily, what has you so upset?" Donovan asked. "I haven't seen you this upset since the day we found your missing office equipment."

"How can you tell?" Lily asked as she led him to a shade tree where they sat down on a nearby bench behind Doc and Granny's kitchen porch.

"I have been watching you for some time, and you have a habit of cupping your left hand, running your thumb across your finger-tips like you are trying to gather your thoughts in some sort of order. In the meantime, you are aware of your surroundings; and it appears there are two little questions that are driving you to distraction."

"And those two questions are?" Lily asked, a bit affronted.

"'What if,' and 'what am I missing?'"

"Thank you. Thank you. Thank you, Donovan." Lily jumped up, her face and eyes lighting up as though some-one had just handed her a fantastic gift. "Love you." She added, as she stood in front of him and leaned down and kissed him so close to his mouth that he was awe-struck. "I will see you. I have to find Lori."

***

"Looking for me?" Lori asked.

"Yes." Lily replied. "The Lookout?"

Lily and Lori walked calmly behind Doc's garage, unlocked it, slipped inside, and relocked it. Lily grabbed her binoculars from their Foursome practice room, and Lori pulled down the attic stairs. Once they were up the stairs, they pulled them back up.

"We may have to go out on the roof-rail," Lori suggested. "Tell me what you are seeing."

Lily agreed. "We are looking for proof that someone rode partway, and then blended in with everyone here and around the immediate ranch buildings. I have adjusted the focus, and now I want you to look through this lens. There is something I have lined up with the peak of the bunkhouse. Tell me what you see."

"Okay," Lori agreed. "Are you certain you don't have to readjust it some more? Wait. You said the peak. When I gently raise it to the distant skyline, is that a tent?"

"Now slowly scan to the right," Lily suggested, "Are there one or two horses tied up in the shade? Is that your phone vibrating?"

"It's Will. Three words: *Where are you?*"

"We better answer him," Lori said. "I'll keep my eyeballs stuck right here."

Lily clicked yes on his next question: *The Tower?*

"Remember the first time we were there with Granny and confiscated Granny's Old Gray Mare and the mare knew where that spring was, so Doc named it the Old Gray Mare Spring. Will is here with Storm and Hunter."

273

"Darn. There goes our secret hideout," Lori added. The attic had never felt this crowded, until the guys showed up. "Pull up the stairs, guys."

"All right, girls," Will asked, "what have you found?"

"Are you aware of where the Old Gray Mare Spring is?" Lily questioned.

"I have heard that story so many times," Hunter added. "The first time Mom and Granny lost my big sisters, right?"

"Let me see what you've found," Will asked.

"Lily located it," Lori directed. "You won't have to adjust it, just line it up with the top peak of the bunkhouse."

"Storm, get out my most recent binoculars. All right, Lily, try this. Your eyes are better than mine," Will remarked.

"Wow," Lily exclaimed. "I think I could read their lips. One guy looks like Madison described today, but I don't recognize the other guy. Lori, you are better at that than I am. Look!"

"Double wow," Lori exclaimed. "Can we get a picture with this? Hunter, Storm. You both have to look through this, and we'll need to check out the landscape. Is this the reason Doc had windows put in his attic?"

"Did you contact Aunt Brandi?" Lori questioned. "I knew if the two of you had a bee in your bonnet, especially after what Lori discovered in the stables, your Aunt Brandi would have had my license," Will added.

"Brandi and Doc are on their way," Will announced.

"Doc," Lori encouraged, "You need to see this."

"All right, Aunt Brandi," Lily suggested, "to save time, line the shot up with the top peak on the bunkhouse, then slowly and gently raise it up."

"I never thought I would need anything like this," Brandi commented, then added, "Will, order me one of these, pronto. Doc, this is posted as private property, which means they also cannot camp or hunt here without the owner's permission."

"There will be a lot of people here this weekend. I can't take a chance that someone might get hurt. I want them arrested."

But by the time Buck arrived, they were gone. "Other than a smoking campfire and the backsides of three horses, what am I supposed to be looking at?" Buck asked.

Chapter 15

While Will scanned the surrounding area beyond the trespassers' tent, they had folded up the tent and left behind a swirl of dust from the Rover, the memory of a very distinctive hat and frustration that someone had slipped through the protective net he, Buck, and Doc had programed for the entire ranch.

As they left their observation spot, Doc asked Will, "It appears someone knows our schedule well enough to be several steps ahead of us. Any ideas?"

"Ideas? I have some questions for Buck," Donovan inquired. "When did you replace the tires on Doc's Rover?"

"About two weeks ago. Why?"

"Well, I'm not a mechanic by trade; but when I went to start it, the gas tank was empty, the spark plugs are loose, and the tires are bald."

"Thanks for bringing this to our attention," Buck replied.

"We need your help," Will added.

***

The following morning the Carriage House was as busy as a beehive. The first group to arrive was the Shadow Angels and business owners for an emergency meeting. The Four Aces and friends helped arrange the photos and directed guests to the Carriage House.

Will took charge and announced, "The kitchen counters and these two banquet tables are covered with photos on file from numerous businesses and offices, numbered from one to one-hundred, collected over the past decade, and some as recent as yesterday."

"There may be duplicates, perhaps taken in different locations. The majority were taken in the Turtle Crossing area, but don't let that question your identification."

"The locations are alphabetized. The O'Reilly Ranch has been dealing with poisoned feed for their stabled horses, mechanical equipment stolen, attempts to unlock stock gates, fence cuttings, and the O'Reilly Ranch bunkhouse was broken into, ransacked and wranglers' personal items were stolen. However, this wasn't the only area caught on security cameras."

"We would appreciate your name and phone number in case we have further questions. Lt. Brandi Carpenter and Officer Jace Carpentier from Sunrise has offered support for the Annual BBQ at the O'Reilly Ranch and are just a phone call away. We will be adding additional security as needed."

What Will did not announce was that Madison Grace and Harmony Faith would be guests at the Victorian, not

277

only for their safety, but because Granny didn't have any guests at the Cradle of Flowers shelter anyhow.

It hadn't taken long for the parents of Pied Pipers, Harvey and Bart, to legally adopt Little Missy and Baby Blue when the boys' mom presented a photo of her sister's children with Harvey and Bart in a photo she had taken a few weeks earlier. They were family.

Little Miss Sunshine, who Harvey and Bart had rescued after the tornado, was in a loving licensed foster care private home.

Two hours later, Will, Lt. Brandi, Jonothan, Jace, and residents of the Victorian finished sorting through the results of the photo questionnaire. "What or who are we missing?" Lori questioned.

"Denver?" Lily asked. "You have a comment you want to add?"

"Yes. When I was working the rodeo circuit for a few years, I realized I was good at recognizing and recalling names and faces."

"What are you not saying, Denver?" Lori requested, just after eye contact with Lily.

"Are you suggesting one or more of these men are regulars at rodeos and the race track?"

Denver nodded, "They're trouble."

"Why here and why now?" Doc asked.

"Is it tied to Eight Mile Centre?" Lily asked.

"We're still looking for a connection," Doc replied.

***

Meanwhile, the Shadow Angels worked in teams as they got reacquainted with Granny's Estate and the layout of the immediate grounds. A segment of her barn had been converted into a garage where two of their cars were parked.

Anyone observing them would assume she was showing how the recently erected fence and gated segment had been added to protect children that were at times "in-residence."

What was unusual was the children's blackboard and corkboard in the playroom. They were now covered with maps of Granny's Estate, Doc O'Reilly's Ranch, and the kennel where retired German shepherd, Rosie III, was training one of her own pups for the canine corps.

This included the Shadow Angels who were most excited about a crash course on how to keep in touch with their new cell phones. They were used to working in silence, night or day, as were Will's men in blue and Buck's wranglers. However, they all could feel how this new connection would save them a lot of time, including provide a measure of safety.

Their first night was quite a surprise for one of Will's men in blue who had skipped the first day's training. Therefore, Wendy and Marcie caught and held one of them because he didn't know that day's password. He was embarrassed and shocked, especially before he could warn his buddy who was in handcuffs by two seventy-two year old women, Willi and Opal.

Granny had promised Opal and Willi to expect her just at twilight and that she would ride the fence line from Doc's, straight into her estate driveway. Buck knew she was planning to ride out but was surprised when Will practically flew out of his mobile headquarters with his wife Wendy. Buck joined them.

When they walked in Granny's kitchen door, it was all they could do to keep from laughing. "Which one of you lost the bet?" Will demanded.

"We both did," Jeremy replied.

"To Storm!" The other added.

"You also missed a meeting," Buck guessed, "just like a couple of my men. It appears Granny lassoed two of my men and made them walk back to the bunkhouse, where she had written the day's password on the chalkboard and softly stated, "Memorize it," and quickly erased it.

"Lives may be at stake here. Okay?" Buck remarked, demanding their attention. "Everything you do reflects not only on each of the people here, but your own life, too. Please. Get it together. Where are your manners? Are your apologies still in your hip pocket?" Buck asked.

The men had never heard or seen their boss in tears of disappointment and anger.

"Granny, Ladies, I deeply apologize," which was echoed by Buck's and Will's men.

"Tonight's happening is not to be repeated," Will demanded. "Granny, are you spending the night here?" When she nodded, he continued, "Men, come with me."

Will looked them over and said, "Line up in front of this map and the blackboard." Granny wrote the day's password, and another one for after midnight. When they turned around, they faced the Shadow Angels dressed all-in-black. As they moved out of their way, they bowed. The passwords disappeared.

"Back to work, men," Buck ordered.

Will looked at Buck and suggested, "Out of curiosity, instead of taking the highway, why don't we cross the road and take a short-cut instead?" But he stopped in the night shadows of Granny's huge oak tree and stared in amazement when they spotted two vehicles parked side by side with just their parking lights on, engines running, and facing opposite directions. However, they were too far away to hear what the occupants were saying.

Will motioned for Buck to take the reins of Granny's horse, as Will turned away and sent messages to Granny, Marcie, Doc, Brandi, and the team that was on duty at Granny's Estate and Doc's Ranch.

Denver was the first to reply when Granny asked, "Where are you?

"Denver, here. I am about twenty feet from Ginger's Corner-post on the home side which marks the property line between Doc's and Ginger's farm.

"Granny's front drive," Will answered. "The Oak across from Ginger's Corner-post."

"Gotcha," Buck whispered. "Is the Sheriff waiting for backup?"

"Probably," Will replied. "But they are parked right beside two of the twenty-four *No Trespassing* signs Doc posted this week. Well, here comes the posse!"

Will immediately sent out another message, "Stand Down."

They had almost walked into trouble and quickly realized they were not prepared to drive or even walk through a seldom used knee-high grass thoroughfare between

Doc's and Ginger's this evening without backup.

The Turtle Crossing Sheriff's deputy pulled out after making note of their drivers' licenses, proof of ownership of the vehicles, a search of their vehicles, and sent them on their way with a warning. "This is private property! And I am certain you noticed two three-foot *No Trespassing* signs right beside you. The next time you will be issued a ticket, a two-hundred dollar fine, and possible jail time."

She backed into Granny's driveway and waited until they left, headed north. Before Brandi left Granny's driveway, she motioned Will over to her vehicle and said, "I will let you know if anything shows up about these men. They appear to be on the up and up; however, I am pretty certain we have fingerprints on two of them from that Sunday interruption at Lily's building at Eight Mile Centre. I also didn't want them to know we now know who they are, but I'm not buying that their reason is to purchase Ginger's property. It might be interesting to know why they think it's for sale. Doc will not be happy about this. He purchased those forty acres after Ginger's husband died because she had spent all their savings on his care. She needed money to live on and pays Doc a token amount for rent."

"Thanks," Will added. "We will be in touch."

After she pulled out towards Turtle Crossing, Will and Buck walked across the road and noted that this was not the first time vehicles had not only parked here, but had driven farther because even in the moonlight, they could see where the ground had been disturbed with footprints and vehicles.

"I can't believe they were this close to Doc and Granny's house," Will remarked.

"What am I smelling?" Buck asked.

"Cigar butts," Denver remarked, as he spotlighted several along the fence row.

"The same brand we found at the driving range." Buck said.

"I'll walk with you; but, first, stop and turn around. I am questioning if they are unaware that not only is this Doc's land, but straight across from Granny's lane. Just in case you are wondering what I am doing out here this evening, I heard something out beyond Doc's willow tree. It was just a cat, but the lights from one of those cars was actually the swoop of a spotlight. So I decided to track along the inside of the fence-row. Hey, they couldn't see me with all this growth in the fence," Denver added.

"That explains why you just happen to be carrying a rifle?" Buck asked.

"Yes, Sir," Denver replied.

"You are lucky none of my men knew about this," Buck warned.

"They know where I am. I didn't want to take any chances."

"Did you ever get close enough to hear the men who were parked here?" Will asked.

"No. They played music too loud on the radio, then would talk."

"What are you scanning the ground with your flashlight for?" Buck questioned.

"Something fell out of one of the cars when they

opened and quickly closed the door. All I found is a colorful cigar band, a cellophane wrapper, and stench of a cigar butt. Have you seen anything on your side?"

"No," Buck replied. "We've been a little busy although I just phoned the bunkhouse and asked a couple of the wranglers to keep watch out here the rest of the night."

"Buck is right. This includes all of us," Will remarked. "Be on the alert; and unless someone's life is at stake, Brandi is asking us not to intervene."

"But, if the need arises…" Denver left his unspoken thoughts dangle in their minds. "Are we still on for a meeting at five a.m. at Granny's Estate?"

Will nodded and Denver tipped his hat at the wranglers as he left to get a few hours of shut-eye.

***

At breakfast, the conversation was heated when Will filled Doc and Granny in on the rest of what had happened the previous evening. "We are pushing Denver here because he has plans to help get Lori and Lily away for a day or two."

"You know once we fill up parking space in the field behind my barn for our annual BBQ," Doc commented, "Granny and I thought her place would be ideal for parking the overflow."

"You know," Denver hesitated to comment, but continued, "after what we found last night, it might be a good idea to park the pickup trucks in the field at Ginger's Corner post before parking at Granny's."

"We'll take a look at that in the daylight," Doc agreed, "after we check out Granny's barn."

The moment they stepped inside the barn, Denver remarked. "This is quite the surprise, Doc. When did you start smoking cigars again?"

"That's the same thing that got our attention last night, too," Will said. "Who in their right mind smokes in a barn?"

"Hey!" Storm announced. "Look what we found stored in these bins. Where did this stuff come from? You planning something, Doc?"

"Saws, ropes, belts!" Doc's face was steaming. "Granny's woods. Someone plans to make a fortune cutting down trees her daddy and granddaddy planted and nurtured, all native oak, walnut, cherry, and hickory."

"Since the reunion, Madison and Harmony have stayed overnight a couple of nights a week and parked in Granny's garage. Otherwise, it's been empty. However, with the Shadow Angels staying here, at least no one else can move forward with their plans for now," Doc added.

"This barn was built with timber they cleared for their homestead," Granny commented. "So, has my barn been used as their headquarters? Henry used to brag that someday he would own my entire estate. But just because he is gone now, it doesn't mean he didn't sell the idea to someone else."

Granny needed to do some research on her own and thought, Henry. She had let her guard down regarding him before. I need to find out who inherited or bought his motel.

Once outside, after Will had left a few state of the art listening devices, he suggested, "Hunter, Storm, Denver, aren't you scheduled to pick up your ladies for your outing today?"

"Yes, Dad. But are you certain you want us to leave? Lily, Lori, Donovan and the three of us will all be leaving."

"You've all got cell phones now. We'll keep in touch," Will replied.

"What about Jonothan?" Hunter asked as he swept his hands towards the back yard and tapped at Will's clipboard. "It gives me the willies. After we beamed in on those guys that were camping at the Old Gray Mare Spring recently, someone could just as easily be watching us."

"As soon as we return to my office, I'll call Marcie," Doc said, "because she is the best when she has a camera in her hands. Especially when Jonothan does the flyovers."

***

Madison and Harmony could have slept in the Victorian master bedroom, but during a tour of the Victorian chose to sleep on the top floor. "I never thought I'd sleep in a fancy attic," Harmony said as they were unpacking their luggage.

"Me neither," Harmony replied. "I am looking forward to seeing the GreatStone Castle in Sidney tomorrow. I have always thought of castles in Europe, not here in Ohio. I suppose we should get some sleep. We have to get up really early."

***

As planned, Denver, Hunter and Storm picked up Donovan in one of Granny's cars and drove to the

Victorian to meet Lily, Lori, Madison Grace and Harmony Faith at six-twenty a.m. and parked Granny's vehicle in the first garage near the Carriage House.

"It's not going to be easy," Hunter said. "Our ladies are not to know about what happened last night and this morning."

"Thanks for filling me in," Donovan nodded in understanding, "but that is a very tall order."

As they loaded up, Lily announced, "Lori and I drew straws. I am driving our Uncle Charlie and Aunt Sara-Beth's Long Van Road-Trek Overnighter to Sidney, and Lori will be driving it back."

Hunter didn't comment, but smiled when he spotted his Mom and Dad's new Lincoln.

"Where are you going, Storm?" Madison asked.

"To get Hunter's and my overnight bags."

"No need," Harmony commented, as she offered the bags to Storm.

"Knowing how my sisters plan things, I'm not surprised. Thank you, ladies."

Hunter announced, "We are ready to depart," as he and Storm scanned the Victorian grounds.

"It's okay," Madison said "Harmony and I have become amazing bird watchers."

"I'm not a bit surprised," Hunter nodded and smiled at Harmony.

"Denver," Lori said. "We're taking a different route than usual, just so you, can see the historic cabin your ancestors built on the O'Reilly Ranch in the early 1900s."

"It really doesn't look like much," Denver said. "Wait

a minute. I recognize that guy I just saw standing by my Great-Great-Grandpa's cabin," Denver said.

"I'm calling Doc," Lily announced, as she made eye contact with Lori. They felt it. They really were back in force.

"We'll take care of it, partner," Doc replied. "Thanks. Will is on the phone, as we speak, with our favorite pilot. You all enjoy your day now, okay?"

Denver was amazed at the animation in Lori's voice and the sparkle in her eyes. He smiled. "May I assume that your shorthand conversation makes sense to you and Lily, but I don't have a clue what just happened in that communication," he teased. Then he remembered what Donovan had suggested. *Be patient. Don't assume. Remember, trust is a two way street, to be earned, not granted.*

Thirty minutes later, the Foursome and their friends met for breakfast at Aunt Tressie's new country home which, like her, was gracious and homey. The exterior and interior were comfortable blends of old and new.

"Welcome, welcome, welcome," she greeted. Her floral, pastel kaftan drifted around her ankles as she hugged Hunter and the ladies and shook hands with Storm. "Hunter, you look more like your Uncle Sheldon every time I see you. You must know, Miss Bea called me and suggested we meet. After you fill your plates, you can ask away. If your coffee pump thermos needs refilling, we can take care of that, too."

"Is there any legal way Henry could take Granny's historical estate away from her?" Lori asked.

"NO," Tressie replied. "I asked Bea that same question

this morning. As you may know or not know, Bea grew up in Turtle Crossing County. Granny's parents' estate was the first property deeded in the county. Her family's cabin was built uphill from the Turtle Crossing River. And Doc's cabin had earlier been a well-known shelter stop for the Plains Native American Indians because of the natural spring nearby. A tributary of the Turtle Crossing River meanders through his ranch and Granny's Estate."

"I don't recall seeing a spring," Denver commented.

"Oh, yes," Lori added. "I'll have to show you sometime."

"I look forward to it." When he smiled and winked at her, Lori turned away towards the window to hide her blush.

"So," Donovan questioned. "What is it Jonothan can do to help?"

"Donovan," Aunt Tressie asked, "have you looked at the aerial view of Doc's ranch and Granny's estate?"

"I never studied them. Why?"

"Imagine how much more they can see with binoculars," Lily suggested.

"And if they do a flyover at Doc's and Granny's," Harmony pointed out, "then they can compare new film with what they took after the tornado went through."

"Thank you, Harmony," Lori praised. "I was so busy on the phone and with the animals, I totally missed that."

Madison requested, "Aunt Tressie, how are you and Little Miss Sunshine getting along?"

"I think she heard your voices," Tressie remarked.

"May we go get her?"

"Of course."

"Hello there, Little Miss Sunshine," Harmony crooned. "We know you didn't just fall from the sky."

"You know," Donovan commented, "one of Isaac's patients from Sunrise filed a missing person's report with the Sunrise police regarding her sister. The story is that her sister had called weeks ago, all excited about a surprise and sent her an envelope marked *Do not open until your birthday*. Her birthday was the day of the tornado and the envelope and that day's newspaper ended up in her junk mail basket. When she found it, she started making phone calls. She said it was like her sister and her husband just disappeared. Her comment was, 'People do not just disappear.'"

"Aunt Tressie," Lily questioned, "have you taken any photos of the baby?"

"Yes. Do you want to see them?"

"Yes," Lori and Lily agreed.

"I believe it's time to phone Aunt Brandi."

"Okay," Lori suggested, "and I'll call Aunt Marcie." Lily and Lori continued taking notes.

Donovan and Denver looked at each other and then at Lily and Lori and shrugged their shoulders in acceptance.

"We'll see what we can find out and will stop by, on our way home, Aunt Tressie," Lori added as she embraced her favorite great aunt.

Harmony handed the baby to Hunter and waved bye to her. Each of the men thanked Tressie for the breakfast and the visit.

"You need anything, though, you'll call right?" Hunter

suggested as he hugged the baby and handed her back to Tressie.

As soon as they drove out of Tressie's driveway, Hunter recalled, "The day before the tornado, Rev. C. W. was expecting a couple who had called and asked if he could marry them after the Sunday morning service."

"Did they show?" Storm asked.

"I don't know. But it would make sense to find out."

"I'll say what you two are thinking," Madison remarked. "Little Miss Sunshine might not be an orphan after all."

Storm clasped her hand in his and suggested, "I know you want to start making phone calls right away, but C.W. will not discuss something like this on the phone if at all. Am I right, Hunter?"

"Well," Harmony glanced in the rearview mirror at Madison. "There was a time when Lily and Lori would have jumped ahead immediately to get the answers, but Lori mentioned something to me in the office this past week about people's privacy and all that stuff."

"Thanks," Harmony added. "As I was saying the words, I started questioning myself."

"Hey, ladies. This is our day to relax," Hunter announced. "And, enjoy our visit to GreatStone Castle."

"Wow!" Madison exclaimed. "It is so beautiful! It's a real castle!"

"And like Lori mentioned," Harmony added. "It really does set on top of a mountain in Sidney. It is also the county seat of Shelby County."

When they drove around to the front, Madison was

overwhelmed, "Oh, wow! Look at the traffic down below. In my mind, I pictured it in the countryside."

"I know we're here for little Allie's birthday party and her mom Sarah's wedding engagement," Madison said.

"Yes," Harmony added, "they were at Granny's Cradle of Flowers shelter for a few weeks until she found a job and an apartment. Now here they are, for a fancy party. Nice."

As they gathered in the parking area, Lily remarked, "Donovan is going to find out where we should wait since we're a bit early."

"They suggested we can walk on the grounds or wait on the front porch," Donovan announced.

"Lori, did you say they have garden weddings here as well?" Madison asked.

"They do," Lori replied. "We can walk that way."

"Great. I want to savor every moment," Harmony said as she and Hunter followed Madison and Storm.

Denver tugged on Lori's arm. "Hey, beautiful. You have been pretty quiet this morning," he whispered, as he brushed her hair back from her face. "Don't worry, they will call us if they get in a tight spot. Furthermore, you haven't taken a day off since you arrived at Doc's," he added, as he kissed her on the cheek.

"Is that an order from Doc?" she asked.

"Not an order, sweetheart, just a suggestion," he added with a smile.

"You make it easy," Lori agreed, her eyes soft with a certain smile she had reserved just for him. "This is all so new to me."

"We're learning together," Denver commented and thought, *On a sweet, summer day with Lori, I really can see a possible future.*

They gathered on the front porch and entered the GreatStone Castle. Lily turned to speak to Donovan, "I didn't notice the details in these Gold Walls the last time we were here. And the Sitting Room is so warm, cozy and more relaxing than the Parlor."

"You're right," Donovan said. "The Parlor is more dignified, like your Pease Victorian, with its antiques."

"We totally agree with you, Sis," Hunter added as they turned towards the Reception/Staircase Hall.

Harmony nodded towards the birthday girl, Allie, who was standing in front of the eight-foot mirror like a scene from *Alice in Wonderland.* Her mom, Sarah, stood nearby smiling.

Madison turned to Storm and smiled. "They look so different."

"Remember? Happiness and lack of fear can do that," Lily commented softly.

Donovan heard the pain in her voice and Denver didn't miss Lori's momentary sad expression, but just as quickly they smiled and applauded Sarah and Donovan's friend, Andrew, as they joined Allie in a photo pose together.

As their hostess commented on the brilliant red carpet on the stairs, Lori recalled, "We were just leaving here a month or so ago while a bridal party was running through their last practice."

Denver squeezed Lori's hand and whispered, "I bet

you and Lily have dreamt of your wedding day since you were little girls."

Denver's comment was left to dissipate like shadows of sunlight through the branches.

Donovan had pictured Lily by his side several years ago, but she had been as skittish as a horse facing a rattler.

The ten-foot oval table was gaily decorated with colorful cupcakes and miniature pink roses for Allie's third birthday and was well lit by the sparkling crystal chandelier in the centuries old Castle Dining Room.

The waitress was dressed up like Raggedy Ann because Allie had felt safe sleeping with the Raggedy Ann cloth doll Granny had given her the day Sarah and Allie had arrived at C.W.'s church and Granny's Cradle of Flowers Safe House.

After they ate soup, sandwiches, ice cream, and cupcakes, Sarah suggested, "Allie, how about we sing Happy Birthday while you blow out your candles, then we'll go outside on the porch so you can open your gifts."

"I make a wish?" Allie asked.

"Of course," the waitress replied as she lit the candles. Allie blew them out immediately and waited until everyone finished singing.

"What was your wish?" Madison questioned.

"That I would have a daddy to love me and mommy. So I asked Mr. Andy to be my daddy."

"And I said yes," Andrew replied as he gave her a kiss on the cheek.

"And I said yes, when Mr. Andy asked me to marry him," Sarah added.

As the waitress boxed up the extra cupcakes and decorations, Andrew asked Donovan, "Can you clear your calendar and be my best man in about six months?"

"Sure," Donovan replied. "Have you already set the date?"

"Not yet," he replied as they continued towards the front entrance.

"Donovan," Lily said, "If you're going to visit with Andrew, the hostess suggested she could finish the tour on the second floor."

"Of course," he replied, uncertain what was on her mind, as the ladies followed their hostess up the Grand Staircase.

"The history in these rooms takes one back in time but with today's amenities," Harmony commented.

"And with a foot stool to climb into this ornate bed," Madison added.

"Oh, what a view," Lily commented as Lori joined her at the window.

"What was that phone call about?"

"Will wants us to think about staying away for another night."

"He didn't say why?"

"No." Lily replied. "I think we all need to talk about the phone call I just received from Will." All eight of them pulled up chairs on the northwest corner of the GreatStone Castle front porch, and Lily repeated Will's request.

Looking around their group, Lori smiled and suggested, "I think our Foursome just became the Double

Foursome. Who is interested in pooling all the pieces of information each of us has and mix it with suggestive possibilities? We can title it our First Research and Rescue. We find and prove that Little Miss Sunshine is not an orphan."

"A nod of approval would be sufficient!" Lily added. "Hunter, would you or Storm like to call Will? Find out where he needs us to stay and—"

"And, stay away from. We'll keep in touch."

"So," Hunter asked, "neither of you is comfortable being this far from home with all that has been happening either, are you?"

The twins replied, "No."

"What do you have in mind?" Storm asked, as he looked right and left, including each of the Double Foursome.

Chapter 16

The Double Foursome had parked their vehicles at a turnout along the old Sunrise/Turtle Crossing Road, which had been re-routed to a two-lane bridge, spanning the Turtle Crossing River. This no-outlet county road still curved along the river and bypassed the covered bridge at Oates Park, which had been deeded back to the Oates Family Estate.

"We need more solid information," Lily suggested.

"I feel it too," Lori agreed, then turned to Hunter and Storm who nodded their agreement.

"Harmony?" Lily asked. "What do we have on the what-we-know list?"

"The police report of a woman who called to report her sister missing. Her sister had called the day of the tornado and said she had exciting news, to expect her that afternoon as soon as they replaced a tire on their car."

"Of course," Lori added, "the police can't share any names."

"A tire?" Donovan questioned. "Denver and I noticed an auto-sized tire covered in debris, plastered against the raised railroad bed."

"It wasn't too far from where you found a lady's purse," Denver remarked.

"The Pied Piper brothers said," Harmony noted, "they found the baby before they arrived at Granny's covered bridge where they spent their first night after the tornado. We've scanned a hundred-foot area around the river and the bridge."

"I took a photo of the tire," Donovan added because it appeared to have rolled into the railroad bed. "The rim is still on the tire."

"These metal detectors have latched onto quite an interesting collection," Storm commented. "We have a wedding band, a diamond engagement ring, a necklace, two watches, three pocket knives, numerous patterns of fancy silverware, a bag of coins, newer looking lug nuts and empty gun shells."

Suddenly Storm's voice changed, "I suggest, ladies and gentlemen, that we continue looking at our maps and motioned towards Sunrise because we are picking up danger signals."

"Ditto," Madison confirmed Storm's suggestion. "I caught unusual reflections west of here. My binoculars look more like a camera."

They quickly stashed their papers in the bags hanging from their waists and loaded up in the vehicles they had parked in the shade.

"C.W. just returned my call," Hunter explained as

they pulled out onto the highway. "He is at his office in Eight Mile Centre and suggested we park behind the church. He will let us in the back door."

After they shared the outline of their search and rescue plans, Rev. C. W. smiled at their enthusiasm and determination, and wrote down the names of two couples he had married that weekend. Then, added, "Here are the keys to two of my vintage vehicles, with new engines that are needing some mileage on them."

***

"I contacted Will after your call, C.W., and he agreed. Apparently someone called the local news that a bunch of college students were spotted with metal detectors, searching the field where the tornado went through outside of Sunrise."

The four couples had left the church with their metal detectors in hand. C.W. added the names of the two couples he had recently married, in Hunter's envelope. However, C.W. also included an invitation for premarital counseling in the envelopes for Lily and Donovan, and Lori and Denver.

Lori drove to C.W.'s farm/estate and Hunter drove the other vehicle. "I've never been on this route before," Denver said, looking left and right.

"Well, these two curves were straightened on the new four-lane which made Uncle Henry really upset because the new route shut off immediate access to his motel," Storm stated.

"It looks like he's doing well right now," Denver remarked. "The 'No Vacancies' sign is lit up."

Lily's phone rang. "That was an interesting group of vehicles at Henry's motel we just passed," Harmony reported, "two of the six are out-of-state. We only got two partial plates because they were covered with mud, while two others, looked like they were covered with a sign. The others were squeaky clean. Perhaps rentals."

"Thanks," Lily replied.

From the time we were children, Great Uncle C.W.'s home has always been my favorite place to visit," Hunter stated. "We'll have to bring you back here when we have more time," he said as they drove back C.W.'s long lane and parked behind his house.

"Yes," Lori added, her voice stilted, remembering a childhood abduction.

"Just follow our lead," Lily said as she unlocked C.W.'s back door and turned on a few lights. "His directions are: Help yourselves to his roaster of lasagna and loaf of home-made sourdough bread his neighbor recently delivered."

Lily, Lori and Hunter quickly had servings on paper plates lined up on the plank table, including a pitcher of ice cold milk and water. "Oh, I love these bench seats," Harmony added as they scooted to make room for others.

Everyone except Storm was still taking in the feeling of having stepped back into the eighteenth century.

By the time they were seated, Storm announced, "Someone is coming up the lane, ah, I recognize C.W.'s headlights." But just in case, Storm drew the filmy lace curtains closed. Unbeknownst to the younger guests, Lori had relocked C.W.'s kitchen door as soon as their Double Foursome was inside.

"Am I in time for prayer?" C.W. chuckled, knowing full well one of them would have said a prayer before taking a bite.

"Right on time," Hunter replied.

After the prayer, Lily added a reminder. "We're on a tight schedule now, so eat first—talk later."

Hunter drove C.W's vintage station wagon, and took the graded stone drive that led them out onto the highway where they normally turned left to go to Winthrop, but they turned right towards Sunrise and Uncle Kristopher's photo lab.

"Lori," Lily asked, "isn't there a white church on the corner of Stoney Road where we turn?"

"Yes," Lori said. "I think we pass a cemetery first, though. It's the third road on our left. Right?"

"Yes," Hunter agreed, "according to C.W.'s map."

"I never drove to Uncle Kristopher's place because we were usually riding with Aunt Marcie," Lily recalled.

"I've been here a few times with Dad," Hunter added. "This is it on the right. His private photo lab is behind his garage. Uncle Kristopher rarely shares the location of his lab with anyone."

Kristopher was waiting for them, and shook hands with each of the Double Foursome.

"Lily, Lori, Hunter, Storm, and friends," he asked, "how close are you to solving your current search-and-rescue case?"

"You know," Lori began, "it's like we're missing something crucial."

He hugged the twins and suggested, "Patience. Please

don't hesitate to contact me about anything though okay?"

"Thanks," Lily said, as they glanced at photos drying like laundry on a clothes line.

"Does this family photo have anything to do with your search?" Kristopher asked.

"Oh," Hunter commented, "You should see the stuff we've collected with C.W.'s metal detectors. Everything from rings and coins to a tire, but no car."

"Yea," Storm added, as he felt vibes from Hunter that still surprised him. "Who knows how many years this stuff has been buried or tossed from a truck, car or passenger train."

"You know, as an attorney and your uncle, I am amazed. Are the four of you aware of how strong your connection is? And, may I add, I'm certain I've met someone who favors the person in that photo. If it comes to me, I'll call you, Storm. Good luck. Turn out the lights and lock the door when you're finished."

Kristopher had been a successful attorney a number of years, and respected the fact that this group was not ready to share the reason why they were here. But there was no way he could not have offered to help them with an ongoing project, whether Storm was working part-time for him or not.

He had to admit, whenever his nieces were involved, they, like their mom, didn't sit back and assume someone else would take care of things.

"What if Kristopher remembers who the woman is in that photo?" Lori suggested. Let's just do a slow drive-by again where you guys found those shiny chrome and rustic steel lug nuts." They loaded up and headed to the other side of Sunrise.

"Harmony?" Lori asked, "What does the medical field do to identify people? You know, besides fingerprints and teeth? I'm used to working with animals with types of brands, etc. Photos?"

"Even though C.W. gave us two couples' names, Donovan and I went through the telephone books for the entire surrounding counties and came up empty," Denver said.

Madison continued, "We called the Sunrise Clinic which is linked to the Turtle Crossing Medical Hospital. Nothing."

"Should we go there in person?" Harmony asked.

"That's a good idea, but I'm going with you," Hunter stated.

Each couple chose a location. "Should we meet at Alex's Welby Mansion B & B for our evening meal and stay overnight?" Lily asked. "Before we go any farther," Lily and Lori stopped simultaneously and faced each other, "let's pray together." They joined hands and repeated the Lord's Prayer aloud, then separated into groups, metal detectors in hand.

Lori, Denver, Hunter, and Harmony quietly studied their map as Lily, Donovan, Madison and Storm returned to the ditch, downhill from the tire tracks. "Stop, guys," Lily said. "Just stand still for a moment, please. I heard a tiny bell."

"You're right, Lily," Lori added. "It's directly ahead of you."

"There is something sparkling in the sunlight on a branch of that straggly shrub," Denver said.

"Wait, Lily," Donovan suggested. "Let me hang onto you." When she reached out over the ditch and grabbed it, the bell rang louder.

"This appears to be a veteran's dog tags," Denver stated. "But why the bell?

"What is the name?" Lori asked.

Rubbing his thumb across the metal tag, Donovan read, "Martin D. Miracle, with his number."

"This sounds like one of the names C.W. gave us," Hunter added. "We need to phone Great-Grandpa Charlie. Because of his military experience, he'll know who to contact that might know how to locate this person."

"Donovan," Denver asked. "Didn't we see that last name in the Sidney directory?"

"Yes!"

"Lori," Denver asked, as he took her by the hand. The urgency in his voice was apparent to everyone. "Remember, when I talked to you about searching for my family, I talked with C.W., and he suggested that some hospitals were taking footprints and fingerprints of newborn babies and the moms. Sometimes families request it at baptisms. Hunter, has he mentioned it to you? Perhaps if C.W. sees these dog tags…"

"Great information," Lori agreed.

"We need to contact Aunt Brandi," Lily said. "We might need her help. We need to decide as a group what our next step should be."

"I feel we should move on this as soon as possible."

"I agree." Hunter nodded.

"Should we have all parties involved meet at Aunt Tressie's? With the promise to protect the Four Aces?" Lily asked.

"I know if someone had worked so diligently to take care of my child and spent this much time to find me, I would be graciously thankful," Madison added.

Lori phoned Aunt Tressie regarding finalizing a meeting with the apparent parents of Little Miss Sunshine yet today and still protect themselves at the same time.

"Lori," Aunt Tressie suggested, "Please put your phone on speaker so you all can hear this. You can keep your identity as the Four Aces by not mentioning it at all."

"Congratulations. You have handled this, your first real case, with determination, expertise, and compassion. I suggest you use your Mother's life story. About how your Great Grandmother stole your mom at the age of six—took her to a children's home and left her there with a false name and birthdate. She told no one."

Donovan and Denver were awestruck. Harmony and Madison hugged with shared tears.

The Double Foursome were the first to arrive at Aunt Tressie's home and parked behind her house to allow room for the rest of the invited guests. Inside Tressie's combined living room and dining room, the Double Foursome rearranged the furniture to allow seating for everyone.

Lt. Brandi Carpenter and Attorney Kristopher Donnelly had worked together and followed up with proof that Martin D. Miracle, his wife, Audrey, and their daughter, Little Miss Sunshine, was named Summer Miracle at birth.

Rev. C. Warren had the baptism papers ready to be picked up, however, the family had never stopped back. In addition, their marriage had been recorded and was also in his file.

Lt. Brandi had telephoned Martin regarding their plans, and was asked not to share this information with anyone, including his wife.

When Mr. and Mrs. Miracle arrived, introductions followed. Martin introduced Audrey to Lt. Brandi Carpenter, Kristopher, Lily and Hunter as her research associates. Lori, Madison, Harmony, and Storm stayed in the kitchen so as not to overwhelm the Miracles and have the chance to entertain baby Summer.

Donovan and Denver went out onto Tressie's shaded deck and delayed an uninvited guest, Kristopher's wife, Nancy, who informed them she was Audrey's sister. The windows were open so they could hear Audrey tell her story, however Nancy wasn't known for her patience.

Tressie greeted the Miracles with a mixture of apprehension and joy. Lily and Lori served tea, coffee, cheeses, crackers and fruit.

Lily asked Martin, "Are you still interested in selling the motorcycle you had promised your wife you would sell for a down payment on a new or used car?"

"Yes. I still need to sell it," Martin replied.

"That horrible tornado stole our car with our baby girl inside!" Audrey exclaimed.

"Audrey," Aunt Tressie asked, "what is your memory of that day?"

"Audrey, before you start," Lt. Brandi Carpenter asked,

"do we have your permission to record your response to Tressie's questions?"

Audrey hesitated, looked at Martin, and, when he nodded, she replied, "Of course."

Audrey glanced around the room and began, "We left Martin's parents' home in Sidney that morning with a full day planned. Martin's mom and I packed an old picnic basket, and a cooler."

"Our first stop was an appointment with Rev. C. Warren. I had always wanted to be married in a little country church. We were married three years ago by a Justice of the Peace because there wasn't time to plan anything else as we started working at our new jobs the following day."

"Martin's parents had heard of a charming chapel at Eight Mile Centre. That was a special moment for both of us. We had Summer baptized that day, as well. Perhaps things would have never happened the way they did if we had just stayed at the covered bridge, but it was on the way to my sister's house in Sunrise. I had called ahead and told her we expected to arrive around five o'clock that afternoon.

"Then we had a flat tire. Summer was getting a little fussy, so I fixed her a bottle, put her in her car-bed, and left the car doors open to a nice breeze. Martin was even working in the shade of the car.

"Then suddenly it got really quiet and still." Audrey teared up, dried her eyes and nose, took a sip of iced tea and continued, twisting a fresh tissue to shreds. "First, the sky was the weirdest yellow/green color. Then it turned black. There was the sound of a tea kettle that became as loud as a train. Martin grabbed me to the ground and rolled us into a ditch.

"We must have blacked out because when we awoke, we were covered in mud and sticks and plastered flat against the Chessie Railway Railroad Bed. Martin said he heard the growl as that nasty tornado took our car with our baby girl, Summer, still inside."

"In case you're wondering," Martin added, "a train engineer said they had been clearing the tracks of rolls of roofing, siding, trees and branches. That's what he thought we were, just another muddy branch."

Lily, Lori, Hunter, and Storm had commented about the flattened grasses near the tire in the photo Donovan had taken of the tire and flattened-grass-imprint of two people? Donovan shivered and felt relieved that the imprints weren't ghosts or spirits after all.

The Double Foursome knew the distance from the place where Martin's dog tags and deep tire tracks were found to the railroad, and murmured, "Thank You, Jesus."

"A woman called yesterday," Audrey continued. "She was yelling and demanding if I knew anything about the Sunrise Tornado. She wasn't real nice, so I told her we didn't know anything."

"That would have been me!" Kristopher's wife, Nancy remarked, as she marched through the kitchen to the dining room, her anger barely controlled. "I am your sister after all! The least you could have done is call me and let me know you were still alive!"

The silence in the room was like a tomb. Audrey stared at her sister. "Your remark alone is why I didn't."

"Uncle Kristopher?" Lily asked, as Lori, Hunter, and Storm joined and stood with her, including Aunt Tressie and Lt. Brandi Carpenter with her canine German-Shepherd, Rosie V.

"Sit down!" Kristopher demanded, "This isn't about you!" he said to his wife, then continued, "I am here representing Martin, Audrey, and Summer Miracle, at the request of the people standing. Their diligence left nothing to chance that Summer Miracle would not grow up an orphan."

"Martin?" Audrey turned to her husband and asked. "This is the reason you wanted me to show your mom why we had that picture of our fingerprints and Summer's footprints and photo as a Christmas gift to her?" Looking around the room, Audrey added, "Martin's mom was adopted and hasn't been able to find any record of her family."

When Nancy started to get up, she noticed that the dog had not taken his eyes off her, so she begrudgingly shredded her tissue and stared at the sister she had thought was gone forever.

"Aunt Tressie?" Kristopher asked.

"All prints are a match," she replied, as she handed him a folder. "Thank you, Lt. Carpenter, for your assistance as well."

"Mr. and Mrs. Martin Miracle," Tressie began, "I would like to introduce you to our mystery guest. Today is the result of this family and their friends who never gave up searching for the two of you because their mom was six years old when she was separated from her twin brother and Dad and grew up in a children's home. She was eighteen years old before she was reunited with her family." Tressie nodded to Martin.

When Harmony carried Summer out, she smiled and started her usual jabbering; but this time she added, "Da-Da-Da-Da." As Martin hugged her close, bravely holding back tears, he carried their daughter into the parlor where Audrey was sitting, talking to Lily and Lori about her wedding and Rev. C.W. But, when she turned and saw Martin with a baby girl, she squealed with her hand over her mouth, so as not to frighten the baby.

"Audrey, look who our mystery guest is."

"Martin, is she really our baby girl, Summer?" Audrey asked, as Martin moved swiftly across the room, Summer reached her arms out and jabbered, "Da-Da-Da." But when Audrey held Summer in her arms, she felt and looked for the mole behind her daughter's right ear. "Summer, Summer," as tears fell. "You're alive. You're alive! How can this be?" She kissed Summer's fingers, the top of her head; tears flowed.

"Martin, how long have you known?"

"For certain? About an hour."

"But there hasn't been anything in the papers."

"No," Martin continued. "This family and friends kept her safe while they searched for us. Can you believe two young boys, a crazy rooster, and God saved our baby girl?"

"I want to tell everyone about this!" Audrey announced.

"Your thanks are sufficient," Hunter commented. "Have you heard of the 'Cradle of Flowers'?"

"Yes. It's a shelter for abused women and children. It works because silence is safety? Is Rev. C. Warren your group's mentor?"

Hunter just nodded. When Martin took his daughter, she reached for his mustache and pulled his dog tags out of his shirt, shook the bell until it rang, and giggled.

Martin smiled, and said, "When my mom was adopted as a baby, both of her booties had a bell on them. She asked me to fasten one of them with my tags. The bell didn't ring until Summer was born. And she loves it."

"Consider our request forgotten," Martin said softly.

"By all means," Audrey added, smiling at Hunter and then Martin. "I'm not used to having someone to lean on," she exclaimed.

"Can we hold her for a moment?" Harmony asked.

When Martin nodded, Summer squealed when Harmony took her.

Audrey turned into Martin's arms and cried. "Honey," Martin soothed. "It's okay. May I explain?"

When Tressie nodded, Audrey continued. "We were already engaged when Martin was offered a job out of state, on graduation day. We left against my parents' wishes and were married by a justice of the peace in another state the following day."

Tressie approached them and handed Audrey a folder with a picture of Summer inside. "Your daughter has been doing well on goat's milk. This is her menu, and this is the name and number of the owner of Gertie, the goat. Her feed and care are all listed here. You mentioned earlier that you have housing for Gertie, so when she's no longer needed, you can return her to the owner which is listed here as well."

"Audrey, Martin," Tressie said, "Enclosed in this envelope is the names and address of the boys who found and cared for Summer the day after the Sunrise Tornado. We notified the boys' parents that Summer, Little Miss Sunshine, is now with her parents, but thought you might like to write and thank them. They understand the need for discretion."

"This is my business card if you need a babysitter," Harmony added, bravely holding back tears of joy.

"This is my business card if you are in need of chiropractic care," Lily added, "or if someone approaches you with needs that require discretion."

"This is my business card if you have a pet that needs the care of a veterinarian," Lori suggested.

"Lori," Kristopher began, "I know there is no way I can ever repay your entire group. I am so very proud of you."

"You finally figured out who the picture reminded you of?" Lily teased.

"Oh, that Audrey and my wife Nancy are sisters?" Kristopher teased back. "Nancy was terrified."

"We understood that," Lori replied.

Nancy raced to Audrey's side and, while the two embraced, Harmony handed Summer to Madison for a moment. Madison asked, "Perhaps when you and your family get settled, could Harmony and I and Aunt Tressie visit Summer? She was so easy to love."

"Aunt Tressie," Lily said. "We're going to leave. We'll

see you at the BBQ at Doc and Granny's tomorrow?"

Kristopher shook hands with Donovan and Denver, as well as Madison and Harmony; but all the rest shared hugs. Followed by Audrey as she shook hands with each of them. As they prepared to leave, Kristopher stopped them to relay a message: "It is safe to return to the Victorian this evening. See you at the BBQ tomorrow."

"It appears your Foursome just became eight. You've inherited the desire to help others and joined an alliance with others who perform great deeds, anonymously. Just because. God Bless."

Chapter 17

The banner for the O'Reilly's Annual BBQ and Veterinarian Animal Hospital Celebration, Friday, July 4th, 1986, had been stretched across the road for two weeks. Parking areas had been roped off by sections the day before.

The original Shadow Angels directed the setup of tables and chairs for seating, and service tables for condiments, fresh veggies, fruits, salads, and desserts. The scent of pork roasting added to the anticipation of the gathering of friends and neighbors, and the chance to tour the Animal Hospital.

Shannon and Wendy had posted samples for the guests to enjoy in the lobby of the Animal Hospital. They were certain the sketch of Gracious Gertie, the goat, was certain to draw smiles and conversation, which included profiles of some of the Tornado Pied-Piper parade. Shannon and Wendy were scheduled to offer a sketch or profile of visitors for a small fee.

Will and Buck stopped Denver and asked, "Why don't you join your friends this evening? We've got everything under control here."

"Thanks," Denver replied. "I'll let Donovan know I will be arriving at the Welby Mansion B & B earlier than planned and ask him where I should park."

"Donovan?" Denver asked, "Will and Buck suggested I leave early, so where should I park? In the boat-docking lot? Sure I know where it is. I'll be driving my truck, of course."

Denver was unaware he had stopped outside under Granny's kitchen window.

"Denver!" Granny called out. "Take my black Lincoln."

"Did you hear that, Donovan?"

"Ah, Denver? Take your time."

"Denver," Granny hesitated as she joined him on the back porch. Her eyes teared up, and she continued. "With your black hair, shower-wet, with a bit of a wave, you look so much like…"

"I know. Like Doc when he was my age? Thank you for your patient, cautious guidance, and believing in me, Aunt Rose."

Granny was so stunned, she smiled and hugged him. "No one has ever called me Aunt Rose."

"It's okay then?"

"Absolutely."

Doc had pulled in his drive from Granny's Estate in her Lincoln she drove to church every Sunday morning. He stopped outside the screen door when he heard Denver's comments to Granny, which was a surprise because he seldom talked about anything but Bronc and the horses.

"I want you and Doc to know that I am in love with Lori."

"Have you told her that?" Granny asked.

"Not yet," Denver replied. He blushed and added, "Every time I start to, I stammer and the moment's lost."

Doc intervened, "This beauty is gassed up and ready to go." As he handed the keys to Denver, he commented, "Did I ever tell you what happened that gave me the courage to ask Granny to marry me? Another guy came into the picture, and I couldn't stand seeing him with her, in my place. I almost lost her before I ever told her how much I needed her in my life."

"Thanks, Doc. Lori reminds me that God has a plan, but it's still up to us. I'm helping Donovan move into the Victorian Carriage House. I might spend the night there, but will be here early tomorrow for your big day, unless you need me this evening, for anything, just call, okay?"

Doc nodded.

Denver started to pull out of the drive when he noticed that the door to his farrier office was ajar. He knew he had locked it just before he picked up his luggage. Just in case, Denver pushed Doc, Buck, and Will's special hot button number on his phone and was glad he had his 45 in his holster.

He took several deep breaths, hit the light switch, revealing Cousin Arther, rifling through his things. "What are you doing in my private office?" he demanded. "And who do you think you are wearing one of Jim Leonard's

Will Fox Blue Uniforms? And, what do you plan to do with my Farrier tools? Sell them? You do know it is against the law to steal another man's property, right?"

The surprise took a bit to wear thin and Arthur the jerk was allowing his cocky, none-of-your-business side to show as he considered his options. "What's it to you what I plan to do with this junk? You really aren't as smart as you think you are. At least your daddy always had money. You know, I do believe I saw a photo of you recently. You were wearing a pretty fancy new western hat. I have a couple of friends that should be here any minute. So, I'll just be going now. "

When Denver felt a response on his phone, he ordered, "Carefully drop the rasp and trimmers, or I will shoot them out of your hand."

"You wouldn't dare! That might bring your friends in here and I just might use that rifle you got there on the top shelf before you could blink."

Jim yanked the door open, with Will at his side. "So, Cousin Arthur. We've been wondering when you would show your hand."

"I'm not alone, cousin."

"It appears you are right now," Jim replied. "Drop the tools. Try anything at all and Denver and Will have the right to shoot. Did you think the 'No Trespassing Signs' didn't pertain to you?"

"You have to know you have broken several laws recently, including the one you are apparently in the middle of right now."

Will and Jim had Arthur tied up and were marching

him out the door when Brandi took charge. "I will need you to go through your office to make certain he didn't take anything."

As soon as they left Denver's office, locked it and Brandi's men wrapped yellow tape across the door of his office, Denver picked up his blanket of tools and turned around, Doc put his arm around him, and commented, "Drive safe."

"We'll talk later," Granny said softly. "Donovan called because he was worried. He is waiting for you. Just drive up to the Welby Mansion B&B guest entrance."

"Thank you, Aunt Rose," Denver replied. "I'll just grab my extra overnight bag out of my truck." He stashed his tool-blanket in the inside tool chest in place of his overnight bag and set the lock and alarm he and Aunt Willi had designed.

"Just who sold you this truck? Willi?"

"Yes, I better leave my rifle where it is. You know I'm licensed to carry?" When she nodded, he added, "If you're real nice, I will show you a bit more about my truck."

"Look forward to it. But you should know Doc and I have no secrets."

After Denver left, Granny called Brandi. "If you spot a handsome young man driving my black Lincoln, my nephew, Denver O'Reilly, has my permission."

It was a full twenty-five minutes later that, someone who sounded like one of her deputies, put in a call with Granny's name on the license plate.

"I sent out a blanket notification," Brandi said. She could have let the call go, but something about the call didn't sit well, and she got the attention of the two deputies she trusted for undercover work.

Turtle Crossing's finest arrived at the Welby Mansion B&B from the rear and parked in the owner's parking space before Denver arrived. They called in the vehicle that was parked in the Fishermen's Lot. The report was quick in coming.

"The owner of that vehicle is Dr. Dexter Franklin. Interesting," Brandi remarked. "He had an emergency surgery around three this afternoon."

When Denver pulled in behind Donovan, he started to get out of the car when Donovan stepped up to the Lincoln and suggested, "Pop the trunk for these two boxes of books and follow me to the Victorian," he added. "I've already checked out. Hunter and Storm will be waiting for us at the gate."

"We have a unit following Donovan and Denver," Brandi said. "Has your video been running at the Welby Fisherman's parking area?"

"Yes. The driver and a passenger got out of the vehicle and smoked a cigarette."

A surprise message came on their phones, "This was a false alarm, boys, we're pulling out." Two Turtle Crossing vehicles drove out the front drive, turned around, and pulled back in. However, Brandi's undercover vehicle stayed where it was. When the driver of Dr. Dexter's car drove out, Brandi's followed, and were surprised when they stopped at Doc's ancestor's cabin.

The passenger got out as Lt. Brandi's muddy sedan with out of state plates drove on by.

But Brandi recognized Dexter's brother, Calvin, in the driver's seat when the interior light flashed on before the door closed, which made her question whose case he was working on.

However, Unit Two followed the driver back to Turtle Crossing and parked in Dr. Dexter's reserved parking space at the hospital. No one left the vehicle. But patience paid off. The driver had apparently fallen asleep.

Dr. Dexter was tired and didn't care who heard him. He yelled, "Calvin! Where did you drive my car? I just filled the tank and it's down to less than a quarter. This is the last straw. You can walk. Tomorrow you're moving out!"

When Dexter arrived home, a light was blinking on the answering machine. "Dexter," his mom announced, "we're staying at the Welby for the holiday weekend. Hope you'll have time to meet up with us tomorrow at the O'Reilly's BBQ around three. Bring Calvin if you get the chance. Bye."

***

Donovan and Denver arrived at the Victorian, unaware they had been tailed the entire time. Lori and Lily were adamant that Granny's vehicle would be out of sight and secured it in one of the empty garages.

"My, oh my, Denver, you appear to be rather mellow," Lily remarked, smiling.

He knew she was teasing and replied, "Driving Granny's dream of a car was smooth and quiet compared to my truck."

"Wait," Doc drew up a layout of the grounds for his BBQ the following day.

"Hey, Lori," Lily pointed at the square, marked in chalk in the Animal Hospital Lobby.

"This is where Mom and Wendy plan to offer sketches or profiles for a fee. The funds will be for the county animal shelter."

"Here," Denver stopped and handed Lori a note from the Shadow Angels.

"Okay, Ladies," Lori read, "this is in Aunt Tressie's handwriting. They will be dressed as Western Gals and helping Granny until we arrive, which means they will be visible and working/invisible, just in case they're needed for security."

"Denver," Lori asked, "did you or Donovan remember to eat today?"

Denver looked at Donovan and replied, "We have been rather busy."

Before Lily could even ask, "Well, someone had to give our approval for Doc's sake, so we couldn't turn down his offer," Donovan shrugged. "The smell doesn't do it justice. Because we just happened to be there and had never experienced his cooking. This was just his roaster sample for tomorrow's BBQ which will be roasting all night."

Hunter looked at Donovan and Denver and suggested, "Enough said, you two."

***

Doc O'Reilly's Annual 4th of July BBQ Festivities were well underway. It was around noon with a clear blue sky. Numerous vehicles from nearby counties had been arriving for at least two hours. Most were eager to tour the Grand Opening of The Doc O'Reilly Veterinarian

Animal Hospital, with the nameplates on the offices of Veterinarians' Dr. Matthew D. O'Reilly and Dr. Lori Anne' Donnelly, on the doors.

Many looked forward to Doc's Annual BBQ Celebration on the 4th of July. Children were always anxious to see the horses in the stable and nearby pasture.

Hunter and Storm had been helping Denver with families and children asking questions about what's involved in owning their very own horses. Denver believed in showing, rather than just talking, and asked Hunter and Storm if they could collect his Farrier tool bundle from his office in the barn.

They had just gone inside Denver's office and closed the door when they overheard a heated discussion outside in the temporary parking area. One inside wall of Denver's office was still in the unfinished stage, a slatted original section with half-inch spaces between. However, the hay loft windows were open for cross ventilation.

"Calvin, I don't know why you are so upset. You saw that I have two flat tires and can't get new tires until Monday."

"Come on, Sarge, or is it Smoke? I don't plan on staying long," Calvin said.

"That's okay. I just want to take a look at this place in the daytime."

"Well, then, we'll have to stop by O'Reilly's Animal Hospital if you want one of those famous' artists to sketch you, since you keep telling me how handsome you are, or maybe not," Calvin challenged.

Shannon and Wendy had been working steady for

over two hours and the line continued two car lengths out the door of the lobby of the Animal Hospital. Lily, Lori, Opal, and Willi had been kept busy entertaining the children while they waited.

However, when Sarge Carpenter and Calvin Franklin strolled into the lobby of the O'Reilly Animal Hospital, Lori mentioned to Lily, "I know people do change after a few years, but this is quite a surprise. I'll be in my office for a few." She didn't know what to think, but Calvin's walk, his military posture, his decent direct eyes was quite a change from the old challenging, brash attitude.

His clean-cut, bleached-blonde, butch haircut had also thrown her off, but still he was with Sarge. That alone spelled trouble. But the memory of the comment Calvin had made to her after she had made a fool of him that day in study hall after he had tripped Lily had haunted her. He had whispered, "Someday, I'll make you sorry."

Lori had learned from practice, talking to oneself had usually become one and the same as talking to the Lord. When Lily tapped on her office door, Lori had made her decision. They looked at each other, both knowing what needed to be done without even discussing it.

Calvin was surprised to suddenly be left alone. Unaware of when Sarge had taken his interest from the donation jar to a sketch one of the artists had completed.

"Calvin, do you have a few minutes?" Lori asked.

He was shocked. Without turning around, he replied, "I am surprised you have the nerve to even speak to me." His voice was a bit rustic and shaky.

"I would like to apologize for letting my anger override

my common sense that day in study hall, but you had hurt my sister."

Calvin gripped his hands together so tightly, his fingers were going numb, as he slowly turned to face the only person who had ever made a fool of him. After all, he had been proud that everyone in school was afraid of him, except the Donnelly Twins and his brother, Dexter. They were the only people who made him feel accountable.

Certainly not his parents. He could do no wrong where they were concerned. When he finally turned to face her, Lori was surprised at how approachable he appeared.

"What do you get out of apologizing to me?" he asked in an uncaring fashion.

"Closure," Lori replied. "It's never too late to mend fences."

"I will never admit this to anyone else, but I deserved what you did to me that day. Dexter was the one I was aiming for, not Lily," Calvin replied.

"We put that together a long time ago," Lori added.

"Really? Odd that no one else did. Thank you for that. I accept your apology, and if your sister will accept my apology, as well," Calvin added, just as Lily joined Lori.

"Thank you," Lily nodded in compliance. "Enjoy the rest of your day."

When Calvin started to leave, he stopped and turned around, "Lori. Lily. Thank you both for today," he continued as he handed them his business card.

They were speechless, when they read, *Calvin Franklin, Owner – Karate Classes – Self-Defense – Wrestling Referee. Sunrise, Ohio.*

"And Sarge?" Lily asked.

"We were friends in school. I'm just his transportation today." Calvin replied, glanced at his watch, and quickly joined Sarge.

"Just drop me off at Uncle Henry's Motel," Sarge said.

"I thought you needed to pick up your truck in Turtle Crossing."

What Calvin didn't see was a horse trailer hooked up to Sarge's pickup truck parked alongside the separate unit Sarge was renting.

Before Calvin pulled back on the highway he sent Will a message. *Be on the lookout for Sarge. I left him at Henry's Motel. He is up to something. Call me if you need anything.*

***

Opal and Jewel had just delivered cookies, strawberry shortcakes, and colorful platters of raw veggies, and were headed for their chairs in the shade when Opal cupped Jewel's elbow and whispered, "Don't you dare pass out," when two young men walked. Okay, strolled past them.

"So," Jewel remarked, "did you see him, too? That young man, really isn't Henry. He really is dead. Do you suppose my ex-husband sent his spirit to haunt me?" Jewel inquired as the two of them plopped on a nearby bench in the shade behind Doc and Granny's house.

"Wow! There ought to be a law against any young man being that handsome, and nice, and polite! Don't you agree, Opal?" Aunt Jewel suggested.

"Well, he's nearly a carbon copy of Henry in his younger days," Opal admitted.

Willi and Tressie joined them with a tub of cookies to

share and teasingly commented, "We've just come from Doc's Animal Hospital where we had our profiles done," Willi said. "And, just so you know, the young man who favors Henry is his great nephew, Sarge. He also goes by the name of Smoke."

"And," Opal asked, "the tall guy with Sarge?"

"He was pretty quiet," Tressie said. "Marcie took photos of Sarge and he actually posed. He took his western hat off and finger-combed his hair. What a big showoff. As you can see, he considers himself a ladies' man."

"But, I overheard some talk in Turtle Crossing that he has a mean streak," Tressie added. "I haven't heard anything about the tall guy with him."

"Then why would Doc invite them?" Jewel asked.

"I understand," Opal said, "that he is a mechanic at Georgie Johnson's Garage. George told Will that if Sarge messes up one more time, he's fired," Opal repeated. "Even if he is Henry's great nephew. Apparently, something happened at Sadie's."

"That's not good," Jewel recalled, as she squeezed Opal's hand, "George and Sadie were classmates and dated back in the day. He won't stand for their nonsense."

"Hey, you two sharpies," Marcie directed. "Smile!"

"Bring that camera in any closer," Opal chuckled, "and you'll see my tonsils."

"Bear with me," Marcie begged. "I'm focusing in on movement in the hillside behind you. Please, Opal, can you pick that weed flower on the ground and to your left. Action, please." However, from habit, she took three more shots.

Jewel loved the theatre and suggested, "Distraction you requested to my left. There's my hanky," Jewel encouraged. "I would hate to lose it. My grandma embroidered a butterfly in the corner of it and mailed it inside my thirteenth birthday card."

Marcie turned around and took Opal's picture, forgetting she had the camera set for distance beyond and unknowingly revealed Ginger's nephew close to the stables.

Turtle Crossing was used to seeing Marcie with a camera. "Donovan," Marcie nodded. "Good to see you. Have you seen Kristopher?"

"As in Kristopher the attorney? Yes." Donovan replied. "He might be over by the Animal Hospital."

"If you see Lily or Lori," Marcie continued, "I have a couple of questions."

"Right," Donovan replied and headed back towards the Animal Hospital. Shannon and Wendy's line extended beyond the driveway. However, when people stopped by and viewed the results that were posted for pickup later in the day, several asked if they could sign up for an appointment later in the month.

He could see Shannon and Wendy were also busy answering questions about the Animal Hospital and how nice it was to see the Donnelly Twins were back and commenting on the mural in the lobby and the Veterans' Wing of the Museum. Willi was kept busy passing out cookies and drinks while people stood in line.

"Can someone give you a break?" Donovan asked. "Marcie requests you and Lori in Granny's kitchen."

"Are we on someone's radar?" Lily asked.

"Hard to tell with all these people," Lori replied, "however, here comes Troup. There's our answer. Good thing we wore our reversible vests and jeans under our skirts." Troup sidestepped around people like he had sniffed someone he truly planned to either take down or disappear from.

Once inside Granny's kitchen, Marcie was quick to show pictures of Sarge and Dexter's brother, Calvin. "Compare these sketches." Lori suggested as she spread the one of Sarge and of Calvin, with your photos, Marcie. What is so surprising is the difference in the two sketches of Calvin. This one was while he was arguing with Sarge. The other one he posed for."

"But, most of all, this is what caught my eye," Lily added. "Calvin's initials. As you know, many people change their signature when they become a doctor, or business owner. But, why would Sarge sign his DAF for Dexter Allen Franklin? Calvin Alan Franklin signed his CAF. They both signed our yearbook and initialed their class photos. However, Calvin's initials today are an artistic CAF similar to his business logo, but not anywhere close to the past or the paperwork on my equipment. Strange. Does Sarge think we don't know who he is or that he was never here?"

"Good question. I also accidently picked up a photo of someone who looks like Ginger's nephew out by the stables," Marcie added. "Ginger said he was MIA from the military. He is walking with a cane and a limp."

"I've notified all my men. Buck will put all of his on

alert, and Brandi has been notified," Will said as he joined them. "One thing is in our favor, the sky keeps looking like rain, so a lot of people aren't sticking around as they usually do."

"Uncle Will, Lily and I are headed back over to the Animal Hospital to help Mom and Wendy."

"Catch you two later," Marcie added, as she followed them.

"There you two are," Hunter admonished as he and Storm joined them.

"Just follow our lead," Lily encouraged. "We'll share new info as soon as we can."

"Well, one good thing," Storm informed them. "Sarge and Calvin left in a huff. Sarge tore his sketch in half and threw it in the trash barrel."

"That Wendy is so talented. We just gave Uncle Will the extras she practiced on."

"Another thing," Lori started, then nodded, when she saw Ginger's nephew struggling to walk on the stone driveway. He was gaunt, pale, and Lori was certain he was in pain with every step. His Aunt Ginger hadn't heard from him for over a year, however she hadn't given up on him. But it still was imperative they treat him like a stranger until he proved otherwise.

"We'll see what we can do." Hunter grabbed Lori's hand and approached him.

"Hi!" Lori greeted. "Have you seen the new Animal Hospital?"

"That was my destination," he replied. "But I was surprised to see those dark clouds move in so early, and

I've had a bit of a challenge fighting the crowds. I should never have left my crutches in my car."

"Do you mind if we walk with you?" Lori asked.

"You're the Donnelly twin who just finished Veterinarian College, right?"

"Yes."

"Are you her brother, Hunter?"

"I am. Would you like a tour today or were you headed for your vehicle? Either way, we can bring your vehicle around for you whenever you need it."

"Thanks. I have had to sit down quite often, so it has taken me longer than I expected."

All the while, Lori and Hunter were on alert as they walked with him. "Have you had a chance to visit with your Aunt Ginger?" Lori questioned.

"I couldn't find her at her farmhouse. Is she okay? I was disappointed. The place was a real mess."

"When were you there?" Hunter inquired.

"This morning. That's why I came over here. I thought I would get a chance to talk with Doc, but he has been so busy, I hated to bother him."

"So how long have you been in the States?" Lori asked.

"I was in a veterans' hospital for over a year."

"Have you had anything to eat today?" Hunter questioned as Will approached them.

"Actually, no."

"If you don't mind, "Will suggested, "we just happen to have a wheelchair here, and one of my men did a stint in the military. He will make certain you get some food in you."

Storm joined them, and inquired, "Did you ever get hold of Ginger?"

"Yes. She's on her way," Will said, as they left Ginger's nephew with Doc and headed towards the Animal Hospital. "Paul is who he says he is. I just got the printout."

"Shannon, did I hear that Troup did not bark or growl at Calvin like he did with Sarge?"

"You heard about that, did you?" Shannon commented as Will was working his magic and suggesting the visitors move inside or cut their visit short due to the weather.

The Foursome joined him as requested. "Rain is expected with this wind and dark clouds," Will said as they were handed reschedule dates.

The sun was short of an hour of setting, and as people left, tables and chairs were folded and stored inside the Animal Hospital. Food had been moved onto Granny and Doc's enclosed back porch, the clouds lifted, the wind calmed, and the sky cleared.

"I don't like this calm," Granny commented. "It is almost too still."

Denver had Bronc out in the paddock, and several people were milling around, relaxing after the big day, rather glad they hadn't planned any fireworks and dance this year.

Suddenly, his voice changed. "What are you doing here? And where did you come from?" he demanded.

"You know, I've had so much fun keeping you all guessing," Sarge laughed as he released a rifle from the sheath that hung from his saddle. "I've had the best time of my life, so, the way I see this going down is this. After I marry the widow Ginger who owns the property behind me, get rid of you, Doc O'Reilly, and Will Fox, I will be the richest landowner in the county."

"Of course, I want this stupid horse. What did you name him anyhow?" Sarge asked, raising his voice another octave. "He needs a few more lessons."

Denver felt Bronc's fear. His ears perked up. His muscles tensed. When Sarge glanced towards Bronc, Denver couldn't believe that Sarge really was aiming at Doc and Will across the paddock. When Denver heard and saw him shift the bullet into the chamber, his itchy finger on the trigger, Denver knew he had to stop him at all costs and dove at Sarge.

Immediately following the loud crack of the rifle shot, there was a strange ricocheting *ping, ping, ping* and then silence. Reminiscent of golf balls ricocheting when hit just right in a stand of trees between two fairways.

The first ping ricocheted off the steel wrapped electric pole, replaced after the tornado, between Doc and Will. The second ping hit a new brass handle on the stable door. The third ping glanced off of Denver's Dad's rodeo buckle Denver had heat-hammered into a cross.

Denver crumpled from the impact of the bullet as it grazed off the cross in his hat band and, in return, was buried in Sarge's hand. Sarge howled, releasing the rifle as blood dripped from his hand.

Bronc moved in and planted one foot on Sarge's leg forcing him away from Denver. Sarge kept yelling, "Get this stupid horse off my leg!"

The Double Foursome moved swiftly, silently, like watching a silent movie in slow motion. Meanwhile, Harmony had scrambled through the stable medical bag and followed Lori's instructions. Because Denver's head was at an odd angle, Madison folded a blanket that had blown off the fence gate and placed it beside his head for support.

While Lily blindfolded Sarge from behind, Hunter grabbed a rope from the lasso competition and tied Sarge's other leg and arm together, Madison wrapped Sarge's hand with a roll of bandage, as Lily tied his own neck scarf around his mouth, firmly shutting him up.

"Don't move," Donovan growled. "Bronc's next step could be your pretty little face." Then, Donovan, like everyone else, crawled away and moved farther out of Bronc's sight.

Donovan sat on the fence where Denver usually sat every evening, and played the only song he had learned on the harmonica he had purchased at an estate sale in Sidney. The sweet, hauntingly mellow "Home, Home on the Range" drifted on a slight breeze and hovered in the air Bronc was breathing, a calming memory of his friend.

Lori's concentration had never wavered except to glance at Harmony Faith. Harmony signed that Denver was alive. Lori carefully watched as Bronc's withers relaxed. His ears slowly turned to pick up any and all sounds.

Bronc was protecting Denver. Anyone observing this scenario recognized it except a steaming mad Dr. Dexter Franklin. "I'm the only doctor here," and while pointing his forefinger on his chest said, "I demand, I *demand*—and what is that weird sound? Music?"

Before anyone else moved, Granny stepped forward and although tears clogged her throat said softly, "Shut up, Dexter." It was all she could do not to rush out there and hug Denver. No one had ever called her Aunt Rose before.

In another lifetime, Dexter knew he would have laughed in a woman's face, but he had heard rumors about Granny but the look in her eyes and her stance gave credibility to a woman who had gained his respect, something he was not known to give women in general.

Lori had yet to physically touch Bronc, but her soft voice was like a chant—a special language as she encouraged him to follow her. Lily had aligned herself directly beyond and behind Bronc.

Bronc hesitated to lift his back foot from Sarge, but possibly because there had been no sound or movement, Bronc followed Lori into the stable through the door Hunter had opened.

While Hunter closed everything in the stable, Lori raced to Denver's side calling his name, but he didn't respond.

Storm had met and guided the Turtle Crossing Rescue Squad, minus flashing lights and siren, to where Denver laid and they had waited as Storm explained the situation. Then, the squad took over, quickly checked his vitals and prepared him for transport.

Sarge was transported in a Turtle Crossing cruiser and read his rights. Lt. Brandi Carpenter confiscated the rifle and cordoned off the entire area as a crime scene.

"Everything by the book!" she demanded as everyone was interviewed except for Lori and Doc and Granny, who had accompanied Denver in the ambulance to Turtle Crossing.

***

Brandi sat alone in her cruiser momentarily, stunned by what had just happened. The stabled horses were restless, but she couldn't bring herself to check on them.

Will had lingered, drawn to the area taking his own photos. The rifle reminded him of Sarge, who attacked like a snake.

Brandi was troubled. Something about the rifle. The identifying name and numbers. New in appearance. Rare as a Special Edition. Stolen. Could that be it?

Will approached her cruiser. "Want to talk about whatever has you stymied?"

"Not yet. I will certainly share it with you when all the pieces of this puzzle fit. Wait a minute, Will. When was the last time you saw Troup? Better yet, where did you last see Troup?"

"With Bronc. Before Ginger's nephew, Paul arrived."

Will phoned Tressie and asked, "Brandi and I are near the stables. Something doesn't feel right. Is Shannon with you?"

"I'm right here, Uncle Will, with Buck and a couple of his men. We'll be right there."

"Odd. We were just on our way to check on the horses," Buck said as he joined them.

"Okay. I can't open this door into the stables. Something is blocking it."

"Thoughts?" Will asked.

"Do you know where the stable dimmer light is?" Buck asked. "I'll look in the window and be ready with my flashlight. Signal with the dimmer if you see anything suspicious."

"I will count to ten after I unlock the door," Will said.

"This door is unlocked too," Shannon noted when a cloud moved past the moon.

The moment Will touched the dial, the horses upped their movements, and Shannon whistled a soft melody. Will had his forty-five in hand and held onto Shannon as they started to move down the aisle. Shannon scanned her flashlight in the rafters and they both stopped when Buck hit the blinkers on his flashlight and lit up the area that had blocked the door.

"Buck," Doc asked, "why are the lights on in the stables?"

"It's Troup. He is hurt bad."

"Mom?" Lori asked.

"It's Troup."

"Miss Lori, Doc is with us. We brought a gurney to help you move Troup if need be."

"Thanks. Mom?"

"Right here. "

"Troup is alive," Lori reported to Doc. "The boys are helping me load him up."

After surgery, Doc, Lori, Buck and assistants were all seated in the recovery room, with Will, Shannon, and Brandi.

"Trackers and their dogs found a female cat not too

far from her kittens. It appears she was shot also. The question is, why shoot Troup?"

Chapter 18

Donovan leaned against the fence, his lips and hands still trembling, as Denver was immobilized and gently placed on a gurney. Denver's breathing was even, but shallow, his muscular body was so frighteningly still.

Lily was torn. She wanted to be there to support Lori; but when she glanced at Hunter, it surprised her that their connection was so easy, as he held both hands out and raised that one eyebrow. Asking her, to make a decision, Lori or Donovan.

She threw him a kiss. He nodded. And, as she turned towards Donovan, Storm pulled his vehicle up beside Hunter. Lily knew they were headed to the hospital.

As she approached Donovan, she realized he hadn't moved from the fence since the ambulance had left. A dark cloud moved eastward, and the full moon lit up the entire area, including shadows the security lights could not reach. He read the compassionate, caring expression on Lily's face, just moments before she leaned her head on his shoulder and wrapped her arms around him.

Donovan gripped the fence that had kept him from throttling Sarge. Splinters were embedded in his hand where he had gripped an old section of the fence. He released the fence and hugged Lily, sucking in deep breaths of the cooling evening air and the floral scent that was Lily.

"He's got to make it, Lily," Donovan's deep baritone voice was clogged with unshed tears. "He really is a good man. You know he is the first good friend I have acquired in years. I can't imagine how Doc and Will must feel knowing he saved their lives. And Lori. He is in love with her, you know."

"I know. Hunter, Storm, and the girls will be at the hospital. As well as Doc and Granny." Lily added.

"What did Granny do? Drive herself?"

"No. She slipped into the front seat of the ambulance when they weren't looking."

Donovan brushed Lily's hair back away from her face, then kissed her with a longing he had been unaware of needing, especially when she responded in kind.

"I know this moonlight is supposed to be romantic," Lily smiled. "And I hate to spoil it all; but before we go to the hospital, I think we need to eat and fill the warmer carryall with sandwiches and chocolate chip cookies."

"It's nice just holding hands. Like we are admitting we are a couple," Donovan said as they arrived at Doc and Granny's kitchen and shared their plans.

"No surprise we think alike," Opal suggested. "Why don't you eat while we wrap up something for the family so they don't have to leave the hospital for something other than a snack this late in the evening."

Tressie chuckled. "Lily, it appears you still can't eat cotton candy without getting it in your hair, unless you're starting a new hairstyle of pink and blue?"

"Nah!" Donovan teased. "Today she had some help. There was an average of twenty to twenty-five adults, waiting in line with their children. They had a choice of having a sketch or a profile, alone or with siblings or parent and child. The results were astounding, and this lady here and Lori were helping Shannon and Wendy corral the little ones, cotton candy and all."

"You appear to be having quite a problem holding your BBQ sandwich, Donovan," Lily remarked. When she turned his hand over she was astounded.

"Donovan!"

"I'll take care of these splinters. Later. Just one problem. Can you drive, Lily?"

When they arrived at the Turtle Crossing Hospital, they knew the moment they saw Lori's face that the report about Denver had not changed. And they all knew Lori had been waiting for Lily's arrival. The two went into an empty family waiting room to talk.

"Lori, have they allowed anyone to see him yet?"

"Just Doc and Granny."

"They won't let you see him because you're not family?"

"I saw him briefly when they took him somewhere for tests and when they brought him back to his room," Lori added. "I think the one nurse knows Granny, so they made certain I was in the hall. Lily, he just looks like he's sleeping, but they can't say when he might wake up. The strange part is they can't find anything wrong except he has a concussion."

"Try eating that sandwich, Sis. You haven't had much all day. You know, I think Donovan would tell them he is Denver's brother if allowed. Did you know they had spent that much time together?"

"Honestly. No. I mean, I was impressed that Denver took the time to teach Donovan to play the harmonica, but he surprised me today. You know, I think I could eat Doc's BBQ for breakfast," Lori added as she finished her sandwich and coffee.

"The hospital is asking us to leave," Hunter repeated. "Look who gets to go home with his hand all bandaged-up."

"I see someone took care of the splinters for you," Lily teased.

"Yes, the nurse said I would not be permitted to see Denver if I didn't because it was an invitation for infection."

"I'm going to stay at the Carriage House with him tonight," Hunter added.

Donovan just shrugged his shoulders. "It appears your brother can be a little bossy when he wants to, as well," he said with a smile.

"He didn't want you to know just how deep those splinters were," Hunter said. "It has to be soaked with Epson Salts to draw out any fragments she might have missed. Less chance of infection."

***

A few days later, Donovan stopped by Lily's office at Eight Mile Centre a little past seven before breakfast and was not surprised to see that she was with a patient, with two in the waiting room.

"Donovan," Madison asked when he walked in the door. "Are you here as a patient or to set an appointment?"

"Patient," he replied.

"Sign in here, please," Madison suggested. "Oh. And, don't you dare break her heart again. Have a seat please." Then she turned her back on him and answered the phone.

"Donovan?" Lily asked when she read over his complaints. "Why me? Why not Isaac? This date was the day you helped me move my new equipment in here. Why wait so long?"

"I don't have a job. Isaac doesn't have enough patients to warrant needing three chiropractors."

"Three?"

"Isaac's son, Andrew, started this week."

"How long has his son been back?"

"Isaac was vague about that."

"I see. On your stomach please," she asked. "Have you had problems with this shoulder in the past?"

"Yes."

"On your back. You knew you had two ribs out?"

"I suspected," Donovan replied. "You are very good, by the way."

"I'll need to see you in three days," Lily ordered. "Have you been icing it?"

"No."

"What have you been doing?"

"Thinking of you. Of us."

"Donovan, did anything else happen?"

"Doctor-patient privilege?" he asked.

"You know the answer to that," she chuckled.

"I bruised it when I tried to ride Bronc. Denver told me to make an appointment with you. He said you helped him when Bronc bucked him off, too." Donovan waited until she was finished with her diagnosis and treatment notes before he broke the silence that ensued. "Can you ever forgive me?"

"I've been trying. Honest I have," Lily replied. "What are you going to do now?"

"Would you consider mentoring me?"

"Really? The student mentoring the professor?"

"Yes. Working with you has become a dream of mine."

Lily couldn't recall ever hearing him mention working with her. "You're serious?"

"Very."

Lily's stomach tensed up and she forced herself to keep distance between them. Silence demanded she make eye contact with him. The look in his eyes was so compelling, they both smiled and Lily suggested, "We have to talk."

"Where?"

"Why not the Pease Carriage House? You're already moved in there, so we could have privacy."

"Madison," Lily suggested, "Since I don't have any more appointments today, would you please close up for me? I will be at the Pease Carriage House. We need to have some alone time to iron out…"

"Well. It's about time," Madison whispered. "I'll make certain you have that privacy, unless something happens with Denver or the family, though."

"Thanks. Oh, wait. Lunch is on me. I'll pick up my takeout. On second thought. Can you call them and double my order?"

***

When they entered the Carriage House, Lily exclaimed, "Donovan, I love the way you've made the Carriage House look more like a home than a gathering place for a crowd. So, you went shopping for not one but two kick-back chairs?"

"Denver and I went shopping together. The reddish brown is Denver's. The black one is mine."

After they ate, Donovan suggested, "I will start from the first time I ever saw you. It was at the Ohio State Fair in the garden produce aisle of ribbon-winning Pumpkins weighing hundreds of pounds, but it was you that fascinated me. I couldn't take my eyes off you."

"Then your twin Lori called you and reminded you she wanted to see some of the horse shows. But first, you still wanted to see the Butter Cow and get some ice cream. I wanted to talk to you, but my mom was busy. So I offered you my balloon. When you accepted it, your Dad called you away."

"I talked my mom into seeing a cow made of butter and she had it marked on her map, so we followed you and your family and were in line just as you were leaving with ice cream cones. You smiled at me as you approached, and I told you I was going to marry you someday. When someone greeted your Dad, 'Mr. David Donnelly. Good to see you.' They shook hands. And by the time we got our ice cream, you were gone. That's how I knew your name."

"I remember a blue balloon," Lily recalled. "I shared it with Lori in our room when we returned home. You were wearing a shirt the shade of your blue turquoise eyes. Not many children wore sunglasses, but when you took yours off, I was fascinated with the color of your eyes. And, I normally didn't talk to strangers. How did you know I was Lily and not Lori?"

"I can't explain that, but when I handed you the balloon, you hugged me and whispered, 'Thank you.' And when I told you I was going to marry you, do you remember what your response was?" When Lily shook her head no, Donovan added, you said, "I'm too young to get married, silly. Only my paper dolls get married. But like you, our paper-doll grooms had no name, so all of you are named Mystery Man."

"Lily. Really? Mystery Man?"

"Well. I didn't know your name," she replied.

"The next time was years later. When was the last time you were at the Winthrop Summer Theatre?" Donovan asked.

"I remember their production of Romeo and Juliet like it was yesterday," Lily replied. "Lori and I had made reservations early, and then she had to cancel, so I left her ticket at the front desk."

"I was one seat from the aisle when I noticed an old friend I hadn't seen for a while, and when she motioned, I left my jacket on my seat and joined her for a five-minute visit, then returned to my seat just as the theatre started filling up, except for the empty seat on the aisle."

"The lights had dimmed, and I stood up twice to let people through to their assigned seats when an usher stopped at my aisle, shining his light to reveal the row and seat number, just as the curtain opened. Twice, I folded my seat back and stood in its space, so people could get through. Each time the person in the aisle seat stepped down a step in the aisle, but he never spoke a word."

"However, when the lights were turned on between the first and second act..."

Donovan waited, as she appeared to be gathering her thoughts, but he recalled the happening.

"I glanced up at movement two rows up and six seats to my left. This giant of a woman, dressed to the nines, was not mindful of the people who had to duck out of her way. A woman's hat sailed down to the stage.

Her luggage-sized handbag was looped over her arm and swung out over two rows in front of her, and was headed my way when the man in the aisle seat put his hands on my waist and pretty much lifted me into the aisle and down a few steps out of her way. He whispered in my ear, 'Hello, again, we can't have you falling now, can we?' When the giant determinedly turned to plow towards the aisle, I felt the breeze of her bag and steamy, strong alcohol on her breath. I was caught in the moment, and my heart stopped when I looked into the most beautiful blue turquoise eyes ever. Then a woman yelled from the top row, 'Hey, Handsome!' That's when the man from the seat on the aisle asked, 'Will you be okay?' Then he moved to the top row. His concern surprised me. However, what has bothered me for years is where his hands had been at my waist, I was left with warm, tingling, indelible feelings. And there have been several times when I have wondered..."

"Lily, please honey. No tears! I had no idea. I looked for you after the play was over, and you had already left. I had no idea you felt what I did that evening," Donovan added, as he put his arms around her. "Lily, honey, you weren't eighteen yet and the woman I went and sat with was my cousin."

"Really? Really? But how did you know I wasn't eighteen?"

"My cousin recognized you and reminded me that I had no business dating anyone under eighteen."

"Donovan," Lily asked as she held onto his hand, "perhaps you could explain the week this man named Michael and I spent at that honeymoon vacation split condo? The door to his side was blue, and mine was green. He reminded me of you, except he wore glasses, had a mustache, and five o'clock shadow beard. When he guided me onto the dance floor, my fingers were electrified when he held my hands as we danced. Since then, I've dreamed about waltzing to 'The Tennessee Waltz' too many times to count. A couple on their anniversary had requested it. Michael sang to me, as well. This mystery drifts through my memory from time to time.

"The next morning, it was like the man I knew as Michael never existed because he left without a word, a goodbye, or let's keep in touch. And when I returned to class, a man known as Professor Michael D. James, was teaching one of my classes. He was wearing different glasses for a few weeks, and then only sunglasses when out on campus. No mustache or beard. Do you have a twin?"

"No. By the expression on your face, I get the feeling you recall that week as well. But, no matter what, not once did you ever attempt to make eye contact with me until recently. And I am left with this feeling of putting my personal life on hold, or move on, because I have no way of knowing you won't just turn around and leave. Again. I don't know if I can trust this person who has drifted in and out of my life like a pair of seasonal shoes."

When Donovan saw Lily was chilly, he removed his powder blue button-down-the-front, cable knit sweater and settled it carefully around her shoulders. His scent, and his after-shave wrapped around her.

Just for a moment, it was his warmth on her shoulders, her neck and arms. She sighed, and just as quickly, shrugged off the dream and his sweater. Her heart accepted the maybe someone, someday thoughts and she walked over to the Carriage House patio door.

"I refuse to play this now you see me, now you don't game anymore," Lily confided.

"Lily, will you please allow me to explain?" he asked as he turned his back on her to gather his thoughts and put into words he prayed she would accept.

"Do you remember the day we refer to as the arrival of the Pied Piper and your response to Little Miss Sunshine?"

When he turned back around, he let out the breath he had been holding. Lily's arms were unfolded, so he pulled up a chair and sat facing her. "I was petrified of wedding bells after watching my parents selfish marriage battles, and whether I could father a child wasn't of any interest to me then. I carry in my heart the look on your face as you cradled that baby in your arms. But was crushed by the knowledge that I can't father a child for you. When I add your feelings about being as much drawn to me as I have been to you."

When Lily nodded her head, he continued. "Then add this magnetic reaction we have for each other; I have not just fallen in love with you, sweetheart. I believe I fell in love with you that day at the Ohio State Fair."

Donovan reached in his pocket and held the ring in his hand. "I have carried this ring for several months, but until now, I was unaware of what really stopped me. It would have been so unfair of me to ask you to be my wife until you knew that all the plans you and Lori have had for years, namely your weddings and children, could or couldn't happen. But what if the tests I just had done, prove otherwise? Perhaps if you meet my parents, you would have a better understanding about my family and me. Having shared trust and belief in God and spending time with you and your family and Denver has opened my eyes and my heart."

Lily had never seen this uncertain side of Donovan and was hesitant to interrupt him.

"I've stayed in the background. Sometimes just watched you from afar. Other moments when I felt included in your world are the ones I treasure. Bottom line honey no matter what I say or do," he asked softly, daringly. "Do you ever need anyone? I'll walk away if that is what you want. No matter what the test reveals."

Lily reached out and clasped Donovan's hands in hers, her heart in her throat, "I would love to meet your family. As I told you earlier, your Great-Grandfather's debt is not yours to settle." Then, she drew him closer and kissed the back of each of his hands, never losing eye contact with him.

"So, does this mean our love for each other is rock solid?" Donovan asked.

"Absolutely!"

"In that case, you need to know, after that night we stayed at the Pease Victorian, I asked Lori, Hunter, your Mom and Dad, and Will for their permission for your hand in marriage."

"I can't believe they kept this from me, all this time."

He got down on one knee and asked, "Lily Anneé Donnelly, will you marry me?"

"Yes," she replied softly, as he placed the ring on her finger.

"Are you certain you are ready to commit your life and your future with mine, knowing what you now know?"

"Yes, I am," Lily replied. "You said you just had some tests run to find out if you can father a child. So, was this the first time you have questioned the validity of that report?"

"Yes. I was in grade school when my mom told me."

"I was with my Great-Grandpa when he had a

fender-bender auto accident. The emergency room doctor insisted on running some tests, and I remember the ER nurse was filling in as a trainee for someone else. They were really swamped because it was the first of the season snowfall which meant icy roads and sidewalks."

"What type of injuries did you have?"

"Great-Grandpa bruised his jaw on the steering wheel, and I bumped my head on the window and door handle. He didn't believe in seatbelts. We both had a concussion."

"You remember the day I saw you with Little Miss Sunshine, I told you it broke my heart? That was the evening I asked Denver if he could teach me to play the harmonica. I wanted to cry, and there wasn't anyone to share this pain with. He had told me that playing relaxed him and Bronc. He also said that Will agreed that it was smarter than picking a fight with someone, and less painful."

Donovan placed a 33 vinyl record on the record player he had acquired at the same estate sale as the harmonica. As the music played, he twirled her around, brought her close, and kissed her on her right cheek, then her left, backed her away, and again drew her close. Neither of them was aware of who moved first for the kiss they both had dreamed would surely happen someday.

"Lily, if there hasn't been a change in Denver when we stop at the hospital, what do you think about meeting my mom and dad? We could leave early in the morning, eat lunch with them, and return home here before sunset?"

"I like the way you think. Please understand, I was on my own in college, except when Lori and I talked on the phone. I would like nothing better than to spend more quality time with you."

True to his promise the day before, Donovan drove from the Carriage House to the Victorian for breakfast. He knocked and Lily called out through the screen door, "French toast, bacon, and strawberries. Hot coffee, iced tea and oatmeal chocolate chip cookies, to go as you requested. Come on in."

"Why is it," Donovan asked, "You never cease to amaze me?"

"Thanks. So, do you think this cool, snowy-white seersucker, baby-soft, pleated skirt with swirls of lavender blossoms sundress will be suitable for today?" she asked, as she twirled around in white strappy high-heeled sandals and straw hat. "Plus matching jacket, I might add."

"I didn't think to ask yesterday, but do you want to drive my Lincoln instead of putting miles on your rental?"

"Sounds like a great idea. The local dealership is checking on a few leads for me." What he failed to mention had more to do with his finances than she could ever imagine.

Lily handed Donovan the keys, smiled, and slipped into the passenger seat.

"Your trust is greatly appreciated," Donovan added, as he leaned her way and kissed her briefly on the lips. He smiled and drove out onto the street, thinking perhaps he should have introduced her to his parents before he asked her to marry him.

***

An hour later, he announced, "Well here we are. The house I grew up in is the white house with black shutters, with brick on the front and sides."

Donovan pulled in the drive, but no one opened a door to greet them. Lily hesitated asking, but reached over and touched his hand which she noted was clutching the steering wheel, even though he had turned the engine off and removed the key.

"They don't expect us for at least another hour," Donovan said.

"Okay," Lily asked, "you must have had a reason for arriving early?"

"I do. I plan to move most of my belongings out today, even though they're expecting me to return to teaching."

"Do they know we're engaged?"

"No."

"What are you really afraid of? Donovan, come on. I'm here for you. You have to start trusting me, sometime. I love you, Mr. Donovan Michael James!"

"Thank you."

"Okay. Let's get this show on the road," she suggested, as she opened her car door, but waited for him to assist her out of the car, as he had in the past, when he met the description of the almost-perfect gentleman.

The moment he stepped inside the front door, he gripped Lily's hand. And she turned, moved into his arms and hugged him. The silence felt strange as they glanced around the room when he turned on the light.

"Nothing has changed. The same furniture is still where it has always been for thirty years. Follow me. I'll show you my room."

"What can I do to help?" Lily asked. His dress shirts and

trousers were on hangers, evenly spaced a half-inch apart. She hadn't even noticed the suitcase he retrieved from the shelf above the hangers and opened on the bed. Within fifteen minutes his clothes, books, and personal items had been retrieved and loaded in the trunk of Lily's vehicle.

Once back inside, Donovan appeared to be looking over the numerous books shelved in the living/dining room area. "Can I help you find something?" Lily asked.

"I'm looking for my journals."

"Book titles appear to be filed alphabetically. How are your journals marked?" Lily asked. Then she spotted a group shelved on the floor level partially behind a desk. "Shine your flashlight back here again," she suggested. "Is this what you're looking for?"

He counted the odd-sized notebooks as he loaded them into an oversized briefcase on wheels. "Those two are different," Lily remarked, but they have your name plastered on the outside."

He leafed through them and literally threw them in his briefcase with his journals. Then he quickly wheeled it out and loaded it in the trunk.

"Do you still expect them?" Lily asked as she held up a family group picture. "You look very stern in this photo," she teased. "What's wrong?"

"I'm still undecided as to whether or not I should have involved you in this mess," he mumbled.

"Donovan, there is a brown car and a local police car in the drive."

"This is so like them."

"And the two women on foot. Neighbors?"

"Oh, yes."

"That voice! The one we heard in Sidney?"

"Afraid so."

"Donovan?" Lily asked. "Don't you dare drop those shoulders."

When he noted the warrior look in her eyes, he replied, "Honey, you have no idea how much I love you." He wrapped his arms around her and gently kissed her.

The moment Donovan's parents and the neighbors burst in the front door, Donovan was kissing Lily. The neighbors yelled, "Arrest them, officer," but shut up when they saw it was Donovan with some tall beautiful blonde with a ring on her finger. Recognition and a look they had never seen in Donovan's eyes. The look of love.

The local police officers asked Donovan's dad, "Are you requesting charges be filed against your son?"

"No," Donovan's dad replied. "Donovan. Good to see you again, son. Who is this woman? And why is she here? Pretty fancy car you are driving there, son."

"Donovan," Officer Brown asked, "do you know a man named Will Fox?

"Yes. Why?"

"Well...he and I were at a luncheon when the call came in and he recognized the license plate and description of the Lincoln out front. He vouched for you, unequivocally."

"Mom? Dad?" Donovan suggested. "I knew you wouldn't understand how my future wife's family stick together. So, first of all, I would like to introduce you to my fiancée, Lily Donnelly. And, as such, she has the right to know if the man she loves unconditionally, deserves to know if you have replaced the twenty-five thousand dollars you borrowed from my local bank account."

His parents sat down. "You must be mistaken," his dad sputtered. "But you go back to teaching and it's yours."

"No. I don't plan to go back to teaching, no matter what little stories you 'leak' to the press. That includes you and your neighbors, Mother."

"Son, I was hoping you would have learned all about this woman by now, and turned to look at Lily. "Well! Little Missy," his mother spat out, eyeing Lily like she was yesterday's trash. "Did he tell you he can't father any little orphans for you?"

A dozen comments raced through Lily's mind, but any comment had to come from Donovan himself. She just prayed Will hadn't been close enough to reply.

"Mom, Dad," Donovan announced, "I am no longer your puppet. You have a good life. I have my own plans. Let's go, honey," Donovan added.

As Lily slipped her hand into his, she whispered, "We missed a couple of your journals on the top shelf."

The doorbell rang. While the neighbor girl asked to give Lily a gift, Denver retrieved the rest of his missing journals. The one felt rather thick but he didn't have time to look as he untucked his shirt and slipped them into the back of his trousers.

When they left, Lt. Brandi was in the lead, followed by Donovan and Lily, with Will and Hunter bringing up the rear. Storm had joined Lily and Donovan.

"First of all, Lily," Storm asked, as he leaned over the

back of the front seat. "What is in the gift box? Look quickly before we leave the city limits. Here wear these rubber gloves. No need for a cover-up here, OK?"

"Donovan, does this teapot have any meaning to you?" Storm asked.

"No."

"False bottom? Notes on the back? What about your journals?" Storm asked.

"One of them felt thicker than the others."

"Okay if I take a look while you drive?"

"Sure. I just recently closed all my accounts and investments, retitled them, and changed my residence."

"Totally, how much are we talking here? How much is missing?"

"You know what? I am embarrassed to admit it, but at least seventy-five thousand, or more. Why?"

"Do you have proof of all of this?"

"Yes. I've been on the phone off and on for over two weeks," Donovan replied.

"Who has been helping you?" Storm asked.

"Richard Warren. He's president of the bank in Winthrop."

"Did you hear all that, Dad?" Storm asked, as he held up his phone so Donovan could see it.

"You've been talking to my Grandpa?" Lily asked.

"I didn't know that in the beginning. Hunter suggested I should see him."

"Dad," Storm phoned Will and Lt. Brandi. "Can we pull over at that rest area we passed on our way to that earlier meeting here an hour ago?"

"Donovan," Storm suggested, "I see why this one journal of yours was so thick."

When Will and Brandi joined Storm in the back seat of Lily's Lincoln, Storm asked Donovan, "Is this your signature on this withdrawal paperwork of two other banks, inside these two envelopes? They are from accounts in your name."

"Thirty thousand dollars in one and forty-five-thousand in the other," Storm added.

Will and Brandi asked Donovan the same question. "You didn't give your parents the legal right to withdraw cash from your personal accounts?"

"No. As soon as I read my bank reports, I called Mr. Warren and he immediately moved the balance into a new account in Winthrop, and The Turtle Crossing City Bank and Savings. I'll call Mr. Warren. Can we stop in Winthrop on our way back home?"

***

Lily and Donovan arrived back at the Victorian, ate leftovers, and headed to their favorite couch with hot chocolate. "Are you too tired to talk?" Lily asked.

"You know, I feel at home wherever you are," Donovan replied.

"Do you have an explanation for your mom and dad doing what they have done to you?"

"I am so glad you suggested explanation, rather than excuses. The truth is my dad and my Uncle Sebastion James, my dad's brother, have never gotten along for as long as I can remember. The bits and pieces of their arguments usually ended with how my Uncle was wasting his life as a chiropractor instead of teaching on the college level."

"My parents have continued this criticism with me after my Uncle passed and left whatever he had to me. They were angry that he left his estate to me with no mention of my dad in his will."

"So, what are your plans?" Lily asked

"I need to visit the property, but not until Denver recovers."

"I can't recall hearing you being the optimist here," Lily teased.

"Is there any other way?" Donovan replied, with a smile.

Lily's phone rang. "Excuse me. That was Hunter. The family is insisting that we bring all your journals inside the Victorian and that you stay overnight with me here."

"I don't need to ask why?"

"They are trying to cover all the possibilities, considering…"

"Considering what my parents have been doing for years?"

***

The following morning, Lily and Donovan arrived at church together, but held off showing her engagement ring to anyone. And found hiding their excitement wasn't easy when Lori's concern and fear that Denver would never be the same driven, fun loving person he had become.

Harder still after she and Donovan held hands and prayed together before breakfast.

However, Lori was focused on Denver's failure to respond at all. It was apparent Lori had not been eating well. She had lost weight and had already drawn two more holes in her belt to keep her jeans up. Denver had been in the hospital over a week. The Donnelly family sat with the O'Reilly family for church on Sunday.

Lily felt compelled to reach out to Lori for Denver after Sunday Church service when her friends' connection-prayer surprisingly built momentum.

The weight of a hand on her shoulder gave her the strength and courage to pursue answers to a nagging quandary of questions. With a leap of faith, her belief in the Lord Jesus Christ settled calmly in her chest.

Lily felt Lori's connection and discomfort. Having lived her life on a rollercoaster of feelings with Donovan, Lily understood Lori's frustration and regret that she had held off telling Denver how much she loved him before he was injured at Doc's.

Lori had stifled a scream inside her chest when she saw Denver lying so still on the ground. And afterwards, every time Lori closed her eyes, she battled with the knowledge that he might never leave the hospital alive.

She squeezed Lily's hand and whispered, "I can't lose him. All those monitors and he still hasn't opened his eyes."

Lily put her arm around Lori and guided her to the hospital chapel. As they kneeled at the altar, and prayed, they were filled with an unusual expectant energy. Lily gently turned Lori around and stated, "We are going to use this anointing oil that Dr. Kate described and pray for Denver's recovery."

"Wait a minute here," Lori pleaded. "We—meaning you and me?"

"Yes. What can it hurt? We're not overthinking this," Lily said.

"I agree, but since when have we ever allowed hesitation to stop us?"

Lily smiled, winked at Lori, and suggested, "Because every time we bite into a chocolate chip cookie…"

Lori saluted Lily and proceeded. "The crunch in the first cookies we ever mixed up was not nuts, but egg shells." Lori giggled.

"But, we followed Grandma's recipe," Lily recalled. "Add eggs. It didn't say break eggs and toss the shells."

With a smile on her face, Lori agreed. "You're right!"

Lori gripped Lily's hand as they entered Denver's room. Lori called his name several times, but there was still no response. Then she leaned down and kissed him on the cheek, swallowed her tears, and nodded to Lily. Their plan was to complete a circle, with Denver as the main focus between them.

Facing Denver as they had planned, one on either side of his bed, Lori slipped her left hand into his and prepared to join her right hand with Lily's left. They both smoothed the anointing oil on Denver's forehead. Lily placed her left hand into Lori's right hand and her right hand soothingly on his left shoulder.

Then, closing their eyes, with heads bowed, they began praying aloud the 23rd Psalm as their parents had taught them. "'The Lord is my Shepherd…'" At *Amen,* Lily and Lori opened their eyes.

When Denver squeezed Lori's hand, Lily kept gently massaging his left shoulder. His lips trembled as he struggled to speak. His heart rate changed on the monitor. He blinked his eyes and stared at Lori, struggled to smile, and squeezed her hand again.

Lori whispered, "Thank you, Lord Jesus," and kissed the back of his hand, never losing eye contact with him.

Lily was stunned. Her hand was still on Denver's shoulder. His hospital gown was wet. Perspiration beaded the hair on his head and his mustache.

Lori's and Lily's hands were still warm as medical personnel rushed into his room and shooed them out. The moment they stepped out of his room into the hall, they were met by their mom, dad, Hunter, and Storm.

"Let's go into this other room so the two of you can have some privacy. We'll be right outside this door," their Mom said in a soothing, yet forceful, voice.

As soon as the door closed, they unexpectedly felt a bit shaky and sat down, facing each other. Tears fell like a bursting dam. Drying their eyes, Lily placed her hand on Lori's forehead, and Lori did the same to Lily.

"Our hands are really warm," Lori remarked.

"I know," Lily replied.

Their mom knocked on the door, opened it a crack, and asked, "How are you doing?"

"We're fine, Mom," Lori replied. "Can we see him yet?" Shannon shook her head no.

"Hunter?" Lily motioned him inside their room.

"Lily," Lori inquired, "so, the Lord Jesus Christ healed Denver—through us—just as Dr. Kate said he might?"

"Isn't it amazing, Hunter?" Lori asked.

"Yes," Hunter replied. "Lori, if you're up to it, the doctor thinks Denver is looking for you. The doctor's orders are: only one family member at a time."

Lily stood in the doorway of Denver's room while Lori went back inside. Lily was stunned when she recognized the depth of abiding love in Denver's eyes for Lori.

She felt overwhelmed remembering the times Donovan had looked at her with the same feeling of genuine devotion after a late morning walk.

Later that evening, when he reached across the table, encasing her prayerful hands in his, her heart had beat faster and they danced several dances together.

***

Denver was starting to fall back to sleep, when he tugged on Lori's hand to pull her towards him and Lori whispered in his ear, "I love you, Denver Avery O'Reilly, "and brushed her lips against his cheek. When she backed away, tears gathered in his eyes. "You're tired, but I won't be far," she whispered, as the nurse motioned her to leave.

The moment Lori left Denver's room, Lily gripped Lori's hand and drew her back into the private room. "We have to talk before the family returns with food. Sis," Lily implored, "Hunter was just inside Denver's room and I assume he was praying with us—but not certain."

Hunter knocked on the door and stepped inside. "Rev. C.W. is with me."

"C.W?" Lori pleaded, "We need your help."

"At your service. I understand the Miracle of God just happened. How are my lovely nieces feeling?" he asked.

His tentative question and gentle hug soothed them. "This mystery of the ages is in your heart. The need to understand, to be the Lord's intermediator."

"I'm overwhelmed," Lily replied.

"Understandable," he said, gently holding their hands in his. "The most important point is Denver is alert and expected to fully recover. Now shall we pray?" They prayed their favorite prayer and felt the power of the Lord still within them.

"C.W., Lily, Lori," Hunter added, "I prayed before and after your healing prayer session for Denver."

***

The following morning, Lily and Lori settled onto the couch for two across from C.W. in his Chapel office.

"Good morning, ladies. I have the list of questions you asked Hunter to deliver, but would still like to hear them from you personally. The last report about Denver yesterday was good. Have you heard anything this morning, Lori?"

C.W. had watched his great nieces grow up; and, when he asked Lori about Denver, her shoulders relaxed a bit and her hands moved as she began explaining Denver's condition.

"He is doing so well in therapy," she explained. "His doctor suggested releasing him in Granny and Doc's care."

"That's great news. First of all, I am impressed with the Strength of your Faith in God. God works in mysterious ways. It's a mystery even to me."

"So, you're saying Denver's response to our prayers and the anointing oil had to do with our belief that God would help Denver wake up from this coma?" Lily asked.

Lori clutched Lily's hand and said, "We're not studying to be in God's ministry like Hunter is. So, why us?"

"You were chosen. God led you to know what to do. I repeat, God works in mysterious ways."

"Really?" Lily added. "But, we weren't certain what we were doing. Hunter's comment was, 'Just think. If you hadn't taken that step, it would have been an unopened gift.'"

"And, how did that make you feel?"

"Well, I was so worried about Denver, I couldn't think straight; but Lily just pushed forward."

"I just reminded you, about other things we used to do together, Sis."

C.W. clasped his hands and smiled. "If God is to work, He first has to be in you to work through you. He is alive. You are God's messengers, His Legs and Arms here on Earth."

"But," Lori recalled, "When we asked Dr. Kate how to go about the special prayer, she said to trust that God would guide us."

"Then," Lily continued, "God would decide how we dealt with the aftermath."

"Are you ready to talk about that?" he asked.

"We both cried," Lori replied.

"Our legs were a bit shaky," Lily added. "And, besides that, our hands were still warm for a couple of hours."

"But," Lori continued, "Perspiration poured off of Denver's head, his rough beard, his mustache, and hospital gown."

"Did that frighten you?"

They looked at each other and back at him, and shook their heads no.

"This is a miracle," he said reverently.

"Granny said she feels like it was a Spiritual Healing."

"In our everyday life, as we converse with others—it's the way Christ Jesus would have you do it. And should you do this again, don't be upset if you don't feel the same, or have similar results—for God may feel you can handle the aftermath feelings."

"I just praise the Lord. Thank you for sharing and don't question God's plans or thoughts. God answers prayers."

"But," Lily asked, "I was confused and hurt when I shared this with a close friend, and her response was disbelief and then she rattled some medical stuff and said it was just psychological."

"Don't be disappointed. Don't throw in the towel, if after anointing someone, and they die anyway."

C.W. was quiet for a moment. "Understand. There will be others who will not believe, but nobody will believe in you unless you believe in yourself. God will let you know when He needs you."

Chapter 19

As Denver continued to fulfill the routine his physical therapist had scheduled, she was impressed at how quickly he had recovered. What she didn't know was how hard he had worked before the coma to catch up with two of the original Foursome, Hunter and Storm.

But Lori was his focus, his determination to fully get back his strength, physically and mentally. When he turned his calendar from September to October, his cellphone rang. "Donovan, I was just grabbing my luggage and headed your way. Do you need me to pick up anything at the market?"

"No, thanks. Before Lily and Lori left for their shopping trip early this morning, Lily dropped off her recipe file. But Sadie also gave me her secret chili recipe. This whole place smells like it too. See you in a bit."

Denver dropped his luggage inside the door of the Pease Victorian Carriage House and turned left to set Aunt Rose's dessert carrier on the kitchenette counter.

"Did Granny put something in each of those five layers? I smell cinnamon, apple, pecan and chocolate."

"You know how she is. She's afraid we might starve otherwise. Doc and Granny treat me like the son they never had, however for some reason, I feel more at home here than I do at the O'Reilly's.

"You know you're always welcome here anytime. Is that why you wanted to leave your kick-back chair here?"

"Well, I still sleep in the bunkhouse for one thing, and I hate to admit this, I have a phobia about sleeping anywhere but the main floor."

"I see. And all the bedrooms here are on the second floor. What else is going on?" Donovan asked as he handed Denver a mug of coffee, with a piece of cherry pie. They had just settled in their chairs when Donovan inquired, "Have you asked Lori to marry you yet? You've had her ring as long as I had Lily's."

"I did. I talked to her Mom and Dad, Hunter, Lily and Uncle Will if they approved of Lori becoming my bride. They all approved. Lori and I work together every day and every time I think about marriage, I freeze."

The carriage house was as quiet as walking on the beach at sunrise, when the refrigerator dropped a half bucket of ice cubes. Denver drained his coffee mug and turned towards Donovan, and struggled in a tone that concerned him. "What if I never get my memory back? There are some things I still can't remember."

"Are you referring to the 4th of July?"

"Yes. Every once in a while I hear a pinging sound, metal on metal, a rifle shot, and see Doc and Will waver in the distance—appear as in a mirror reflected image from the side of the rifle that looks familiar."

"Have you shared this with anyone?"

"No. Why? I just wish the nightmare would stop."

"You know, I overheard Will tell Brandi that he and Doc were blinded by a momentary flash of the sun reflected off that rifle which blinded them. It took them awhile to piece together what had happened."

"They were busy trying to save my life." Denver's voice was but a whisper as he rocked back in his chair looking a bit lost. "It would have been ironic if the rifle that almost cost me my life, turned out to be the one that my Dad gave me on my fifteenth birthday. And was later stolen."

"I had kept it hidden under my bed in the original box and wrapping paper and later shelved this same empty box in my Farrier Office. When I reported it missing to Brandi, she took a photo of the box. Has Brandi released a report regarding the rifle?"

"No. I've heard these things take time."

Denver refilled their steaming coffee mugs and continued, "Thank you, Donovan. You're like the brother I never had and I think I just might beat you at Double Solitaire after all."

The following morning over breakfast Denver asked, "When did Lily say they would be back?"

Donovan smiled and said, "Two days. I know you don't play golf, but what about fishing?"

"Never tried that either, but always wanted to. Doc and Granny talked about it, but we never seemed to find the time."

"While you were singing in the shower, I called David, our ladies' dad. He has everything we'll need and is anxious for an outing. We won't need a fishing license because it's on private property."

Denver had always heard fish hooks could be a bit tricky and prayed he could focus on fishing today because he couldn't wait to see Lori. "I noticed Lily was wearing your ring, but am surprised Lori hasn't even mentioned it."

Denver finished pulling on a faded ball cap and retrieved Lori's ring he had carried in his pocket for two months, then hesitantly asked, "Donovan, have you and Lily set a date for your wedding yet?"

"Lily mentioned Christmas,"

"But that's five months away!"

Donovan smiled and nodded.

Epilogue

Five Months Later—December 1986

Lily and Lori had arrived at GreatStone Castle Wednesday, December 16, 1986, around three p.m. Madison and Harmony had joined them to give credibility to their last-minute shopping spree out of town.

"Uncle Kristopher, how can we ever thank you for setting up this unusual situation for us?" Lori asked.

"Come on," he replied, looking from one twin to the other. "I consider it an honor to be asked to officiate at one of your weddings. Lily, you've met Donovan's parents and I've read some of the threatening letters his parents have sent recently, and you are also aware of some of the laws they have broken.

"Lori, I doubt you've forgotten the condition Denver was in when he arrived at Doc's. Even though his Dad's gambling debts have been paid in full, Denver doesn't trust that group. You look surprised. Sorry. I thought you knew about that."

"No. But that's okay."

"By the way, you ladies look lovely as usual," Kristopher added. "Would you like to look through the paperwork again?"

They both shook their heads no.

"I couldn't be prouder of you if you were my own daughters, and just so you know, I've grown to respect Denver and Donovan."

Smiling, they replied in unison, "We think they are pretty special too."

As soon as Kristopher left them, Lily grabbed hold of Lori's hand and asked, "Are you nervous?"

"Yeah. Excited too," Lori replied. "It seems strange, though."

"You mean because Hunter and Storm aren't here to be a part of this crazy scheme."

"Oh, I think they just arrived."

"Where?" Lily asked, looking around the Christmas Holiday swags, lights and decorations. "So, I wasn't wrong, but we weren't the only ones who assumed they would be here."

"No." Lori agreed. "You weren't wrong. At least we will have more privacy at Mom's Great-Grandad's Winthrop Estate. That will be nice."

"Hunter. Storm. It's great to see you both," Lori greeted, taking a calming deep breath. "We'll see you later."

As the twins climbed the stairs to the dressing room, Lily asked Lori, "Has Uncle Kristopher explained everything to you? He prefers we sign the papers before midnight and leave the GreatStone Castle. That's the business side," Lily added.

"I know, Sis. Denver and I have said goodnight more than once. But keeping our promise to wait until our wedding night has not been easy."

"So have Donovan and I. It became much harder when Denver was hurt and in a coma. We questioned and prayed regarding waiting to consummate our love for each other when tomorrows can be so fragile."

"Are you two ready to slip into your backup wedding dresses?" Madison asked as she and Harmony removed the white and silver dresses for the brides.

"Just so you know," Harmony added as she finished zipping Lori's dress, and with arms opened wide said, "Look at you. Amazing. No belts. No buttons. No jewelry, and both of you are glowing."

"Madison and I feel honored to be included in this evening's festive wedding. Not many couples would go to such lengths to not only protect each other, but your families as well."

"In case our guys haven't said anything to you," Madison said, "Storm and I will be driving one couple, and Hunter and Harmony will be driving the other when we leave."

"This way you can have some privacy on your way to your next destination," Harmony added. "Your grooms are waiting. A bit impatiently, I might add."

***

Lily and Donovan had just returned to the Pease Victorian from their honeymoon weekend after their secret first wedding at GreatStone Castle. "I'm certain all of our wedding photographs will be memorable," Lily remarked.

The parlor was lit by soft colorful lights from the fragrant Blue Spruce Christmas tree, and Donovan had just placed a recording of "Waltz Across Texas" by Ernest Tubb on the record player.

"May I have this dance, Mrs. Donovan James?"

"Yes," Lily said softly, as she melted in his arms. "I still feel as though this past weekend was just a dream. Why did we fight so hard to find ways to not say yes to each other?"

"Honey, I really don't know," he replied. As he twirled her around, her ankle-length flared skirt swirled and caught on a leg of the Pennsylvania-built miniature black pot-bellied stove. When it tipped against the fireplace, the bottom door and lid flew off.

When Donovan tightened the loose leg, Lily prepared to replace the lid when a short, fat sock fell out.

After pulling out over a half dozen IOU receipt stuffed socks, they found a letter addressed to Donovan's great-grandfather, Michael James, who had left a specific Bayonet Sword as collateral for his loan. It was marked, Paid-in-full, and signed Isaac R. Pease, Sr.

Enclosed with the letter was a flyer featuring Isaac's storytelling presentations using this Model Argentino 1909 Mouser Sword Bayonet that represented military using similar swords. At the bottom of the flyer was written: *A special thank you to Michael James for the loan of the above sketched bayonet.*

"You remember what tomorrow is?" Lily asked, smiling when they finished their dance.

"Yes ma'am," he replied. "Somehow, getting married in the church the day before Christmas has me intrigued. Which reminds me, it's about time for Denver to bring Lori here and then I will join him at the Carriage House for the rest of the evening. I look forward to seeing you in church tomorrow, sweetheart," he added as they kissed and the doorbell rang.

***

Early the following morning the ladies were in the Pease Victorian, and the men had gathered in the Victorian Carriage House. There was a bustle of excitement at both places. The bridal party room looked like a bridal beauty shoppe. Each dressed in matching robes and slippers as the hairdressers took over part of the kitchen.

Madison and Harmony found a quiet corner in the front parlor to enjoy the smorgasbord of food the Shadow Angels had insisted the young ladies might need. "Decorating the church was so much fun," Harmony remarked as she prepared to dip a strawberry into a fruity dip and held it aloft. "Are you ready to go through all this preparation for your wedding?"

"If it is with Storm, yes! What about you?"

"I don't think I would have a choice," Harmony replied. "Remember meeting the Carpentiers from Sunrise?"

"Just at the GreatStone Castle wedding shower," Madison replied. "I like Jace, but when his mom Pearl, and sister Samantha found fault with the food and the gifts, I almost bit my tongue to keep from smiling when Brandi gave them a choice to say something nice or zip it and leave!"

375

"They listened, though, didn't they?" Harmony smiled.

"Hello Girls," Great-Grandma Fox, Will's mom, greeted as Richard Warren's wife, Eileen set a snack plate of cheese, crackers and grapes on the table beside her. She smiled and took a sip of her cold drink.

"I've heard a lot about you, Madison. My Great Grandson, Stormy, just can't quit talking about you."

Madison blushed and replied, "Thank you. Yes. Today is a very special day for all the family."

"Shannon, you favor your mom, Summer, with your hair styled back and up," Grandma Fox remarked. "It's days like this when I feel closest to her, and am reminded of her absence more."

"Thanks, Grandma," Shannon replied.

"Madison, Harmony, can you make certain the rest of the attendants are ready? You all look lovely," Shannon added, her hands trembling.

When Shannon started to introduce them to Great-Grandma Fox, Madison winked at the attendants who were all in their twenties. Harmony glanced up and saw Hunter waiting at the door.

Nodding at Grandma Fox, Shannon continued: "This is the Maid of Honor, Marcie, and Bridesmaids: Sheldon's daughter, Amber Beth-Eden Donnelly; Will and Wendy's daughter, Summer Jewel Fox; Mason and Autumn's daughter, Allison Ellen Davies; Friends and Associates, Harmony Faith Forever and Madison Grace Ball.

"Ladies, our dresses, shoes, and personal luggage have been delivered to the church," Shannon continued. "By the way, everyone did an awesome job decorating the church. It is beautiful and will remain for the Christmas Pageant."

"Mom," Hunter teased, "your ride is still waiting. Grandma Fox is riding with you."

"What about the girls?" she asked looking around the room.

"They left fifteen minutes ago. We're locking up and will meet you at the church," he added, as he hugged her and whispered, "Everything is going to be okay. Try to relax. I love you. I would kiss you on the cheek, but I don't want to mess up your makeup," he teased, and she smiled.

"Amber," Hunter stated, "you will be riding with Harmony and me."

"Allison and Summer," Storm announced, "You will be riding with Madison and me."

"Hey, big brother," Summer teased. "I understand Dad has had his hands full with other Warren Family weddings, but surely you don't expect any problems with this wedding?"

Storm wished he hadn't even glanced at his dad in that moment because it resulted in chill bumps running up his spine and settled in his neck and shoulders. Storm felt Hunter's response as well. "Dad," Storm asked, "may Hunter and I have a copy of your itinerary?"

Will pulled sheets out for each driver and ordered, "Follow them. Lt. Brandi Carpenter has approved them. There are NO detours. Keep your phones on speaker phone and report any traffic delays or anyone darting in and out of traffic."

Harmony and Madison went into the Four Aces mode and turned on their phones before they fastened their seat belts. The attendants felt their 'awareness,' and felt safe as a result. However, because they had heard about some of their escapades, they remained silent but watchful.

Meanwhile, Marcie was driving Lily and Lori to the church in her Marcie's Flower Delivery truck. "I hope getting married a week ago at the GreatStone Castle hasn't spoiled a do-over for you today?" Marcie asked.

"Not at all," Lori replied. "I can't wait to start our honeymoon; you know, just the two of us, with some uninterrupted time. Denver said while he was still in a coma, he heard people tell him they loved him, and he heard Lily and me when we prayed aloud for him. He said he truly believes there is a heaven. That he saw it, but hearing my voice..."

"Lily?" Marcie questioned. "I totally agree with Lori. But when Donovan asked me how many children I would like us to have, I was overwhelmed. The possibility that we could have a family, you know? Of course, our conversations are pretty special to us."

"Thank you both for sharing. Your thoughts are saved in my heart," Marcie replied, as she pulled into the delivery entrance of the church.

"Marcie," Lily inquired, "can you share any info that Will is on the lookout for?"

"I will share this much. Sarge has been singing like a canary. They're expecting the King Pin will show his hand and surprise us all. The Sunrise police and those in retirement are on the lookout for him." Marcie didn't have the right to say more, and her heart went out to his family.

Sheldon Warren was driving Denver and Donovan in Marcie's Catering Truck. "How are the two of you doing?" he asked.

"I take it," Donovan replied, "You know we were married at GreatStone Castle a week ago?"

"Yes," Sheldon replied. "I understand you both had your reasons?"

"Yes," Donovan answered. "My parents have sent Lily and me threatening letters insisting Lily sign a prenuptial so they can inherit my Uncle Sebastian James' estate, should I die. But Sebastian had a fantastic attorney. His will prohibits my Dad ever getting a penny, no matter what."

"Denver?" Sheldon questioned. "So, how has Kristopher Donnelly helped you?"

"He made out our wills the same day of our wedding. What a relief."

"Here I thought the Warren family had the brass ring on weddings. What am I saying? This should be expected. This is a Warren family wedding!"

Doc and Granny delivered the groomsmen to the church: the Best Man, Shannon and David's son, Hunter James Donnelly; Marcie and Sheldon Warren's son, Kristopher Charlie Warren; Brandi and Jonothan's son, Jacob Fletcher Carpenter; Autumn and Mason's son, Alex Daniel Davies.

C.W.'s church was packed and no one minded that their purses were searched, and didn't mind waiting outside in the cold white tent before filing in for the wedding. That's one thing that came in handy. One could pack more people into pews than chairs. The twins had always wanted a Christmas wedding.

The bridesmaids' dresses wore ankle-length, short-sleeved dresses, with a bodice of red velvet with removable jacket and candy-apple red high-heeled boots. The groomsmen wore black tuxedos, white shirts, red satin bow ties and cummerbunds. The grooms' tuxedos featured tails, white shirts, and red satin vests outlined in black with black bow ties.

The brides' princess style gowns were organza over white poly-satin. The bodice was appliqued with satin embroidered Venice lace roses, swirls and fine fern framed the sweetheart neckline. Layers of Crystal pleated ruffles and Venice lace covered the chapel length train. Segments of the embroidered satin had been applied by hand to the full sheer sleeves with four-inch buttoned wristbands.

The brides' white hats were covered in the same lace as the dress with a veil of bridal illusion flowing down the back. The removable veils were fastened to red satin head bands. They wore high-heeled white boots and ankle-length red wool capes for their trip from the church to the Reception Hall which was set up with cameras inside and outside.

***

Will didn't tell the families they had brought in security guards on loan from several nearby towns because their warning tips had come from several reliable sources.

Calvin Franklin usually worked undercover as a deputy with Jace Carpentier with the Sunrise Police Department. He had found he had a love for acting and had played bit parts with the Winthrop Theatre. He had become a master undercover artist for Jace when assigned as a rookie.

The town of Sunrise was used to seeing Calvin Franklin at his favorite bar because they not only served the best loaded hot dogs in town, he had become a very good listener here. He was just finishing his meal when in walked his Dad, Delbert Franklin, whom he hadn't seen for over ten months. But Delbert wasn't here to see his son.

Calvin had seen his dad drink and complain that his sons were lost to him forever because they would rather serve in the military than work with him. They were still lazy. But this time there was an anger-laced calmness about the set of his dad's jaw when he bragged, "The Donnelly twins will soon be widows. I personally made certain her office equipment was rerouted permanently," he added under his breath.

But, who would take him seriously? Calvin knew his dad was not drunk. He would have to call this in to Jace.

The clock behind the bar chimed the noon hour. Delbert didn't order his usual burger and fries; he ordered whiskey. Calvin had heard the same old stories before but waited until his dad looked his way. When Delbert fingered his shot glass, he didn't see Calvin as he melted into the shadows and left.

Later, however, Calvin was working on measurements of recording devices and cell phones in the field when his dad and mom stopped by his brother, Dexter's house unexpectedly and were unaware Calvin was there because he had walked from his property to Dexter's.

Now he was stuck in the basement until they left or went to bed. He had always heard you never hear anything positive when overhearing conversations, but this broke his heart. It shouldn't because he had heard it before, or perhaps it was when the tone of his dad's voice changed.

"I can't expect any more help from that Sarge kid because he's still in the local jail. But those Donnelly twins are going to rue the day they took my boys away from me. All these guys I had hired to do a few jobs for me and they either disappeared, quit on me, or ended up in jail."

"Now, Delbert," his mom suggested, "those girls were hurt that day, too. That has been years and years ago."

"You weren't there. I saw it happen. They all lied. I'm the one who always tells the truth. I've always been there for Calvin. You're the one who spanked him, just like my dad did me."

She knew she would be wasting her breath, clarifying that Delbert's dad was mean, and more than once left bruises on Delbert's arms and legs. His school teacher had kept notes and reported it, but nothing was done, according to him.

"Delbert, you've never understood that children need discipline with love, which reminds me, are we going to the Donnelly wedding?"

"You can go with Dexter. I'll be helping a crew setup a huge tent outside the church. You remember now, those brides will become widows. Oh, and you make certain your baby son is too ill to attend. He quit listening to me when he chose to follow Dexter into military school over working with me."

Calvin watched from the basement window as his dad drove out the drive and rushed barefoot up the stairs; but stopped just as quickly when he heard his mom dialing the telephone. "Opal, this is your Third Wheel calling."

"Are you back in town for the wedding?"

"Yes. I'm at Dexter's home. If your Jonothan is there, have him pick up your extension. You always said…I heard the extension, please just listen. Delbert is planning to make the twins widows right after the wedding. He will be working with the tent crew at the church. He's on a rampage. Of course, he could change his mind, since he doesn't trust me with anything. That's why I filed for divorce a week ago. He plans to frame our son Calvin for everything, starting with his signature. Can we meet somewhere?"

"We'll send you a cab."

"Thanks."

"Alley?"

"Yes."

"Deer Tracks set?"

"Yes."

When Opal and Brandi hung up, they flew across the room together, notebooks in hand. Memories of Turtle Crossing's Shadow Angels were hush-hush about a new member. A secret agent known only as Third Wheel, which also explained where she had heard one of their terms, Deer Tracks. She had apparently glued tracking medallions in his dad's new cowboy boots, his dad had insisted his mom needed to polish.

Calvin waited and was shocked. He would never have recognized his mother, Florence Franklin, except for her walk. Makeup. High-heeled boots. A very expensive wig and suit. A beautiful red-head who could have walked onto any movie set and look like she had lost thirty pounds in thirty minutes in her stylish, tailored suit.

Calvin locked up Dexter's home, set the security system, walked to the back of Dexter's property and past his own rusty bucket, junk-yard vehicle which was scheduled to be towed.

He walked at least one-hundred and fifty feet in the alley, punched in the code on the gate of his fenced property, and a few minutes later pulled out of the alley on his all-black Harley motorcycle, thankful for the dry pavement. As an officer with the Sunrise Special Patrol, he was appropriately dressed with shoulder harness, badge and tuxedo under his all-weather garb. He was one of several working security for the Donnelly wedding and reception.

Calvin arrived early and parked his motorcycle under a partially enclosed carport behind the church. He was a brunette today. And per the brides' request, he, like all the other ushers, would be in a black tuxedo and wearing white gloves to separate them from the bridal party.

He recognized Will's men and Jace's Sunrise crew as they continued to look in every nook and cranny for the unusual. One of those attractions was the paper-doll display, of Lily and Lori as brides and their groomsmen within a glass enclosure. He would bet everything right down to the miniature Christmas lights and bouquets of bright red Poinsettias and miniature Christmas trees would match today's wedding, described nearby in the stack of programs.

Surrounding it was music of "I'll be Home for Christmas," "Silver Bells," "O Come All Ye Faithful," and "Silent Night."

Calvin made himself useful whenever someone needed something and walked several visitors to their designated seats. All the while, he continued to check the white wedding tent that had been installed shortly before he arrived, while cautiously shadowing the grooms.

***

"Did you read the back of Calvin Franklin's business card?" Denver asked.

Donovan turned the card that he had found in his tuxedo pocket over and read, Second Chances.

"Donovan?" Hunter asked.

"Sorry. I was just trying to recall where I've seen this before," he added. "Ah." He smiled. "You no doubt already know. C.W. explained about the stained glass window of Jesus seated with little children in his previous Chapel that separated and broke when they were transporting it here. The hem of his robe is scattered with flowers designed from the broken pieces and signed, Second Chances."

Denver caught Will's expression in the mirror across the holding room for the groomsmen, remembering the lesson Will had repeated to him shortly after his arrival at Doc O'Reilly's Ranch. *Doc and Granny are giving you a second chance. Don't mess it up!*

Calvin had never been to a church wedding where he knew the family. One would have had to be blind to not see such devotion and love when Lori mentioned Denver's name or Lily when she mentioned Donovan by name. But especially the way Denver and Donovan treated their brides with such precious, tender respect and love.

He was stunned! He knew these two women were as honest as the day was long. Are they proof that love is still a possibility?

The Christmas decorations of tiny silver bells, poinsettias, and white roses lined the altar and the aisle, while Christmas music played softly inside and outside.

The wedding party walked in to Purcell's "Trumpet Tune" which was followed by Wagner's "Lohengrin," better known as "Here Comes the Bride."

The wedding went as scheduled. The reception went smoothly. The honeymooners kept silent about their destination. And no one else needed to know about the wills and prenuptial that had been signed a week earlier.

Afterword

After a court hearing Delbert Franklin's wife, Florence's divorce became final. Delbert Franklin was slapped with so many warrants, he would probably spend a chunk of his life in prison due to his own miscalculations.

When he blew a tire on Calvin's rust bucket junkyard vehicle, he hit a fence, slid down an embankment and was trapped with the equipment he had made plans for, which blew up in and out of the trunk. It was said he was lucky. Though he might disagree, except when he enjoyed a cigar now and then.

***

Delbert's decision to wear Calvin's Motorcycle boots had been his first mistake. They slowed him down because they were too big. But what he was unaware of was, these were the boots Calvin had been working on—fit with special microphones to record and forward information to the Sunrise and Turtle Crossing Detective's office. They also saved his life after the accident.

387

While Delbert was pinned inside the vehicle, he rattled on and on about his plans that had gone awry and all the money he had wasted on four specific men. Including Sarge, who had not only not gotten the job done with Denver, but hadn't returned the rifle that he, himself had stolen to cover the money the kid's old man owed him.

What he didn't know was that his carelessness with a certain brand of cigars had placed him in the wrong place at the wrong time anyhow.

However, when Delbert purchased old Henry Carpenter's motel before Henry died, Delbert had been so ecstatic to be within just a few miles of the O'Reilly Ranch that he signed his wife's name on the title. Let her get stuck with the back taxes and repairs. The motel didn't get enough traffic to break even.

Months later, Florence Franklin found the deed to what she had always referred to as Henry Carpenter's Motel, in her name. After visiting it, she was thrilled. Her head was spinning with ideas and second chances. But first, she planned to clear out Henry Carpenter's stash of cigars.

Genealogies

Donnelly

Robard J. Donnelly m. Rose L. Fields
        I

I	I	I	I
Charles Donnelly	Kristopher Donnelly	David J. Donnelly	Marcie M. Donnelly
SaraElizabeth Carpenter	Nancy A. Jordan	Shannon Warren	Sheldon Warren
I	I	I	I
David J. Donnelly	Jacob Donnelly	Lily Anneé Donnelly	Amber Beth Eden Warren
Marcie M. Donnelly	Jordan Donnelly	Lauri Rose Donnelly	

Warren

Winthrop Warren (WW) 1st.m.   Cecil Warren (CW) m.
E. Tessa Montgomery {m. annulled}   E. Tessa Montgomery 3rd. m.

Winthrop Warren (WW) 2nd. m.   E. Tessa Montgomery 2nd.m.
Constance Stephanie Strange   Tom Sands
    I   I
Richard C. Warren 1st. m.   Wendy Warren Sands m.
Summer Eden Fox   William {Will} Fox
    I   I
Sheldon Warren   Storm Thomas Fox
Shannon Warren

Carpenter

Henry Carpenter	Tressie Carpenter	Jacob Joseph Carpenter	aka	Joseph {Joe}Jacob Carpentier
Jewel Hendrix	Fletcher Brown	Opal Fields		Pearl E. Peltiers 2nd.m
I		I		I
SaraElizabeth Carpenter		Jonothan Arden Carpenter		Jace Carpentier
Charles J. Donnelly		Brandi Elaine Davies		Samantha Carpentier
I				
Marcie M. Donnelly				
David J. Donnelly				

Welby / Erne

Daniel Welby	Allen B. Ern	Mason Davies {cousin of Brandi)
Ellen Winters	SueLynn Winters	Autumn Winters Johnson
	I	I
	Ariel Ern	Allison Ellen Davies
	Alexandria Lyndsay Ern {Alex}	
	Jamie Johnson	
	I	
	Autumn Winters Johnson	

Acknowledgments

A special thank you to the following:

Reverend Joe Sopher

A 1948 graduate of LaFayette-Jackson High School in LaFayette, Ohio. He was the minister of Seybert United Methodist Church in Bellevue, Ohio when he retired. He answered my numerous questions regarding faith and belief that God heals and answers prayers.

He asked if I was going to put this information in my next novel. I agreed. He then added: "People could be in a different place in their life—but may remember reading what you have written."

Charles Bates

Curator of Transportation (Railroad Archives) at the Allen County Museum, Lima, Ohio.

Amy Joseph

Amy has been riding horses since she was five years old. Her favorite was a quarter-horse named Ivy. She competed in barrels, trail class, horsemanship and halter. She was an Allen County 4-H Advisor and was a Judge for a horse show.

Janet Burkholder Stark

Janet shared her experiences with care and training horses, and photos of her mom when she was in competitive showmanship with her Chestnut Morgan Stallion.

Jim Campbell

Jim attended the North Carolina School of Farriers—and allowed me to observe as he gave a two-and-half year-old quarter-horse and a 20-year-old mare a pedicure.

Editor—Cheryl Mueller, Ph.D.

Cheryl is published in several genres and has attended numerous workshops and taught student groups in the U.S.A. and abroad. Her favorite is several years of Paris Café Writing. She is an experienced world traveler, lifetime student, educator, consultant, and editor.

Editor—Jan Romes

Jan has authored 27 novels in the romance and humorous fiction categories.

The Inklings' Writing Group of Bluffton, Ohio

A very special thank you to: Cheryl Mueller, Christina Walton, Eugene McCall, Jan Romes, Linda Strahm, and Pat Rodabaugh for their continued support and encouragement.

I would also like to acknowledge the following invaluable research sources used for this book: *Storey's Horse-Lover's Encyclopedia* by Jessie Haas, *An English and Western A to Z Guide* by Lisa Hailey and Edited by Deborah Burns, and *Horse Care Manual* by Colin Vogel.

About the Author

Marilyn R. Stark graduated from Northwestern School of Commerce in Lima, Ohio. She has spent most of her life, writing and updating the family history of immediate and extended families. She also continues to mail over one-hundred annual Christmas Newsletters for her husband's family history.

For six years, Marilyn was a Feature Writer for *The Senior's Beacon* (which is out of print). She also wrote and recorded a monthly radio commercial for same.

Marilyn's previous novels include *The Flutist and The Dancer*, *The Pianist and the Locksmith*, *Broken Arrows/Broken Promises*, *Trails End Isle and Wings*, and *Safe Passage in Masquerade*.

She researched and wrote a coffee table book, compiled text and photos for *A Pictorial History of Lima, Allen County, Ohio*. She researched and wrote for *The Allen County Historical Society, The History and Purposes of Allen County Institutions, Buildings and Government*.